Lautaro's Spear

A Novel

Scott R. Larson

www.ScottLarsonBooks.com

To

Teresa and Maggie
always and ever

Dayle
for support, help, generosity,
and enduring, loyal friendship

Many thanks to

Dayle Moss
for editing assistance and feedback that not only made
the final manuscript better but also never failed
to put a smile on my face.

and to

Michael Morrow and Marcella Peralta Simon,
whose interest, encouragement, feedback, ideas,
and investment of time not only encouraged me
to continue the story of Dallas Green but also
helped to form, refine, and validate the story,
while making the book's writing
a less lonely project.

Contents

1   Knocking   *1*

2   Saturday   *3*

3   Linda   *9*

4   Lana   *20*

5   James   *31*

6   Marty   *41*

7   Justin   *51*

8   Golden Gate   *60*

9   Knocking Again   *67*

10   Buzzing   *69*

11   Over   *78*

12   New Plan   *83*

13   Old Scotch   *93*

14   Fright   *103*

15   Flight   *109*

16   Deauville   *118*

17   Calvados   *129*

18   Valérie   *139*

19   La Galoche   *147*

20   Declan   *153*

21   Dino   *164*

22   Logan   *173*

23   Bordeaux   *182*

24   Ángel   *192*

25   Armagnac   *204*

26   Trains   *213*

27   More Old Scotch   *222*

28   Berlin   *230*

29   Fulda   *240*

30   Lukas   *250*

31   Fall   *257*

32   Birthday   *266*

1
Knocking

HOW LONG has the damn knocking been going on?

I do not know how long the knocking has been going on.

I only notice it now because it keeps getting louder and louder. It is so loud now, I cannot ignore it anymore.

Someone is pounding on the door. Pounding hard. Pounding frantically.

I have no idea what time it is. Or what day it is. Or what year it is. I do not know where I am. I do not know how old I am. I do not know where I live.

I am totally confused.

I am in bed. That must be why I am so confused. I must have been asleep.

I get out of bed. I walk in the direction of the knocking. I know where I am now. I am in my apartment. Someone is knocking on the door of my apartment.

I open the door.

A woman with black hair is standing there. It is Marisol. She is so much older than the last time I saw her. She is terrified. A child is standing next to her. He looks like he should be in about the third grade. His shirt is dirty with smudges and stains. He is holding an ice cream cone.

"Marisol, what the hell is going on?"

"Let me in. He is after us. If he finds us, he will kill me."

"Who are you talking about? Who will kill you?"

"Carlos. My husband. I could not stay there anymore. He is involved in bad stuff. Very bad stuff. I could not think of anything else to do except to come to you. You have to help us. You have to."

It is all so confusing. I cannot think clearly. I do not know what I am supposed to say or to do. I just stand there looking at the little boy. The ice cream has been melting while he stands there. Finally, as if in slow motion, the ice cream slips to one side of the cone and then off the cone. It falls and goes splat on the floor. The boy looks at the ice cream on the floor, and his lip trembles. His eyes start to water. I can tell he is trying hard to hold back the tears, but the tears begin to trickle down his cheeks anyway.

"What's his name?"

The question annoys her.

"I told you. His name is Carlos."

"No, I mean *his* name."

I point to the little boy.

"Oh," she says.

She looks at him with very sad eyes.

"His name is Antonio. I named him Antonio."

She looks at me again. Her eyes are full of desperation. So much desperation that it scares me. I still do not know what to do.

"Do something, Dallas. He will come after us. If he finds me, he will kill me. If he finds me here, he will kill you too. He is into very bad stuff. You must do something. Please. Do something."

I should do something. I know that. But I have no idea what to do.

"What do you want me to do, Marisol? Tell me. What do you want me to do? I'm sorry, but I don't know what to do. Please tell me what to do."

Now the phone is ringing, but it seems so very far away. Where is the damn phone? Who is calling me? Why do I feel so damned confused?

2
Saturday

"YOUR PHONE is ringing."

"Mmmm."

"I said, your phone is ringing."

I turned over. I didn't want to hear about it.

"Aren't you going to answer it? It might be important."

Where was I? What happened to Marisol? And little Antonio?

"What were you dreaming about anyway? You were jumping around like someone was chasing you."

I could hear it clearly now. Yeah, the phone was ringing. I looked at the clock on the nightstand. I stumbled out of bed and into the next room where the phone was.

"So, who calls somebody at eight o'clock on a Saturday morning anyway?" asked Lana, as she pulled back the covers that I had half dragged onto the floor.

"Farmers. Or people who live in a farming town. It's probably my mom."

My voice was scratchy. I did my best to clear my throat as I picked up the phone.

"Hello?"

"Dallas?"

"Yeah?"

"Dallas Green?"

"Yeah?"

"Dallas, it's me."

"Who?"

"It's Linda. Linda Jefferies."

My head was still trying to deal with Marisol and little Antonio. It took a moment to be able to think about Linda. I finally started waking up enough to think halfway normally.

3

"Oh, Linda. Hey, how are you? I, uh, haven't heard from you in a while."

"I know. I've missed you."

"Where are you calling from? Are you…?"

"I'm here. Here in Frisco."

"Uh, people here really don't like it when you call it Frisco."

"Oh, well, I'm sorry, mister big city big shot," she laughed. "Excuse me. I'm here in *San Francisco*. My friend Patty and I decided to come up for the weekend. We're staying at the St. Francis. Do you know where that is?"

"Yeah, it's on Union Square. Everybody knows where it is."

"Yeah, I guess they would. It's just that this place is so big. I don't know how people here can figure out where they are going. Anyway, it's a really fancy place. We're pampering ourselves. I figured we deserved it."

"Oh, cool. So, uh, how did you get my number?"

"Your mother gave it to me. How do you think? I hope that's all right. I just thought it would be nice to see you. It's been so long. Remember when we used to have so much fun when you were living in Bakersfield?"

I remembered all right. Whenever Linda and her husband Wayne would have a fight or sometimes when he went away on one of his weekend hunting or fishing trips, she would leave her daughter at her mother's and come over to my apartment for a visit. The excuse was always that we were reminiscing about Lonnie, about how much we were missing him since he died. It was really just an excuse to get drunk together. That was okay for a while—until the time we had a little *too* much to drink, and one thing led to another, and we wound up falling into bed together. In my drunken state at the time, it was like a dream come true because all through high school I had dreamed of a night exactly like that one. Back in those days I had been so in love with Linda that it hurt. The only problem back then had been that she was going out with my best friend.

When we woke up the next morning, I felt like shit. I was disgusted with myself for having tried to relive my old, high-school fantasy. The truth was that I had already gotten over Linda a long time before. On top of that, I was there in bed with some other guy's wife. And not just any guy. Everyone knew that Wayne kept guns in his house. Not very bright, Dallas. After that little incident, I got more and more paranoid. Sometimes I would wake up late at night in a cold sweat, freaking out that he was going to come after me with one of his hunting rifles. The more time went by, the more jittery I got, all the time looking over my shoulder. I stopped answering the phone in case it was Linda—or Wayne. After a while she

4

must have gotten the hint because she stopped calling me. Finally, when enough time had gone by, I managed to forget about the whole thing—until the next year when I heard that Linda and Wayne had gotten divorced. Then the paranoia started again. I kept wondering if she had told him about us and whether that had something to do with their breakup. I started looking over my shoulder again. I was a complete mess, and I swore I would never get involved with a married woman again. That was around the same time that I finished at Cal State Bakersfield. I did not have any full-time work. Just some part-time freelance sports photography for the Bakersfield newspaper, which didn't pay all that much. The time seemed right to think about maybe moving somewhere else. I had promised myself that, as soon as I had enough money saved up, I would go back down to Mexico. It would be just like after I graduated from high school. Time for another escape.

"Yeah, Linda," I said, "Those were some good times in Bakersfield all right. Seems like a long time ago now. How are you doing?"

"Really good. I'm selling real estate now. Can you believe it? Who would have thought? And the amazing thing is, I'm really good at it. I love it."

"That's great, Linda. I'm happy for you."

"You know that Wayne and I split up, right? That's been a couple of years now."

"Yeah, I think I did hear that."

"It hasn't been easy all of the time, but it's a lot easier now that the kids are older. And Mom's great about taking them if I have to work late on the days Wayne doesn't have them. It's kind of a crazy life. Every so often Patty and I just say, hey, it's time for the two of us to get away for a break. Sometimes we go to Pismo. Sometimes we go down to L.A. This time we thought, what the hell, let's go to Frisco. Sorry, San Francisco."

"Sounds good, Linda. So, what are you guys going to do while you're here?"

"Well, Patty has a friend who lives in Marin. They're going to meet for dinner, but I said I'd take a rain check and let the two of them catch up. So…"

I gritted my teeth.

"I was wondering if you wanted to get together. You know, catch up on old times. It's been ages since I've seen you. There's so much to catch up on. You must have all kinds of news."

I glanced back toward the bedroom. Lana had gotten on top of the covers and was lying on her stomach to have a better view of me. She was listening to everything and grinning like the Cheshire cat.

"Yeah, sure, I guess we could do that."

"Well, try not to sound too enthused. You don't have to if you don't want to."

"No, no, it's fine. No, it would be great to see you again. Sorry if I sound out of it. I was fast asleep when you called. I guess I'm still not completely awake."

"That's great, Dallas. I'm really looking forward to it. Patty and I are going to see Alcatraz and a few other things, but we should be back by six o'clock. Do you want to come meet me here at the hotel?"

"Yeah, that sounds good. Six o'clock at the St. Francis. I'll see you then."

As I hung up the phone, Lana's grin had gotten bigger.

"So, you have a date for tonight. And here I was worrying that you were going to be desperately lonely without me."

"She's somebody I went to high school with. I haven't seen her or talked to her in years. She was the last person I expected to hear from."

"So, was she your girlfriend? Do you two have a history? Give me all the dirt."

"She was Lonnie's girlfriend."

The smirk on Lana's face faded.

"Lonnie who died?"

"Yeah, Lonnie who died."

She went quiet for a moment. But just for a moment.

"Sorry. I know that's a sensitive subject for you."

Then, in a split second, she went from her relaxed, teasing mood to panic.

"Jesus. Look at the time. I have to get going. I'm going to be late."

She jumped off the bed and went looking frantically for her bra, panties, and other clothes, which had somehow wound up in various random locations on the floor.

"Gary absolutely hates it when I'm not there to meet him at the airport."

"Do you have to go?"

"What a question. You know I do, Tex."

"I hate it when you leave."

"It won't be too bad this time. Gary has another business trip in just another week. I'll see you then. In the meantime," she said with a wink, "have fun with your old girlfriend."

"She wasn't my girlfriend."

"Well, if you're not interested in her," said Lana, bending her limber arms behind her to clasp her bra, "maybe you should go look up that woman you were dreaming about. What kind of name is Marie Soul?"

"Was I actually talking in my sleep?"

"You sure were. I thought you were going to jump out of your skin. You were frightened out of your wits. Maybe it was that movie we saw last night. It was pretty creepy."

"Yeah, you'll have to watch out or I might wind up breaking through the door with an axe like Jack Nicholson."

"So, who is she? This Marie Soul. She certainly had you excited."

"That's kind of a long story."

She sighed.

"Yeah, that's one thing I've learned about you, Tex. Your stories are always long. Too long to even start. Anyway, you can tell me next week."

She stopped pulling on her clothes just long enough to give me a quick kiss on the mouth.

"Be glad I'm not the possessive type. You're free to do whatever or see whoever you want for the next week. Any other man would love to be in your situation."

I did not love my situation. Watching her get ready to leave filled me with dread. The nights I slept by myself—and that was most nights—were black and endless. I dreaded being alone in my apartment, especially in bed at night. I didn't know what was wrong with me. I knew it was not normal, but it had been like that for an awfully long time. At night, when I was alone, there was no hope. I was in a constant state of irrational fear. If someone asked me to explain what I was afraid of, I would not be able to because it made no sense. I just knew that every minute until the sun came up was endless torture. Except when Lana was there. It was only when we were making love that the fear and the sadness disappeared—for a while anyway. And when Lana was not there, I felt completely alone in the world—and like I always would be for the rest of my miserable life.

"Do you at least have time for some breakfast? I could make us some coffee. It would just take a minute."

"That sounds wonderful," she mumbled as she put on lipstick in front of the mirror. "But I'm completely out of time and you're not helping. I'll see you next week."

She sat on the bed just long enough to put on her shoes, then stood up. Before I knew it, she had disappeared out the door. My heart sank.

The walls of the apartment closed in on me. The air was suddenly so thin that I couldn't catch my breath. My heart pounded in my chest. I shut my eyes tight and forced myself to breathe slowly. Sometimes that helped. Sometimes.

This isn't normal, I thought. *What the hell is wrong with me? Why can't I just be like everyone else? Other people don't go through this whenever they are alone, do they? Why can't I just be like everyone else?*

In my mind, it was as if there were a giant black crater where my soul should be. It was a huge, gaping hole, like the one they were digging a few blocks from my apartment. Just as that hole was devouring streets and buildings and businesses and apartments, the black hole in my heart was consuming all the happiness I should have been enjoying in a great city with a great woman like Lana.

In the light of day, I could at least take my mind off my black thoughts by doing some work. I had a lot of photographs to develop in the makeshift darkroom I had set up in the closet. That would keep me busy for most of the day. I put my new Def Leppard tape in the cassette player, made some instant coffee, and began mixing my chemicals.

Despite my feelings of dread at night, the good thing was that, once I did finally manage to fall asleep, I usually slept through the night without waking up. I was hardly ever bothered by dreams. Either I did not have them or else I did not remember them.

The dream about Marisol was something new. I wondered if it meant something.

3
Linda

THOUGH IT made me sad to realize it, I really did not want to see Linda again.

As I walked from my apartment up to her hotel, I wondered why she had bothered to call me. She was probably just being friendly or courteous. Maybe she was curious. It was probably just a coincidence that she happened to come to the city and, after all, I was probably the only person she knew here. Still, I could not get rid of the nagging feeling that maybe she thought—now that she was single again and, as far as she knew, I was single too—maybe we could pick up where we had left off. That thought made me nervous. And the fact it made me nervous made me sad. How could I have been so crazy in love with her in high school and now not even want to see her again? Maybe she just brought up too many memories. After all, I would never be able to see her again without being reminded of Lonnie. And I was doing my best not to think about Lonnie, even though it was impossible. High school was ancient history, and I had a new life now in a different place with different friends. And I had spent more than enough time thinking about and missing Lonnie. But now I only wished I could put all that behind me. Seeing Linda would bring it all back again.

It was not a long walk from my apartment to Union Square, but it was like crossing into a completely different world. South of Market, where I lived, was full of warehouses, garages, and apartment buildings. There was every kind of workshop, from flag sewing to casket making. There was even an automotive shop operated completely by women. It was mostly working people living in my neighborhood, people who had lived there for years. But there were also some of us who were young and single and who were living there because it was cheaper than most other parts of the city. There were white people, black people, Asian people, just about any other kind of people you could think of. I guess you could say the area was kind of run down, but it did not seem that way when you lived there awhile. Life in the shadow of the freeway that connected to the Bay Bridge was never going to be the suburbs, but for me it was now home. The bad part was all the digging and construction work going on for the new convention center.

Only a few blocks away was Market Street. Once you managed to get across the expanse of Market, it was a completely different world. North of Market was full of glistening hotels, theaters, and department stores. Everyone there always seemed to be dressed to the nines and spending endless amounts of money. Every time I got over there, I found myself wishing I had put on a better shirt.

As I got closer to the hotel, I did my best to think positively about this unexpected date. Maybe when I actually saw Linda, I would be glad to be there after all. Would it be the worst thing in the world if she was interested in me? At least it would actually be possible to have a normal relationship with her now—and not have to sneak around when her husband was out of town. Really, I was just kidding myself if I thought there was going to be any future with Lana. I picked up my pace as I made my way to the hotel entrance.

I walked into the lobby and had a look around. I wondered if she had changed much in the four years since I had seen her and whether I would have any trouble recognizing her. Almost immediately she sprang excitedly out of a chair near the door.

"Dallas!"

"Hi, Linda."

She was giddy, like a little kid.

"I can't believe it! I can't believe it's you! I've missed you so much. And you haven't changed a bit. You still look like you're eighteen. You haven't even cut your hair or anything. And you still have all your hair. Wayne is almost completely bald. God, I'm so happy to see you!"

She put her arms around me and hugged me so tight I had to catch my breath. I wanted to return her compliment, but I was not very good at lying. She was heavier now. I guess I should not have been surprised that she looked like someone who had given birth to two children. After all, that is what she was. For some reason, despite wondering if I would recognize her, I still expected her to look like I remembered her—not older. Personally, I didn't feel any older. Whenever I looked in the mirror, I never seemed to change. It was strange to think of people back home getting older while nothing ever seemed to change for me.

"You have to tell me everything. All about your life. Mom says you're a big photographer for some important magazine here. It must be so interesting."

"Well, I'm just working for a weekly newspaper. It's okay, I guess. It's not really that big a deal."

"Just as modest as ever! I can't get over how good you look. San Francisco must agree with you."

"Want to get a drink? We can go to the bar here. Or I know a place a few blocks away that isn't so busy." *Or so expensive*, I thought.

"That sounds great. Take me someplace where you would normally go. I want to find out everything about your life now."

"Do you mind walking a few blocks?"

"Sounds like fun."

I led her five blocks down Geary Street. She kept stopping to pay attention to her feet.

"I think I wore the wrong shoes."

"You look nice. That's a pretty dress you have on."

"Yeah, well, I thought I would pull out all the stops. I never get to go anywhere nice in Bakersfield. This is my big night out for the year."

She looked a bit doubtful when we arrived at a door with only the word BAR above it.

"Is this it?"

"Yeah, is this okay?"

"I suppose. It's just that there were so many nice places down by the hotel…"

"Yeah, but this place has character," I said as we went in, "and you see some really interesting people. What'll you have?"

"Do you still drink tequila?"

I had not had tequila for a long time. The question reminded me of the main reason she and I had gotten into trouble before.

"How about a beer? Have you had a Steam beer?"

"No. Sounds good."

I got us two Anchor Steams, getting verbally abused in the process as usual by the bartender. That was a lot of the place's attraction. I joined her at the table where she had taken a seat. Blondie was singing "Call Me" on the jukebox. That was another reason I liked this place. It had an old-fashioned jukebox, just like the one in the café back home where my family went out for dinner as a special treat once a month. Linda seemed to read my mind.

"Do you ever miss home?"

I thought about her question as I sipped my beer.

"Not really. There's a lot more jobs for what I want to do here than down there. And I definitely don't miss the San Joaquin Valley summers.

Sometimes, in August here, I actually have to put on a sweater. And the place gets so socked in with fog you can't see anything. I've gotten used to smelling salt in the air. I don't think I could go back to living in a place that's like a desert. Besides, there's so much to do here."

She looked a bit sad. I could not tell if she was comparing her life to mine, or maybe she had been hoping that I someday might move back home.

"So, what about you? Tell me about the real estate business. Are you actually selling houses?"

She smiled.

"Yes! Can you believe it? A couple of years ago, when Patty was selling her house, she asked me to help her. I started learning everything I could about property and real estate, and I found I liked it a lot. After Wayne and I split up, I took a class and went for my real estate license. I've been working out of Bill Norris's office for the past year. I mean, I'm not getting rich or anything. After all, the economy is really bad, and it's a tough market out there, but I've been doing well enough that I could afford this weekend away. It's great to be earning my own money and not having to rely completely on Wayne's child support payments."

That reminded me, I had not asked about her children.

"So, how old are your kids now?"

Her face brightened.

"Bonnie will be five in two weeks. She's so excited. She'll be starting kindergarten in September. Ryan is two-and-a-half. He's a real bundle of energy. I can't keep up with him."

"Wow, they're so old now."

Bonnie had been just a baby when Linda first started coming to see me in Bakersfield. I did a quick calculation in my head to figure out when her son was born. It would have been a half-year after I finished at Cal State, and a year-and-a-half after I had slept with Linda.

"I'm sorry that it didn't work out with you and Wayne."

"I'm not."

"I hope… I mean… I guess I always wondered… Did it have anything to do with…?"

"With what?"

"You know. Us. That time."

To my surprise, it took her a moment to catch on to what I was talking about. Finally, somebody turned on the lights.

"Oh. That. No, it didn't have anything to do with you. Is that what you thought?"

It had totally caught her off guard that I would have wondered such a thing.

"No, I had plenty of reasons to divorce Wayne. He was an asshole. Imagine. I was pregnant with Ryan. Bonnie was still in diapers. I was overwhelmed with taking care of the two of them. Then I found out he had a girlfriend. You know all those times he went away, supposedly hunting and fishing with his buddies? Most of those times he was with his little slut."

"Wow. I had no idea."

"I tell you, I went through hell, Dallas. It was a rough time. There were times I wanted to pick up the phone and call you. You know, cry on your shoulder, like in the old days. But somehow, I just couldn't. Anyway, it was better that I worked it all out myself. I came out of it a lot stronger. I mean, I'm tired all the time, looking after the kids and trying to work, but at least I'm happy now. I really am."

"I'm glad to hear that. You deserve to be happy. You know, I've always cared a lot about you. I don't know if Lonnie ever told you, but back in high school…"

"You had a big crush on me. Yeah, I knew. I didn't need Lonnie to tell me. I always knew. You were so cute. And you kept hanging around with the two of us anyway. Most other guys wouldn't have done that. You were such a nice guy."

My cheeks were burning.

"I wasn't that nice a guy. If you and Lonnie had known the thoughts that were going through my head…"

"Don't be too hard on yourself. You were about the nicest guy I knew in high school. You were always such a good friend to Lonnie. You always did your best to keep him out of trouble. Of course, that was impossible. Hey, you want to know something funny?"

"Yeah?"

"Now that I've spent a little time with you again, I can see something is different about you now."

"Different how?"

"It's hard to say exactly. It's just something about your voice sometimes and a look you get in your eyes. It makes you seem like Lonnie. That never used to be true before, but now it is. Isn't that weird?"

"I seem like Lonnie? Really?"

"Yeah, kind of. I mean, you're still you. You've always been a lot different than him. And you still are. But every so often there will be a look in your eyes or an expression on your face that reminds me of him."

"That *is* weird."

"Actually, it's kind of nice. It's like a part of him is still alive—inside you. As long as you think about him and don't forget him, he will always sort of still be around."

I decided not to tell her about the strange fantasy I had sometimes—the one where I imagined that Lonnie was actually still alive somewhere. She would have thought I was crazy.

"Anyway," she said, "that's enough talk about Lonnie. That's all water under the bridge and a long time ago now. Let's talk about the here and now. What else is new with you? Are you seeing anyone?"

My brain froze for a few seconds. I had not told anyone about Lana before, but there was no reason not to tell Linda.

"Yeah, I'm seeing someone. Her name is Lana, and she's really great."

Linda's smile brightened.

"Dallas, I'm so happy for you! That's wonderful. So, should I be expecting a wedding invitation anytime soon?"

"I think I'll get us a couple more beers."

When I came back to the table, she was like an animal ready to pounce.

"So, tell me everything. I want all the juicy details. What is she like? How did you meet her? When is the engagement? Come on, don't hold back."

"Gee, there isn't all that much to tell…"

"Men are so bad at giving out important information. You should have brought her along tonight. I would love to meet her. I bet *she* would answer all my questions. I hope she doesn't mind you being out with me."

"No, she's not the jealous type. She was more than happy to see me going out tonight."

"What did you say her name was?"

"Lana."

"Lana! What a glamorous name. I bet she's named after Lana Turner, the movie star."

"I don't know if she's named after anybody. I like to think she's named after Superboy's girlfriend."

She laughed. "Oh, so you're Superboy now."

"No, that's not what I meant."

She sighed.

"You haven't changed a bit. I bet you're still reading comic books. How long have the two of you been going out?"

"Let's see, almost two years now."

"Two years! And you still haven't put a ring on her finger? What's wrong with you? How did the two of you meet?"

"Uh, did you ever meet my friend Keith?"

"I don't think so."

"I knew him at Cal State. We were in the same Spanish class. Anyway, he's the one who convinced me to move to San Francisco. He's the reason I got my job. We were sharing an apartment here in the city until he met Amy and they got married. Lana is Amy's cousin."

"So, where is she tonight?"

"Uh, she had things she had to do. She's always busy with something."

"Two years is a long time. It must be pretty serious."

"I think we're both happy with the way things are. I wouldn't hold my breath waiting around for that engagement announcement."

She studied me intently as she took a sip of beer.

"You know, you're just like my brother Michael."

"What?"

"You and he are the same. Neither of you wants to grow up. He hasn't settled down either. He doesn't have a steady girlfriend. He just enjoys himself all the time, going out with his friends and throwing parties. I don't think he'll ever grow up. Or you either, for that matter. I guess the two of you are just a couple of confirmed bachelors."

Now I was the one studying her. Did she really not know her brother was gay? Or did she just feel that she had to pretend for my benefit? After almost three years in the city, I had met so many gay guys that it did not even seem strange anymore. I had even stopped letting it bother me when I got whistles while walking around my neighborhood from the guys in the leather vests and biker caps. Maybe some people back home would be bothered that Michael was gay, and maybe it bothered me when I found out and Lonnie nearly killed him. It did not bother me now, though.

"Everybody's different," I said. "Not everybody is cut out for a wife and kids and an 8-to-5 job. So, how is Michael anyway? I haven't seen him since I gave him back his camera that I had swiped and took to Mexico."

"I'm worried about him, Dallas. Lately, he seems to be sick all the time. He has a cough that he just can't seem to get rid of. It doesn't seem to be going away."

"I wouldn't worry. There seems to be a flu or something going around. A lot of people have been sick lately. I'm sure he'll be okay."

"I hope so. I do worry about him. I wish he had someone to look after him."

"Maybe he does. Maybe he just doesn't want to tell you."

"Well, that would be silly. But I suppose it's his own business. He's as settled in Los Angeles as you are here in San Francisco. I'm afraid our little town is dying on the vine. Everyone our age seems to have moved to Bakersfield or farther away."

"Look at the time. You must be starving. Dinner's on me, Linda, and you can pick the place. We can go back to Union Square if you want."

"You should pick. This is your city. I wouldn't have any idea which places are good. You decide."

"Nope. If you leave it to me, you'll just wind up in some weird place, like this bar. Pick a nice place where you can show off that pretty dress of yours."

We finished our beers and headed back down Geary toward Union Square. It was already starting to get dark, and the air was brisk. I wondered if the evening had turned out like Linda had wanted or whether she was disappointed.

"I can't get over how cold it is here," she said, "compared to Bakersfield. Does it ever get hot here?"

"Sometimes, but not very often. At least not hot like Bakersfield. Not in the city anyway."

"No wonder you like it here so much. You never did like the heat."

"Yeah, I guess so."

Pretty soon we were back at her hotel.

"So, where have you decided?"

"I don't know, Dallas. I have no idea."

"Well, I suppose we could…"

"That one looks nice!"

We were standing in front of a restaurant called Balthazar's. I looked through the windows at the linen tablecloths, the shiny silverware on the tables, and a waiter dressed in something like a tuxedo. I did my best not to look panicked.

"Well, if you want to. I probably should have gotten more dressed up."

"Don't worry about that. Our money is as good as anybody else's. Let's see if we can get a table."

I was calculating in my head how much dinner for two would cost in a place like that, and I hoped I had enough on me. I wanted to show her a nice time.

Before I could say anything else, Linda was already in the door and talking to the host. He was telling her they were booked up for the evening, and I felt relieved. I was apparently off the hook—or so I thought. She kept insisting and, to my surprise, he finally wound up giving us a tiny little table off in a dark corner.

"That was impressive," I told her. "I would have given up and gone somewhere else. It can be hard to get into places around here without a reservation."

"I guess it's just part of my real estate training. You can't always take the first answer you get. Restaurants often save a few tables, even on a busy night, for special customers."

We had barely sat down before a tall thin man appeared. He was elegantly dressed. He had a moustache, and his black hair was perfectly combed.

"Good evening," he said with an elegant accent. "My name is Richard. I shall be looking after you this evening."

To my relief, he did not look down his nose at me. In fact, he made us feel quite comfortable.

"I love your accent," said Linda. "Where are you from?"

"England, ma'am. London actually. May I interest you in an aperitif?"

"Let's get a bottle of wine," said Linda.

"Would you care for a claret? I have a Saint-Émilion I can recommend quite heartily. I also have some other bottles of Bordeaux that are quite nice."

"Is Bordeaux good?" asked Linda.

"The best, I can assure you."

"Let's get some Bordeaux," said Linda enthusiastically.

"Very good, ma'am."

"I just love the way English people talk," said Linda as Richard went to get our bottle. "He sounds so high class. Like a lord or an earl or something."

"He's probably putting it on. He's probably from Oakland or San Mateo."

The service was not what you would call fast, but the food was very good. The price of the wine was nearly as much as our dinners. This was definitely not the sort of place where I would usually eat—not even with Lana. She was what you could call rich—she lived in a big house in Hillsborough—but she was always happy to go to the funky little places I liked. Linda, on the other hand, was enjoying this expensive restaurant and chatting with Richard the waiter. I liked the fact he knew to leave us alone when we were eating, and Linda liked the fact that, when he did come to our table, he was happy to talk with her and answer her questions. I noticed that he pretty much avoided answering any questions about how or why he

17

had come to America. I was just happy Linda was getting the fancy night out she had wanted.

When the bill came, I braced myself for the bad news. Before I could pick it up, Linda grabbed it.

"I'll look after this," she said.

"You can't do that. I told you I'd pay. This is my treat tonight. I want to."

She grinned as she pulled a credit card out of her purse.

"No, I'm the one who invited you out, remember? I made a big sale last week. That's why I'm splurging this weekend. I can't tell you, Dallas, how good it feels to have my own money. Divorcing Wayne was the best thing I ever did. Buying you a nice dinner is my way of saying thank you."

"Thank you?"

"Yeah. You don't know how much your friendship meant to me. I mean, during that year when I was missing Lonnie and fighting with Wayne all the time. You probably didn't know it, but you kept me sane."

No, I did not know that.

"Anyway, my life is great now and, even though I am tired all the time, I am really happy now. Maybe for the first time in my life. And I'm trying to show my appreciation to people who were there when I needed them."

"I didn't do anything great, Linda. You were the one helping *me*. I was missing him too. I wish you would let me pay."

"Not a chance, mister. Besides, I bet Lana has you spending big money on her every night of the week. It's time someone treated you for a change."

If she only knew.

After dinner, I walked her back to the hotel. I thanked her and said good night in the lobby. She gave me a big hug and a kiss on the cheek.

"It was so good to see you, Dallas. It's great to see you doing so well and enjoying your life. And I'm so happy that you have someone special in your life. I'll be waiting for that wedding invitation."

"Good-bye, Linda," I said. "Thanks again for dinner."

I watched her disappear into an elevator.

I felt stupid now having thought she might have come to the city because she was in love with me. What an idiot I was—as usual. Strangely and unexpectedly, I was finding myself feeling kind of sad that she hadn't.

The evening had gone by very fast, and now Linda had vanished back into the past. Who knew if I would ever see her again? As I stood there, I felt the temperature drop. While I was with her, I had felt normal—even happy. Now that I was alone again, I could feel the darkness all around.

Now I would go back to my apartment by myself. One more time I would face the all-consuming blackness of my nights.

4
Lana

I WAS lucky to have a job in the city. In fact, I was lucky to have a job at all. The economy was so bad that lots of people I knew could not find work.

I never would have been living and working in San Francisco if I had not become friends with Keith when I was at Cal State. I could tell from the first moment I met him that Keith was a real go-getter. He was in my Spanish class, and we usually wound up sitting next to each other. One day after class, we got to talking about why each of us was in the class. For some reason, I felt comfortable with him, and I found myself telling him about my trip to Mexico. I even told him the part that I had not told anybody else—about my crazy idea of learning Spanish really well and going down to Monterrey and finding Marisol. Maybe, I thought, there was some possibility of picking up where we had left off that night in Guaymas—now that she was over eighteen.

My story made him laugh. He had a completely different reason for learning Spanish. He was planning on a career in marketing and knowing Spanish was a good skill to have in business in California. He had a big plan for his life all mapped out. He was going to be a millionaire by the time he was thirty. That made *me* laugh because I did not have any plan for what I would be at the age of twenty—and that was my next birthday.

The reason, I suppose, we got to be friends is that Spanish was not very easy for him, while for some reason I picked it up without much trouble. He latched onto me with the idea of us helping each other study. That really amounted to me helping *him* study, but I did not mind. Studying with someone else just made me learn it that much better. Also, it was good to have a friend. I did not know many people in Bakersfield, and doing stuff with him was more interesting than going home to my parents' on the weekends.

Of course, being friends with Keith was nothing like my friendship with Lonnie. You only get one chance in your life to have a friendship like I had with Lonnie. Besides, Keith and I were very different. He came to class in slacks and a neatly ironed shirt with *The Wall Street Journal* under his arm. I showed up in jeans and a tee shirt. He kept his hair short and neat. Mine hung down to my shoulders. The two of us must have looked pretty odd together. He always looked like someone heading to a job interview. I must have looked like I was the guy who was there to mow his lawn.

In spite of being different, we got along just fine. He liked to go out drinking on Friday nights, and he could really hold his liquor. It was times like that—having contests in some bar to see who could drink the most— when it nearly felt like having Lonnie back again.

During our last semester, Keith started talking about going to San Francisco. He had been researching some companies up there and was sure that he could get in at one or the other of them. He had already put a résumé together and had his letters of recommendation lined up. He had even compiled a list of people with hiring authority at the various companies he was targeting.

"You should come up there with me. It would be great. We could share an apartment, split the cost of living. San Francisco is a wild city. We'd have a blast."

"Yeah, but what would I do there? Where would I get a job?"

"One of the places I'll be applying is a new publishing company. I'll bet they could use a photographer. If they saw your portfolio, you'd be in like a shot. Your stuff is really good."

"They must have lots of photographers already in San Francisco. Why would they want to hire someone like me?"

"Have you not learned anything at all by spending time with me, young man?" he asked jokingly. "You're just as good as anyone else. It doesn't matter where you come from. You just have to believe in yourself. You have talent. Most of what sells people is having confidence. Don't talk yourself into failure when you have a stack of photos as beautiful as yours. Besides, what else are you doing in June?"

"Well, I've been saving up some money. Remember my crazy idea of going back down to Mexico? I've been planning it for a while now. I already have my passport."

"Cool. I wouldn't mind a break before starting work. Where in Mexico were you thinking of going? Cabo? Puerto Vallarta? Hey, maybe we should live it up and head to Acapulco."

He had completely forgotten my story about Marisol.

"Actually, I was thinking of going to Monterrey."

"Monterrey? Monterrey, Mexico? What's there?"

"A girl," I answered sheepishly. "At least I hope she's there."

"Right. I kind of remember now. So, is this actually something serious between the two of you?"

"No." I laughed, a bit embarrassed. "It's not the least bit serious."

"But you've been keeping in touch with her?"

"Not really. I mean, no. Not at all, actually."

"So, how do you know she's still there? Or that she doesn't have a boyfriend? Or a husband?"

"I don't."

As I listened to myself, it became obvious even to me how crazy this all was. Still, Keith was doing his best to find a reason to come along.

"Monterrey. Is that on the coast?"

"No."

"So, there's no beach or anything like that?"

"No, it's just a big city. It's 135 miles from Laredo, Texas. From what I've read, it's got some nice mountains close by, though."

"So, how far away would the nearest beach be? I mean, where could we go once this chick has shot you down and you actually want to go enjoy yourself?"

"The Gulf of Mexico is only a couple hundred miles away."

"Okay, tell you what. This has all the signs of being the worst trip ever, but I'll go with you just to keep you from having the most boring time anybody had in Mexico ever. Do whatever it is you need to do in Monterrey, and after that we'll head for the beach and kick back. Then we'll head to San Francisco and find us a couple of good jobs. Does that sound like a plan?"

"Yeah, that's definitely a plan."

The less said about that trip to Mexico, the better. It was lucky that Keith and I did not end up killing each other. It was very different from traveling with Lonnie. I suppose I was not very fair to Keith. First, I dragged him to a place that was not exactly a tourist destination, and then I made him hang around with nothing to do while I went through telephone directories. There sure were a lot of Carvajals, and none of them wanted to talk to me on the telephone. Asking local people in bars if they knew any Carvajals who had a daughter named María Soledad did not turn out to be productive either, but at least it was more fun. What I had not prepared myself for was the sheer size of Monterrey. The population of the city and its suburbs was in the millions. Keith tried to be patient, but he finally went a little crazy just tagging along as I wasted day after day getting nowhere. Finally, he had it out with me and said he was taking a bus down to Tampico and that, if I had any brains, I would go with him. As stubborn as I was, I finally managed to see that he was right. I was getting nowhere in my search for Marisol, and I did not want to be left in Monterrey by myself.

Tampico felt like the end of the world—in more ways than one. The buildings dated back to Spanish colonial days, and they looked like they were being suffocated by all the lush tropical vegetation. We went to Miramar beach, and that was okay. It was obvious that Keith wished he was at one of the beaches on the Pacific side, like Puerto Vallarta or Cabo San Lucas. We made the best of it, lying out on the beach during the day and drinking way too many margaritas at night. All the while, I kept scanning the Mexican tourists, thinking I might get lucky enough to spot Marisol on vacation. Of course, that never happened. There was one good thing that came out of that trip to Mexico. I found that my Spanish classes—and practicing the language in Bakersfield's Mexican restaurants and bars—had paid off. While I could not understand or be understood by every single person I met, I was able to get by most of the time without having to ask people to speak English to me. That felt like a pretty good accomplishment.

Once we got back home, Keith made sure we did not waste any more time. Before I knew it, we were moving our stuff into a small two-bedroom apartment in San Francisco. The first few weeks were very discouraging. I spent days walking into the offices of any companies I thought could possibly use a photographer. I filled out a lot of applications and left a bunch of résumés. Keith had helped me to make a résumé so that the two of us could get them printed at the same time. He even got them printed professionally. It was not cheap, but Keith promised me it would be worth it. Maybe it was for him, but in the end it made no difference for me. The only thing that got me a job was Keith. It hardly seemed like it took any time before he had gotten hired by the advertising department at a weekly alternative newspaper that was just getting started. He was going out to work every day, and there I was still pounding the pavement trying to get an interview.

Then, one day, he came home and told me that the paper needed a photographer, that he had put in a word for me, and that I needed to go into the office with him in the morning because I had an appointment for an interview. Somehow, I think the job was mine even before I did the interview. It had definitely not taken Keith long to find his footing at that place. Anyway, I was lucky to get that job. It was not the best pay in the world, but the work was interesting. Mostly I spent my time going out with writers and taking shots of people they were interviewing or of places mentioned in articles they were writing. Sometimes I got sent out on my own. Every once in a while one of my photos wound up on the cover. When that happened, it was a real feather in my cap.

As for Keith, the world was his oyster. I was sure it would be no time at all until he was running the paper. I never understood how anybody could stand going out every single day and trying to sell stuff—like advertising—but Keith thrived on it. Every time he got a new account, he made a copy of the first page of the contract, circled the client's name red, and hung it on the bulletin board next to his desk. The board was always entirely covered.

Keith was definitely good at his job, but he was not leaving anything to chance. Before I knew it, he was dating Amy, who was not only a feature writer for the paper, but who also just happened to be the daughter of David, the owner and editor of the paper. Luckily, she had her own place, so they were mostly sleeping in her apartment. Our little flat would have been pretty crowded for three of us. I knew it was only a matter of time until Keith would be moving out altogether, and then I would have to either figure out how I would cover the rent by myself or find another roommate. It was not easy to find places to live in the city. Everything was really expensive.

Finally, the inevitable day arrived. Keith and Amy announced their engagement. It had all happened so fast. By comparison, I think I had had a grand total of three dates in the entire time it took for Keith to meet Amy, go out with her for the better part of a year, and then get engaged. I found it hard to meet women. I suppose I lacked confidence because the city was such a big place and everything was so expensive. My money barely stretched to cover the rent and utilities. There never seemed to be enough left over for taking someone to a nice restaurant. Keith and I always joked that the city was a bachelor's paradise for straight guys because women were always complaining that most of the men they met were either married or gay. The ratio between single straight women and single straight men definitely favored the men. Those odds did not help me much, though. That is, until Keith and Amy's engagement party.

Amy's parents had a cabin on the peninsula, up on La Honda Road. The party was mellow and relaxed, not at all stuffy like I thought it might be. It was not a big affair, mostly just close friends and family. It was not that interesting for me since the only people I knew well were Keith and Amy and, besides, I had to be on good behavior because the boss and his family were all there. I would have ducked out early, but I needed Keith to drop me off afterwards in the city. So I spent a lot of the evening sipping on a longneck bottle of beer and trying not to look too conspicuous.

"You look like you're having about as much fun as I am."

I looked around and saw a woman with one of the best smiles ever. She was a few years older than me and gorgeous. Unlike a lot of the women there, she was not wearing too much makeup or a really expensive dress. Her hair was reddish brown, and her face had a few light freckles. Her eyes were green, a much more intense green than mine. I could not stop looking at her smile.

"Oh, it's all right," I said. "I just don't know many people here. Everybody else seems to know each other already."

"Yes, it's all very incestuous. You must be one of Keith's people. Your side is massively outnumbered."

"Yeah, I'm Keith's roommate—at least for a while longer. None of his family was able to make it, so I'm the only one of his people from Bakersfield."

"You're from Bakersfield?"

"Well, not exactly. I'm from a little town not too far away from there. Keith and I went to Cal State together. That's where I met him."

"Yes, I thought I detected a twang."

"Twang? I don't have a twang."

"Yes, you do. You sound like one of those country western singers. Like Buck Owens. Isn't he from Bakersfield? I actually like country music. None of my friends do, but I enjoy it."

"I don't like country music much. Never have. Lonnie and I were always into hard rock."

"Is Lonnie your girlfriend?"

That made me laugh. It had been a long time since I had heard anybody make that mistake.

"No, Lonnie's my best friend. I mean, he was. He's dead now."

"I'm sorry."

'It's all right. It's been four years now. I guess he just wasn't cut out for getting old. Kind of like James Dean. You know, too fast to live, too young to die."

"You're funny. I bet he got teased as a kid. You know, a boy named Lonnie. By the way, I'm Lana."

She put out her hand for me to shake, and I took my time letting it go.

"Hi, Lana. I'm Dallas."

She broke out laughing.

"You're kidding, right. Dallas?"

"Yeah, that's my name."

"Like that new TV show?"

"Yeah, and the city in Texas."

"I bet you get teased about that."

"Yeah, I've always gotten teased about my name. A TV show with the same name will probably just make it worse. I hope it won't be on TV for very long. Otherwise, it could end up being the worst thing to happen to me."

"Except for your friend dying."

"Yeah, except for my friend dying."

She could not stop laughing.

"I'm sorry. I don't know why I said that. That was a terrible thing to say. It's just that... You have to excuse me. I just get really weird sometimes. I have an odd sense of humor. I'm always offending people with it. I really don't mean to be laughing about your friend."

"It's okay. It actually was pretty funny. Lonnie would have gotten a kick out of it. He had a pretty strange sense of humor too. I bet he's having a good laugh about it right now."

"Do you think he's listening to us?"

"Yeah, well, maybe. I don't know. But I used to talk to him all the time. It was kind of weird. It was like he was actually there. Not so much anymore. I guess I'm getting used to him being gone."

"Yeah, I feel the same way about my grandmother. I talk to her all the time."

"Oh, when did she die?"

Lana burst out laughing.

"I'm sorry. She's still alive. I don't know why I said that. It's just that she's so old, I sometimes think about her like she's already dead. Does that seem weird?"

"Yeah, it kind of does."

That made her laugh even more.

"Well, that didn't take long. I only just met you and you already know what a whacko I am. Tell me, Dallas, do you smoke?"

"Sometimes."

"I could really use a cigarette. Do you want to go outside for a smoke?"

"Sure."

Actually, I had not had a cigarette since Lonnie died, but I was definitely going to have one now if it meant being alone outside with this woman. We slipped out of the cabin and walked down the road under the trees. She pulled a pack out of her purse.

"Do you want one of these or do you have your own?"

"I'll have one of yours, thanks. And I'll take a light from you if you don't mind."

"Do you really smoke?" she said as she touched the end of my cigarette with her lighter. "Or are you just trying to impress me?"

"I used to smoke some but mainly because Lonnie always insisted. He didn't like to smoke alone."

I took a puff and exhaled.

"I've actually kind of missed it. It's hard to maintain my bad habits without Lonnie around."

She threw her head back and exhaled a large puff of smoke. She looked very glamorous, like an old-time movie star.

"Do you mind if I ask how old you are?" she asked.

"How old do you think I am?"

She looked me up and down, and there was something animal-like about her eyes that made me shiver.

"Well, you have to be over eighteen anyway, so I wouldn't be breaking the law."

"Breaking the law? What are you planning to do with me?"

"We'll see. I'm guessing you're twenty-two, twenty-three?"

People were always thinking I was younger than I was.

"Nope."

"Don't tell me you *are* eighteen. Don't tell me you're *seventeen!*"

"Do you really think I'm a teenager?"

"No. You're too wicked to be that young. What are you? Twenty-four, twenty-five?"

"Yeah, I'm twenty-five. Twenty-five going on sixteen. So, do I get to ask how old *you* are?"

"Old enough to be your, uh, big sister. How old do you think I am?"

"I don't know. Twenty-six?"

I deliberately tried to guess way under. Things were going pretty well, and I did not want to ruin it by guessing too high.

"Yeah, that's right," she replied with a big smile.

"Really?"

"No."

"Are you going to tell me?"

"You're going to think I'm ancient."

"No, I won't. It's just a number anyway. I can already tell how old your body is."

"Why, you filthy thing. You've been looking at my body? You should be ashamed of yourself."

"Don't change the subject."

"Thirty-two," she said. "Are you going to look at me like I'm your mother now?"

"I've never looked at my mother like this. I can't believe you're not in your twenties. You look really fine."

She got that look in her eyes that women sometimes get when a man says something that pleases them a lot. It was like some kind of thrill was running from her heart to her brain. She stopped laughing and became more serious.

"A guy like you has to have a girlfriend—even if her name isn't Lonnie."

"I am so girlfriend-less it is not even funny. I've never really had a girlfriend. Ever. At least not a real one."

"Not a real one? Does that mean you had an imaginary one? Or an inflatable one?"

She started laughing again. I loved the way she laughed.

"Do you want to go somewhere?" I asked her.

"We are somewhere."

"I mean somewhere else."

"Like where?"

"I don't know. Anywhere."

I tried to think of someplace, and then I remembered that once Keith and I had driven out of the city and down Highway 1 past Pacifica and Half Moon Bay. There were some nice beaches down that way.

"Let's go to the beach."

"You mean, just leave the party? Now? Together?"

"Sure. Why not? I don't know about you, but I'm pretty sure no one will miss me."

She looked doubtful. I could tell she was weighing what she wanted to do against using her better judgment. It was all playing out in her eyes. Finally, she broke into a huge grin.

"Okay, let's do it!"

"Cool. Just one thing, though. I hope you have a car."

"Of course. Don't you?"

"No, I don't need one in the city. I came with Keith. I know he won't mind one bit if he doesn't have to take me back there."

"Then this is your lucky night, Tex."

"Nobody calls me Tex."

"If your name is Dallas, then I get to call you Tex. Them's the rules if you want to ride in my car, Tex."

"Tex it is then. Let's go."

"I should go back in there and say goodbye to Amy and Keith."

"Cool. Then everyone in there will know that I'm the one leaving with the hottest chick at the party."

"On second thought, let's just go."

She had a tiny cherry red MG Midget convertible. We climbed in, all giddy like a couple of kids ditching school. The little car zipped down the mountain road toward San Gregorio. We had to shout at each other to be heard over the wind.

"I can't believe we're doing this," she screamed.

"Me neither," I yelled back.

"So, what were you like back in Bakersfield?"

"What do you mean?"

"I mean, I've never been there, but my idea of it was always that it must be pretty boring."

"Yeah, I guess it kind of was."

"So, what did you do there? I mean, for fun?"

"I dunno. On Friday nights Lonnie and I would cruise up and down Chester Avenue. Mostly I just remember working. During the summers and school breaks."

"Working at what?"

"Mainly working on my dad's cousin's farm. You know, chopping cotton, driving a tractor. During harvest, I would get to take cotton to the gin."

"Gin?"

"Yeah, the cotton gin."

"Cotton gin? Really? Well, I guess you learn something every day."

"You never heard of ginning cotton before?"

"No, I never thought about how they made gin. I sure didn't know they could make it out of cotton. That'll be something to think about when I'm having my next martini."

I got caught in a fit of laughing that lasted so long I thought I would faint from lack of breath. Lana looked at me like she thought I had gone crazy.

"What's so funny?"

When I finally caught my breath, I said, "You don't make gin from cotton. Not the gin you drink. You gin cotton to get rid of all the seeds. You never heard of Eli Whitney?"

"How would I know? I've never been on a farm. I don't know what goes on there."

"I think I'm going to like being friends with you. You're awful funny."

"I'm going to like being friends with you too. I've never known a cowboy before."

We laughed all the way to the Pacific Coast Highway. We stopped at a little store along the way and picked up a couple of fire logs and a bundle of kindling, as well as a bag of marshmallows and a bottle of red wine. Then we cruised along the coast until we spotted a nice deserted beach. She parked the car, and we grabbed a blanket out of the trunk and followed the trail down to the sand. I made a campfire, and soon we were huddling next to it for warmth and toasting the marshmallows. There was a full moon just above the horizon, the air was cold and smelled of salt, and a constant low rumble of waves broke on the surf. It definitely felt like the best night of my entire life.

We passed the wine bottle back and forth and laughed about everything. When we were too tired to laugh anymore, we just sat quietly, looking at the flames.

"So, Tex," she said finally, "why did you bring me out here?"

"We came in your car, so it was actually you who brought me."

"Don't try to evade responsibility. This was your idea. We're all alone out here. You have me at your mercy."

"Somehow," I said as I moved my lips close to hers, "I think I'm the one needing mercy."

The best night of my life kept getting better. As we kissed, the faint trace of her perfume smelled like roses and her warm mouth tasted slightly of salt. Before long, we were eagerly exploring each other's bodies, and our clothes came off in spite of the chill in the air. We made love for what seemed the entire night. At some point, we fell asleep.

The sun rising over the mountains woke us. That and the morning chill that felt colder than the night. It was not until the sun was fairly high in the sky that Lana got around to telling me why she had been at the party by herself. Her husband was away on a business trip.

5
James

AFTER WORK Keith and I would go out sometimes for a drink at one of the bars near the paper's offices. As time went on, Keith got into the habit of working later and later, and he was less inclined to go out after work. Shortly before their wedding, he and Amy bought a house in Marin, and his main preoccupation at the end of the day was how long it would take to get across the bridge. After they were married and when Amy got pregnant, there was more pressure on him to get home at a reasonable time. In hardly any time at all, Keith had gone from being the guy I hung out with to just a guy I happened to know at work.

Keith's new situation did not do much for my social life. Sometimes I would find someone else to go out for a drink with. Usually, though, I just went home or sometimes stayed at work late to use the darkroom for developing my own personal photographs.

One night as I was heading out the door, James from the production department collared me.

"Heading home, Dallas?"

"Yeah, I am."

"Do you have time for a drink? I'll buy."

He caught me by surprise. James had never before shown any interest in talking to me, let alone buying me a drink.

"Uh, where were you thinking?"

"I don't mind where. You can choose."

"Okay, I suppose so. How about Shelby's, across the street?"

"That's fine. Just let me shut down my machines."

I could not figure out for the life of me why James would want to have a drink with me.

As soon as we settled into a booth at Shelby's with our drinks, he started talking.

"Dallas, since you joined us, I have been extremely impressed with the quality of your photography. You have a lovely eye."

"Uh, thanks, James."

I would have returned the compliment, but I did not actually know a lot about what James did. I know he was mostly a typesetter and spent a lot of time at his keyboard retyping articles from the writers. He also did some paste-up. He had a reputation for being very fussy about his work.

"You guys in production do a good job too," I said. "The paper always looks good. Nice and clean."

"I believe you take photographs for yourself as well as for the paper?"

"Yeah, I'm always shooting photos. Anything that catches my eye. It's kind of second nature now. I shoot lots of stuff that the paper can't use. I just do it for myself."

"Do you have portfolios of all your work? I would really like to see more of it."

As much as I liked getting compliments for my work, I was starting to feel a little uncomfortable.

"I don't know. I mean, it's kind of personal stuff that I just do for myself."

"If you don't want people at work seeing it, I could come over to your place. I don't mind. I would like to see it all."

"Uh, well…"

"Yes?"

"It's just that, well…"

"Is there a problem? I don't think David minds you using the darkroom for your own projects if that's what you're worried about."

"No, it's not that. It's, well…"

I had no choice but to be direct.

"You know I'm not gay, right?"

He looked stunned for a moment, but then he laughed.

"Don't worry. You come across as nothing but straight. And for what it's worth, you would not be my type anyway. I'm not sure you would be any man's type."

"What's that mean? Are you saying there's something wrong with me?"

"No, no," he said, "you are not actually a bad looking fellow."

He reached across the table to my shoulder and fingered the ends of my hair.

"It's just that we'd have to do something about your stuck-in-the-sixties look. You can almost just about get away with it because you look young, but we would need to cut that hair and style it a bit. And burn those clothes. Are those the same clothes you wore in high school?"

My cheeks were burning. I sat back against the seat so that my hair slipped out of his fingers.

"I know I'm not the best dresser or anything, but I'm happy with the way I look. If it keeps gay men from coming on to me, then so much the better."

Defensively, I thought about the guys in my neighborhood who sometimes whistled at me At least *they* seemed to find me attractive.

James sighed.

"Why do straight men always think that every gay man in the world wants to jump their bones? Do you all have to think so highly of yourselves?"

"Are you saying gay men don't come on to straight men?"

"Not in my experience."

"Well, in my experience I've been hit on quite a few times. Well, not constantly or anything. But it happens every so often."

"Well, good for you. Yes, I'll concede that there are a few deluded souls out there who actually see it as a challenge to seduce a straight man—or at least a man who thinks he is straight. I assure you, that is the exception rather than the rule. I cannot imagine someone like you being troubled by gay men."

I was actually feeling a little annoyed. The conversation had begun with me worrying James was going to make a move on me. Now my ego was hurt because I was not good enough for him. I took a swig of my beer.

"Okay," I said. "I'm sorry I misunderstood you. So, why are you asking me all these questions about my photos?"

He laughed again.

"Yes, your photographs. I assure you that my interest in them is purely professional. Can I trust you with a secret?"

"Sure."

"I'm serious now. I do not want this getting out at work. I have to ask for your utmost discretion."

"Don't sweat it, James. I can keep a secret."

"The thing is, you see, I'm going to be leaving the paper. I don't know when exactly but probably sometime in the next couple of months. I am in negotiations to buy a print shop in Seattle. Thankfully it looks as though it is all going to work out. With any luck I will soon own my own business."

This was a complete surprise to me. I had not had any idea that James was interested in anything beyond his job at the paper.

"Hey, good for you. I hope it all works out for you, James."

"Once I get set up, I want to start my own alternative weekly up there. If that happens, I am going to need to hire people. I will be needing a photographer."

"Wow. This is a bolt from the blue. You want me to go work for you in Seattle?"

"Nothing is definite at this point. I just want you to think about it. I do honestly admire your work. It would give me a lot of confidence in the whole project if I had someone of your caliber shooting the covers."

"There must be photographers in Seattle."

"Yes, of course there are, but I know you and your work. It would save a lot of time and effort not to have to look for someone while I am still getting on my feet. The fact is I know I could rely on you, and I think we would work well together."

"Man, this is something I just wasn't expecting. I'll have to think about it. I mean, I like it a lot here in the city. I wouldn't know anybody in Seattle. Doesn't it rain a lot up there?"

"Yes, it does rain a fair bit. Is that a problem?"

"I don't know. I've never lived anywhere rainy before. And what about that volcano that erupted a few weeks ago? Isn't the place all covered with volcanic ash?"

"I don't think they got the worst of it. Anyway, when the recovery finally kicks in, Seattle is poised to be one of the best places in the country economically. Boeing is already coming back. And trust me, things are a lot cheaper up there than they are down here."

"You've really researched this, haven't you?"

"Yes, I have. No need to give me an answer this minute. As I say, things still need to be finalized. I just want you to think about it. I will let you know if and when I can offer you a job."

"This is great, James. Congratulations. And thanks for the heads up. The next round's on me."

We had a few more rounds as we sat there talking about his plans and ideas for his printing business. We talked about his ideas for a paper and what sorts of stories and features we might do. It felt good to know someone thought so much of my work and my ideas. I was starting to feel like a success.

Eventually, somehow, the conversation worked its way back to my dress and grooming habits.

"So, do you really think I should get my hair styled?"

James's hair was cropped short. He had a receding hairline, and the way he trimmed his hair made him look almost bald. He had a moustache and goatee that were so tightly trimmed they almost looked painted on. I definitely did not want to look like him.

"Maybe not styled. Just cut shorter and neater. You should definitely use a conditioner, to give it more body. If you wanted to let me make you over, I am sure I could make you quite the stunner. You really are a handsome fellow, you know. Not matinee idol handsome, I mean. But you have good eyes with nice long lashes and good cheekbones. If you were just a bit tidier, you could be amazing. Do you want to put yourself in my hands?"

"I don't know. It would be too weird."

"What would be weird about it?"

"You know, having a guy do all that hairdresser stuff to me—like I was a woman or something."

"You let a man cut your hair, don't you? I mean, assuming you ever do actually get a haircut, that is."

"Yeah, but that's different. Besides, I'm pretty sure my barber is straight."

"Why should that matter?"

"Well, because it does. Having a gay guy washing my hair and doing all that other stuff with his hands. I mean, wouldn't that just be turning him on? It would be for him like it would for me to be touching a woman. It might just be asking for trouble."

"So, you still have this idea that every gay man is lusting after you?"

"Well, that's kind of the whole point, isn't it? They like men."

"And you like women. That doesn't mean you lust after every woman you come across, does it?"

"Well…"

By this time the beers were definitely having an effect on me. I was getting kind of silly. I could not tell if James was getting silly too or he was being his usual self. He seemed to be the same no matter how many beers he had.

"Are you comfortable with gay people, Dallas?"

"Yeah, I guess. I mean, as long as they don't, you know, try anything with me. Live and let live, I say. What they want to do with each other is their own business. It just seems kind of sad."

"Sad?"

"Well, you know, living their lives knowing they will never get married, have kids," I said, staring down at my beer bottle. "It just seems like they miss out on a lot."

"Yes, it is indeed sad when one has to keep his love life secret from other people. I suppose it is not unlike, well, let's say being in a relationship with a married woman, eh?"

My head jerked up.

"What?"

I could tell by the look in his eyes that he knew something.

"Don't worry," he said. "I'm not in the habit of spreading gossip. In fact, I usually do my best to avoid listening to it. It's just that I wasn't able to avoid hearing something about you and David's niece being seen in a few different places. I assure you, I'm not judging you at all, but in the future you may want to be just a little more discreet."

"Jesus. Does everybody know?"

"No, no. I haven't heard anyone at work mention it. And I think I would have if there were any such scuttlebutt. No, I've gotten my information from other sources. As I say, you have nothing to worry about with me. I am very open-minded about these things. I just thought you should know."

"Well, thanks. I guess we should be more careful. I mean, it's not what you're probably thinking. We really are in love. It's just that she's waiting for the right time to tell her husband."

"Yes, I'm sure she is."

"So, I guess I didn't need to worry about you knowing I was straight. You must think I'm some kind of idiot."

"Is it that important for you that people know you're straight?"

"Well, yeah."

"You know, Dallas, I am starting to suspect that you may not be entirely comfortable with your sexuality."

"Oh, I'm comfortable with it all right," I laughed. "I'm *very* comfortable with it."

Yes, I was definitely getting silly.

"Let's play a little game. Do you mind? I want to make a point."

"A game. What kind of game?"

"It's a thought experiment. A mental exercise. It is meant to get you thinking a different way, to get a new insight into yourself. Shall we give it a go?"

"Sure, why not. I like a good game. How do you play it?"

"I am going to invent a situation. You have to take this situation seriously and answer my question with complete honesty. Are you game?"

"Sure. Hit me with your best shot. By the way, speaking of being comfortable with my sexuality, that Pat Benatar is one fine woman."

That gave me a good laugh, but James was losing patience with my silliness.

"So, you will answer seriously and honestly?"

"Yeah, yeah. I am nothing but honest. Shoot."

"Okay. Here is the situation. Aliens from another planet kidnap you. They are performing an experiment and they have total control over you. They give you an ultimatum. You must have sex with a man or they will kill you and everyone on earth."

"Goodbye, earth!"

"You have to take this seriously. You have to have sex with a man or you will die and everyone you know and love will die. But they allow you to choose who it is. They allow you to pick any man in the world. It can be a movie star or a pop star, or it can be one of your friends or just someone you know. You just have to say who you pick and they will bring him to their flying saucer. Once you have sex with him, they will erase both your memories, and neither of you will ever know that it happened. But you have to choose. Otherwise you and everyone else will die. Who do you choose?"

I drained my current bottle of beer.

"What kind of stupid game is this anyway?"

"It is a thought experiment. It is just to get you thinking about something you do not normally think about."

"You got that right. This is definitely something I do not think about."

"So, who do you choose?"

"I told you. It's goodbye, earth."

"You are not being honest. Do you honestly expect me to believe that you would let yourself and everyone else die rather than have a brief experience that you would not remember anyway?"

"I don't like this game. Let's play something else."

"Think about all the people in the world you love. Your parents, your brothers and sisters, your girlfriend, all your friends, your relatives. Would you really let them die?"

"It wouldn't be me killing them. It's the aliens' fault."

"They'd still be dead. Do you want that? Do you want to die?"

"I think I need another beer."

"You are probably already thinking of someone. The moment I posed the question, someone's face popped into your head. You know it did. You promised you would be honest. Just tell me who it is. I probably will not even know him."

"This is too weird. I don't want to be thinking about this. I don't like this game."

"Just say. And then it will be over. As soon as you say, I will go and get you another beer."

"It's too weird…"

"You see his face. Just say his name."

"Too weird…"

"I won't laugh or tease you. I promise."

"Do I have to?"

"It doesn't matter to me. It's about being honest with yourself."

"You're not going to leave me alone, are you?"

"I promise, tomorrow we will have forgotten we ever played this game. It won't matter."

"It's just too weird."

James began to stand up. I did not know if he was leaving or just going to get more beers.

"Okay. Okay. Justin."

"Who?"

"Justin."

"Who's Justin?"

"He makes the coffees at Flaubert's."

"Why him?"

"Because he looks cool. He looks the way I wished I looked."

"Describe him to me."

"He's young, maybe around twenty. He's tall and skinny. He has shaggy black hair and deep blue eyes. He kind of looks like Mick Jagger."

"At Flaubert's you say."

"Yeah. He works the espresso machine. The only reason I know his name is because sometimes I listen to him talking with the other people at the café while I'm waiting for my coffee. He talks about being in a band. He not only looks like a rock star, he probably is a rock star. I just get jealous sometimes looking at him. I bet he gets laid anytime he wants."

"Oh, yes, I think I know the one you mean. I've seen him. Yes, he is quite nice. Well done. I approve."

"There's nothing to approve. I don't even know him. I was just playing your stupid game. What was the point of it anyway?"

"As I said, it was just to get you to see things in a different way. The point is, underneath it all, even straight men see other men in a sexual way—even if they do not want to admit it to themselves."

"Are you saying I'm queer and that I just don't want to admit it?"

"No, that is not what I am saying at all. My point is only that you and I are not as different as you might like to think. That's all. You don't have to worry about it. My little experiment has not affected your testosterone level one bit. Go forth and breed all you want."

I was sorry I ever agreed to play James's game. I promised myself that I would never fall into that trap again. I let him buy me one last beer, and we found other things to talk about. I did my best to get Justin out of my mind. I felt like an idiot. I should have just refused to play. But now I had said Justin's name out loud and I could never unsay it. The sooner I forgot about the whole thing, the better.

Forgetting about it, however, turned out to be harder than I had thought. The next morning on my way into work, I stopped at Flaubert's for coffee to go, as usual. When I walked through the door, the first thing I saw was Justin standing behind the counter at the espresso machine. I could not look at him directly.

"The usual?"

"Yeah, the usual. Thanks."

As he ground the coffee, I looked around everywhere except at him. Eventually there was nowhere else to look. I watched him tamp the grounds in the metal coffee filter. His sleeves were rolled up, which menat I had to see the muscles flex in his forearms as he worked. He absent-mindedly ran his tongue over his enormous lips, as he attached the filter to the machine. He blew a lock of black hair away from his eyes as he began to steam the milk, then closed them. Somehow he knew exactly when the milk got to the right temperature, and his blue eyes reappeared from beneath his long lashes. It did not seem fair that a guy should be so good looking.

It suddenly dawned on me that he was looking at me.

"Everything okay?" he asked.

I realized he was looking at me because I had been staring at him.

"Uh, I was just thinking, you do a really nice job making the coffee. It always comes out great."

He broke into a big grin. Whenever he was in the middle of making coffee, he invariably had a serious and earnest look on his face. Most other times he usually had a silly grin. It was a nice smile. He had a slight overbite, but his teeth were otherwise perfect.

"Hey, thanks, man."

It was the truth. The coffee at Flaubert's was the best coffee I had ever had. My daily latte was a treat I looked forward to every morning. I would be lost without it.

I paid for the coffee and dropped all of the change into the tip jar.

Unfortunately, I thought ruefully, *I might have to start getting my coffee somewhere else. Damn you, James. I think you've made getting my coffee here too damn weird.*

6
Marty

THE BAY Area was just one of those places where weird things kept happening.

Things definitely got weird after I moved there. Maybe weird isn't exactly the right word. More like tragic. I had been living there a year when a congressman from San Mateo County went down to South America to investigate a commune set up by a preacher from the city. As the congressman's group was leaving Guyana, he and four others were killed in an ambush at the airport. Only one week earlier, he had been trying to get Patty Hearst's sentence commuted, and now he was dead. As if that was not crazy enough, everybody in the commune killed themselves by drinking poisoned Kool-Aid. The whole Bay Area was in shock, but the craziness still wasn't over. A week later, a guy who had recently quit the Board of Supervisors shot and killed Mayor Moscone and another supervisor. For people in the city it felt as if the whole world had gone completely crazy. Nothing made any sense anymore. For me it was as if the heart had been ripped out of the city—and in a very real way. It was as though the gaping hole down the street from me was where its heart had been. Machines were clawing at the dirt, making the hole grow bigger and bigger. All the old buildings—and the people who worked and lived in them—were gone. Just to make sure nobody would forget why the city's heart was ripped out, the hole would be filled with a convention center named after Mayor Moscone.

In a strange way, being there through all those crazy things that happened bonded me to the city and made me feel like a real part of it. It affected all of us in the same way, and nothing would ever change that. It did not matter that I had not always lived there. Everyone I knew in the city was from somewhere else. Either they were from somewhere else in California or from somewhere in the Midwest or from the East Coast or from other countries. We were all part of the city.

I loved the city. The sea breezes and the smell of salt in the air made it feel like always being at the beach. It reminded me of being a kid and escaping from the valley heat to Pismo Beach. Moreover, the city was full of wonderful characters. On my days off I spent hours walking all over the city. Camera in hand, I walked block after block, filling up a roll of film nearly as soon as I had bought it. Some days I left the apartment early in the morning and did not return until it was dark. I walked up and down steep hills. I shot views that had been shot countless times before, and I shot ones that maybe nobody had bothered to photograph before. Sometimes I walked as far as Golden Gate Park or the Sunset District or all the way to the Presidio and the Golden Gate Bridge. People might have thought I was odd because I spent so much time by myself, but I did not mind being alone. It gave me plenty of time to think. Besides, it never felt like being alone. There were always plenty of people around. That is the thing about cities. They are full of people. I never felt alone during the day—only at night. I did not mind going home to an empty apartment, as long as it was not dark yet. If nothing else, there was always the seagull that sat perched on the second floor window ledge across the street. No matter when I came or went, he always seemed to be there. I always looked for him and was always reassured to see him there.

The neighborhoods in the city were all different. Each one had its own great buildings and interesting people. The Financial District was full of business types and the affluent, although it also had its share of buskers and mimes and, inevitably, panhandlers. Chinatown was like being in a foreign country. So was the Castro, at least to me. People there dressed every which way and sometimes you did not know if you were looking at a man or a woman. Fisherman's Wharf was always jammed with tourists. The Haight was still full of hippies and flower children. It was as if it was still the 1960s. And don't get me started on the Tenderloin. Of all the areas, the place that kept drawing me back was the Mission District. If going to Chinatown was like visiting Asia, then the Mission was like being transported to Latin America.

Sometimes—not too often—I would slip into a church there and sit way in the back while the priest was saying Mass. I usually tried to be there when the Mass was in Spanish. For some reason I just liked the Spanish one better than the English one. Every so often I would put a few coins in the box and light a candle. I did it for Lonnie even though the last thing Lonnie would have wanted was for me to say a prayer for him in a church. I do not know exactly why I liked to do it, but for some reason it made me feel good.

I liked hearing people speak Spanish in the Mission, and occasionally I would overcome my shyness and strike up a conversation with somebody I did not know. Sometimes I got complimented on my Spanish, which made me feel good. Even more than the language, what drew me to the Mission was the food.

I had developed the habit of treating myself to a meal out on Sundays. If I was short of time, I just wandered down to Hamburger Mary's on Folsom Street, where the burgers were great. The sign over the entrance, which read "Enter at Own Risk," seemed appropriate, as some of the place's stranger denizens eyed me up and down.

When I had more time, I headed for the little restaurants and taquerías of the Mission. There was so much amazing food. It was like being in Mexico—definitely better than the Americanized stuff you found in some parts of the city. I made a point of ordering my food in Spanish. That may or may not have been the smart thing to do. Sometimes the food I got was so spicy hot that I could feel blisters forming in my mouth. The question was always, did they give me the extremely *picante* stuff because they thought I knew what I was getting? Or were they just teaching a lesson to the gringo showoff?

Generally I had little trouble conversing in the restaurants, which were usually family-run—as long as the discussions were kept simple. Some people, though, were just plain hard to understand. Obviously they had not learned *their* Spanish in California classrooms. They sounded nothing like the audio tapes in the Cal State language lab. Their accents varied depending on what part of Mexico they were from or, in many cases, what country they were from. Not everyone was from Mexico. There were quite a few people from Central America and even some from South America. During my months of visiting the Mission I must have chatted with scores of people from all over.

That is how I met Marty.

Walking down Mission Street one Sunday, I decided on a whim to explore a side street I did not know. The street was deserted and, to be honest, I was just a little nervous. As much as I liked the area, there were parts of it that could be kind of rough. I nearly decided to turn around when I spotted one of those little nondescript hole-in-the-wall places that often turn out to have great food. The place was quiet, and I was not sure if it was open. The door was unlocked, so I went in. I did not see anybody at first.

"*Hola*," I called out. "*¿Alguien aquí?*"

A stocky middle-aged man ambled out of the kitchen.

"Yeah? What can I do for you?"

Usually people were happy to respond to me in Spanish. Sometimes they took one look at me—like this guy—and just automatically answered in English.

"*Buenas tardes*," I said. "*¿Tiene un menú?*"

He grabbed a menu off the counter and extended his arm to indicate I could have my pick of the three small tables. The look on his face suggested boredom.

"Here you go."

The place was so quiet I wondered why it was even open. I sat down and studied the choices on the menu between the red and green salsa stains. It was surprisingly promising. It was not limited to the usual tacos and enchiladas. Menudo was on the menu. He also had mole poblano as well as pozole and a few things I had never heard of before. I had a good feeling about the food—if not the atmosphere.

"So, what can I get you?"

"*Yo tendré la carne asada a la tampiqueña por favor.*"

"You speak pretty good Spanish," he said without looking all that impressed. "You learn it in school?"

"Mostly. But I spent some time in Mexico. I had a friend who kept trying to teach me the language."

As he stepped back into the kitchen to prepare my food, he continued to talk to me through a window.

"That's the best way to learn. You have to live in the country, talk to the people. Where were you in Mexico?"

I guessed that most of his gringo customers—if he had any others— would answer that question with places like Tijuana or Puerto Vallarta. I prepared to impress him.

"I traveled the whole length of the country, from Baja California all the way down to Chiapas."

There was no reaction on his face, as he intently and vigorously chopped the steak meat. An entire minute went by before he responded.

"That's a hell of a long way. How were you traveling?"

"My friends and I drove as far as Michoacán. Then we took a bus into Mexico City. I traveled the rest of the way in a Jeep with an Irish guy I met."

"And this friend who was teaching you Spanish, where was he from?"

"I'm not sure exactly where he was from originally. He mostly grew up in L.A. That's where we picked him up. He wanted a ride to Hermosillo, but he ended up coming with us as far as D.F."

"You still in touch with him?"

"No. I only heard from him once after I got home. He sent me a postcard from Santiago, Chile."

"Did you say Chile?"

Now, finally, he sounded impressed—or at least suddenly interested.

"Yeah, he went there with a couple of guys he met in Mexico. That was just before the military takeover. I never heard any more from him after that. I've always wondered what happened to him. I didn't have any way to try to get in touch with him."

"So, he was there in '73?"

"Yeah, as far as I know. I was really worried about him when I read in the newspaper about all the stuff going on down there. It sounded like a lot of people were getting killed or arrested or just disappearing."

"Yeah, we did one hell of a job on Allende all right."

It was a strange thing to say. Maybe by "we" he meant the United States. After all, it was well known the U.S. government had supported the Chilean military.

I said, "You sound like you were actually there yourself or something."

"So, how do you want your meat cooked?" he asked over the hissing of the oil as he tossed the strips of beef onto the grill.

"*Medio cocido, por favor.*"

"Medium it is. So, you ever think of going down to Chile to look for your friend?"

"Yeah. I thought about it a lot. But I didn't have any idea where he was down there. And, to be honest, the idea of going to a country so far away—especially one with a military dictatorship—was kind of intimidating. And a trip like that wouldn't be cheap. I did try writing to the family in Mexico of the guy he went to Chile with. We stayed with them when we were in Michoacán, and they were really nice. I never heard anything back, though. I don't even know if I had the right address for them or if they even got my letter. I couldn't think of anything else to do. I just hope Antonio is all right and living his life out there somewhere. The only thing is, if he is okay, I suppose the fact he never got in touch with me again must mean he forgot about me."

The guy did not say anything else for a while. He just stared down at his grill as he aggressively worked the meat with his fork.

Finally, he said, "That's tough. It doesn't sound like there would be much of a paper trail on him. It could be hard to track him down."

He was lost in thought, as he kept working on the food. The smells wafting out of the kitchen made me feel suddenly famished. The aroma was a glorious mixture of grilled steak, garlic, jalapeños, cilantro, and lime. It had been a while since I had been so impatient for a meal.

"Antonio, huh? What was his second name?"

"I don't actually know. The way he came along with us on that trip, it all just sort of happened. We never bothered mentioning our last names to each other. I've kicked myself a million times ever since that I didn't ask him what his full name was or more about his life. In a way, I guess it doesn't matter. You see, he used a different name when he went to Chile. He used the birth certificate of his friend's dead brother to get a Mexican passport. He was going by the name Miguel Pérez Rivera. If there is any record of him down there, I'm pretty sure that's the name it would be under."

"Hmm. I might ask a friend if he can dig up any info for you."

"A friend? What kind of friend do you have who could find out something like that?"

For the first time he smiled. He even winked at me.

"I know a lot of people in a lot of places. You never know what one of them might be able to tell you if you just ask them."

"Hey, if you're serious about that, I mean, if you're not just being funny, I would give anything to know what happened to Antonio. It was one of those friendships that, you know, it didn't last all that long, but I've never been able to forget about him. You know?"

"Yeah, I know. Here's your food."

He walked out of the kitchen holding a steaming plate with a towel. He set it down in front of me and said, "There you go. Hold on. I'll bring you some tortillas."

The wonderful smell of the carne asada was incredible. What was this amazing food doing in such a dingy, out-of-the-way place? How come there wasn't a line out the door of people wanting to get in?

"What will you have to drink?"

"Don't suppose you could mix up a margarita?"

"Nah. I don't do cocktails. Not here. How about a nice cold Negra Modelo?"

"Sounds good!"

I took a bite of the meat. It was so tender I thought it was going to melt in my mouth. The spices were so good it was like eating Mexican food for the first time. I could not believe I was the only customer in the place.

"This is great," I told him enthusiastically. "You must get a lot of people in here for food like this."

The praise did not impress him. He simply shrugged.

"I do all right. I like to cook. I'm not looking to get rich. I just open the place when it suits me. My regular customers know when I'll be here."

"Well, I intend to be one of your regular customers."

"No problem. I like to see a young guy like you enjoy his food."

He held out his hand.

"I am Martín. My friends call me Marty."

"Well, Marty, I think this is the beginning of a beautiful friendship."

He laughed.

"So, you like *Casablanca.* Good movie. There's no one like Bogie. Never will be anyone like him again. He was one of a kind."

I savored every mouthful of that meal. It was so good I nearly wept when I got to the last bite. As much as I would have liked to hang around and talk some more with Marty, it was getting late and I had a long walk home.

"How much do I owe?"

"Let's see, $4.50 for the carne asada and another buck for the beer."

I had enjoyed the food so much that, after getting my change, I left a dollar on the table. I thought he would be pleased, but he picked it up and handed it back to me.

"You don't need to tip. I'm not a waiter. I'm the owner."

"I just wanted you to know how much I liked the food."

"Don't worry, I can see you liked it. I could tell by the way you were eating it. That's good. You know, you don't look like you eat enough. You should definitely put some meat on those bones, kid. When you come back, I'll give you extra portions. On the house."

This had turned into one of the best days I had had in a long time. It was so lucky that I found that place. The only sad thing about it was that there was no one to share it with or to talk about it with. I really missed Lonnie right then. He knew his Mexican food and he would have appreciated how good that food was. He definitely would have loved that place—if I could ever have gotten him to come to the city in the first place. I got sadder thinking of all the things I had done and experienced the previous six years and how Lonnie was frozen in time—now and forever—at the age of 21.

Poor Lonnie. He always got the short end of the stick. It killed him that his father left and never made any effort to see him again. Then he had to put up with a stepfather he hated. He drank too much and always got into trouble. Then he got drafted and had to go into the army. Then he died. Compared to him, my life was near perfect. When I was at Cal State, one of the books I read was *The Picture of Dorian Gray* and, in a strange way, the picture in that story reminded me of Lonnie. It was as if Lonnie was *my* picture of Dorian Gray. I got all the good stuff, and he got all the bad stuff.

I thanked Marty for the food and told him I would definitely be back.

From then on I made a point of walking down to Marty's restaurant most Sundays and trying every single thing on the menu at least once. I never ceased to be amazed how quiet the place always was. Sunday afternoon was definitely the best time to go there because I usually had the place to myself. Sometimes Marty's friend Leonides would be there, just hanging out with him, but usually it was just me.

Leonides was a strange bird. Tall, thin, and gangly with longish black hair dangling from under an old-fashioned fedora, he looked to me like a walking scarecrow or maybe a toy skeleton all dressed up. He wore thick horn-rimmed glasses over his beak of a nose and appeared to be in his fifties. I never heard him speak any English, and he never talked to me, but he and Marty would have long involved conversations in Spanish about everything and anything. They often talked about what was going on in various Latin American countries. It was entertaining to watch them converse because they enjoyed listening and talking to each other a lot. It was the only proof I had that Marty even spoke Spanish since he never spoke to me in anything but English.

Every so often, when they got onto a subject that Marty considered somehow sensitive, he would point in my direction and say half-jokingly to Leonides, "*Cuidado, hombre. Ese joven nos entiende. Él sabe muy bien castellano.*"

It made me feel good that he thought I was following their conversations with no problem. In fact, I was getting only about half of what they were saying, but that still seemed pretty good to me. Their accents were different from the way I had heard Mexican-Americans talk. I wondered if Marty and Leonides were both from the same country and, if so, what country it was. At first I had assumed Marty was Mexican-American, but as time went on I was pretty sure he was neither American nor Mexican. He was not interested in talking about himself, and I was not very good at asking direct questions.

On the afternoons that Leonides was not around, I sometimes got Marty to talk about some of the countries he knew about. He had an opinion on every one of them. For instance he said the Mexican Miracle had about run its course and the ingrained corruption of the PRI was about to catch up with them. A lot of his opinions were pretty right-wing. He thought the military takeover in Argentina was necessary, though the generals were carrying it too far and were too heavy-handed with the Montoneros and the

ERP. He thought Pinochet was doing a good job in Chile and that the upcoming constitutional referendum would show that he was sincere about returning the country to democracy. While he condemned the people who had killed Óscar Romero during Mass in El Salvador, he added that the archbishop "had really been asking for it." His harshest words were for Fidel Castro. He insisted that history would show that he was the worst of Latin America's dictators and that the boatlift from Mariel was proof of it. Throughout all his commentaries, there was always an insinuation he had some kind of extra information that most other people did not.

I never tried to argue with Marty when he got off on one of his rants about this country or that leader. He had a lot more facts at his disposal than I did, and I knew I had no hope of winning a debate against him—even if I thought he was wrong. It was easier just to sit back and listen to him while I ate his delicious food. At the end of the day it did not matter to me what he thought. People are entitled to their own opinions. I knew that pretty much everybody I worked with at the paper would peg him as some kind of reactionary conservative crackpot.

In spite of his politics—or maybe because of them—Marty fascinated me. I did not know what to make of him. Did he really have all those connections that he kept hinting at? Or was he just a bluffer who was good at sounding like he knew everybody and everything? I had no way of knowing. At least not until the day he landed a bombshell on me. On one of my Sunday afternoon visits, I walked in and took a seat as usual.

"What'll you have today, amigo?"

"I think I'll have the enchiladas de mole poblano, Marty."

He disappeared back into the kitchen, and I could hear the usual sounds of him getting my order. Then there was a new sound. I could have sworn it was the rattling noise of ice in a cocktail shaker. Before I knew it, he was back out in front of me setting a large rimmed champagne glass on the table. The rim was salted.

"Compliments of the house."

"You made me a margarita? I thought you didn't do cocktails here."

"For you I'm making an exception."

I took a sip. It was ice cold and contained a strong kick of tequila. It did not taste like a lemonade slushy the way many restaurant margaritas did. The lime juice tasted fresh squeezed. I could also detect a healthy dose of Triple Sec.

"*¡Excelente, señor! ¡Muchas gracias!*"

Soon he was back with the enchiladas.

"You've really outdone yourself, Marty. What the hell are you doing here anyway? You should be working in a big fancy place. You could be making a fortune with your cooking and mixology talents."

"That sort of thing don't interest me. I like working small. Seeing the smile on a face like yours once in a while is all I need."

"Well, the world's loss is my gain. I'm just glad I lucked into finding you."

He stood there smiling for quite a while. His eyes twinkled.

"Say," he said, "you know that friend of yours? The one you went to Mexico with and then he went on to Chile?"

"Yeah, Antonio. What about him?"

"You said you never knew his last name?"

"That's right."

"It's Vega."

"What?"

"His name is Vega. Antonio Vega."

Then he vanished back into the kitchen, leaving me sitting there with my mouth hanging.

7
Justin

I DECIDED it was stupid to stop going to Flaubert's just because James had made it all weird with his stupid game. Even if I could not quite bring myself to look Justin in the eye whenever he was handing me my coffee, I knew there was no reason for me to be embarrassed. Sure, guys—well, straight guys anyway—do not usually go around pointing out men they think are attractive, but James had a point. It did not have to mean anything. It was not like I had a crush on Justin or anything. I just wished I looked as cool as he did. That's all. I put James's silly game out of my mind and moved on.

What I had not counted on was that James had not finished playing games with me. A week or so after my "date" with him at Shelby's I came out of the darkroom at work, and someone said, "Hey, Dallas, there's someone looking for you up front."

That was unusual. No one ever came into the office looking for me unless I was expecting them. I had no idea who it could be. I quickly washed the chemicals off my hands and went up to the front. Standing on the other side of the counter was Justin from Flaubert's.

"Yes?"

"So, this is where you work?"

"Yeah."

"Cool. So, you're Dallas Green?"

"That's right."

"It's funny. I see you, like, every morning, but I never knew your name before. I'm Justin."

"Yeah, I know. I mean, I've heard people calling you that in the café."

"So, you're a photographer?"

"Yeah, that's right."

"I was talking to your friend. You know, James?"

"You were, were you?"

"Yeah. Nice guy. He said you were working on a project."

51

"Uh, what project was that?"

"He said you were doing an art spread about Bay Area bands and that you were looking for some bands to photograph. It just so happens I'm in a band. I was wondering if you would be interested in photographing us."

"James told you this, huh?"

"Yeah. I hope it's all right me coming here to see you about it. I just thought since you're a regular at the café, you might not mind. I mean, you probably have lots of bands already lined up, probably better known ones than us. It would just be so cool if we could get into a paper or a magazine or something. Or just have some professional photos for our own publicity. We could pay you for them. I mean, if they're not too expensive. It would help us out a lot. I'd really appreciate it. I might even be able to slip you a free coffee now and then, you know, when the boss isn't looking."

I was only half-listening to what he was saying. At the moment my mind was focused on the various ways I might kill James.

"Yeah, well, I don't know whether that particular project is going ahead or not. I'll have to let you know."

"Sure, I understand. Thanks for listening to me anyway. It's just so hard to get anywhere with music in this city. There's so much talent and competition around. It's hard to get noticed and get gigs. You know, ones that pay anything."

I kind of felt sorry for him. I had built up this image of him in my head of being so cool and perfect. I had completely missed the fact that he was only just a kid. He didn't see himself as a rock star at all.

"No problem. Hey, let me know sometime when you're playing somewhere and I'll come listen to you—and maybe shoot some photos then."

"Hey, that would be great! Say, we're rehearsing tonight. Do you want to come and watch? Maybe you could take some pictures of that?"

"Yeah, okay, I guess I could." I grabbed a pencil and notepad. "Just tell me where and what time."

"Thanks, man! I really appreciate this. If I can ever do you a favor, just let me know. Anything at all. Just name it. You're my new best friend. Really."

"Don't get carried away there. You might want to know me better before you start offering me carte blanche."

"No, I mean it. Anything at all. Just ask. I definitely owe you. Anything at all. No matter what. Anything."

Please stop saying that, I thought.

"Thank you," he said. "I'll see you tonight. Just make sure to knock loud on the door. We don't always hear when people show up. We get pretty loud."

That evening I went to the address he had given me. It turned out to be only a couple of blocks from my apartment. It was upstairs in an old warehouse. Just like he had said, nothing happened at first when I knocked. I knocked louder, and then again. Finally, a short Asian guy with glasses opened the door.

"Yes?"

"Hi, I'm Dallas. Justin asked me to come watch and maybe shoot a few photos."

"Right! The photographer! Come in, come in."

I followed the guy in. He re-joined the others in the middle of the space and stood behind a microphone. Two guys with guitars were on either side of him. Justin was behind, surrounded by drums.

"Rad!" he shouted. "You made it. Guys, this is Dallas. Dallas, this is Johnny, Terry, and Rick."

He pointed at each one in turn with a drum stick.

"And I'm Justin. But you knew that already. Let's play something for him, guys."

They began to play some heavy metal. They were okay, but they weren't exactly Iron Maiden. I didn't recognize the song, and my guess was that it was something they had written themselves.

"Nice," I said when they had finished. "What do you call yourselves?"

Justin pointed to his bass drum with one of drum sticks. There was a logo painted on it that read, "ÜberVenge."

"Cool name," I lied. "Play another one. I'll get some shots."

I walked around for different perspectives—kneeling on the floor, climbing halfway up a ladder that was against the wall, stuff like that. The four of them were definitely playing to the camera, hamming it up when they saw the lens pointed in their direction. They definitely thought they were some hot stuff. After playing five songs—which I guessed was the entire repertoire—they were eager for my opinion. I gave them plenty of compliments. I could see why they were having trouble getting gigs, but there was no point in hurting their feelings.

"Thanks, man!" said Justin. "Think you got anything there you can use?"

"Yeah, I think so. I can't promise that they will get published, but I'll be happy to make you some prints."

"Rad!" said Rick.

"Hey, does anybody want to go get a beer?" asked Justin.

The other three said they had to go to work early in the morning.

"How about you, Dallas?"

"Uh, okay."

"Cool. I'll get my jacket."

Down on the street we said goodbye to the other three.

"A couple blocks from here there's a bar we go to sometimes," said Justin. "If the right guy is working, he never IDs me."

"How old are you?"

"I'll be twenty-one in two months. The stupid liquor laws are a real pain. Say, are you old enough to buy?"

Like everybody else, he thought I was younger than I was.

"Yeah, I can buy. Tell you what. I actually live just a couple of blocks from here. Let's pick up a six-pack and drink it at my place. It'll be cheaper that way."

"Cool."

Justin was impressed with my apartment, though it was about the size of a postage stamp.

"This is such a cool pad. I wish I lived in the city."

"Why? Where do you live?"

"With my parents. In Mill Valley. It's so boring there. I spend the night in the city whenever I can instead of going home after work. Terry is cool about letting me crash at his place. And sometimes, when we have a gig, I get lucky afterward. There's almost always some woman who will take me home. One time I went home with a woman who told me she had slept at least once with every single drummer from every single band in the city. She said she was taking me home with her to keep her perfect record. Man, what a night that was. She was really good in bed. Really experienced, you know what I mean? I mean, she was, like, *really* old. I think she was twenty-seven."

"That's pretty old, all right."

"Yeah, there's nothing like an older woman."

"My friend Lonnie used to say that men start their lives coming out of a vagina and then spend the whole rest of it trying to get back in. I think he might have been talking about you."

Justin laughed.

"Lonnie sounds like one righteous dude. Hey, it was really nice of you to come listen to us and take all those photos. I owe you, man."

"Don't worry about it. I had a good time."

"So, what do you do for fun. I mean, when you're not out photographing struggling heavy metal bands?"

"Not that much. Mostly, I just like to walk around the city and shoot lots of photos, mostly for myself."

"So, would you like to hang out? I mean with me? The other guys don't have as much time as I do. Todd and Rick are always with their girlfriends, and Terry works all the time."

"Yeah, I guess we could."

What a strange world it was. A week ago I did not know this guy at all, and I had a completely different picture of him. Now I knew all kinds of things about him, and we were suddenly buddies. We were going to be hanging out together.

Justin and I got into the habit of going out for a drink at least once or twice a week. Sometimes we would go hang out at the bar where he could get served, and sometimes we would just take some beer back to my place. Hanging out with him actually turned out to be an okay way to pass the time. The only annoying part was that sometimes, when he met me at work, James would spot us and give me an obnoxious smirk.

Justin's and my tastes in music were pretty similar, and we spent a lot of time listening to records from our music collections. Sometimes we went to see one of the bands he liked. It never seemed to dawn on him that I was six years older than he was. At least not until the night he dragged me to see a band called Dead Kennedys at the Mabuhay Gardens in North Beach.

They had just finished a song called "When Ya Get Drafted" and he yelled at me over the noise of the crowd, "Hey, that reminds me. Did you hear the news?"

"What news?" I yelled back.

"About the draft!"

"What about it?"

"They're bringing it back."

"Really?"

"Yeah, it was on the news. Carter has started up the draft again. This thing with the Soviet Union is getting serious. First, he boycotts the Olympics. Now he's starting up the draft. We're going to have to get registered."

He was totally freaked out. I just laughed.

"What do you mean we, white man?"

"You'll have to sign up too. It's the law. We're fucked, man."

"I don't have to sign up."

"You don't? Why not?"

"I already signed up. A long time ago."

"You did? When?"

"I signed up when I turned eighteen. It was the law back then too."

He looked totally confused.

"What? How old are you anyway?"

"Old enough to have barely missed Vietnam."

"Jesus. I knew you were older than me, but I didn't think you were *that* much older."

"Yeah, I know. I should be hanging out with your dad instead of you."

"So, you're not worried about getting drafted?"

"Nope. Besides, I don't think they call up guys over the age of twenty-six."

I put my hand on his shoulder as a gesture of reassurance.

"Don't worry. I don't think they'll be sending the army to Afghanistan anytime soon. They learned their lesson in 'Nam."

I thought maybe Justin would see me differently when he realized how much older I was. Maybe he would even lose interest in hanging out with me altogether, but it did not seem to matter to him. We kept on spending time together, and I eventually introduced him to the pleasures of tequila. Occasionally, I would buy us a bottle of Scotch to drink on a Saturday night while we dimmed the lights and put on some Black Sabbath. Justin would return the favor by sharing joints he had bought from a friend of his in Marin. After enough shots, I would sink into my chair and pretend I was eighteen and that Justin was Lonnie.

One Saturday night he took me to a party his friend had told him about in the Haight. When we walked into the house, we were met by a wall of haze and smoke. This was definitely the granddaddy of all pot parties. For a long time we stood there, wondering if we should go in. I stared into the fumes and tried to make out how many people were there and what sort of condition they were in. Some were sprawled over chairs. Some were stretched out on the floor. A few were sitting upright on the floor. A couple of them were actually on their feet. Jefferson Airplane's *Surrealistic Pillow* was playing on a turntable. It was like 1968 all over again.

"Some of these people are completely wasted," said Justin. "Look at that guy over there."

He was pointing at a wiry guy with long stringy hair sitting on the floor by himself in a corner. He looked as if he had been there for hours, and it was kind of sad. His eyes were glazed and he was talking to himself. I kept staring at him.

"Hey, I know that guy!" I said.

"Really?"

"Yeah, I went to high school with him. His name's Steve. Steve Barton."

"You and that guy are the same age? Are you sure? He looks really old."

Justin was right. Steve's hair was much longer than mine, but that only made it more obvious how much of it he had lost. I never felt more like Dorian Gray than I did in that moment.

"I'm going to talk to him."

I sat on the floor next to him.

"Steve?"

"Huh?"

"Steve, it's me. Dallas."

"Huh?"

He was really out of it.

"Dallas Green. We went to high school together."

He finally started to focus a bit.

"Oh, Dallas! Hi, man. Hey, what are you doing here?"

"I just wandered into this party with a friend. I'm living here now. In the city."

"Cool. Man, I haven't seen you in a long time. How long has it been?"

"It's been nine years, man. I haven't seen you since that time Lonnie and I crashed at your place in San Diego."

"Oh, yeah. I remember that. You and Lonnie showed up at the apartment. Not too long after we moved in. You had that Mexican kid with you."

"That's right."

"Man, what a night that was! Did we get shit-faced drunk or what? Man, those were some good times. So, how's Lonnie doing anyway?"

"Lonnie? Jesus, didn't you hear? He died."

"Oh yeah, right. Come to think of it, I did hear that. There was some story about him. I'm trying to remember. Oh yeah. Damn. I heard he went to 'Nam. Heard he died a hero. Threw himself on a grenade and saved a bunch of men. Who would have thought, huh? Ol' Lonnie McKay turning out to be a hero?"

"Where the hell did you hear that bullshit story?"

"I forget. Someone told it to me. I don't remember exactly."

"Well, it's bullshit. Lonnie never went to Vietnam. He died in West Germany."

"Germany? Really? Nah, that can't be right. Why would he be fighting Germans? We ain't had to fight any Germans in a long time."

"He wasn't fighting Germans. He died in a road crash."

"Car crash, huh? Yeah, well, I'm not surprised. Lonnie always was a crazy driver. Too bad though. I always liked Lonnie."

"He wasn't the one driving. He was in the back of a truck."

"Damn, well, that was fucked. They should have let Lonnie drive. He may have been crazy, but he usually came out all right when he was doing the driving."

"Steve, what are you doing here? Where's Tina?"

"Oh, didn't you hear, man? We got divorced. A long time ago. Shit, I don't even remember how long it's been now."

"What about the baby? Tina was expecting a baby that time we saw you in San Diego."

"Yeah, we had a little girl. You should have seen her, man. She's beautiful. Don't see her much these days, though. Tina's kind of pissed at me because I got a little behind in child support. It's just so fuckin' hard getting by in this economy. There's no jobs anywhere. The economy's totally fucked. And all Carter has done is tell us to turn down the heat and put on sweaters."

"So, where's Tina now?"

"She got married. Last I heard they were living in Clovis. The guy she's married to is a real prick."

"Sorry to hear all this, Steve. I really am."

Steve stopped talking. He looked as though his mind was drifting off again. I didn't particularly want to talk to him anymore anyway. Seeing him this way was kind of depressing. I looked around for Justin. I finally spotted him on the other side of the room. He was standing there talking to a girl with long blonde hair. I had no idea what they were saying to each other, but no matter what Justin said, she laughed like it was the funniest thing that she had ever heard in her life. She was a lot shorter than him. She just kept looking up at him and smiling and doing her best to make sure he did not look anywhere else. I wished that, just once, at a party a girl would look at me that way.

If he doesn't go home with her, I thought, *then he is an idiot. I sure would. She's beautiful.*

Justin leaned down and whispered something in her ear. She got a big smile on her face, and then they both made their way to the door.

Well, that's that, I thought. *I won't be seeing Justin again tonight.*

God, I wished I had his looks and his life. He did not seem to worry about anything. I bet he never stayed awake all night because every dark thought in the world would not let him sleep.

"Say, Dallas?"

"Yeah, Steve?"

"I was wondering. You know, I'm a little short. I've been washing dishes down at Mancini's, but they haven't needed me the past couple of days. I was just wondering, you know, if you could help me out a little. I swear I'll pay you back, just as soon as they give me some work again."

I dug into my pocket. I found a five-dollar bill and handed it to him.

"Thanks, man. I really appreciate this. I'll pay you back just as soon as I can. You don't have to worry."

"Yeah, sure," I said. "No problem. Well, I've got to be going now. Good to see you, Steve. Take care of yourself."

I got to my feet. He still had the sawbuck in his hand, and he looked like he was starting to nod off.

"Good luck," I said, just to be saying something while I walked away.

I figured there was no point hanging around now that Justin was gone. I might as well just head home. I did not look forward to spending the rest of the night alone. I would have given anything if Lana would have been waiting for me back at my place.

8
Golden Gate

IN ADDITION to the Mission District, my other favorite walk on a Sunday was a long one. That is why I did not do it very often. It would involve walking down Lombard Street—not the twisty part but the long straight part heading west—out to the Presidio and then across the Golden Gate Bridge. When the weather was clear, the view was spectacular. The city, its skyline dominated by the Transamerica Building, was magnificent. The water, such a breathtaking distance underneath, sent chills down my spine. On the bridge it was always cold. When there was fog, it was like being high up inside a cloud. The bridge's huge cables disappeared into the mists above as if they were connected to a different world. When I got to the halfway point, I liked to stand there and think. There were usually lots of people walking or cycling on the pedestrian path, but every once in a while I seemingly had the whole bridge to myself.

One particular evening I set out from my apartment later than usual. As I walked down Lombard, I listened to a tape I had just bought for my Walkman, *Armed Forces* by Elvis Costello. It was not the sort of music I usually listened to, but I liked it a lot. As usual, I wondered what Lonnie would have thought of it. There had been so much new music since he died, if he were to somehow come back, he would have real trouble catching up with it all. What new bands would he have liked? Which ones would he have hated? It was always one or the other with Lonnie. There was never anything in between. One thing I knew for sure anyway was that he would have hated disco with a passion.

That day I was missing Lonnie more than usual. I was lonely for him, and I was lonely for Lana. Gary was not going away on as many business trips as before. That is what she told me anyway.

Listening to "Accidents Will Happen" for the third time that day, I thought about how my life had become one long fruitless search for a Lonnie replacement. Of course, no one could actually replace him. You only get to have one friend like that in a lifetime. After you get to a certain point in your life, no new friend will ever really know the real you. He will never know what you were like as a kid or as a teenager. We get too good at hiding away the parts we do not want other people to see, the parts that embarrass us. I tried telling myself to grow up, to just deal with it. This is life, after all. Besides, if Lonnie had still been alive, he and I might not even be friends anymore. We had already started to drift apart by the time we got back from our trip to Mexico. Me going to college and him going into the army only set our paths further apart. One of the last things he said to me before he shipped out was that college was a waste of time and only suckers went to school any longer than they had to. When he got out of the army, he said, he would show me how real money was made. If he were still alive, I wondered, would he have ever come up to the city to visit me? Of course, he would have—at least once in a while. Would it have been the same though? Probably not.

Because Lonnie died when he did, our friendship was frozen in one particular moment forever. Because he was gone, there was a huge hole in my life where that friendship had been and which would never be filled. Sometimes I liked to fantasize that Lonnie was not dead at all, that he had somehow faked his death and was hiding out in West Germany or somewhere else. In my fantasy he was laughing at me and at everybody else because we all fell for his one last best joke. There had been rumors for years that Jim Morrison did not actually die in that bathtub in Paris, and now there were people saying that Elvis Presley was still alive. Wouldn't it be great if Lonnie had actually pulled it off? I would have given anything for it to be true.

For a while I thought Linda was filling the empty space, but that blew up pretty fast. Anyway, she was the absolute worse person to be my Lonnie replacement. After all she was the one who most reminded me of him. The night I slept with her felt like I was cheating on Lonnie.

Later I thought Keith might be my new Lonnie. He and I did have some good times together. He could almost keep up with Lonnie in the drinking department. Still, he was no Lonnie. Keith was too serious about everything: about work, about making money, about life. Of course, once he met Amy, it all changed anyway. Whereas Lonnie never allowed a girlfriend to monopolize his time, once Keith met Amy, it was as though I hardly ever saw him again. Who could blame him? I would have done the same in his place.

When I met Lana, I thought maybe she was the answer. Not only was I in love with her but the two of us had fun together. A lot of it was the same silly, getting-into-trouble kind of fun Lonnie and I used to have. She and I would have been good friends even if we had not been lovers. I wanted to be with her all the time. Being so limited in the amount of time I could spend with her was torture. Maybe she would finally become my real Lonnie replacement, my other half, my alter ego. That was not what she was now, though. We simply spent too much time apart.

As for my new friendship with Justin, it was something totally unexpected. I did not take it very seriously at first. I expected him to get tired of hanging out with me fairly quickly. I figured he had plenty of friends his own age, but apart from his bandmates he did not seem to. Even so, I expected it would only be a matter of time until he had a steady girlfriend and would disappear like Keith. So far, though, that had not happened. He had his occasional one-night stands, but beyond that he seemed perfectly content to spend time with me. God only knows why. Could he not see how uncool I was? One day he surely would and after that I would doubtless never see him again. Believing that made me pretty sure he was not going to be my new Lonnie. I just could not see him and me still being friends in our thirties or in our forties. Not the way Lonnie and I would have been, regardless of how much we might have drifted apart in our day-to-day lives.

As all these thoughts churned in my head, I came to the same conclusion I always came to. There was no replacing Lonnie. That hole was just always going to be there.

I approached the south end of the bridge. I looked at Fort Scott below and then at the line of cars filing past the toll booths as they came into the city. I was glad pedestrians could cross for free. The sea wind buffeted me as I walked high above the channel connecting the ocean with the bay. Most of the car traffic was in the far lanes, and it was barely moving. Everybody was coming home from their weekend outside the city. It was now late enough that I was the only person on the walkway. I looked over toward the city and watched more and more buildings reveal themselves. It was dark and many of the windows were lighting up. I took a shot with my camera.

That makes only one million and one times now someone has taken that exact same picture, I thought. Still I could not help myself.

The farther I walked, the more I became aware of the gulf of empty space underneath me. The south tower and its cables loomed high above me. To either side there was dark emptiness. The water seemed a million miles beneath me. I thought about the fact I was standing over the San Andreas Fault and how the city had nearly been destroyed seventy-four years earlier. That was a quarter-century before they built the bridge.

What would happen to this bridge if that earthquake happened again right now? I wondered.

I had begun shivering. I walked faster in an effort to warm up. Soon I was at the center of the bridge. Usually, I would walk all the way to the Marin County side to have a good look from the viewpoint over there, but it was getting too late. I decided to stop where I was. It would be late before I got home, and I had to go to work in the morning. I began to shiver again as I looked at the bay, at Alcatraz and at the outline of the Bay Bridge.

I did not want to go home. No, it was more than that. It was actually a dread that, the more I thought about it, began to turn into panic. I knew exactly what lay ahead. On the rare nights that Lana could spend the entire night, I could just about manage to keep the darkness away. On all too many nights, though, the darkness was endless. I would lie in bed, while the minutes and hours dragged on endlessly. My heart would be consumed with dread—even though I could not explain why. I would lie there with my eyes closed, feeling like a child afraid of a monster in the night. I could not explain to myself—let alone anyone else—what the fear was. Was it the fear of death and its certainty? Maybe it was the fear of the *uncertainty* of death—of knowing that it would come but not knowing when or how. Would it be drawn out and painful? Would it be sudden and unexpected and over before I knew it? The total lack of power and control was fueling the fear. That and the prospect of being completely alone forever. It was the fear of no longer existing and knowing that my non-existence was inevitable. It was knowing that there was absolutely nothing I could do about it. It was a fear of death so strong that it was also a fear of living.

This is not normal, I thought. *There is something seriously wrong with me. I need to get help. But how? How can I possibly talk to anybody about this? Where would I find the words? Where could I possibly get the courage? Me, the biggest coward in the world.*

My nights could not always have been like this, could they? It was hard to remember a time when they hadn't been—at least some of the time. It did not happen every single night. Sometimes I went days or even weeks with no problem, and I would think, *Hey, I finally have this thing beat.* Sooner or later, though, late at night it would all come back again. I could make no sense of it. There were times, like the nights I spent with Lana or when I went out drinking with Keith, that I was actually happy. And then there were the nights when the darkness and hopelessness were unbearable.

At least I could usually get through the daytime with no problem. I was always busy enough that I did not have a lot of time for thinking about what might be coming at the end of my day.

Today was different. At that particular moment I could think of nothing but the dread that was coming. I stared down at the black water far below, and it occurred to me that I was in a place that was famous the world over for people like me. People who were at end of their rope. People who gave in and gave up. I kept staring downward. Was the answer right there in front of me? I could end the terror once and for all at this very moment. It would finally be over.

Of course, that was crazy. If the root of my problem was the fear of death, where could I possibly find the courage to choose to die? No matter how bleak things might be, I was too much of a coward. The thought of climbing over the railing and letting myself fall through the cold air for what would probably seem like forever to the hard and frigid impact of the flowing waters below made my legs buckle. I honestly thought I might collapse on the walkway. I was too much of coward. There was no escape from the dark prison of my mind.

With that thought, I should have felt the relief of having weathered another crisis, but I was getting tired of crises. I was cold. I wanted to start moving again, but I was frozen there. The thought of the night's coming dread held me there. My heart accelerated until it pounded inside my chest. I seriously thought I might die then and there from a heart attack. It was as though my body, disappointed I did not have the courage to take action, was going to make itself die anyway. For a few seconds I honestly believed I was in my final moments.

My mind flashed back to a conversation Lonnie and I had once had. We had been talking about the fact that so many famous rock stars died at the age of twenty-seven. Brian Jones, Jimi Hendrix, Janis Joplin, Jim Morrison. There were so many of them. It was downright eerie. What was it about that age? Were their lives so interesting and so full of talent and accomplishments that they only needed a bit more than a quarter-century to live a full and complete life? Did their coolness entitle them to stop living in their twenties and be young forever, never to endure old age?

Idiot that I was, I wondered why that random memory—of all my memories—should pop into my head. Then it dawned on me. Of course, twenty-seven was the age I was now. That number, which had always seemed so far in the future, had snuck up on me. Now everything made sense. I was consumed with the thought that this was the year I was meant to die. It was crystal clear. Strangely, this came as a relief, as if I did not have to worry about it anymore.

I stepped up to the railing and leaned over. The long distance down to the water no longer frightened me.

"Hey, Lonnie!" I yelled at the darkness. "I hope you have a bottle of tequila handy! I'm coming to drink the whole thing with you!"

I lifted a leg and swung over the top of the railing. In just a couple of minutes I had gone from abject fear to a weird sort of elation. I could not believe how good I suddenly felt. I only needed to make myself go the rest of the way over the railing. My problems would be over. The thought of seeing Lonnie again actually made me smile.

I'm doing way too much thinking, I thought. *I should just count to ten and then do it.*

I started counting—backwards. *Ten, nine, eight...*

An icy blast of wind hit my face. For some reason it made me laugh out loud.

Seven, six, five...

I thought about my camera. I did not want it to get destroyed by the water. I took my leg off the railing, lifted the camera strap over my head, and set the camera down on the walkway. I tried to leave it in a way that it would not slide or get knocked over the edge. Back up went the leg.

Four, three, two...

I stared at the camera. I hoped someone would find it. Someone who liked to take photographs. Maybe someone who really wanted a camera but could not afford to buy a good one. I wondered what they would think when they developed my photos. Would they like them? Would they wonder who owned the camera and why he left it there in the middle of the bridge? Would people ever know what happened to me? Would my body be found and identified? What would people at work think about what I did? What would Lana think? And Justin? And my parents?

One...

I sank down until I was sitting on the walkway and covered my eyes. What had I been thinking? Would I have really done it? What was wrong with me? Was I crazy? No, that was not the right question. The right question was, exactly how crazy was I?

I was back to my old dilemma. I was too scared to go on, but I was too scared to stop. Another night of dread was too much to bear, but the thought of falling through the air and experiencing pain and death was too much to bear too. There was no solution. There was no hope.

My brain divided itself into two different people—the one who wanted to die right now and the one who did not. They argued back and forth. They each tried to convince each other that the other was wrong. The debate felt like it was going on for hours. Finally, a compromise was reached.

Look, one of them said. *You are going to be twenty-seven for six more months. You have plenty of time to die like a rock star. Give it until the day before your next birthday. Give it until December. If things are not any better by then, you have permission to come back here and throw yourself off. Come back on the day before your twenty-eighth birthday. Then, if you still want to, fly through the air. Go out like a rock star. Go see Lonnie again.*

That seemed like a good compromise. That gave me six months to get used to the idea of never being twenty-eight. It gave me six months to do everything I ever wanted to do but had never gotten around to. And it gave me six months to say all the things I needed to say to all the people I needed to say them to. Instead of spending so much time being full of dread, I could actually look forward to the next few months. And I would not have to worry about Christmas shopping ever again. I would be gone the night before Pearl Harbor Day.

I felt as if a huge weight had been lifted from my shoulders—at least for the moment. I picked up my camera and got to my feet again. I looked toward the city. With the wind blowing on my face, I closed my eyes and took a long deep breath of sea air.

Then I started the long solitary walk home.

Home to yet another night of fear.

9
Knocking Again

HOW LONG has the damn knocking been going on?

I do not know how long the knocking has been going on.

I have heard this knocking before. This has happened before.

Someone is pounding on the door. Pounding hard.

I am confused.

What time is it? What day is it?

I get out of bed. I walk in the direction of the knocking. I open the door.

The woman with black hair is standing there. It is Marisol. It is always Marisol. The child is standing next to her.

"Marisol," I say, "What is going on?"

"He is after us. He is still after us."

"Why is he after you? What has happened?"

"Carlos will kill me. He will kill you. He knows. He knows everything."

It is still confusing. I still cannot think clearly. I still do not know what I am supposed to say or to do. I look at the little boy. His ice cream cone has been melting while he stands there. Finally, as if in slow motion, the ice cream slips to one side and off the cone.

"Why did you name him Antonio?"

"For you."

"Why for me?"

"Do you not know? Do you not understand? After all this time do you still not understand?"

"Understand what?"

She grows angry.

"*¡Hijo de puta!*" she yells. "*¡Después tanto tiempo aún tú no entiendes? ¡Qué idiota!*"

Even though she is angry, even though she has called me a son of a bitch and an idiot, I am strangely happy. It pleases me that I can understand her Spanish.

"*Mi amor, ¿dónde fuiste tú? ¿Por qué no regresaste tú? Yo te esperaba, pero tú no regresaste. ¿Por qué? Por la gracia de Dios díme por qué.*"

"I don't understand. How was I supposed to return? I did not know where to find you. I tried. I really did. I went to Monterrey. I just didn't know how to find you. What else was I supposed to do? I never got to say goodbye to you. I never got the chance to get your address, your phone number. What was I supposed to do?"

"Now it is too late. Carlos knows everything. Everything."

"What does he know?"

"He knows who Tonio's father is."

"Isn't Carlos Antonio's father?"

"*¡Tonto! ¡Imbécil! ¿No entiendes tú nada?*"

Gradually it dawns on me.

"You mean he's mine?"

"Who else?" she says. "*¿Por qué piensas tú que yo le puse el nombre Antonio?*"

I look at the boy's face. His big brown eyes look up at me. He looks so terribly, incredibly sad. It breaks my heart.

"Tell me what I am supposed to do, Marisol. Tell me what I am supposed to do."

She is speaking, but I cannot hear her.

There is a buzzing sound. It is drowning out her voice.

"Talk louder," I tell her. "I can't hear you. Please talk louder."

The buzzing sound gets louder. It drowns out everything. I cannot hear her. I cannot hear anything.

Except for the buzzing sound.

10
Buzzing

WHERE WAS the buzzing sound coming from?

I was so confused.

It was the buzzer to the door of my apartment building. Someone was down on the street pushing the button next to my apartment number. In the dark I looked in every direction until my eyes finally found the soft red glowing numbers on the clock. It was nearly 3:15.

My heart raced. It was always racing when I woke up at night. Who was looking for me at this time of night? Should I answer the intercom? Was I really awake?

If I answer the intercom, I wondered in a daze, *will I hear Marisol's voice?*

I studied details of the room until I was satisfied this was the real world and not some dream world. I concentrated on getting control of my breathing.

The buzzer sounded again.

Must be some drunk, I thought, *or some punks joking around. Why else would anybody be pressing on my buzzer in the middle of the night?*

I tried ignoring it, but it did not stop.

Might be some sort of an emergency, I thought. *Maybe someone is hurt or in trouble.*

I got up, went to the intercom by the door, and pressed the button.

"Hello?"

My voice was scratchy. I cleared my throat.

"Dallas?"

"Yeah?"

"Dallas? It's me. Justin."

"Justin? What's up? Is everything all right?"

"Sorry to bother you, man. It must be pretty late. I don't even know what time it is."

"It's 3:15, man."

"Wow, it's later than I thought. Or earlier."

He laughed self-consciously at his joke.

"Hey, I'm really sorry about this, but can I crash at your place tonight? It's kind of a long story, but you'd be doing me a big favor."

"Sure, I guess. I'll let you in."

I pressed the button to release the lock on the building's front door. Then I opened the door to my apartment and sat down to wait. After a few minutes Justin appeared with a sheepish look on his face.

"Hey, I really appreciate this."

"No problem. What's the story?"

"This woman came into the café today, I mean yesterday. We hit it off really well and I ended up meeting her after work. One thing led to another and we wound up at her place. It was great."

"Cool. Sounds like a good time."

"Yeah, it was. I was there a long time. I thought I was staying the night, but then about the time I'm ready to go to sleep she says I can't stay. She says, 'It's been fun but you need to go now.' I don't know what the deal was. Next thing I know I'm out on the street. I've missed the last bus to Marin, and then I remember that Johnny is out of town so I can't crash at his place. I was stuck. I was thinking, man, looks like I'm going to be sleeping on the street. Well, that sucks. Then I thought about you and the fact that your place was right around the corner. Hope you don't mind. I'm really sorry I woke you up."

He was rambling a bit and slurring some of his words. It was pretty obvious he had done a fair amount of drinking.

"No problem, man."

I looked around. Unfortunately for him, my apartment was tiny.

"Sorry," I said, "I only have one bed. You can sleep on the couch if you want."

He looked at the couch, and we could both see it was nowhere near as long as he was. Also, the cushions were pretty worn.

"Uh, do you have a blanket?"

"Sorry. I don't get many overnight guests—at least ones who sleep on the couch. I suppose you can have the blanket off my bed. It's not that cold tonight."

"No, I don't want to take your only blanket, man."

He kept looking around, like maybe he thought I had an extra bed somewhere I was not telling him about. Finally his eyes settled on my bed.

"Uh…"

"Yeah?"

"Uh, would it be weird if I slept in your bed with you?"

The question surprised me. It was a double bed all right, but it still seemed pretty small for two guys.

"I guess not. I mean, I don't mind if you don't."

"Cool. My brother and I used to share a bed all the time. It'll be like being kids again."

With no delay, he pulled off his tee-shirt and dropped it on the floor. Then he undid his jeans and stepped out of them in two seconds flat. Obviously, all those nights with the drummer groupies had allowed him to perfect the art of losing his clothes at a moment's notice. He was not the least bit self-conscious. He looked even skinnier naked than he did with his clothes on. You could see every tendon in his arms and legs and every rib in his torso. His legs were hairier than I had expected.

He slid into the bed and pulled the blanket and cover over him. I stood there a moment, trying to catch up with everything. Then I got back into the bed, doing my best to hug my edge and not accidentally brush against him. The two of us were lying back to back.

"I appreciate this, man" he said. "I owe you."

"Don't worry about it. Sorry your night got cut short."

"That's all right. The morning after is always kind of awkward anyway. It's just I hadn't thought about where I would go afterwards. I just didn't expect to get kicked out like that. I guess that's just life in the city."

I lay as still as I could. I wanted to go back to sleep, but now I was wide awake. A soft light shone through the window. The full moon had risen above the building across the street, and now that was distracting me. There was no telling how long it would take to get sleepy again. I thought about James and what a big laugh he would have if he could see me at that moment. It was as though he had somehow arranged for this to happen just to play with my mind.

I heard Justin breathing behind me. He clearly had no trouble sleeping, and I envied him. I could swear I could feel heat radiating from him. It was like being next to a pile of clothes that had just come out of the dryer. I rolled over so that I was facing his back. I moved the cover so that I could see his back. His shoulder blades were perfect. His whole back was perfect, like one of those statues I had seen recently at the Palace of the Legion of Honor. I wondered what my back looked like. I was pretty sure it looked nothing like his. It was all bony with a few freckles and a blemish or two. His was like a bar of Dove soap. He shifted slightly, and I watched the muscles in his back move. I would have traded my body for his in a heartbeat.

71

The more I studied him, the more fascinated I became. I sat up slightly. I had never been in a position to stare at length at another guy. That is the sort of thing that can get you teased or maybe even punched. Now, however, I could look at Justin all I wanted. I could compare myself to him and find ways that we were similar and ways that we were different. I wondered what his skin felt like. Would it feel any different from a woman's?

What the hell, I thought.

I reached over and touched the ends of his hair. His long straight black hair looked so cool. My hair never shined like his. My hair was a nondescript brownish color and always looked greasy. His hair always looked clean and bright. I ran my fingers through it.

God, I wish this was my hair, I thought.

Having drawn closer to him, I had expected him to smell bad. He was a guy after all, and by his own account he had been having sex all night. I expected him to smell of sweat and dirt. The opposite was true. He smelled good. Really good.

"You smell like lemons!" I said.

I had not meant to say that out loud.

"Huh?"

"I said, you smell like lemons. That's really weird."

"I do?"

"Yeah."

"Huh. Oh, it must be the dish soap."

"Dish soap?"

"Yeah. I was washing dishes."

"You were?"

"Yeah. After we had been going at it for a while, she went into the bathroom and stayed there for a really long time. I got bored waiting for her to come back, so I got up and went into her kitchen. There were a whole lot of dirty dishes, so I washed them."

"You did?"

"Yeah."

"Why?"

"I dunno. I guess it's just a habit. I wash dishes all the time. It's one of my jobs at Flaubert's. I always finish my shift by doing all the dishes left over from the day shift. I don't mind doing it. In fact, I kind of like it."

While he was talking, I touched his back. He did not react at all. I could feel the air moving in and out of his lungs while he talked. His skin was not exactly like a woman's, but it was not that different either. It was tighter and did not feel quite as smooth as it looked.

In the moment immediately before my fingers touched him, I wondered if I would like how it felt. I wondered if it might even get me excited. I mean, more excited than I already was from exploring something new and different. My body and my mind reacted in a way I had not expected.

As my fingers made contact, the most wonderful feeling of complete and utter peace came over me. It was amazing. All the fears, shadows, and darkness melted away. I felt the kind of relief I usually only felt when making love to Lana. It was not sexual, or at least it did not seem to be. Once my hand touched him, it could not be moved. It wanted to stay there forever. I did not want the feeling of relief to end.

My fingers sank deeper into his taut skin. I massaged the area around his upper spine. It occurred to me that neither of us had spoken for a while.

"Uh, what are you doing?"

"I'm rubbing your back."

I did not stop.

"Uh, why?"

"Sorry, I can't sleep. I thought I would do this for a while. I mean, if you don't mind. It's something I do for my photography."

"Your photography?"

"Yeah, it's kind of hard to explain. I'm planning to take some more pictures of you. Ones just of you. I find I can get a better shot of someone if I have a tactile connection with them. It's just something some photographers do to relate to their subject. You don't mind, do you?"

That explanation was complete and total bullshit, which I had just made up. It did sound like something one of my photography teachers might have said, though.

"Wow, that's really cool. You really are an artist. You must know everything there is to know about photography. It must be nice to know so much about something like that. Me, I don't have a clue. Not even about music really. Yeah, go ahead and keep doing it. It feels good. I was just kind of surprised when you started."

"Guess you didn't realize what kind of weirdness you were getting yourself into by dropping in here in the middle of the night."

"This is fun. I like hanging out with you a lot."

I kept massaging him. Now that I had started, I could not stop. The area getting massaged grew gradually larger to include his shoulder blades and lower back and eventually the tops of his shoulders. I ran my fingers along the back of his neck. The more the massaging had gone on, the better I felt.

Strange thoughts went through my mind. I wondered if I could arrange to have Justin in my bed every night, so I could do this all the time. I thought about asking him to move in and be my roommate. I thought about telling him he would not even have to pay rent or utilities. I would pay all the bills if he would just let me rub his back every night. He would think I was crazy, but it would be worth it if I could just have some peace at night. Could I explain that to him? I mean, in a way that did not make me sound crazy? No, of course not because I *was* crazy. There was just no getting around it.

While all these thoughts were going through my head, Justin was silent. Finally he spoke again.

"Uh…"

"Yeah?"

"You know I'm not gay, right?"

I laughed out loud.

"Yeah, that's pretty damn obvious."

Of course, it was entirely natural that he would have started wondering about me. It occurred to me that I had never given Justin any idea what my love life was like. I had never told him about Lana because I just did not want to get into the whole thing about adultery and whether it was right or wrong or any of that. The result was that there was a major part of me he knew nothing about. One time I had tried to tell him about Marisol, but he treated it like a joke. He was sure my story about a night of passion in Mexico was about me hiring a prostitute. It was just too much trouble to get him to understand how serious the whole thing had been for me.

Now I looked at myself through Justin's eyes and considered what he actually knew about me. Seeing it from his point of view, the only thing he could have concluded was that either I had no sex life at all or else I had some reason for keeping my sex life a secret.

"I mean, I don't think there's anything wrong with being gay," he said. "I mean, I have some gay friends, and it doesn't bother me or anything. I think people should be free to do whatever they want, you know? It's just not *my* thing."

"Yeah, that's pretty much how I feel too."

I moved a little closer to him so that I could do my massaging more comfortably. Neither of us spoke for several minutes.

"I've never done anything with a guy," he said.

I think he was inviting me to talk about my own sex life, but I just said nothing.

"Lots of women, of course, but no guys. I mean, there have been guys who wanted to do things with *me*, but I just wasn't interested."

I continued the back rub in silence.

"It's just that I like women, you know?"

Still rubbing.

"But I guess I do get curious sometimes."

The conversation was now going in a direction I had not expected.

"I mean, sometimes I wonder what it would be like. You know, just to satisfy my curiosity. Just to know if I'm missing anything. The problem is, I never thought it was something I would ever be able to make myself do. I mean, the idea of sex with a guy is kind of gross. You know?"

I wished Justin would go back to sleep, but he seemed pretty awake now.

"But you're different."

My ears perked up.

"I mean, if I was going to do it with a guy, I suppose I might be able to do it with you. You're just, well, you're just really cool."

"I am definitely not cool."

"No, seriously. I really like you. You're a neat guy and, well, I hope you don't take this the wrong way."

"Take what the wrong way?"

"You're not really like a guy?"

"I'm not like a guy?"

"No, I mean, you're a guy all right. It's just that you're the kind of guy I would like if I were into guys? Does that sound crazy?"

"No," I lied.

"Sorry. Now I've made it all weird. I'm not confessing my love for you or anything. It's not like that. It's just that, well, if you ever wanted to, you know, do anything—just for the hell of it, you know, like an experiment or just messing around, well, I might be interested in trying it. Just for the heck of it. You know, nothing serious or anything. Does that sound totally crazy?"

I did not know what to say. What a weird situation. Touching him gave me such a feeling of peace that I would have done pretty much anything to keep the connection from breaking. But would I actually go as far as having sex with him? I could not imagine what that would be like. The idea frightened me.

Maybe it had something to do with my religious upbringing. I do not mean being brainwashed into thinking sex—or even just certain kinds of sex—was sinful. I had gotten over that hangup a long time ago. Still, for some reason I was not like other guys I knew. Most of them—Lonnie was a prime example and Justin was another—would nail anything that moved. If they could get a woman to sleep with them, it did not matter if they knew her or even liked her. Me, though, I had to be in love. The act of making love was just too personal. Something so personal about me—and about the other person—got revealed in the moment when all the emotion was released and when all control was lost. I did not want to see Justin in that moment. More to the point, I did not want him to see *me* in that moment. It was just too much to share with him. Yes, maybe I could close my eyes and pretend he was Lana or Marisol and maybe that would work. Hell, I might even enjoy it. But I knew the moment I touched some part of him that did not feel right the spell would be broken and I would be overwhelmed with humiliation.

As I lay there, I knew the logical thing to do was just explain to him why I was touching him, I should just tell him about the horrors that came to me every night and how having my hands on him kept them away. To do that, though, would be as big a revelation of weakness as letting him see me have an orgasm. There was no way I could ever tell him or anybody else my shameful secret. I would have to take it to the grave.

I had taken so long to answer him that Justin gave up waiting and started talking again.

"I don't mean tonight or anything. Hell, I'm too wasted and too drained after my night with—what was her name again?—to do anything tonight. I'm just saying, if some night you wanted to get together and, you know, just mess around, I might be interested. I mean, if you are. Probably just only one time though. Hell, maybe after I sober up, maybe I won't be interested at all. Who knows?"

"Yeah, we'll see."

Justin did not talk anymore after that. Pretty soon I could tell by his breathing that he was asleep. I wondered how much of this he would remember in the morning. I wondered how much of it *I* would remember. I continued rubbing his back until I could not keep my eyes open anymore. I silently promised myself that someday soon I would go find James and strangle him. When I got too tired to continue the massaging, I relaxed and left one hand resting on his hip. At last sleep began to overtake me. I savored the feeling of not feeling afraid. I savored something else as well.

Justin thinks that I *am cool.*

I felt like I was in junior high again—except this was so much better than junior high. When I was in junior high, absolutely *no one* thought I was cool.

My last thought, as I drifted off, was to wonder what twisting and turning our two bodies might do as we slept. Neither of us would have any control over our dreams or how our sleeping bodies might react to them. Would we have a rude awakening in the morning to find one of us on top of the other? Like the way Lonnie, much to his amusement, found Antonio and me that morning in the woods in Michoacán?

I had no need to worry. I woke in the morning to find myself alone in bed. I looked around the apartment, but there was no sign of Justin. In fact, there was no evidence whatsoever he had ever been there. I seriously wondered whether the whole thing had not been some weird dream.

11
Over

EVERYTHING CHANGED in August.

I was at work and about to take some new film into the darkroom when someone told me I had a phone call. I set the rolls down on a table and picked up the phone.

"Dallas Green," I said.

"Dallas, it's me."

This was strange. In all the time we had been together, Lana had never called me at work before. We both knew it was a risky thing to do. After all, I worked with her uncle and her cousin.

"Hi" I said in a low voice, trying to sound casual while I looked around to see who might be within earshot. "What's up?"

"We need to talk."

"Okay. When can you come over?"

"Can I come tonight?"

"Yeah, of course. What time?"

"As soon as you're home. You tell me."

"I can be there by six."

"I'll be there waiting."

The sound of her voice worried me.

"Is everything okay?"

"Dallas, It's over."

"Over?"

"I'm leaving Gary. My marriage is over."

I was stunned.

"Don't you have anything to say?"

My brain was still frozen.

"Wow."

"That's it? Wow?"

"Sorry, it's just that you caught me by surprise, and this isn't exactly the best place for me to be talking. We'll talk tonight. Okay?"

"Okay. And, Dallas…"

"Yeah?"

"He knows about you."

"He does?"

"Yes. Everything is out in the open now. It's for the best. No more lies. See you tonight."

I hung up the phone and stood there in shock. This was the last thing I had expected. I remembered how paranoid I had been about Linda's husband Wayne coming after me with one of his rifles. I wondered if Gary owned a gun.

I grabbed my film rolls and rushed into the darkroom. I could not concentrate on developing them, though. Instead I just stood in the dark, trying to get my breath. This should have been good news. For more than a year I had dreamed of Lana and me being together and having a normal relationship.

When everything settles down, I told myself, *this will be for the best. Everything is going to work out for me and Lana. This is a good thing.*

If this was what I had been wanting for so long and if it was for the best, I wondered, then why was I terrified? Why was I consumed with sheer panic? As much as I tried to convince myself that Lana's news was something to celebrate, I felt like a cornered animal. What would she expect from me? Would she expect me to spend the rest of my life with her because her marriage was over? What about her kid? I had never even met her son. Would she expect me to be his new father? Suddenly the thing I had been dreaming of felt like a huge trap. I needed to run away.

I took a few long, deep breaths in an attempt to lower my heart rate. Then I walked out of the darkroom and into the production area. I found James and began to bombard him with questions.

"James, what is happening with your Seattle plan?"

He looked around warily.

"This is not really the best time or place to be discussing it," he replied with annoyance.

"Things are different now. Something's happened. I am ready to move to Seattle now. Immediately. How soon will you be starting things up there?"

Not one bit happy, he looked around and satisfied himself that no one would hear our conversation.

"Things are on hold. I have been having trouble with the financing. The economy is terrible and the banks don't want to lend to anyone who actually needs the money. The loan officer actually told me—can you believe this?—that maybe things would improve after the election—if Reagan wins. Can you believe that?"

James could not stand Ronald Reagan. He had been appalled when Reagan won the Republican nomination. "I had to put up with eight years with him as governor," he had said, "and there is no way I or the country will survive if he becomes president." His only comfort was that it looked like President Carter would be re-elected pretty easily.

"To answer your question, I don't know how soon I will be able to move forward. What's your hurry anyway? I didn't think you were interested in moving."

"I just need to get away. I've had it with the city. I think I need to try someplace else."

He studied me curiously.

"Did something happen? Perhaps with that cute young thing from Flaubert's. I've seen the two of you out together a few times now. Are you possibly learning something about yourself that you're not quite comfortable with?"

"No, no, it's nothing like that. Look, I think I may be moving to Seattle really soon even if you don't. Just keep me posted on your plans. It would be good to have a job lined up. Okay?"

"Well," he said with an arched eyebrow, "*something* is definitely going on with you. I would love to know what."

"Yeah, I'll tell you about it in Seattle," I said as I headed back to the darkroom.

Yes, that is what I'll do, I told myself. *I'll quit my job and move to Seattle. I'll start over up there. It will be a fresh beginning. I'm not going to be trapped.*

First, though, I had to see Lana. There was no avoiding it.

When I got home, she was sitting on the step in front of my building, looking as serious as a heart attack.

"Sorry I didn't get here sooner," I said. "I didn't mean to make you wait."

"It's okay. It gave me some time to think. It's just so good to be out of the house."

We went up to my apartment. I looked in the cupboard to see what I had. There was not much there. I poured us two small glasses of Canadian Club whiskey. I felt bad about getting so upset by her news, especially now that I saw how upset she was.

"Are you okay?"

"No, not really. Gary and I have been married seven years. That's a long time. That's a lot to throw away, but I've never been happy. Not really. He's just not there, physically or emotionally. You know what I mean?"

"Yeah," I said, though I could not say I knew exactly what she meant.

"I just couldn't go on. I mean, I deserve to have a life too. It's fine for him to travel all over the world and then come home and expect us to be the perfect family. But what about me? What about all of the things I always wanted to do?"

I tried to put my arm around her, but she pushed it away.

"It's my turn now," she said. "I'm going to do what I want for a change. It's going to be about me now."

"And what do you want?" I asked.

"I don't know. I have to figure it out. I need to take some time."

I felt rotten. All I had been able to think about was myself and about escaping. Now I wanted to do something for her.

"Move in with me. We can figure it out together."

She looked exasperated as she glanced around my apartment.

"Here? No, don't you understand. This is about *me* now. It's not about Gary, and it's not about you. It's about me now. I'm going to take Jason and go to my sister's in Petaluma. I suddenly realized I don't even know my son. He spends more time with Sylvie the *au pair* than he does with me. That has to change."

I had been sleeping with this woman for more than a year, and I had never met her son.

I said, "I always thought someday you and I would be together. Once you've divorced Gary, that can happen. We can finally be together. Always."

She looked irritated.

"I'm just now getting out of a relationship. You want me to immediately go into another one?"

"I thought you and I *were* in a relationship."

"You thought this was a relationship? Oh, you are a poor dumb cowboy. We had fun, Dallas. Really we did. But it wasn't a relationship. It was not like living together. It was not like having a child together. You just got the fun part. That's what made it nice for both of us. No worries, no cares, no responsibilities. It was just fun. But I need more than that now."

"But... I love you."

She smiled at me sympathetically.

"And I love you. But you never thought we were going to be together like a married couple, did you?"

A minute before I had been ready to beg. Now my pride took over.

"No, you're right. It was fun while it lasted. I knew that. I just wanted you to know that I was here for you. That's all. It's no big deal."

"Who knows?" she said. "Maybe when I get my head together, I will decide you are what I want. Maybe someday we can be together for real. Who knows? All I know right now is that I need time and space to figure everything out. And I need time to get to know my son. Who knows what will happen later on?"

"Well, I hope you figure it out. And I hope that you're happy. That's all I want for you—to be happy."

"Okay, well, I guess this is goodbye then."

Suddenly this was it. Just like that. This might be the last time I ever saw her. My insides were caving in, but I was determined to act like nothing major was going on. I did not want her to see me as weak.

Then I thought about what it would be like alone in my bed that night.

"I don't suppose you could stay with me for just one more night?"

She gave me a sideways glance.

"I'm booked into the St. Francis. Jason is there with Sylvie, waiting for me. I have to go."

She put her arms around me and kissed me.

"I really am going to miss you, Tex. You'll never know how much you meant to me. You were just what I needed at just the right time. But now I need something else."

She kissed me again.

"Go out and have a good time. I know you will. There are plenty of women out there who will appreciate a nice red-blooded American boy like you."

Then without another word she left. Suddenly she was out of my life. Just like that.

I spent the next few hours listening to Pink Floyd and Led Zeppelin and finishing the bottle of Canadian Club.

12
New Plan

DESPITE THE terrible headache I had the next morning, I forced myself to get out of bed and go to work. It helped that I had a definite plan in mind. Even though, in hindsight, my panic the previous day about getting out of the city seemed so very stupid, I was determined to go through with my plan to move to Seattle. Now it was for a completely different reason. Instead of running away from Lana, I would be running away from all my memories of Lana.

I had come to love the city and to feel a part of it. I was heartbroken at the thought of no longer walking its streets, up and down its hills and seeing the bay and its bridges. I would miss all the great places I had found for food and drink and for watching the huge, crazy cast of characters that made up the city's population. All those things, however, were now all reminders of Lana. All the places in the city that I loved were now either places where she and I had been or else places where I had hoped one day to take her. My life had turned upside down, and I needed a fresh start. I needed to take action immediately. If I did not, I might lose my nerve and I would end up regretting it.

I went into work determined to hand in my notice to David. Quitting my job would force me to move forward. Then I would give notice to my landlord. Then I would go to Seattle and start over. I had never been in Seattle before and I did not know anyone there, but I convinced myself that was just what I needed. With any luck, James would get his loan, start his printing business, and hire me. If not, I would find something else. If that did not work out and I could not make a go of it in Seattle, I could always move back to Kern County. If that was my only alternative, it would be plenty of incentive to make things work out in Washington.

When I got to work, I went straight to David's office. He was always there in the morning before everyone else. I knocked on his door, which was halfway open. It was always halfway open. He prided himself on his open-door policy. David looked up at me from his desk.

"You got a minute, David?"

"Mr. Green. Just the man I wanted to talk to. Give me about twenty minutes, if you don't mind. I'll come find you."

He looked serious. It was unusual that he would want to talk to me. I wondered if I was in some kind of trouble. Could he have heard about Lana and me? Needless to say, he would not be happy that I might have had something to do with the breakup of his niece's marriage. Maybe he was going to fire me before I got the chance to hand in my notice.

Cool, I thought. *If he fires me, I might be able to draw unemployment while I'm looking for a job in Seattle.*

I went to the darkroom and tried to pass the time, but it was hard to concentrate. I replayed my conversation with Lana over and over. I wondered, if I had said something different, maybe I could have changed her mind. To stop thinking about that, I tried to think of practical things, like what I needed to do in order to move to a different city. Waiting for David felt endless. It had definitely been more than twenty minutes. More like an hour and a half. Finally I heard his voice behind me. He had materialized like a ghost.

"Sorry to keep you waiting, Mr. Green."

For some reason he called everyone by their last names even though we all just called him David.

"I'll see you in my office now."

I was surprised how nervous I was following him back to his office. It did not matter what was going to happen since I had already made up my mind to quit my job. Still, nobody likes to be fired—especially under awkward circumstances.

He settled into his chair, leaning way back and resting his hands on his knee. David was kind of a stuffy guy. He always wore a suit even though he was okay with the rest of us dressing casually. What little hair he had he kept neatly trimmed. He always spoke as if he were trying to sound English. I guess you could call him kind of a snob.

"Well, Mr. Green," he began. "I have to say, you've been doing a very nice job with the photographs. We have gotten consistently good comments on your work. I do not have to tell you how important the quality of the artwork is to the look and credibility of a magazine."

He always called it a magazine, although it was really a newspaper.

"Thanks, David."

"An opportunity has come up. One of our advertisers has approached us about funding a major special supplement, and it will be very heavy on photography. It is not an exaggeration to say that it will succeed or fail on the quality of the photography. It will be a lot of pressure on you particularly. Are you ready for such a challenge?"

It looked like I was not getting fired. In fact, it looked as though I was going to be getting more work, maybe even more money. This did not fit in with my plan. On the other hand, after the disappointment of the night before, it was nice to feel appreciated.

"Uh, yeah. Sure, David. I'm always looking for a challenge, especially when it comes to my photography."

"That's good. Now the next question I have to ask you is: do you have a passport and is it in date?"

That was not a question I had expected, but I only had to think a few seconds. I had gotten a passport to go to Mexico with Keith that time, and it still had seven years left on it.

"Yeah, I do."

"Excellent. I need you to bring it in to me as soon as you can. We need to submit it along with some paperwork to the French consul so that you may work as a journalist in France for a period of one week."

"France?"

"Yes. Tell me, are you familiar with the Deauville Film Festival?"

"Dough ville? Uh, no."

"Deauville is in Normandy. For six years now they have been holding a film festival there dedicated to American cinema. And this year you will be attending. What do you think of that?"

"I, I don't know what to say. This is kind of the last thing I expected."

He smiled at me indulgently.

"Yes, I understand. France is not one of the usual beats for our humble little publication, but it so happens we have a new advertiser who is willing to fund two of you to go to Deauville—but under one condition."

"And what's that?"

"Are you familiar with the filmmaker Logan MacCaul?"

"I can't say I am."

"Yes, well, I suppose most of his work is before your time. At one point he was the toast of New York and Hollywood. His first film was considered a work of genius that was going to redefine cinema as we knew it. He made two more films that were well received... and then nothing. He essentially went into seclusion. He refused to take calls or answer letters. He never gave another interview. The mystery around him—on top of the scarcity and quality of his work—made everyone that much more desperate to hear from him. People have clamored to see more of his work, but there has been nothing for years. He lived in France for a few years. Then he came back to the States to live in seclusion on a farm up in Lake County. That's only two hours away, but journalists eventually stopped going up there. All visitors have been turned away unceremoniously for years."

"What does that have to do with me going to France."

"There is a rather persistent rumor out there that MacCaul has managed to make a brand new film completely in secret, without anybody getting wind of it—at least until now. Furthermore, it is rumored that he will show it next month in Deauville. Our new advertiser is a major film buff with a Logan MacCaul obsession. He has offered to fund an entire supplement covering the film festival on the condition that it play up the Bay Area angle by including an interview with MacCaul along with a photo spread."

"Sounds like this guy MacCaul may not want to be photographed."

"I am hoping he will be willing if he indeed has a new work to publicize, but you are right. His history suggests he will be camera shy. That is where I am counting on you to do whatever you have to. Please understand how important this is, how much money is involved. If you succeed, the prestige from such a coup will make our humble publication's name known nationally and internationally. It's a lot to place on your shoulders. That's why I need to know you have what it takes to get this done, one way or another. Are you game, Mr. Green?"

"You said two of us were going?"

"Yes, you will be working with Melanie Francis. She will do the interview. She will make the contact with him. With any luck you will only have to tag along and be ready with your camera."

I tried to maintain a positive expression, but the truth was I hated Melanie Francis. She was the most unpleasant, pushy reporter I had ever met. On the other hand, if anyone could actually bluster their way into seeing someone who did not want to be seen, it was probably her. Anyone standing in her way usually ended up as roadkill, so I had made an art of staying out of her way. Having to work closely with her for a week was not exactly my idea of good time.

"Sounds good," I lied.

"That's what I like to hear. I'm counting on you, Mr. Green. You won't let me down, will you?"

"No, sir."

"Very well. We'll be talking more about this as the time approaches. In the meantime you may want to begin researching Logan MacCaul, including familiarizing yourself with any photographs of him you can find. It's impossible to find recent ones. Oh, you don't happen to speak French, do you?"

"No, but I know some Spanish."

"Well, that certainly can't hurt. The two languages are not dissimilar after all, but you may want to try to pick up a bit of conversational French if you can. And don't forget to bring your passport in to us at the earliest opportunity."

"Yes, sir. Thank you."

I walked out of his office dumbfounded. This was the last thing I had expected to happen. So much for my plan to quit my job and move to Seattle—at least for the time being. I was not going to say no to a free trip to France or the chance to be a part of something likely to bring the paper and me a lot of attention—even if it did mean spending a week working with Melanie. I was no less eager to escape from the city than before, and this new development was simply a delay.

I had not planned on doing any work that morning, and now I was too distracted to start anything. I walked over to Flaubert's to get a coffee. As usual, Justin was working the espresso machine.

"Hi, man," he said.

"Hey."

I had not had much chance to talk to him since the night he spent in my apartment. I had wondered if he would feel embarrassed or awkward about it, but Justin never felt embarrassed or awkward about anything. In any event, we had not talked about it.

He was already making my coffee. It had been ages since he had bothered to ask me what I wanted, since I always had the same thing. I watched him as he tried to shake his dangling hair out of his eyes while both of his hands were busy steaming a pitcher of milk.

"What's up?"

"The damnedest thing just happened. They're sending me to France."

"France? Really?"

"Yeah. Crazy, huh? It was just out of the blue."

"When are you going?"

"Next month."

"How long?"

"Just a week."

"That's cool. I wish I could go to France."

"Do you know any French?"

"I took it in high school, but I don't remember much of it. I wasn't exactly what you'd call a model student. So, are you going to try to learn French before you go over?"

"Maybe just a few words. I'm hoping it will be close enough to Spanish that I can sort of fake it. I think you can check out language tapes from the library."

"Yeah, the main library over by the Civic Center would probably have whatever you need."

As he handed me my coffee, I leaned closer to him and said in a lower voice, "You want to know something crazy?"

"What?"

"I was planning to quit my job today. Before I could say anything, though, I found out about this assignment in France."

"Really? Why?"

"I… I just need to get out of the city. It's time. There's a chance I could have a job in Seattle."

Justin looked flabbergasted.

"Because of me?"

"You? No, why?"

"I just thought you might be weirded out by what I said that night."

I laughed and pointed at my head.

"No, the weirdness is *all* up here. The fact is I've got a *lot* of stuff going on. Stuff I haven't bothered to tell you."

"Do you want to talk about it? Later, I mean, when we're both off?"

"Yeah, it would probably do me good to talk about it. See you after work?"

"Yeah, man, sure."

"Okay, I'll come by for you at closing time. We can go somewhere and get shit-faced."

"Sounds good."

I went back to work, resigned to the fact that, for now, nothing had changed. I was still employed, and all my assignments were still waiting for me. So much for my dramatic break for freedom.

At six o'clock I walked back into Flaubert's. Justin was taking off the apron they made him wear. As we walked out together, I detected the scent of lemons.

"Been washing dishes again?"

"Same as every other day."

"So, where do you want to go?"

"We might as well go to your place. I don't feel like getting carded today."

"I'll sure be glad when you turn twenty-one. When's your birthday again?"

"Just two more weeks. I can't wait."

We stopped at a liquor store on the way and I picked up a bottle of tequila.

"This is definitely what's called for tonight. Now we need to find a store that sells limes."

When we got to my apartment, I put *Led Zeppelin IV* on the turntable and opened the bottle. As Robert Plant belted out the lyrics to "Black Dog," I poured the first two glasses.

"So, what's going on with you man," asked Justin, looking concerned.

"I never told you about my girlfriend Lana."

"You been going out with someone? For how long?"

"For over a year, but it's over now."

"How come you never told me about her?"

"Because I was embarrassed. She's married."

"Wow. I had no idea. I mean, you never said anything."

"Yeah, I know. I guess I just figured there was no point. It wasn't like you were ever going to meet her. It was like she was just a fantasy. I thought we were having a great love affair, but for her it was just, I don't know, extracurricular activity. Something to do for fun. That's what really hurts. I wasted all that time thinking I was honestly connected to somebody, and it wasn't even real. Man, it wasn't even real."

"Hey, don't sweat it, man. She was just one woman. There'll be others. You've got plenty of time. At our age we've got all the time in the world."

There was something sweet about the way he tried to make me feel better. He was like an eager puppy trying to get a crying child to play.

"You keep forgetting I'm not your age. I'm seven years older than you. Most people I grew up with are married and have families. I'm still living the way I lived when I was, well, when I was your age."

"Hey, nothing says you have to buy into all that traditional, materialistic crap. What's wrong with living like you're twenty forever? Who says life has to stop being fun just because you reach a certain age anyway?"

I poured two more glasses of tequila. By this time Jimmy Page was plucking the first strains of "Stairway to Heaven."

"Thanks, man," I said. "You're a good friend."

"The truth is," he said with that intensely earnest look on his face, "you're my *best* friend."

That made me laugh.

"So, what, are we in grammar school now?"

He did not think it was funny.

"I'm serious, man. I'm closer to you than anybody I know."

"Really? Don't you have friends that you went to school with? That you were kids together with? You and I have only known each other a few months."

"No, my family always moved around a lot. My dad was always getting transferred because of his work. I never got to have friends for very long. I guess I made friends in high school after we moved to Mill Valley, but we didn't keep in touch. I was always into different things than everyone else."

"What about the guys in your band?"

"We get along all right and sometimes we do stuff together, but they're busy all the time. They all have girlfriends and jobs during the day. Johnny is cool, but he spends a lot of time with his family in Chinatown."

"Well, I don't mind being your best friend—even though we are both too old to have best friends. I guess you're my best friend too. Two days ago I would have said that Lana was my best friend, but that's all over now. So you're it. Congratulations."

"Sorry if I'm being weird—again. It's just that when you said you wanted to move away from the Bay Area, well, I would get really bummed if you left. I thought it was because of that stuff I said the other night."

"Nah. Don't worry about that. I was actually kind of flattered. Besides, I could tell you were drunk. My friend Lonnie used to say, the whole point of getting drunk is so you don't have to be responsible for anything."

"About your friend Lonnie…"

"Yeah?"

"Don't take this the wrong way or anything…"

"Take what?"

"I know it's sad he died and you miss him and everything…"

"Yeah?"

"You really need to stop talking about him."

"What do you mean? I hardly ever talk about him."

"You talk about him *all* the time. You really need to let him go. I mean, how long has it been since he died?"

"Six years and three months."

"I'm just saying, maybe part of growing up and acting your age—if that's what you want to do—is letting things in the past stay in the past."

"Yeah, maybe you're right."

I decided to change the subject.

"Do you want to hear my latest crazy idea?"

"Sure."

"I told you I was thinking about moving to Seattle, right? James at work has been talking about moving up there and starting a business. That was my escape plan, but now I'm thinking about a different plan."

"Yeah?"

"Since I'm being sent to France anyway, I'm thinking, once I finish my assignment, I might just not come back. I might just stay over there."

"Really? Why?"

"I don't know. It would just be a complete break from everything and everyone here. I could re-invent myself."

"But you said you don't even know French."

"I'll learn. Just like I learned Spanish."

"But you've never been there before. You don't know anyone there. How will you live? What will you do for money?"

"I don't know. I'll figure something out. Maybe I can give people English lessons or something. I don't know. I said it was a crazy idea. Right now that's the way I am thinking."

"Why are they sending you to France anyway?"

"They want me to try to get photographs of some reclusive filmmaker. He hasn't been seen for a long time. Some guy named Logan MacCaul."

"Logan MacCaul?"

The look on Justin's face could not have been any more wondrous than if I had said that I was going to have an audience with Jesus Christ Himself.

"Really? Logan MacCaul?"

"You know him?"

"He's my favorite director!"

"Really? I never heard of him until today."

"When I was in high school, I had this friend who was really into movies. He convinced me to ditch school for a day, and we went to the city to an arthouse theater in the Mission District. There were two movies he wanted to see and that was the last day to see them. The first one was a French film called *Jules and Jim*. It was about two friends in love with the same woman. The two men go off to war and end up fighting on different sides. The second movie was *Tristan's Passage* by Logan MacCaul. I swear to you, it was the best movie I ever saw. It absolutely changed my life."

"Really? It was that good?"

"Yeah, it was. It just spoke to me in a way that no movie ever spoke to me before. It was like he had made it just for me. Ever since that day I have been trying to find a way to see it again. For a long time I looked in the newspaper every week to see if it was playing at any of the arthouse theaters or if it was going to be on television, but I never managed to see it again. I would give anything if I could just see it one more time. Anything."

"It was honestly that good?"

"Yeah! You should ask your friend Keith about it?"

"Keith? I didn't know you knew Keith."

"Sure, I do. Don't you remember? One time you and he and his wife came in for coffee together."

"Oh yeah, that's right. So, Keith has seen that Logan MacCaul movie?"

"Yeah. Another time he came in for coffee by himself, and he said something about the *Casablanca* poster up behind the counter. While I was making his latte, we got to talking about our favorite movies. He said *Tristan's Passage* was one of his favorite films too."

"Wow. Now you have me curious. I'd like to see that movie for myself. Anyway, this MacCaul guy has apparently made a new movie, and they think he is going to show it at a film festival in Deauville."

Justin looked absolutely desperate.

"You have to take me with you."

"God, I wish I could. I rather be going with you instead of the bitch I have to go with."

We kept on talking as the tequila bottle got emptier and emptier and more records got put on the turntable. Justin explained at length why he loved *Tristan's Passage*, as well as discussing some of his other favorite movies. By the time we finished the bottle we were pretty wasted.

"You wouldn't really stay in France, would you?" he asked.

"I don't know. It's just one of those ideas that seems good at the time. It probably isn't very practical."

"I'd really miss you if you didn't come back."

"Yeah, I'd miss you too."

I had started to notice that Justin could get kind of clingy when he was drunk. I wished he wouldn't because it made me feel responsible for him, like he was my kid brother or something. Tonight I did not mind so much. He fell asleep while the two of us sat on the couch. As he slumped against me, I looked down at his perfect hair and long black eyelashes. I still envied him for being so cool looking, and I still loved his lemon smell.

13
Old Scotch

THERE WAS one loose end I definitely wanted to tie up before I left for France. On Sunday I walked down to the Mission District for another of Marty's amazing meals. The place was no busier than usual. I took my seat, gave him my order, and waited for another masterpiece of Mexican cuisine. As he brought it out, I savored the smell. He was always pleased with the smile on my face.

While diving into the food, I got down to business.

"No more games, Marty. I want some answers."

"Answers? I got all kinds of answers. Any answer you want, amigo."

"Yeah, you always say that, but I never get the straight stuff. Is Antonio's name really Vega? How did you find that out?"

"I told you. I know people. I asked around. I just passed on to you the answer that came back to me. That's all."

"Who did you ask? What kind of people? Where are they?"

He looked at me with no small amount of amusement.

"You want to know what kind of people? I'll tell you what kind of people. They're the kind of people that people like me don't talk about too much with people like you. At least not if people like me want to get answers to questions that people like you like to ask. That's the kind of people they are."

Once again the two of us were going in circles.

"But how can I be sure that your Antonio Vega is my Antonio? I mean, you didn't have much to go on. I just didn't have much info for you—at least not the kind of stuff that would turn him up in somebody's filing system. He was just a kid living on the street who tagged along with us to Mexico. And he definitely wasn't using the name Antonio when he went to Chile. It's hard to believe you could talk to these 'people' and they would be able to figure out who he was."

"Yeah, come to think of it, it is kind of far-fetched all right."

"So, did you find out anything else about him? Do you know what happened to him in Chile? Do you know where he is now?"

"Sorry. All I got was a name. From back when he was living in L.A. The cops there had some stuff in their files on him."

"How do you know it's *my* Antonio?"

"I'm pretty sure it's him. The age and other details match up with your story. He disappeared from the U.S. right about when you said he did. Around August 1971."

"How much stock should I put in this information? Should I believe it? Or is it just so much bullshit?"

"Maybe. Who knows? You had a question. I got an answer. How believable is it? You have to decide that for yourself. But I can tell you this much. I believe it. As much as I believe anything in this crazy old world. Is it one-hundred percent certain? Nah, nothing is one-hundred percent, but I would say it's pretty good. You would be surprised at the information out there on people you think are totally off the radar. Nobody can hide completely—especially if they're not trying to hide because they don't think anyone is looking for them."

A shiver went through me. That always happened when I talked to Marty about this stuff.

"You would be surprised at the interesting stories lots of ordinary-seeming people have in their pasts. Here's an interesting one. You ever been in a restaurant near Union Square called Balthazar's?"

"Yeah…" I said suspiciously.

This was a perfect example of the weirdness that went through my conversations with Marty. Balthazar's was the only restaurant in that area I had ever been in. What were the odds of that?

"There's a waiter there. His name is Richard. He's an English guy."

"Yeah, he waited on a friend and me."

"You don't say? Well, don't tell anyone where you heard it, but that guy is a murderer."

"You're joking, right?"

"It's true. I swear it."

"If you know this for sure, shouldn't you tell the police or somebody?"

"Nah, there's no need for that. He only killed one time, and he won't ever do it again. He was a British lord back in England—and a professional gambler—but things just didn't go well for him. He was separated from his wife and children. One night he slipped back into the house and killed the nanny. Beat her to death with a lead pipe. Poor girl wasn't even supposed to be working that night. Not sure if he mistook her for the wife or if she just got between him and the kids. Anyway, he took off and no one has heard of him since."

"And that's him serving food at Balthazar's? That's pretty damn hard to believe, Marty. If that's true, how do *you* know about it. Why don't you tell the police?"

He shrugged.

"That one ain't none of my business. How are the tamales tonight?"

"They're great, like always. So, level with me Marty. What you told me about Antonio. Is that legit? I got to know for sure."

"So, what's so urgent about this?" he asked. "Why are you asking me this again now?"

"The fact is I don't know how many more times I will be coming back here. My boss is sending me to France on an assignment. And I'm half-thinking about just staying there—or going somewhere else."

Marty's eyebrow arched in a way I had never seen before.

"Well, now that is interesting. France, huh? Where in France are you going?"

"Deauville. There's a film festival there."

"Deauville, yes," he said thoughtfully. "Very, very interesting."

"Anyway, I'd sure miss your food if I didn't come back, but things have changed lately. I'm starting to think maybe it's time I got away from the city. I think maybe it's time for me to try someplace new."

For a while he did not say anything. I just kept on eating my tamales. Finally he spoke again.

"Do you like Scotch whiskey?"

"Huh? What? Yeah, I drink it sometimes."

I was about to tell him how Lonnie had introduced me to drinking it, but then I remembered Justin telling me I talked about Lonnie too much and I bit my tongue.

"I have a nice bottle at my place. Very old. Good stuff. Would you like to come over for a drink?"

This was the last thing I expected. I had never thought about where Marty lived, let alone expecting I might be invited there someday.

"Yeah, I suppose. When were you thinking?"

"How about now? I mean, after you've finished those tamales?"

"Now? But don't you need to be here?"

He shrugged and looked around.

"I'll close up. I don't think it's going to cost me much business."

"Well, okay. Where's your place?"

"Don't worry about that. I'll give you a lift. Leonides will drive us."

"Leonides?"

"Yeah, he drives me places. You didn't think I keep him around just because of his pretty face, did you?"

No, definitely not. No one would ever accuse Leonides of having a pretty face.

"Yeah, sounds good. Thanks."

As I finished my food, I wondered exactly what I was getting myself into. After all, I did not know much of anything about Marty. It was strange that, out of the blue, he would invite me to his place to drink Scotch. Marty cleared the table. Then he shut down the kitchen and turned out the lights. We stepped out of the front door. While Marty was locking up, I noticed a 1960s model Chevy—dark blue but otherwise not too different from the one Lonnie and I drove to Mexico—idling in the alley. Leonides was sitting at the wheel, looking as bored as ever. Marty opened one of the rear passenger doors for me and I got in. He went around to the other side and sat next to me, leaving Leonides alone in the front. Without Marty saying a word, he started driving.

I had no idea where we were going. It occurred to me that no one else had any idea of where I was or would have any hope of tracking me down if I happened to disappear. Maybe I should have been more apprehensive, but for some reason I did not feel nervous. After all, I had been eating in Marty's place for quite a long time and, if he were a kidnapper or criminal deviant, I surely would have already picked up on that vibe, right? If he were a kidnapper, he could not have expected to get much, if any, ransom for a nobody like me.

I just sat back and watched the city pass by. We drove north up Mission Street and then Van Ness Avenue, which surprised me, since I had assumed Marty lived in the Mission. It would not have surprised me if he had been living in the back of the restaurant.

The farther we went up Van Ness, the more I wondered if maybe we were going to take Highway 101 all the way to the Golden Gate and leave the city altogether. When we got to Lombard, though, the car made a right turn and climbed up Russian Hill. Were we going on a tour of the city? Was he going to take me down the twisty part of Lombard where all the tourists liked to drive? Instead, the car made a right onto Hyde Street. After another turn or two, it pulled up in front of a house that would have been easy to miss since it was wedged between two large apartment buildings. It did not fit in with the rest of the neighborhood. Most of the nearby buildings were in the familiar San Francisco style with the standard bay windows. This house was what you would call Tudor style, with dark wood trim all over it.

Leonides still looked bored as Marty and I got out of the car. He drove off without ever having said a word. I followed Marty up the steps to the door. I looked back and, in between the buildings across the street, I could see the city's lights and the bay in the distance. Although I had walked all over Russian Hill before, I had never been inside any of the houses, and I certainly did not know anyone who lived there. This was where the city's old money lived, the people who had been here for generations—not people like me or my friends who had all come from somewhere else.

Marty led me into the living room. It was not huge, but everything about it was elegant. The ornaments on the shelves and tables—everything was oak—looked like they must have cost a fortune. The light in the room came from Tiffany lamps. The bookshelves were stuffed with old books, mostly with leather covers.

"Make yourself at home," said Marty. "You are in for a treat."

Marty left the room, and I settled back into an extremely comfortable leather armchair. I detected a faint smell of pipe tobacco. In no time Marty was back with a bottle, a small pitcher of water and two glasses. He made a great show of removing the foil from the top of the bottle. The label looked as though it had been written by hand. He poured a small amount in the two glasses.

"You can add your own water," he said.

"Do you have any ice?"

He looked at me disapprovingly.

"You do not put ice in a whiskey like this. You should not even put water in it, but a little bit is okay—just to cut the taste. It's 25 years old, and it's 100 proof. You can't buy this whiskey, at least not outside of Scotland. It has to be collected in person in Strathspey. The liquor in your glass there is worth about, let's see, about twenty-five dollars or so, depending on the exchange rate between the dollar and pound sterling."

"You mean twenty-five dollars for the bottle?"

"No, twenty-five dollars just for what's in your glass."

He poured just a drop of water on top of the whiskey in his glass, and I did the same. Then he lifted his glass and said, "*¡Salud!*" He downed it all at once. I quickly lifted my glass, said "*¡Salud!*" and drank mine as well. It burned my throat. The intense taste of something very strong and very smoky made my body shudder. I thought I had done enough drinking in my time to be able to handle anything, but this was something different.

"What do you think?" he wanted to know.

I cleared my throat with a cough or two.

"That's some serious stuff. Did the little bit in that glass actually cost twenty-five dollars? Is that retail or is that the bar price?"

He laughed.

"You won't find this in a bar—or in a store for that matter. But yes, buying it directly from the distiller with no retail mark-up, it would run you about a thousand dollars or so for a half-liter bottle. Shall I pour us another round?"

"I, I don't know," I said. "It's kind of intimidating when I know how much it costs."

He laughed again and then delicately dispensed a couple more ounces in each glass.

"Don't worry about that. The money is only wasted if no one drinks it."

As I added the requisite drop of water, he got up and opened a drawer in an oak cabinet. He retrieved a wooden box, which he set on the table. It had a glass top, and I could see it contained cigars.

"Do you smoke?"

"I have a cigarette once in a while, but I've never really been into cigars."

"If you are ever going to smoke a cigar," he said, "this would be the time. These aren't that easy to come by."

"Why? Are they Cuban or something?"

"As a matter of fact, they are."

I had been joking, but he wasn't. The labels wrapped around each of the cigars read, "Cohiba." He unlocked the box with a key, took out a cigar, cut off the tip with an odd-looking knife, and then handed it to me. I put it in my mouth, and he lit a match. He held it with the flame just below the cigar's end. I puffed on it and rotated the cigar, like I'd seen men do sometimes in bars. The smoke's aroma filled my mouth. It made me cough.

"You're not used to it," Marty laughed. "Cigars aren't like cigarettes. I can promise you, though, you will never have a better cigar than that one."

This time around we sipped our whiskeys slowly. I sat back and enjoyed the extravagance of it all. The last thing I had expected, leaving home earlier in the day, was that I would wind up in a place like this, drinking expensive Scotch and smoking Cuban cigars.

"There must be more money in Mexican food than I thought," I said, thinking I was being funny.

Marty laughed but did not respond. He leaned back and contemplated the smoke rings he had blown. He was definitely a man who enjoyed life. After sitting comfortably awhile in silence, he asked a question.

"What's your plan, my young friend?"

"My plan?"

"You know, for your life? Where do you see yourself in five years?"

"Why? Do you have a job for me?"

He smiled.

"If I did, what kind of job would you want?"

"I dunno. I'm a photographer. I suppose I would always be looking for work taking photos."

"That's good. Photography is good. Photographs are important."

"And I'm a damn good photographer. If I do say so myself."

"I bet you are. Would you ever be interested in taking photographs in other countries?"

"Well, I'm going to be taking some in France soon."

"Yes, right."

Noting that our two glasses were dry again, he poured a couple more ounces in each one.

"How would you be, say, taking photographs without anyone noticing you were taking them? You know, on the sly.'

"You mean, kind of like a spy?"

"Yes, kind of like that."

"I don't know. I'm not exactly the bravest guy in the world, if you know what I mean. I kind of like to play it safe. I'm not much of a daredevil."

"Yeah, I knew a guy like that years ago. He thought he was a coward. It turned out he was the bravest of us all. In the end, all it took was a little word in his ear from Mr. Churchill."

I laughed.

"Did I say something funny?"

"Sorry, but yeah. What you said. That's in an Elvis Costello song I've been listening to."

Mildly amused Marty drained what was left in his glass and with a look in my direction indicated that I should do the same. I did. As he reached for the bottle again, I said, "This is turning out to be an expensive evening for you. I don't mind if you have something cheaper to drink."

"Life is too short to drink the cheap stuff," he said, replenishing the tumblers.

He leisurely savored his next sip between a couple of puffs on his cigar.

"So, my young friend, what exactly were you thinking when you walked into Guatemala?"

I was feeling very mellow. It was like a pleasant dream. It took a full moment to absorb what he had said.

"Huh? Guatemala? Who said anything about Guatemala?"

"You *were* in Guatemala, weren't you? I mean, just for a short time and just inside the border, but that was you there that time, wasn't it?"

"I don't understand how you would know anything about that. I never said anything about it to you—or hardly anyone else. Ever."

"Like I keep telling you, kid, I know people. I hear things. The more you learn about the world, the more you realize that there are very few things that someone somewhere doesn't know."

This was creepy.

"So, what else do you know about me? Do you have some kind of file on me or something?"

He chuckled.

"Don't worry. Nobody is interested in you particularly. You're the kind of person who mostly flies under the radar, as we say. You don't leave much of a trail behind you. I'm guessing you don't write a lot of checks or use a credit card all the time."

"I don't have a lot of money to throw around if that's what you mean."

"Don't take me the wrong way, amigo. I'm singing your praises. You're one of the smart ones. I think you're going to do just fine. You're not caught up in all the same stuff that everybody else is. I admire that."

I took another sip of his Scotch, which I was now finding downright addictive.

I said, "Well, I'll probably never be able to afford to drink like this every night, but I don't have any complaints."

"So tell me. You can level with me. Why were you in Guatemala in '71? Were you really just doing a favor for a couple of guys you didn't know? Did you really not know what you were carrying? Or did they manage to convince you that you were liberating the working class?"

"I've never been very interested in politics."

"So, why did you do it then? Why did you take the risk? Was it just for a laugh?"

I had tried to make the Scotch last as long as I could, but I found myself draining the glass again.

"It was about a girl. A woman."

Marty broke into a grin.

"Ah, now it makes sense. Yes, I like this. Tell me about the woman."

"I met her in Guaymas. We had a night together. I was in love. Those two guys in Mexico City convinced me they could help me find her again. That's why I did it. For her. I wanted to be with her again."

Marty smiled warmly as he poured more whiskey. This time he did not bother to measure a finger's width as he had the previous times. In fact, he poured such extravagant amounts I cringed to see how much of the bottle we had consumed.

"Dallas, my friend, you're nothing but an old-fashioned goddamned romantic. I knew there was a reason I liked you. Tell me, what was the young lady's name?"

"María Soledad Carvajal. She was from Monterrey."

"And did you ever see her or talk to her again?"

"No. I went to Monterrey six years later, but I didn't have any luck tracking her down. I didn't 'know people' the way you do."

"Would you like her address and phone number?"

My heart stopped. I would have thought he was just messing with me, but I had heard enough from him to seriously believe that I might be only a few words away from seeing Marisol again.

"Do you have it?"

"No, of course not. But I can ask somebody. Do you want me to?"

For some reason, the idea of finding Marisol again now seemed scary.

"Can you find out just a couple of things for me first?"

"Like what?"

"Can you find out if she is married? And can you find out if she has any children and what their ages are? Their exact ages?"

"Interesting. Okay, I'll see what I can come up with. No promises though. Now can I ask you something?"

"Sure, why not?"

"Tell me about the Irishman."

"The Irishman?"

"Yeah, the guy you said drove you to the Guatemalan border."

"How do you know about him?"

Marty gave me an exasperated look, as if to say, hey, haven't you figured out I know everything about you by now?

"You want to know about Séamus?"

"Is that what he called himself?"

"Yeah, that's what he called himself."

"Interesting that he used his real name with you. You want to know an interesting coincidence?"

"Okay."

"He has the same name as your singer friend?"

"My singer friend?"

"Yeah. Your guy pronounces it Cos-TELL-o, but old Séamus, being Irish, says it COS-tello."

"So, what do *you* know about Séamus? What's he up to these days?"

Marty chuckled.

"There's a lot of people who would like to know that, I can tell you."

Between the strong whiskey and the cigar smoke, I was starting to feel a bit dizzy.

"By my estimate, Marty, I must have drunk about a couple hundred dollars worth of your whiskey. I should probably head home before I bankrupt you."

"Sure, sure. Leonides will drive you home. No problem but, before you go, I need to ask you a favor."

"Why not?" I said. "After all the things you're finding out for me, not to mention the Scotch and the cigars, I suppose it's the least I can do. What do you need?"

"When you are in France…"

"Yeah?"

"Well, I might need you to take a photograph for me."

"Sure, no problem. What do you want me to shoot?"

"I'll have to let you know. It won't be me personally. It will be a friend of mine, but you will know it's for me when he talks to you. Will you do that for me, Dallas?"

"Yeah, sure, like I said, no problem."

He put his hand on my shoulder and gave me kind of a fatherly smile as he drained his glass for the last time.

"I'm not worried about you, Dallas. You're going to do just fine. You're going to be all right. I can tell."

A warm glow was radiating through my whole body as he walked me to the front door. It was as though the Scotch was antifreeze and now it was running through all of my veins and arteries like the radiator and hoses of a car. I was floating on a cloud. He opened the door and I saw the Chevy idling down on the street at the bottom of the steps. Leonides was waiting. Had he been there the whole time or did he somehow know just when to come back?

Damn, I thought, *This has been one strange evening.*

14
Fright

I SAT in the front passenger seat next to Leonides. He had expected me to sit in the back, like before, but I just was not comfortable being driven around like he was my chauffeur. I tried to engage him in conversation but, no matter what I said, his only response was to either nod or shrug. He was not a big talker—at least not with me. He let me give him directions to my place, although I suspected he already knew exactly where I lived.

As the car approached my street, I told him to let me off at the corner. It would make it easier for him to head back and, besides, I felt slightly less paranoid if he did not see which building I went into. He stopped where I told him, and I thanked him. He drove off, and I walked toward my apartment. It was dark and more quiet than usual. As I got to the door of the building, I noticed a man walking in my direction. He was dressed in a business suit, which was kind of strange. Usually, you didn't see business types this side of Market Street and definitely not that time of night. As I was about to reach into my pocket for my key, he called out.

"Dallas?"

"Yeah?"

I had no idea who he was, and I was getting a bad feeling.

"Dallas Green?"

"Who wants to know?"

He walked right up to me and looked me in the eyes without answering my question. He was not particularly threatening, but he made me nervous. He was scrawny with thick glasses. He was mostly bald on top and had a moustache.

"I just wanted to see what you looked like."

"Why? Who are you anyway?"

"I wanted to see what a real asshole looks like up close."

"Hey, man, what's your problem?"

"I had to see if there was something special about you. I wanted to see what you see in the mirror every day."

I was getting angry.

"Look, I don't even know you. Who the hell are you anyway?"

"Who the hell am I? Who the hell am I? You want to know who the hell I am?"

"Yeah."

"I'm the guy whose wife you've been fucking!"

Oh, shit.

He had caught me completely by surprise because he was nothing like I had imagined. This was the last guy I would have pictured with Lana.

"Jesus, man. Look, I don't know what to say. I don't blame you at all for being pissed."

"That's it? You don't blame me? *You* don't blame *me*? That's a fucking laugh. Well, I blame you. I blame you for making my wife cheat on me, for ruining my marriage, for making my son have to go through a divorce."

I wished I had something to say to him, but I didn't. He did not want to hear that I had thought I was in love. He did not want to hear I had never actually thought about him because I had not known him. He did not want to hear that I had not thought about his son because, well, because I just hadn't. It all happened without me thinking. There was nothing I could say. Nothing.

He was standing right up against me, looking up at me because he was about half a head shorter than me. He reeked of alcohol, probably bourbon by the smell of it. He was obviously three sheets to the wind, and he made me nervous. I kept my eyes on his hands, not because I thought he might punch me but because I worried he might have a gun.

"How do you live with yourself, you piece of shit? Tell me! How can you even stand to look at yourself? Do you think you're smarter than everyone else? Do you think you're smarter than me? Were you having a good laugh thinking about how you were getting away with sleeping with my wife? Did you think it was funny? Did you?"

"No," I said quietly. "No, I didn't think it was funny…"

"You know," he interrupted, "you're nothing special. Nothing special at all. That's what really gets me. There's absolutely nothing special about you."

"I know," I whispered, but I don't think he heard me.

"I mean, of all the men she could have had—and a woman like her could have had anyone—she picks you? You!"

He pushed against me. I did not move. He nearly lost his balance. There was nothing I could do but stand there and hope it would be over soon.

"Why don't you say something? Not so smart now, are you? Not so clever now, huh?"

He got himself more and more worked up.

"How did she justify it to you? What did she say about me?"

"Uh, she never really talked about you. Not much anyway. It was kind of like you didn't exist…"

It would have been better not answering his questions, but I guess I felt I owed it to him to at least try.

"That's great! That's just perfect. Did she try to tell you that I was cheating on her?"

"Uh, no…"

"Well, it wasn't cheating. It didn't mean anything. It was just physical and never with anyone more than once. It was always anonymous. I thought she understood. I never had an affair. I was never in love with anyone but her. It's just… just the way I was. I thought she understood."

I had thought the situation could not possibly have gotten more uncomfortable, but I was wrong.

"And you know what, Dallas Green? You know what?"

I said nothing. He was talking loudly. I wondered if anyone in my building could hear him. I hoped no one called the police.

"Every one of them was better than you. Every one of them. I would never have looked at you twice. I can't imagine what she saw in you. You're nothing special."

After all this time, only now was I beginning to understand the fundamental issue in Lana's marriage.

"Nothing special at all. Or are you?"

Without warning he pressed himself up against me and forced me against the wall. Before I knew what was happening, he had grabbed my crotch and squeezed hard. As sickening pain spread through my intestines. He pressed his mouth against mine. The shock of it all nearly made me pass out. My instincts took over while I went into some sort of trance. With all my strength I shoved him away. He staggered backwards and nearly fell. He recovered his balance and stood licking his lips, looking as if he were trying to focus on something. I wiped my mouth with the back of my hand and spat on the ground, trying to get the taste of his saliva out of my mouth. I tried to ignore the pain in my groin.

"You're crazy, man!" I yelled at him. "I don't know what you want me to say, but I'll tell you the honest-to-God truth. I'm sorry. Maybe you won't believe it, but I am really, really sorry for what I did. If I could take it back,

I would. But I can't. I'll never be able to, and I'll have to live with that. But, man, you're crazy. If you come near me again, I'll kill you. I swear I will."

He just stood there, lost in thought.

"Nothing special," he muttered.

I thought about Wayne Jeffries. As far as I knew, Wayne never found out about me and Linda. If he had, there definitely would have been none of this craziness. He would have simply picked up one of his guns, he would have come found me, and he would have shot me dead. Just like that. This was worse.

As I calmed down and the pain slowly went away, I started to feel sorry for him again.

"I think you should go home, man. How are you getting home, Gary?"

The question roused him from whatever he had been thinking about.

"I have my car."

"You're in no condition to drive, man. Give me your keys. I'll call you a cab."

He got angry.

"Fuck you. I can drive just fine. Don't go trying to act like a nice guy with me. I can look after myself."

I tried to talk sense to him.

"Hey, man, take it from someone who has done my own fair share of drinking. You're in no condition to drive. Give me the keys. You'll get them back tomorrow."

"No way in hell, asshole. I've had enough of this. I'm out of here."

"I can't let you go, Gary. Not like this. You're liable to kill yourself or, worse, someone else. Give me the keys."

He pulled the keys out of his pocket. He dangled them in front of me and laughed.

"I'll give them to you on one condition."

"What's that?"

"Let me blow you."

"What?"

"You heard me. If you care so fucking much about me, then let me blow you."

"What? Hell, no. I'm not letting you do that."

"You sure? You don't know what you're missing. I'm really good."

"That's just not going to happen, man. Give me the fucking keys."

"If you're not going to let me blow you, then blow me. Maybe that's what you were wanting to do all along anyway. Let's see if you're half as good as my wife."

Now he had definitely pissed me off, and I lost it completely.

"That's it, man," I yelled at him. "I tried to help you. I really did. But you said the magic words. You're on your own now. All I ask is you don't kill some innocent person out there. Now fuck off."

He staggered down the street. I felt humiliated. I wondered if any of my neighbors had heard or seen what happened. Just then I had a feeling of being watched. I looked around but did not see anybody. Then I looked up at the building across the street. In his usual place on the window ledge was the seagull. He sat there watching me. I had never seen him there after dark before. I wondered if he was looking at me with sympathy or if he was judging me.

I got out my key and opened the door to my building. Once inside, I just stood there and listened. Finally I heard a car roar down the street. Probably a European import by the sound of it. Most likely a 1.4-liter engine. After the noise from the car had died away, I continued to stand there, unable to move. I began trembling, and soon I was shaking violently. I had managed to hold it together until I got inside, but now I was losing it. I was light-headed and thought I might pass out. A sudden coldness came over me. The pain in my groin made my stomach sick, and I fought the urge to vomit. All I could think of was how horrible it had felt, even though it had only been a few moments, when he overpowered me. I could not get the thought out of my mind that, if he had been bigger or stronger, he could have done anything he wanted to me. That feeling of helplessness was what really made me feel sick.

I had walked around the city by myself, often at night, for the previous couple of years. I had never given a second thought to my safety. I was young and male and not supposed to worry about things like that. I was by no means reckless. I knew to avoid bad areas and to be alert to potentially dangerous situations. I had never before felt as though I was in danger. Maybe I actually deserved what Gary had done to me or had tried to do to me. At any rate I had definitely brought it on myself. The result was that, from now on, I would never feel completely safe again. I would always be looking over my shoulder in case Gary would come after me again. If not him, then it might be some crazy stranger if I just happened to be in the wrong place at the wrong time. In a matter of minutes I had lost my peace of mind. I did not even know that I had had it until it was gone.

After a while I finally felt okay enough to walk up to my apartment. As I climbed the stairs, I prayed, *Please, God, don't let that idiot kill anybody out there on the road. That's the last thing I need on my conscience.*

I walked into my apartment and threw myself on the bed. As I lay there, the Scotch I had drunk with Marty caught up with me all at once. I fell asleep with my clothes on.

I remember thinking, *Man, I definitely need to get out of the city.*

15
Flight

THE THING I had not expected about flying was how much waiting there would be.

First there was waiting in line to check in. Then, after arriving at the gate, there was waiting until the plane arrived. Then there was waiting in line to get on the plane. Once on board, there was waiting until the plane finally began to move. Then there was more waiting for the plane to taxi onto the runway and for it to be cleared for take-off.

As the plane accelerated, the force pressed me into my seat. There was a strange sensation when the plane left the ground and climbed, followed by an unnerving feeling of the plane seeming to slow down. So slow that it felt as though it could not possibly remain in the air. A disturbing rumble rose up from the floor, as the landing gear retracted.

"You know, the plane will stay in the air even without you helping to hold it up."

Melanie was looking at my hands clutching the armrests. I was holding them so tight my fingers had gone completely white. I let go and felt the blood flow again.

"Nervous flyer?"

"It's just that it's my first time in a plane. I didn't really know what to expect."

That surprised her. She stopped focusing on the considerable paperwork on her lap.

"Really? Your first time? You've honestly never flown before?"

"No."

"That's kind of hard to believe."

"I just never had to travel anywhere before. I've never been outside of California. Well, except for two trips to Mexico, once by car and once by train. I've never been anywhere else."

"Well, you can relax now. That was the worst of it. In a few minutes a flight attendant will ask us what we want to drink. I'll make sure she gives us doubles."

"Sounds good."

The plane started shaking, and I grabbed the armrests again.

"Don't worry," she said. "We're just going through the jet stream. It will be nice and smooth again in a few minutes."

I had never cared much for Melanie, and the feeling had always seemed to be mutual. Now that we were traveling together, though, she was being very nice to me. I do not know exactly why I had not liked her. It was probably because she always talked about work and she was never happy with the job anybody else was doing. Now that we had no choice but to sit next to each other for a dozen hours, I saw her differently. After all she was an attractive woman. Sure, her blonde hair would have looked better straight instead of in tight curls. And if she wanted my advice, I would have told her to try contact lenses instead of those large black-rimmed glasses. Of course, none of that was any of my business.

Before long, just as she had promised, we were sipping Scotch on the rocks in little plastic cups while munching on honey roasted peanuts. This jet-setting life was not so bad after all. As I finally began to feel comfortable, Melanie suddenly became business-like.

"We need to have a strategy for making contact with MacCaul. I've researched him extensively, and mostly what I've learned is that he avoids the press like the plague. What are your thoughts?"

"Won't we have plenty of time to think about this after we get there?"

"Plenty of time? What planet are you on? We need to think about this now. Once we get there, it's going to be crazy. MacCaul may be our main focus, but there are a lot of other things to consider as well. I will want to get as many interviews as I can. We're going to have to hustle."

Looking at her notes, she said, "There will be tributes to Yul Brynner, Glenn Ford, Danny Kaye, Clint Eastwood…"

"Clint Eastwood? Really?"

"Yes."

"Cool. What movie is he in?"

"Something called *Bronco Billy*. Sounds dreadful. There's also a tribute to Elia Kazan. He's not showing anything, but his wife has a film in the festival."

"*Bronco Billy*? That played ages ago in the city. I thought a film festival would be showing *new* movies."

"Deauville is an *American* film festival. A lot of the movies have already been released in the States. The point is they are new to the French."

"Well, you've definitely done your homework, Mel. Nobody could possibly be more prepared than you are."

"Prep work is just part of it. The important thing is to not lose focus after we get there. To be honest, Dallas, I'm a little worried about you holding up your end. You seem very relaxed about all this."

And there she was—the Melanie that always ended up driving me crazy. It was never enough for her just to push herself. She had to push everyone else too.

"Don't worry about me, Mel. I'll have my head in the game when it counts."

She was exasperated with me.

"Please don't call me Mel, and for your information having your head in the game counts *all* the time. Here. Familiarize yourself with these photos of the major directors."

She handed me some 8x10 headshots. I did not recognize any of them except, of course, for Clint. She pointed to one guy with a beard and glasses.

"You might like this guy's movie," she said sarcastically. "You probably saw his previous one. It was called *The Texas Chain Saw Massacre*. His new one is about vampires."

"Hey, wait a minute," I said. "I saw *Salem's Lot*. It was on television last year. I watched it with Keith and Amy."

"Yes, well, sometimes made-for-TV movies in the U.S. get theatrical releases in Europe. I've written the names on the back of each photograph. I expect you will have them all committed to memory by the time we get there."

"Is there a photo of Logan MacCaul here?"

"Just this one. There are no good recent photos of him. At least none that I could put my hands on."

She handed me a black and white photo of a young man with large, penetrating dark eyes and a very long face. His hair was short and black. His elbow leaned on a table. A cloud of smoke rose from the cigarette in his fingers.

"This looks pretty old," I said. "He probably doesn't look anything like this now."

"Well, it's all we have to work with. I'd say if you ran into those eyes today, *they* would be recognizable anyway."

I stared at his eyes and wondered what thoughts were going through his mind all those years ago. What made him so gloomy?

"Why do you think he stopped making movies, Mel?"

She stopped shuffling her notes and looked up with annoyance.

"Did I not just ask you to not call me Mel?"

"Why? What's wrong with it? It suits you, and it's a lot shorter than saying Melanie all the time."

"Do I have to have a reason? I don't know why. I've just never liked it. Maybe because it makes me sound like a man."

"Don't worry. No one is ever going to mistake you for a man. You're definitely a woman."

She glared at me.

"Please tell me you're not flirting with me."

"What if I am?"

Her face tightened even more.

"You do know what a big mistake you're making?"

I laughed.

"Yeah, I know. Sorry, I was just trying to lighten things up. I didn't mean anything by it."

"The best way to lighten things up for me is to do your share of the work and be ready *before* we get there. Now that you've had your fun, try to go through these notes I've made and then I'll quiz you on the headshots."

I sighed. It was going to be a long flight. Nearly twelve hours according to what the pilot had said over the intercom. I could have done with a nap. I had not gotten much sleep the night before. For one thing Justin had insisted on spending the previous evening with me and having one last drinking session. The poor guy had gotten so attached to me I was starting to worry about him. He actually made me feel guilty about leaving. To make him feel better, I told him I had only been joking about not coming back from France and that made him happy. The truth, though, was that I was still determined not to come back.

Not only did I end up getting to bed late, but a phone call woke me up in the middle of the night. It turned out to be Marty. It sounded like he was calling from a phone booth, but that made no sense. What would he be doing in a phone booth at four in the morning? Only later did I think to wonder how he had gotten my phone number.

"Marty? What the hell? Is something wrong?"

"No, no. It's just I know you are flying out tomorrow and I promised you some info."

"How did you know I was flying out tomorrow?"

"You must have told me."

I was pretty sure I had not, but I let it go.

"What info was that?"

"You asked me to find out about this María Soledad Carvajal."

Hearing her name over the phone in the dark made me seriously wonder if I was having yet another of my weird dreams. I literally pinched myself and decided that I was awake.

"Really? Thanks, Marty. What have you got?"

"You sure you want to know?"

"Why? Is it bad?"

"Nah, it ain't bad. It's just I don't know what you were hoping for."

"I was just hoping to find out how she is, where she is. I guess I just wanted to know that she was okay, wherever she was or whatever she was doing."

"Okay. Well, first let's make sure I have the right woman. She's 24 years old and she's always lived in Monterrey. Is that right?"

"Yeah, that sounds right. So, is she married?"

"Yeah, she's married."

That was the answer I had expected, but it still felt like a punch in the gut.

"Do you have her husband's name?"

"Sure. Cárdenas. Eduardo Cárdenas. He's a bank executive."

"So, his name isn't Carlos?"

"Carlos? No, why? Where did you get the name Carlos?"

"Sorry, forget about that. I didn't actually think his name was going to be Carlos. Do they have kids?"

"One child and another on the way."

"Is the child a boy?"

"No, a girl."

"How old is she?"

"Two years."

"Two years old. You're sure about that."

"That's the info I have."

"No other kids?"

"That's all I have."

"No chance there was another pregnancy… like when she was still a teenager?"

"Well, I suppose anything's possible. I'm not God here. This is just what's in the public record."

"Thanks, Marty. It's… it's good to get the information. This is stuff I've been wondering about for a long time now."

"Glad I could help, kid."

I was about to hang up the phone when another question popped into my head.

"Say, Marty, do you have the name of her daughter?"

"Let's see, yeah. The name is Dalila."

"Dalila?"

"Yeah, that's what I have."

"Really?"

"Really. Why?"

I smiled.

"Dalila. Doesn't that kind of like sound like Dallas?"

"Uh, sure, if you say so. Or maybe it's just a name she liked. So, anyway, you're happy with the info I got you?"

"Yeah, Marty, very happy. *Muchas gracias*."

"So, now that I've done you a favor, you'll do one for me, right? You won't forget about my photograph?"

"Sure, no problem. What do you want me to shoot?"

"You'll find out when the time comes."

"But I'm flying out tomorrow. You should tell me now."

"Don't worry. I'll get word to you."

"In France? How will you know where to find me?"

"Let me worry about that. I just need to know you're ready to do it. Someone will be in touch. When he is, you will know that the message is from me."

"I wish you would explain more what this is all about. I'd really like to know what I'm getting mixed up in."

He chuckled.

"Trust me. The less you know, the better off you are. Don't worry. You won't be in any trouble or anything like that. It's just that, well, it's better when these things are done by someone like you. Someone who doesn't attract the wrong kind of attention."

"Okay, whatever you say. I owe you. I'll do my best."

"I know you will. Have a good flight."

After we hung up I lay awhile in bed wide awake. A strange wave of sadness came over me. In a weird way I was mourning little Antonio. I was actually grieving for a child I had thought I might have but now was pretty sure I did not. This probably meant I was not going to be having those dreams about Marisol and the little kid anymore. It should have been a relief knowing I was not responsible for a little child existing in the world, knowing I should have taken responsibility for him but had not. The child was a phantom, but my sadness was real. In my imagination he had been real. Now I knew I would never see little Antonio in the flesh. I would never tell him who I was or how I met his mother and that we were in love for one glorious night. I would never tell him where his name came from. I would never watch him grow up or teach him English or how to play baseball. There had been a phantom boy named Antonio, and there had also been a phantom Marisol, who had been waiting for me all those years. She was gone too.

My thoughts were interrupted suddenly. The plane was shaking violently. I grabbed the armrests again.

"Shit!" I said. "What's that?"

Melanie was still going over her notes and was not the least bit alarmed.

"We're just going through some turbulence," she said matter-of-factly.

"Do you think the flight attendant would bring us a couple more Scotches?"

She looked at her watch.

"It's too late for that. We'll be landing soon, and we should try to have our heads clear. We will want to hit the ground running, so to speak. I've noticed you haven't spent a lot of time looking at those notes I worked so hard on. I hope you have at least committed all the photos to memory."

"Yeah, yeah, don't worry, Mel, I've got it under control."

She gave me an exasperated look but apparently decided there was no point asking me again to drop my favorite nickname for her. Instead she simply asked, "Do you ever take anything seriously?"

"Sure, I do, but a person can't be serious *all* the time. Life isn't only about notes and memorizing and trying to get ahead of everyone else."

"Why don't you tell me what life is all about then? I'd like to know your thoughts. Really."

"I don't know. I suppose there's something to be said for actually enjoying your work instead of always making it drudgery."

"I *am* enjoying my work."

"It doesn't seem like it. You're always so serious."

"Just because I'm serious doesn't mean I'm not getting satisfaction from what I do."

"Okay, okay. I'm sorry. I'll spend the rest of the time reading over all your notes really carefully. I promise I won't let you down, *Melanie*."

She looked as though she was about to criticize me again but then thought better of it. She put her hand gently on my arm and said, "Sorry. I know I can be a bit of a bitch sometimes. I'll try to ease up… a bit."

"Thanks. That's all I ask."

Just then the flight attendant passed by, and Melanie grabbed her attention.

"Pardon me, Sherry, we'll have two more Scotch on the rocks here please."

Melanie had actually made a point of learning her name.

"Sorry, ma'am" said the flight attendant. "I'm afraid the beverage service has finished."

As sweetly as anything I had ever heard in my life, Melanie told her, "Yes, I understand. It's just that my colleague here has budgeted for a good deal of air travel this year, but he is a nervous flyer. I am sure you could make an exception in this case?"

Sherry looked at me and then at Melanie again and winked.

"I think it will be okay if you drink them fast," she said.

Within a couple of minutes we were sipping our last drinks of the flight. I was impressed—and a little jealous—at how Melanie had managed to get what she wanted. I had a whole new appreciation for her. My mind wandered. Lana was out of the picture. My old fantasy of someday seeing Marisol again was now gone for good. I was feeling free and single in a way I had not for a very long time. Melanie was actually an attractive woman, especially when she managed to stop being so business-like. Also, she was smart. She was definitely going to be very successful. She was not the kind of woman I had ever gone out with before, but now my thinking was changing.

We finished our drinks quickly. As the flight attendant came by to scoop up the plastic cups, I felt the plane begin to descend. The landing could not happen soon enough for me. I tried to see out the windows, but we were in the middle section and there was not much to see. Melanie, meanwhile, kept working on her notes.

Yes, I thought, *I should definitely go out with someone like Melanie. I might even consider going out with Melanie herself, but I know that will never happen. I know for a fact she's in a relationship, and I'm definitely not going to get into that situation again.*

I tensed up as the wheels touched the ground. The plane bounced a couple of times and I was forced into my seat as the pilot stepped on the brakes.

Thank God, I thought. *On the ground again at last.*

No, there would definitely never be anything between me and Melanie. Not only was she in a relationship, but I had actually met her girlfriend Sheila a couple of times and really liked her. The last thing I would ever want would be to come between them—as if that were even possible. Those two definitely only had eyes for each other.

16
Deauville

MY FIRST impression of France was pretty much like my first impression of flying. There was a lot of waiting.

After the plane touched down, it took forever to taxi to the gate. There was another long wait to get off the plane. There was a long walk to get to passport control. Once there, we stood in a long line until a bored-looking man in a uniform spent a minute or two staring at our passports and then stamped them.

"*Bonjour*," I said to him, doing my best to make use of the language tapes I had listened to.

He looked up at me with heavy eyelids, even more bored than before. He gave an epic shrug as he handed my passport back to me. Without uttering a single word, he turned his attention to the person behind me.

There was more walking to get to baggage claim. Charles de Gaulle Airport did not seem much different from San Francisco International, which meant that up until this point France did not seem much different from the United States—except for all the cigarette smoke.

At baggage claim, there was more waiting. Finally, our luggage arrived on the carousel. We grabbed our bags and handed our landing cards to the customs guys as we headed for the exit. Melanie had a suitcase. I had brought my backpack.

"You know, that really makes you look like an American tourist," she said.

"What can I say?" I said as I slipped my shoulders inside the straps. "I like having my hands free."

It was only when we walked into the main terminal that I finally felt I was in a different country. There were people everywhere, and I could not understand what any of them were saying. The language had a whole different sound to it than English or Spanish. People also dressed a lot better than in America—even better than people in the city—and I had thought nobody liked to dress better than people in San Francisco. The smell of cigarettes was everywhere, and it was not the aroma of Marlboros. It was a dark, strong cigarette smell. I had noticed it the minute we got off the plane. The moment they walked through the gate, the French passengers had all grabbed their cigarette packs and lit up. It was as though they had waited for nothing but taking a drag the previous twelve hours. In the arrivals area the smoke was even thicker. I had been around a lot of smokers before, but nobody could touch the French. It seemed like every man, woman, child, and dog in the country had a coffin nail hanging out of their mouth.

I had no idea where we were going or what we should do next. Fortunately Melanie was in charge. She had been in Paris before and knew the ropes. I followed her to a window with a sign that said *Bureau de Change*.

"I'm going to change some dollars for French francs. I advise you to do the same."

I changed a hundred dollars. The francs were bigger than dollar bills and did not fit into my wallet very well, so I just crammed them in the best I could. We walked out of the terminal and down a sidewalk to a bus stop where we waited about a half an hour. There was a smell of diesel from all the buses and trucks.

Melanie spotted the bus we needed, and we pushed and shoved along with everybody else to get on. It was a longer drive than I expected into the city. We passed through some nice countryside before gradually making our way into the city and, finally, the middle of Paris. The streets were narrow. The buildings, squeezed close together, were old and dark gray. All my life I had heard so much about Paris that I somehow expected it to be glittering and bright. Instead, a lot of it looked old and dirty. The cars were small, and the drivers were crazy. There was a lot of honking and occasional shouting. I looked out the window of the bus, thinking I might catch a glimpse of the Eiffel Tower. There was no way I was going to see anything except whatever street we were on. Eventually we got to a plaza in front of a large building with columns. I followed Melanie off the bus and down the street to the train station. There were crowds everywhere. I thought San Francisco was a busy place, but Paris was absolutely crammed with people walking in every direction at once.

Tall and with high windows, the train station was like something out of a history book. A big clock looked down at us from just below the green copper roof. I wondered if there could really be trains inside that building. There was more hustle and bustle inside the station. I was glad that Melanie knew what she was doing because I found it all overwhelming. She bought our tickets and led me to the platform to wait for the train. I would have never figured out where to go.

When the train pulled in, it was every man for himself. That was apparently the standard way of boarding transportation in France. People did not form lines. I did my best not to get crushed or to lose sight of Melanie, all the while holding tight to my camera bag. Once on board, we found a couple of seats, threw our bags up onto the overhead rack, and sat down with relief. In hardly any time at all the train started moving, slowly at first and then gradually faster. At first there was not much to see—just walls on either side, mostly covered with graffiti. Sometimes we got a view of houses and other buildings beyond the walls. Then the walls were gone and we were looking into gardens in the backs of houses. Eventually we were back out in the country. The rolling hills were a rich green color and very different from the dry golden hills of California.

As I settled back to relax, a sudden wave of tiredness came over me. I wondered how long I had been awake and tried to calculate it in my head. I reckoned it was something like ten in the morning back home, which meant that I had been awake more than twenty-four hours by this point. No wonder I was feeling so tired. I looked over at Melanie and saw that she was dozing. I could not believe I was actually in France.

I jerked awake. I did not remember having fallen asleep. Melanie was awake now and looking out the window. She looked quietly happy.

"I love France," she said. "Sheila and I came here on a holiday not long after we moved in together. It's always been a special place to me."

"I guess I haven't seen enough of it to feel like I'm really here yet. Mostly so far I've just seen a bus and a train."

"There's so much to see," she said. "It's such a beautiful country. So much culture. So much good food and wine."

I had never seen her with such a dreamy, faraway look before. She obviously wished she was here with Sheila instead of me. This was my first real glimpse of Melanie without her work personality, and I definitely liked her better this way.

A few hours later we pulled into the train station. The sign outside the window said, "Trouville-Deauville." Melanie leapt to her feet and pulled down her suitcase.

"We're here," she said excitedly.

I followed her out of the train station and onto the street. There was a line of taxis and she walked up to the first one. She gave the driver the name of our hotel. He got out of the car and dutifully put our luggage in the trunk. He wanted to take my camera bag, but I did not let go of it. We got into the car, and he took off down the road like a bat out of hell. I do not know why he was in such a hurry. The hotel was only a mile away.

The hotel was a huge place. It looked strangely like Marty's house on Russian Hill—except a whole lot bigger. Melanie paid the driver, and we walked into the lobby. She handled the check-in. I was impressed with how good her French sounded. At least it sounded good to me. She handed me my room key.

"Are you interested in getting a bite to eat?" I asked her. "Or maybe a drink?"

I was dead tired but, at the same time, we had not eaten anything since getting off the plane.

"I wouldn't mind," she said. "but I'm exhausted. I think I'll go straight to bed. You'll do the same if you're smart. And don't forget. You should have all of those photographs and notes memorized for the morning. We need to be able to recognize who's who at the festival and to recognize Logan MacCaul—if we're lucky enough to spot him."

The old Melanie from work was back. I followed her into the tiny elevator which took us up to our floor. It was extremely slow. I wondered if it would make it all the way up. When the door opened, the hallway was pitch black. Melanie touched a switch on the wall and a series of lights along the ceiling came on.

"Your room's down there," she said. "I'm one floor up. See you in the morning. Let's meet for breakfast at eight o'clock. Try not to be late."

"Okay," I said. "Night."

I went into my room and put down my backpack and camera bag. The room was about the size of a large walk-in closet. There was a tiny bathroom with a toilet and sink and another thing that looked like some weird kind of extra sink on the floor. The room smelled of smoke. I washed my face in the sink and looked at myself in the mirror.

This is my first night in France, I thought. *I don't care how tired I am. I'm going down to the bar for a drink.*

I ran my comb through my hair and then went back out to the hallway. It was pitch dark again. I tried to find a light switch on the wall like the one that Melanie pushed, but I could not find it. I felt my way down the hall until I got back to the elevator and took it back down to the lobby. I could hear the low rumble of people talking and headed in that direction.

The bar was elegant. There was a lot of wood and crystal and the biggest array of all kinds of bottles I had ever seen. I found a stool and sat down. Instantly a thin, serious-looking man in a perfectly ironed white shirt slapped a coaster down in front me and said, "*Monsieur.*"

I tried to remember if I had learned any French words that would be helpful in ordering a Scotch on the rocks, but in the end I just said, "I'll have Scotch on the rocks."

"*Très bien, monsieur.*"

While the bartender was taking his time with my order, I looked around the room. It was full of people, most of them engaged in animated conversations with one another over drinks of various sizes and colors. Most of them were dressed extremely well. I felt like a slob compared to them. As I surveyed the room, I had absolutely no idea what any of them were saying. If they had been speaking Spanish, I might have been able to catch a few words here and there. With French I was hopeless. It was still a strange feeling, being in a country where I had never been before and, for the moment anyway, being completely alone. The language had a different sound than Spanish. There was something musical about it. I liked the sound of French. I just wished I could understand and speak more of it.

Over in a corner two women were having a particularly animated discussion. The older blonde woman looked important, maybe because she wore flashy earrings and a pearl necklace. The younger woman, with long black hair, was dressed more simply. She had big dark eyes with a very friendly look about them. She was as thin as a rail and wore a tight sweater.

God, I thought, *she's gorgeous.*

The bartender set down in front of me a glass containing a miniscule amount of whiskey. There was a single ice cube in it. A few minutes later he returned and plopped down a tiny bowl with a few peanuts.

"Thanks," I said. "I mean, *merci.*"

In Mexico I had gotten to where I could communicate pretty well. It was a good feeling when I could understand what someone was saying and make them understand what I was saying. While I had not yet learned many French words, I was determined to use the ones I did know whenever I could. Right now, though, it did not matter. The bartender was not going to get involved in a conversation with me anyway. He clearly understood me when I spoke English, though he responded only in French.

I sipped my drink and watched the two women. I wondered what they were talking about. Did they have something to do with the film festival? Were they friends who lived in Deauville and decided to go out for a drink on a Thursday night? Was it really Thursday night already? With the traveling and the time difference, I felt as though I had somehow lost an entire day of my life.

I surveyed the room from my perch and imagined who all the various people might be. I liked the buzz of the place. In no time at all my glass was empty.

"*Un autre?*" asked the bartender, who seemed to have materialize out of nowhere.

"Yeah, sure," I said. "I mean, *oui.*"

I looked over at the two women I had noticed before. Yes, the black-haired one was definitely fine. I could look at her all night. I had a little daydream as I watched her. Suddenly, she turned her head and her eyes locked with mine. Because I was so far from them and there were so many people in the place, I had felt invisible. Who would notice me with so many other people around? At least that is what I had thought. Completely embarrassed, I grabbed the drink the bartender had just set down and stared into the glass while taking a sip. I did not dare look back over in the women's direction.

In no time I had downed the second drink. Then the jet lag hit me hard. I worried I might actually fall off the stool.

"How much I owe you?"

The bartender went to the cash register for a few minutes and came back with a check written out with fancy handwriting. The price on the paper woke me right up. My two drinks had cost a fortune. Then I remembered the price was in francs and francs were worth a lot less than dollars. Even so, after I calculated the exchange rate as best I could in my increasingly sleepy head, the price was still pretty steep for such a measly drink.

"Can I charge this to my room?"

"*Très bien, Monsieur. Votre numéro de chambre?*"

I showed him my key with the room number etched into the attached hefty piece of wood—*they're definitely going to make sure no one steals this key*, I thought—and signed the tab. I was now definitely ready for bed. I made my way back up to my room, stepped out of my clothes and fell onto the bed.

The next thing I knew, there was a strange buzzing noise.

It took me a moment to remember where I was. The room looked different, mainly because there was daylight streaming in through its only window. I had slept on top of the bed with my clothes on. The buzzing noise did not stop. I finally realized it was the sound of a French telephone. It was on the night table next to the bed. I picked up the receiver.

"Yeah?"

"Dallas!"

"Yeah?"

"It's a quarter past eight. Where are you?"

"Man. I don't feel like I slept at all. What time did you say it was?"

"It's eight-fifteen. I'm downstairs. You need to get down here right now if you want any breakfast."

"Okay, okay. Just give me a couple of minutes. I'll be right down."

At least I was already dressed. I struggled to get off the bed and staggered to the bathroom. I felt like I had a huge hangover, but I knew this was no hangover. Not on those two measly little Scotches I had the night before. I looked at myself in the mirror and did my best to make my hair look halfway neat. I needed a shave but figured I could get away without one for another day. Even at twenty-seven I still did not have to shave every day. It was as though my body was stubbornly refusing to mature.

I grabbed my camera bag and headed downstairs. I went to where they were serving breakfast and spotted Melanie. As usual, she was poring over a table full of notes. I sat down across from her.

"About time," she said without looking up.

There was a large cup in front of me along with two metal pitchers, one full of thick black coffee, the other full of warm milk. There was also a basket with a small loaf of French bread and a croissant.

"I'm starving," I said. "I might order some bacon and eggs."

Melanie looked at her watch.

"We don't have time. We need to get to the festival office to pick up our credentials. We have no time to waste today."

"Why? What time does the festival start?"

"There are no public events until this evening. It's opening night, but all the activity you and I are interested in will be happening outside the screenings and programs. There are press events scheduled all day long."

I poured myself some coffee and took a sip. I liked my coffee really strong, but this coffee was even stronger than *I* liked. I added some milk.

"*Café au lait!*" I said, suddenly realizing that I had actually begun learning French from the moment I had first walked into Flaubert's in the city. "Hey, this croissant is really good. Even better than the ones Flaubert's has."

"Don't spend too much time savoring it," said Melanie, still not looking up from her notes and not sounding the least bit impressed with my thoughts. "We need to get moving."

By the time the plane had landed the day before, Melanie had gotten to be almost human. I actually thought we were going to get along fine, but she was now definitely back to her usual work self. I gobbled my croissant and washed it down with coffee as fast as I could. I did not want her any more out of sorts with me than she already was. As soon as she saw me drain the last drop from my cup, she gathered up her stuff and stood up. I obediently stood up too and followed her out of the hotel, doing my best to keep up with her pace.

The weather was very much like San Francisco with a cold, stiff breeze bearing down on us. The terrain was a lot flatter though. I could smell the ocean even if I could not see it. I had the distinct impression it was not very far ahead of us. We stopped in front of a large and impressive building that looked like some sort of castle with high windows and columns at the front entrance.

"This is the Casino," she said, pronouncing it "ca zee *no*" the way the French would say it. "This is where we will be tonight for the opening."

She pointed to a large building to our left on the next block.

"That's the Hotel Royal."

She led me in the opposite direction to the other side of the Casino. Across the street was another large sprawling building. It had lots of dark wood trim and looked like something out of a Hans Christian Andersen story. Across the street from it was a miniature golf course.

"That's the Hotel Normandy. Most of the people we are interested in will likely be staying in one or the other of these two hotels."

"Do you think MacCaul is in one of them?"

"I have no idea. It wouldn't surprise me if he isn't holed up somewhere outside of town. On the other hand, it might be easier for him to slip in and out of screenings if he is based close by. It's hard to know. You've committed his face to memory, right?"

"Yeah, his face from a hundred years ago. There's no way to know how much he has changed since then. Is he bald? Did he get fat? Is his face all wrinkled like a prune now? Who knows?"

"Just do your best. In the meantime there will be plenty of other people to photograph—some you might recognize on your own. Let's go get our credentials and our press packets."

The visit to the press office only reinforced my initial impressions of France: there was a long wait, French people were not the least bit interested in forming a line, and everyone smoked. As usual, I let Melanie do all the talking. I was so dependent on her I was starting to feel like I was five years old again. Finally she handed me a laminated badge with a strap to hang around my neck and a folder full of papers.

"Here is a list of photo events," she said. "Use your own judgment as to which ones you go to. Focus on the films and filmmakers and actors that will be of most interest to our readers. If there is nothing interesting going on, try wandering around the two hotels I showed you. See if you can spot anyone familiar. If you even *suspect* that you see Logan MacCaul, shoot first and ask questions later."

"Wait, aren't you going to be with me?"

"No. Why? Do you need me to hold your hand?"

"No, I just thought... I don't know. I just thought we were working together."

"We are, but I'm going to be doing some detective work on my own. It will be easier if I am by myself. The last thing I need is to attract attention by having a guy with a camera tagging along. I'm determined to find MacCaul and, for today anyway, I need to work alone. That's why I was so keen on making sure you had done all the research and studied the photos beforehand. If I manage to get any good interviews, I'll definitely want you to be there. We'll meet tonight at the Casino for the opening night program. In the meantime, you're on your own. Make me proud. *Ciao*."

She walked off and left me standing there. Since we had left the city, I had done nothing but complain about her in my head. Now I was panicked to see her walk away. I had mentally prepared myself to simply follow orders. Now I felt lost in a completely new and strange place. I opened my folder and glanced at the sheet for the first day. There was nothing scheduled for the next couple of hours, so I decided to go for a walk. I went outside and walked into the wind. In just a couple of blocks I was at the beach. It was a nice wide sandy beach, and the ocean was dark blue. Overhead clouds were blowing in my direction. I could imagine I was in California, maybe at Pismo Beach when I was a kid during one of our family vacations.

I walked past the stalls on the boardwalk at the edge of the sand. There was an endless row of changing rooms. The door to each one had a handrail, and I noticed each handrail had a name painted on it. I read the names: William Wyler, Burt Lancaster, Stanley Donen, Stanley Kramer... There were flagpoles along the boardwalk, and the beach was dotted with closed umbrellas. I glanced at the festival program in my folder. The cover was a director's folding chair on this same beach underneath an umbrella that looked like an American flag.

I bet this is nice in summer, I thought.

I was getting cold standing there with the wind blowing off the ocean, so I turned around and walked back. I had noticed in my press information that there was another place besides the Casino where movies were being shown. It was a few blocks the other side of the Casino, so I decided to walk up to it to make sure I knew where it was. I found it with no problem.

It had an interesting rounded shape and was on a narrow street corner in the shape of a triangle. As I headed back again, I noticed a store selling newspapers and magazines. Of course, they were mostly in French, but I found a few things that were in English. They had *Time* and *Newsweek* and a newspaper called the *International Herald Tribune*. I picked up a newspaper and took it to the cashier.

"*Bonjour*," I said.

"*Bonjour, monsieur*," she said pleasantly.

"*¿Cuánto cuesta?*" I asked. I had meant to try asking in French but for some reason it came out in Spanish. "Uh, *combien*, I mean, uh, how much..."

She patiently turned the paper over and pointed to a corner where the prices for all the various countries were printed. The price for France seemed kind of expensive, but I put the money down on the counter. She handed me the change.

"*Merci, monsieur*," she smiled.

I carried my prize as far as the next block and stopped at a café. It had a red sign more or less in the shape of a diamond that read, *Tabac*. I assumed this meant they sold cigarettes. I had been breathing so much second-hand smoke since getting to France I decided, if I was going to be breathing it all the time, I might as well join in. I blamed Lonnie for getting me started with smoking in high school in the first place. I never smoked as much as he did, but after he died I started smoking a lot more. I guess that was one of his habits he passed on to me, kind of like Linda had said that night at Balthazar's.

I decided to try a local brand and pointed to a small powder blue pack with the name Gauloise. I took a seat at a table. Pretty soon a waiter came over and I asked for a coffee. I lit a cigarette from the pack, took a puff, and had a minor coughing fit.

Damn, I thought, *these French coffin nails are a lot stronger than I'm used to.*

I wondered what Lonnie would have made of France. I wished he was there so that we could talk about all the things we were seeing and which things we liked and which things we did not. I wondered what he would have thought of French cigarettes. He definitely would have had an opinion. He and I would have been making jokes about people we saw and how they were different from Americans. If Lonnie had been there, we would have already started drinking. I missed Lonnie.

The waiter brought my coffee. For some reason I had been expecting a normal cup of coffee like I would have gotten in a coffee shop back home, but he had brought me an espresso. There were two sugar cubes wrapped in paper on the tiny saucer. I unwrapped them, dropped them into the inky black liquid and stirred until they dissolved. I took a sip. It was like a shot of pure adrenaline. The sensation on my tongue was the richest, most delicious taste ever, and the sugar was so sweet it brought back memories of sneaking spoonfuls from the sugar bowl when I was a kid. I did not think I could ever be satisfied with any other coffee ever again in my whole life.

I drank my coffee, read my newspaper, and forced myself to smoke the Gauloise all the way down to the end. Though it had only been a day or so since I had left the city, reading the American news and seeing the American comic strips and the American crossword puzzle made me feel homesick. I paid the waiter and left.

In the afternoon I went to a couple of the press events. I stood around with all the other photographers and took pretty much the same photos they were all taking. I wondered why I even needed to be there. My photos were not going to be much different than those of the other photographers. I needed to think of something different to shoot, something more interesting than what everyone else was shooting. As I finished the last shoot, an incredible wave of tiredness came over me. I felt as though I was going to fall asleep right then and there.

Damn, I thought. *So, this is what jet lag is like. I don't think I care much for it.*

I found a place in the Casino where I could get a shot of espresso. I ordered and drank two of them. After a while the feeling of tiredness finally began to pass.

Later on I found Melanie, and we went to the opening. A huge cheer in the auditorium went up when a man about seventy years old crawled out on the stage on his hands and knees. He did not say anything, but he pulled out a whistle and blew on it loudly. The crowd loved it.

It was Danny Kaye.

"Hey," I said to Melanie, "I used to watch him on television when I was a kid. I didn't know he was still around."

Melanie said, "My mother has to watch him and Bing Crosby every single year in *White Christmas*."

I thought, *Wait 'til Lonnie hears that I actually saw Danny Kaye in person!*

17
Calvados

IT WAS no easier to wake up the next morning than it had been the previous morning. At least this time I managed to open my eyes before there was a phone call from Melanie. As tempted as I was to stay in bed, I forced myself to get up. This time I had a shave and a shower. The bathroom was hard to figure out. The shower head was strange, and the water pressure was nearly non-existent.

I went downstairs and had a croissant and a café au lait. I thought about ordering bacon and eggs but decided it was more trouble than it was worth. As I had my *petit déjeuner*, I thought about how I might do some of my own "detective work," as Melanie had put it, to maybe find Logan MacCaul myself. I decided on a plan.

After breakfast I walked up the street to the magazine store I had found the previous day and bought another *International Herald Tribune*. Then I walked over to the Hotel Normandy. Of the two hotels Melanie had pointed out to me, that one struck me for no reason I could explain as a more likely place to find MacCaul. The hotel was huge. It looked like something that would be in Disneyland, like an overdone fairy tale. I walked through the courtyard toward the entrance. From above, rows of small balconies looked down on me. I passed through the large arch entrance with its revolving door and into the lobby, Like my hotel, the look was all dark wood and chandeliers. Some of the windows were stained glass, kind of like an old church. The place was touristy and lavish all at the same time.

I found a place to sit in the lobby. I slipped my camera bag out of sight and settled back to read the newspaper. I read the entire newspaper from beginning to end, while watching to see who came and went through the lobby. I listened for any snatches of conversation I might catch.

People came and went all morning, but none of them looked anything like MacCaul—or like anyone else particularly interesting. There was one guy who walked through with a lot of people around him. He definitely looked important.

You know, I thought, *he looks kind of familiar. In fact he looks like the guy who played Superman's father in the movie. Not his father on Krypton. That was Marlon Brando. I mean, his father in Smallville.*

It was a pretty boring morning. I had decided my great idea of doing my own detective work was a waste of time when I picked up on a conversation at the reception desk. One of the hotel employees was talking to the guy at reception. I had absolutely no idea what they were saying, but it sounded as though they were complaining about someone. I heard phrases like *il est très exigeant* and *il est difficile, non?* Then a woman joined them. She had a pitcher on a tray. It looked as though it might be lemonade.

"Tu vois? Il insiste sur la limonade fraîche pressée. Il se contentera de rien de moins."

Lee moan odd? I was pretty sure that was French for lemonade all right.

"De plus il a voulu changer de chambre plus de deux fois."

"Et après tout ça dans quel chambre est-il maintenant enfin?"

"Trois cent trente-quatre. Note-la bien. Il ne faut pas se tromper."

I was pretty sure I had heard a room number in that exchange. I pulled out my notepad and scribbled, "TRWAH SAHN TRONT KATRUH."

I had no idea what I had written down except that it had to be a number and maybe it was the number of a room in the hotel. I just needed to repeat it to someone who knew French so that they could tell me what it was in English. I wished I knew where Melanie was—she would probably be able to translate it—but I had no idea where to find her at the moment.

I thought, *There must be lots of people around here who speak both French and English. This is an American film festival in France after all. Someone will be able to tell me what number I heard.*

I went into the bar and grabbed a stool. The bartender appeared immediately.

"Monsieur."

I was tired of drinking coffee. I had had a lot of coffee since I had been in France.

"Una cerveza por favor."

I meant to try saying it in French, but it came out in Spanish. That was something that kept happening to me.

The bartender, a short balding man with a thick black moustache, studied me.

"Caballero, a sus órdenes. ¿Qué clase de cerveza desea usted?"

Cool. He spoke Spanish.

I asked him, *"¿De dónde es usted?"*

"Yo soy de San Sebastián. Soy vasco. ¿Y usted?"

"*Norteamericano.*"

I asked him if he was really Basque, and I told him that the best restaurants in Bakersfield, aside from the Mexican ones, were the Basque restaurants. He said he had a cousin who had moved to California many years before. He complimented me on my Spanish, and we agreed that Spanish was a much easier language than French. He said the Basque language was probably harder than either of them. He said that with a big smile. As far as I had observed, the French bartenders never smiled.

"*¿Y su cerveza, señor?*"

I looked at the taps and picked a name at random.

"*Kronenbourg, por favor.*"

"*Muy bien, señor.*"

As he filled the glass, I thought about asking him to translate the number for me. He was friendly and would probably be willing to help me out. In the end, I decided to look for someone else since he did, after all, work for the hotel and I did not want to get him in any trouble. I sipped my beer and looked around. I wanted to find someone who was not connected to the hotel.

The bar was not busy. The few people there did not look like they wanted to be bothered. A woman walked into the bar and sat at a small out-of-the-way table. My friend from San Sebastián went over and dutifully took her order. Soon she was sipping a coffee while leafing through a stack of papers. She had long black hair and there was something familiar about her. Eventually it hit me. She was the same woman I had seen in my hotel's bar the night I arrived, the one who locked eyes with me. That night she had been smiling and laughing. Now, focused completely on her papers, she was all business. I found her every bit as beautiful as the first time I saw her. I wondered if she had noticed me when she came in. I wondered if she recognized me as the guy she had seen staring at her from across the room. I wondered if she thought I was some kind of weirdo.

Damn, I thought, *I wish I had the nerve to talk to her.*

I played out in my head what would probably happen if I did. For one thing, she might not know any English. Or she might cut me down with a withering look and tell me to stop bothering her. The likelihood of getting totally shut down made me think twice about approaching her.

I reached for my pack of Gauloises and put one in my mouth. Before I could think about which pocket had my matches, my Basque friend was over like a shot with a light. He had also brought me a spotlessly clean ashtray.

"Hey, *gracias, amigo*," I said.

"*Por nada, señor.*"

I took a drag on the cigarette. I was getting used to French cigarettes. In fact, I was starting to like them.

What a wimp you are, I said to myself. *You've never met this woman before and you will never meet her again. What's the worst that could happen? What would Lonnie say about this? He'd say I was a chicken shit, that's what he'd say.*

I sucked in more smoke. I had the strange idea that somehow there was a bit of Lonnie's spirit in the smoke. As it passed through my lungs, it felt like Lonnie's nerve coursing through my body. I remembered Linda saying I had become more like him. Surprisingly, she had said it as though it was not an entirely bad thing.

That's it, I thought. *I'm going to do this. I'll do it for Lonnie.*

I tried to think of a good opening line—something that would make me seem friendly and not creepy. The problem was that I did not have any good lines. Lonnie was the one who had the good lines—or at least lines that sometimes worked for him. Lonnie's lines would not work for me. Lonnie was Lonnie, and I was me. I needed my own line. Then it hit me. What an idiot I was. I had the perfect excuse to talk to her. I could ask her to translate the number for me. I could kill two birds with one stone.

I put the cigarette in the ashtray and walked over to her table. As I approached, she looked up. To my surprise and relief, she smiled. It was as though she thought I was someone she knew, someone she was glad to see. I smiled back at her. There was something about her that made me feel that I should have known her already, that we should already be friends.

"*Perdóneme,*" I said. "I mean, *pardon.*"

She stifled a laugh. Her expression turned wary.

"*Oui?*"

She had the darkest, loveliest eyes I had ever seen, but it was the smile on her face that won me over. It was a comfortable smile, the smile of someone happy. The fact that her two front teeth were not perfectly straight did not make her smile any less beautiful. In fact, it made it more so.

"Sorry to bother you. Do you speak English?"

She gave a small, embarrassed shrug of her shoulders.

"*Plus ou moins.* A little."

She pronounced it "leetle" with the lightest of *l* sounds. There were a few light freckles on her face. I was close enough to smell her perfume. It was not particularly strong, but it was definitely my new favorite scent. I glanced at her hands and was relieved to see that none of her fingers had a ring. She looked at me expectantly, as if she thought I would have something interesting to say.

"This is kind of embarrassing," I said, "but I need to find out what something in French means. You see, the clerk at reception must not have realized I don't speak French."

As I spoke, I could hear how stupid my made-up story sounded.

"I mean, it should have been totally obvious I'm not French, right? Anyway, he gave me my room number in French, apparently thinking I would understand him. And I was too embarrassed to tell him I didn't understand…"

My story was becoming increasingly stupid.

"Is the number not on the key?"

I loved the way her *th* sounds came out like soft *z*'s and how "number" came out as "numb bear."

"Yeah, right. You see, someone else has the key. Anyway, I was wondering if you could tell me what the number is in English."

Her smile was comforting. Her eyes had that look some women get when they see a cute child or a puppy.

"*Pas de problème.* No problem. Um, what is the number?"

What a relief. I was home free.

"TRWAH SAHN TRONT KATRUH."

The smile vanished from her face. She stiffened.

"Who told you that number?"

"Uh, the man at hotel reception."

She was not one bit happy.

"There is some kind of mistake. There is not such a number in this hotel."

"Really? Do you work for the hotel?"

"No, but I know the hotel. I know there is not such a number."

I had been so close.

"Okay. Well, thanks anyway, but would you mind telling me what that number is in English anyway? I'm just curious."

"Excuse me. I have some thing I must do. Excuse me."

Trying not to look flustered, she gathered up her things from the table and quickly left.

Damn, I thought. *Of course, I managed to pick exactly the wrong person to ask. Why do I always screw things up?*

I stood there like an idiot for a minute. Then went back to my stool to finish my beer. As disappointed as I was about not getting the room number, I was more upset that I had scared her off. I heard her voice in my head. It had a soft, breathy quality with just a hint of a vibration—not unlike a cat purring. I loved the way it sounded, and I loved the way she pronounced certain words. There was something musical about the French language. I wanted to chase her and ask her to talk some more. I wanted to listen to her—and smell her perfume. I wanted to see her smile—the one she had before I asked her to translate the room number.

I was now convinced MacCaul must be staying in the hotel and that my mystery woman knew about it. I finished my beer and told myself to stop being such a wimp of a detective. I paid the bar tab and gave the bartender a good tip. Then I laid my pen and notepad on the bar and asked him, "*Amigo, ¿puede usted por favor escribir en este papel un número que yo tengo en francés?*"

"*Por supuesto, señor.*"

"TRWAH SAHN TRONT KATRUH."

He winced at my pronunciation, but after doing his own mental translation, he wrote, "334."

"*¡Perfecto!*" I cried. "*¡Muchas gracias!*"

Why did I not just ask him in the first place?

I grabbed the pen and notepad and headed to the lobby. Trying to look nonchalant, as if I were a guest who belonged in the hotel, I made my way to the stairs that led to the guest rooms. I climbed up to the floor designated as the third one—it was actually the fourth one, but that is the French for you—and walked down the corridor. When I found room 334, the door was wide open.

There were two maids folding sheets. On the table was an ashtray full of cigarette butts. In the wastepaper basket were two newspapers, the *International Herald Tribune* and *Le Monde*. It looked to me as though someone had just vacated the room—and in a hurry. The maids looked at me with dull expressions.

"*Monsieur?*"

"Sorry," I said. "I was looking for a friend of mine. I think he might have been staying in this room. Do you know where he went?"

The two women looked at each and shrugged.

"*Désolée, monsieur.* Sorry, no English."

"No problem. *Merci.*"

I went back downstairs, more convinced than ever MacCaul had been in that room and I had missed him by mere minutes. I was definitely close to finding him, and my only hope was the beautiful woman with the magical voice. I had to find her again.

For the time being, though, I was stuck. There were press events I was supposed to be attending and crowds of photographers to push and shove against in an effort to get a decent shot. I had wasted nearly half the day.

I studied the schedule to figure out where I was supposed to be. I caught up with the mob at the next photo shoot. It turned out to be the three guys who made the *Airplane!* movie. They were very funny. They did a lot of joking around and were generally very entertaining. Later on a film festival official explained why the tribute to Elia Kazan had been canceled. Kazan had not come to Deauville because his wife was dying. She had actually made a film of her own, which had just been shown at the festival. The day of its screening happened to be when she died in New York.

That evening as I wandered through the Casino, I looked at all the happy, laughing people dressed to the nines. Some were sitting at card tables. Some were playing slot machines. Many were sitting at tables and enjoying their drinks. It was like one big glamorous party. I could not stop thinking about Elia Kazan's wife. Just because you are a bigshot director and you are famous enough to get a tribute at a film festival, it does not mean that bad things will not happen to you—just like they happen to everyone. It does not mean your wife is not going to die.

I looked for Melanie. There was no sign of her. Jet lag hit me again. This was the time of night it always kicked in. I thought seriously about heading back to the hotel and getting an early night. I made my way through the crowd toward the exit. Then I saw her. My mystery woman was deeply involved in a conversation with a man in a black suit and with wavy gray hair. I stopped in my tracks and waited. The man looked important. He was clearly trying to finish their talk so he could move on to something more important. After a few minutes he gave her a peck on both her cheeks and disappeared. This was my chance.

I walked over to her quickly and said, "Look, I'm sorry. I think I said the wrong thing earlier. I got off on the wrong foot. Can I buy you a drink?"

It took her a moment to realize I was talking to her. She had a thousand things on her mind.

"*Vous êtes très gentil,*" she said. "You are kind. I am very busy now. Another time?"

The remnants of Gauloise smoke in my lungs spoke to me with Lonnie's voice. They told me not to be put off so easy. They told me I had to put myself out there and make my case.

"Please," I said. "*S'il vous plaît.* I really want to talk to you. A lot. I know you are busy. I promise not to take up a lot of your time. Just one quick drink. Then I will leave you alone. Okay?"

I was not sure how well she understood me. Once more and after many years, I thought of the old Beatles song "Michelle." I pleaded with my eyes. I was dangerously close to looking like a fool. I wanted her sweet puppy dog look, but I got a strict mother look. She held up her thumb.

"One," she said. "*Pas plus!*"

I did not delay in case she changed her mind. I asked her to find us seats while I went to the bar.

"What will you have?" I asked. "What will you drink?"

"*Calvados, s'il vous plaît.*"

I had no idea what "calva dose" was, but I ordered two of them.

I found her at a small table and sat next to her. We raised our glasses.

I said, "*¡Salud!*"

She said, "*À votre santé!*"

I took a sip of my drink. It had a real kick to it.

"Hey, that's applejack!"

"*C'est Calvados.* It is a drink from here in Normandy. You must have Calvados when you come here."

"All this is new to me. I don't have a clue about France and Normandy. I need someone like you to teach me."

"I am not of Normandy. You must find a *Normande* to learn about this province properly."

"And where are you from?"

"*Je suis Bordelaise.* I am of Bordeaux."

"Cool. I am of California."

I extended my hand.

"My name is Dallas. Dallas Green. I'm here for the film festival."

She took my hand and shook it lightly. It was unexpectedly warm and nearly moist. The touch of her skin made my whole arm tingle.

"Valérie Destandau."

Every vowel in her name sounded like music to me. The *r* alone was like a chorus of angels.

"Val uh REE," I tried to repeat after her.

She eyed my camera bag suspiciously.

"You are *photographe*?"

"Yeah, I'm a photographer. My paper in San Francisco sent me to get some photos of the film festival."

"I have always wanted to go to California. Do you live near Kell-zay-vill?"

"Where?"

"Kell? Zay? Vill?"

"Kelseyville? I think I might have heard that name sometime. Do you know where it is? Is it in the Bay Area?"

"I do not know. I have never been there. Someday maybe *peut-être*. The idea of California pleases me. I want to go there very much. I want to see the surfing and where they make films."

There was a faraway look in her eyes when she talked about California. I liked it.

"Do you do the surfing?" she asked

"No, I never lived close to the ocean—at least not until recently."

"Is this your first time in Deauville?"

"My first time in Deauville, my first time in France. Are you here for the festival?"

"Yes. I have been in Deauville for every one of them. This is year number six."

"You must see a lot of movies."

"I see all that I can, but I work for the festival. I have not the occasion to see too many."

"Working for the festival, huh? That sounds very interesting. What do you do?"

"I do whatever they need me to do. This and that. I assist some of the guests at the festival."

"The festival only lasts a week. What do you do the rest of the year?"

"I am only volunteer here. My real job is at Bordeaux. I work in a shop, on the rue Sainte-Catherine. I have vacations to come here every year for the festival."

"You must get to meet lots of famous people. Have you met anybody famous this year?"

With a slight shrug of her shoulder, she indicated I should look beyond her.

"*Tu vois cet homme-là?*"

Over at another table I saw a striking man with a distinctively shaped bald head. I also noticed that she had switched from using the word *vous* to using *tu*. I knew from my Spanish we had crossed a familiarity barrier.

"Yeah?"

"He is Yul Brynner."

"Get out of here! Really?"

"Yes, really."

"He was great in *The Magnificent Seven*," I said, pulling the camera out of my bag. "Yeah, come to think of it, I remember Melanie saying something about him being here."

"There is a tribute to him. He is very known in Deauville. He has had a house here many years."

I zoomed in on his head and began to shoot. If he noticed me, he did not react.

"And like you, he is *photographe*. He makes many photos. *Mais maintenant*, I am sorry. I must to go. *Je m'excuse*."

"I'm sorry. Are you leaving because I took his picture? I figured it would be all right since he is in a public place. He definitely must be used to being photographed by now."

"*Non, c'est bien. Je suis sûre qu'il en a déjà l'habitude.* You do not need to worry. I go because I have other things I must do this evening."

"I want to talk with you again. When can I see you?"

"Perhaps for the breakfast?"

My heart skipped a beat. Could she possibly be saying what I wished she was saying?

"*Le petit déjeuner?* Really?"

"If you like. What time do you take breakfast?"

"I don't know, around eight?"

No, she wasn't saying what I had hoped she was saying.

"Where do you want to meet?"

She looked at me as if she found me silly.

"In the hotel, of course. You and I are in the same hotel, *non?*"

She stood up to leave. I stood up and on an impulse did what I had seen people doing all over Deauville. I gave her a kiss on one cheek and then again on the other one. She did not act like she minded or that it was anything strange.

"I will see you at the breakfast," she said. "*À demain*."

As she disappeared into the crowd, a happy feeling came all over me. She *had* noticed me that very first night.

18
Valérie

AFTER SHE left, my head buzzed so much I could not sit still. The jet lag was definitely gone. I went to the bar and ordered another Calvados. It was not my usual sort of drink. I was not into liquor with fruit flavors, but this had a nice kick to it. More importantly, it reminded me—and would always remind me—of Valérie. I kept repeating her name quietly, just to feel the letter *l* on my tongue. I tried to pronounce the letter *r* the same way she did.

After I finished my drink, I went back to the hotel. My mind raced. I could not wait to see her again. I could not wait for it to be morning. Would she show up at breakfast?

I got into bed but, for the first time in Deauville, I was having trouble sleeping. I could not stop thinking about her. Since I had been in France, I had not had been bothered by my fears at night. I had been too exhausted for them. Would they come back once I had adjusted to the time zone? I had no idea, but I was sure of one thing. If I had Valérie beside me, they would be gone forever. I just knew it.

As I finally started to drift off, I thought about the name Kelseyville. I might have seen it on a map of California. Come to think of it, that name might have been located in Lake County.

I had no trouble waking up in the morning. Maybe I was finally getting adjusted to the time zone. Maybe I was excited because Valérie said she would meet me for breakfast. Up and ready in record time, I grabbed my camera bag and headed downstairs.

I walked into the breakfast room and looked around. When I did not see her, my heart sank. I looked at my watch. Ten minutes to eleven?

Damn, I thought, *I* still *haven't changed my watch.*

I stood there fiddling with it, finally turning it ahead nine hours. I had meant to do that for the previous two days, but things kept distracting me. Not having an easy way to know the right time had gotten to be a real pain.

Guess I'm a little early.

As I finished setting the time, a finger softly tapped my shoulder. I turned and saw Valérie's beautiful smile.

"*Bonjour!*" she said in her lovely singsong way.

"*Bonjour* yourself. You made it."

"I said you that I would come. I keep my promise always."

We found a table and sat down. Again my thoughts turned to bacon and eggs. I hardly ever had bacon and eggs for breakfast at home, but there was just something about being in a country where everyone ate bread for breakfast that made me hungry for fried food. In the end I again settled for a croissant. Valérie nibbled on an ordinary piece of French bread with nothing on it.

"What do you do today?" she asked, as she sipped her coffee.

"The same thing I have been doing every day since I got here. Show up at the various press events and otherwise wander around seeing if I can spot anyone famous to photograph. I could sure use your help to spot people. It was cool seeing Yul Brynner last night"

"Perhaps we can have another drink tonight. I will tell you if I see someone famous."

"I would like that. A lot. Do you want to meet at the Casino again?"

"I propose another place. Here I write the address."

She pulled out a notepad and scribbled on it.

"We may see people very known there."

"That's really nice of you. Do you provide this service to all the foreign visitors to the film festival?"

"The ones from California only," she laughed.

Things were going well between us and I did not want to mess it up. On the other hand, I thought I should probably be honest about why I was there. I just hoped it would not ruin things if part of her job was protecting MacCaul's privacy.

"Can I ask you something—about the film festival?"

"*Bien sûr. Pose ta question.*"

"I noticed that there was a screening on the schedule that did not say what movie was being shown—a surprise screening. Do you know anything about it?"

"It has not been announced," she said matter-of-factly.

"But do you know what film it is? Who the filmmaker is?"

She shook her head as she picked up her coffee cup with both hands.

"Tell me if I'm pestering you and I'll stop, but do you know anything about a rumor that's going around? About a new movie by Logan MacCaul?"

I studied her face for a reaction, but her hair hid her face as she stared down into her coffee.

"Do you like the films of Logan MacCaul?" she asked.

"Definitely," I said. "He's my favorite director of all time."

"And what is your film preferred of him?"

Of course, I had seen none of his films. I only said he was my favorite director because I thought it might make her more willing to tell me what I wanted to know. I tried to remember the name of the movie that impressed Justin so much. I wished I had not been drinking so much tequila when he told me about it.

"Well, of course, he hasn't made very many films—at least not that most of us know about. There are just the three of them. Of course, his best one by far is, uh, *Tricia's Passing*."

"*Tristan's Passage*."

"Yeah, *Tristan's Passage*. That one changed my life. Really."

"And how *exactement* did it change your life?"

"It's just that, well, I could relate to it so much. The way the two men were in love with the same woman and then they had to go off to war and they were on different sides and then they came back..."

She smirked at me.

"I think that you are talking about a film of Truffaut, *Jules et Jim*. Not *Tristan's Passage*."

"Oh yeah, I get them mixed up sometimes."

What an idiot. I was just not very good at faking it. In any event, she smiled at me. She reached across the table and tugged my hair.

"*Tu es un garçon très, très méchant*," she said, as if she were scolding a child. "*Il ne faut pas dire des mensonges.*"

I felt like a fool, but I kept going anyway.

"So, is it true? Is he here in Deauville?"

She smiled like the Cheshire cat.

"Because you know all about Monsieur MacCaul, then you know that he prefers not to see people."

"So, he is here—and you know where, don't you?"

She shook her head, her smile still just the slightest bit mischievous, and said, "*Je n'en sais rien. Rien de tout.*"

"Okay, okay. But could you just ask him if he would be willing to pose for one photo? Ask him if he'll do it for a fellow Californian. Maybe I didn't know anything about him before I came here, but tell him that I have a friend back in the city who really *is* his biggest fan of all time and that his movie did change *his* life. Will you do that for me? *Sil vous plaît?*"

"*S'il* te *plaît.*"

"Huh?"

"*S'il* te *plaît. Toi et moi nous nous traitons de toi, pas vous.*"

She was correcting my grammar. She was making sure I knew we were using the familiar way of saying *you*. I was relieved. This meant she hadn't written me off—even though we were now on opposite sides of Logan MacCaul's desire for privacy.

"So, what is *your* favorite movie?" I asked her.

"You mean, *à part de Tristan's Passage*?"

"Is that really your favorite movie?"

"Let us say that the *oeuvre* of Logan MacCaul is very important to me."

"Okay, but what is your favorite movie besides his?"

"That depends. In this moment I say *Un homme et une femme* of Claude Lelouch. Part of it was filmed here at Deauville. It is a film, um, very *sentimental.*"

"Is it one of those mushy romantic movies? I don't like those."

"*Moi non plus.* I do not either. Except when I do. And now it is late. I must go. *Au revoir.*"

"I'll see you this evening. You won't forget, will you?"

"I shall not forget. *Ciao.*"

She was gone in a flash. I tried to hold onto the feeling she gave me when I was with her. She was wonderful. I had fallen hard.

I did not expect to feel this way again. I thought I was too old to get crazy crushes on girls anymore or fall madly in love. I had been in love with Lana, but it was not like this. This was like being on the beach in Guaymas with Marisol—but better. It was better not being so young and stupid. I mean, I still felt pretty young and pretty stupid, but at least now I felt I had more of a clue than I did back then. I just wanted the day to pass quickly so I could be with Valérie again. That night on the Golden Gate Bridge seemed very far away now. I must have been out of my mind. What if I had been crazy enough to jump? Then I would not be here. I would not be in France. I would never have met Valérie. I shuddered to think I could have missed all this. What an idiot I was sometimes.

The rest of the day dragged. At one point I ran into Melanie. She was surprised to see me, as if she had completely forgotten I existed.

"Sorry, Dallas," she said. "I didn't mean to abandon you. It's just that I have been making so many contacts and meeting so many people. I am up half the night every night, typing up my notes and then I am wrecked the next day. I hope you aren't feeling too neglected. Are you getting any good photographs?"

"Yeah, no problem. They bring out the directors and the actors like clockwork. Some of them I know and some I don't. It's pretty interesting, but it's also pretty staged. I'm mostly getting the same photos as everyone else. I did get a candid shot of Yul Brynner last night at the Casino. That was cool."

"Yul Brynner? Really? Nice."

"So, have you made any progress finding out about Logan MacCaul?"

She shook her head.

"Everyone's very tight-lipped. I'm starting to wonder if there was ever any truth to that rumor at all. I hope it's true for David's sake. It cost a lot of money to send us here."

I did not tell her about my own detective work. I was worried nothing would come of it. If I did somehow manage to snap a photo of MacCaul, then it could be a surprise. If not, then at least I would not have gotten her hopes up.

The evening finally arrived. I rushed to the address Valérie had scribbled for me. I walked into the bar. It was packed. I looked around and had a momentary feeling of panic when I did not see her anywhere. I glanced at my watch. I was actually five minutes late. The thought she might not show up depressed me. I looked around again. She definitely was not there. I found a small table and sat down. Before long the *garçon* showed up to take my order. I asked for a Scotch on the rocks and told him to make it a double. When he returned with my drink, I looked at my watch again. She was now twenty minutes late. I pulled out the scrap of paper and double-checked the name of the place and the address. She had also written the time. It said "20.00" which I was pretty sure meant eight o'clock.

I took a sip and said to myself, *Face it, man. She stood you up. A woman like her would have plenty of better things to do in Deauville on a Sunday night.*

I thought seriously about drowning my sorrows. Getting really shit-faced seemed like a good idea, although not at the prices this place was charging. I wondered where I could find a liquor store in this town. Just as I was about to feel good and sorry for myself, she suddenly appeared. She breezed into the place like she did not have a care in the world. Her face lit up when she saw me. She walked over and leaned in to give me a kiss on each cheek—I was really getting to like that particular French custom—and then she sat down.

"*Ça va?* Have you a good day?" she asked.

"Not bad," I said. "Did you have trouble getting away from work?"

Her face was blank. It did not occur to her to explain why she was late.

"*Non*," she said, shaking her head and then looking around. "I like this place very much. I come here often when I am at Deauville."

Apparently, for her—and maybe for all French people—it was no big deal showing up late.

"Yeah, I like it too. It feels more down-to-earth than the Casino."

"Down to earth? *Sur la terre?*"

"Yeah. The people seem more, I don't know, more normal. Not so formal."

"Yes, yes. *C'est ça.* That's it. I like the films at the festival. Not so much the *spectacle*, they make the impression."

She was frustrated.

"My English is not good. It should be more good. *C'est ridicule.* I am here at an American film festival and the Americans cannot comprehend me. It is very difficult."

"Valérie, your English is fine," I said. "It's definitely better than my French—or my Spanish. Don't be so hard on yourself. Tell you what. You can practice your English all you want on me. I'm willing to talk to you as long as it takes."

She smiled at me. The *garçon* came over, and she ordered a Pernod.

"You are very nice," she said. "And how would I pay you for the lessons?"

"Oh, I'm sure we could work something out. We could do an exchange. You could teach me French. It would be a great arrangement."

I saw that faraway look in her eyes again.

"It is funny. I always thought that I would be with an American. Even when I was small. It is funny how things happen."

"Is that why you got involved with an American film festival?"

"Yes, I suppose so. I have always known that America is my destiny."

Was I reading the signals right? We seemed to be hitting it off, and I was completely dazzled by her. It was too good to be true. On the other hand, why shouldn't things finally work out for me? Everyone else managed to find somebody. Why should I be any different? I was definitely ready to be involved with a woman who was not married, ready to be in a normal relationship. Yes, there was the problem of her and me living in different countries, but was not my plan to stay in France and not go back to the city? This could be the fresh start I needed.

"Do you listen to me? Do I bore you?"

"Sorry, my mind wandered there. What were you saying?"

"If I bore you, you can leave," she laughed.

"No, you don't bore me. Not a bit. In fact, I'm fascinated by you."

"*Je te fascine? Oh la la.*"

"Wow. French people really do say, 'oo la la'?"

"Not 'oo la la,'" she corrected. "*Oh la la.*"

Our silly conversation continued for a long time. I was tempted to bring up Logan MacCaul again but decided against it. I did not want to annoy her or make her think that I was only spending time with her to get to him. If I had to choose between my photo of MacCaul and being with Valérie, I would definitely choose her.

Eventually the moment came when she said she needed to go. I grabbed the check, but she insisted on paying for her own drinks.

"It's okay," I said. "I'll buy."

"*Non,*" she said. "We need to be *égaux*, um, equal."

"I really want to. Please let me pay. It's my way of showing how much I like being with you."

She was stubborn, but finally she said, "Very well, but I will pay the next time. *D'accord?* Okay?"

"Okay. If you insist. But it's not necessary."

"It is necessary."

After I paid, we walked out to the street. She turned in a different direction than me.

"Isn't the hotel this way?" I asked.

"I go somewhere else. I see you tomorrow."

"Can I walk you wherever you're going?"

"It is not necessary."

"I don't mind. Really."

"I go alone. Thank you."

I was disappointed. Maybe I was getting ahead of myself, but I had thought, when we got back to the hotel, she would come to my room or invite me to hers.

"*À demain.* Until tomorrow."

"Wait."

I took her by the arm.

"I just wanted to tell you how much I enjoyed this evening. It was really good."

"Yes, it was good."

I kissed her on one cheek and then on the other. Then I kissed her on the lips. She was startled, but she did not resist. My body tingled. I breathed in the scent of her perfume It made my head spin. I would love that aroma forever. I ran my hand through her long black hair. She lifted her hand and put it on my cheek and let it rest there. Her hand had its own scent.

"Your hand smells like lemons."

"Mmm."

"Were you washing dishes?"

"Dishes?"

The kiss was over. I was sorry I had spoken, but I was intrigued by the lemon smell.

"Sorry," I said. "I have a friend who smells like lemons sometimes. That means he has been washing dishes. Because of the dish soap."

This amused her.

"I do not wash dishes when I am at Deauville. The aroma is of real lemons. I made lemonade today."

"Really? For who?"

She looked at her watch.

"I must go. Really. I am late. *À demain.*"

She ran her fingers through my hair quickly and then turned to go. I watched her walk away. I waited until she was nearly out of sight and then began walking.

I had decided to follow her.

19
La Galoche

I KNEW following her was the wrong thing to do. I did it anyway. There were just too many things I had to know. Where was she going at that time of night? Was she going to Logan MacCaul? If so, why so late? I was still playing detective. I still thought she might lead me to him and I could get a photo. It was wrong to spy on her, and it was wrong to use her to get a photo, but I could not help it.

If she was not meeting MacCaul, then I wanted to know if she was meeting another man. I did not know a lot about her. How could I know for sure she was not married? Lots of married people do not wear their wedding bands. Some take them off when they are away from home. I had learned that lesson from Lana.

As I followed her, I took care to leave a good distance between us, though not so much I completely lost sight of her. If she were to spot me, it would be all over. She would never speak to me again.

It was not a surprise she headed to the Hotel Normandy. She walked through the entrance. I approached slowly, hoping to see her through a window. She headed for the bar. Cautiously, I went as far as the lobby but hung back, trying to see from a distance through the doorway. I held my breath, hoping she would not walk back in my direction. How could I possibly explain what I was doing there?

I edged closer until I could see her. She approached a man sitting at a table. On seeing her, he stood immediately. Fortunately, Valérie's back was to me. I had a good view of the man. He was tall and heavyset with shaggy gray hair. He looked like he could be in his fifties or sixties. He appeared anxious, as if he had been waiting a long time. As if she were late. He embraced her in a way that looked to me as desperate. He kissed her tenderly on her forehead. They talked. I was not close enough to hear exactly what they were saying, but I was pretty sure he was speaking English. There was something about his eyes. They were sad. They were large and penetrating.

147

Damn! I thought. *It is Logan MacCaul. It has to be. He's a lot older than in Melanie's photo, but there's no mistaking those eyes. It's him all right.*

My first instinct was to take out my camera and try getting a shot of him, but he was too far away and Valérie was in the way. If I tried to get any closer, they were liable to spot me. There was nothing for me to do but stand there and see what happened. I was amazed to have actually done it, to have found the famous, reclusive Logan MacCaul. What a great story this would be. It would be nice, though, to have some proof that this had actually happened.

The guy at reception was watching me. I must have looked pretty suspicious. I was afraid he would call out and attract attention to me. I put a finger to my mouth and mimed the sound "shhh" while giving him a wink and a smile. I hoped that would be enough to get him to mind his own business.

Valérie and MacCaul were still deep in conversation. He looked anxious, but she was managing to calm him. They hugged again, and she gave him a long kiss on the cheek. They turned to walk toward the lobby. In a panic, I withdrew through the inner doors of the hotel's entrance and hugged the side of the vestibule. If they had been leaving the hotel, they would have seen me for sure, but they went in the direction of the guest rooms. I waited long enough to be sure they were not coming back and then went back into the lobby. The guy at reception was watching me more carefully than ever.

"*Monsieur?*" he said in a tone that was a mixture of amusement and disapproval.

I ignored him while I waited to see if Valérie came back. The longer I waited, the less I worried about her discovering me there. After a half-hour I decided it was stupid to hang around any longer. I headed back to my hotel.

Walking down the street, I had an interesting conversation with myself. I told myself it did not necessarily mean anything that she had met with MacCaul alone and late at night. I told myself it did not mean anything that she had gone with him up to his room. I told myself, it all had to do with film festival business. The hugs and the kisses were no big deal. That was simply the way the French act with everyone. It did not mean anything. They were probably in his room working on the remarks he would make to the audience when introducing his new film. Valérie was a dedicated worker. She was doing it all for the film festival. That was the only reason she was in his room at that hour. Besides, it was none of my business. After all, I barely knew her. She may have let me kiss her earlier in the evening, but that did not mean that we had any kind of commitment to each other.

When I got back to my hotel, I headed straight to the bar. I had hoped my Basque friend would be at the bar, but he wasn't. It would have been nice to see a friendly face.

"*Whiskey écossais, s'il vous plaît,*" I said, "*avec des glaçons.*"

My French was getting pretty damn good—at least when it came to ordering my usual drink.

I looked for Valérie the next morning at breakfast, but there was no sign of her. I set about my usual day of press events and photo ops. I kept my eye out for her all day, hoping to run into her, but I knew from experience that I was not likely to, at least not until evening. I did not run into her, but then I never had when I was out and about during the daytime. The only thing that kept me going was the fact that her last words to me the night before had been "*À demain.*"

I wanted to see her desperately. I had so many questions to ask. I just had to find a way to ask them somehow without revealing I had seen her with MacCaul the previous night. I had to get her to talk to me more, to tell me more about herself.

In the evening I stood outside one of the screenings, trying to get some good photos of people going inside. I was unhappy with the job I had been doing as far as getting interesting and spontaneous shots. There were too many other photographers around. Getting anything unusual or unique seemed hopeless. After everyone had gone into the auditorium, I made my way to the Casino. That is where I spotted her.

"Valérie!"

She was with a man and a woman. She looked in my direction and smiled. She made some excuse to them and came over to me.

"*Salut!*" she said. "*Ça va toi?*"

"Yeah, *ça va*. How has your day been?"

"*Pas mal*. I was thinking of you."

"Yeah? *Pourquoi?*"

"*Je ne sais pas*. No reason *en particulière*."

"Want to go for a walk?"

"Okay. Where?"

"How about down on the beach?"

She looked up at the darkening sky.

"*Ça fait froid.*"

"Don't worry. I'll keep you warm."

She dug her hands into the pockets of her jacket and pretended to be annoyed.

"I shall make myself warm."

We walked onto the sand. She had been right. It was cold there. When the wind kicked up, I put my arm around her. She did not seem to mind.

"*Ça fait* definitely *froid*," I said.

"You are now very good with the *Franglais*."

"The what?"

"*Le Franglais*. You know, when one mixes *le français* and the English."

"Really? That's a real thing? I was just cheating when it came to words I didn't know."

"*Mais non. C'est le Franglais. C'est une* real thing."

"You know, there are so many French things I have heard about my whole life. Now that I'm here, I want to try them all."

"What things?"

"You know, French bread, French toast, French fries."

"They are French things only in English. In French they are just things."

"You know what French thing I would really like to try?"

"What thing?"

"Do you know what French kissing is?"

"French kissing? *Ça c'est drôle. Qu'est-ce que c'est?*"

"I'll show you."

I put my mouth on hers. So far so good. It seemed safe to introduce the tongue. She backed off with a laugh.

"*Quelle audace!*" she exclaimed, though not in an angry way.

"*S'il te plaît*," I pleaded, running my hand through her hair. "*Je t'aime.*"

"*Tu m'aime?* It is not possible. You know me only short time."

"It's true, Valérie. I'm crazy about you."

"I believe you have a girlfriend in California."

"No, no girlfriend in California—or anywhere else. Believe me, I am all yours."

"*Tu me profites*. You go away soon, to California."

"I'll stay here with you. I swear it. That's how crazy I am about you."

"*Tu es fou, tout à fait fou.*"

"I'm *fou* all right. I'm *fou* about you."

I kissed her again. She did not resist. I showed her properly what French kissing was, and she did not seem to mind. We sat down on the sand. Then we lay on the sand. The air may have been cold, but our mouths were warm. I loved the salt smell in the air and the perfume smell on her skin. Our tongues wrestled with no sign of tiring. It was one of those moments you wish could last forever.

Finally she stopped and sat up.

"That is not French kissing," she said, a little out of breath.

"No? Then what is it?"

"*C'est une galoche.*"

"Okay, call it whatever you want. All I know is that I like it—a lot."

I leaned in for more, but this time she pulled back, looking a bit guilty.

"This is wrong," she said. "I should not to be here."

I stroked her hair and said, "I hope you're not about to tell me you're married."

"*Non*, I am not married, but I have, um, a boyfriend."

"A boyfriend, huh? Is it serious?"

"It is enough serious that I should not to be here. I am a very bad girl."

"Tell him you've met someone else. People do it all the time. How long have you been with him?"

"Not very long, but enough long. I love him."

"What about me? Maybe I'm wrong, but doesn't there seem to be something pretty good going on between the two of us?"

"*C'est vrai. Je suis attirée par toi. Je ne peux pas le nier.*"

"Sorry, this conversation is getting too important for me to be guessing what you're saying. Tell me in English."

"It is difficult. Too difficult. I think I love you and him, the two. But this is crazy. I know you only two, three days. *C'est fou.*"

I refused to give up. I heard Lonnie's voice in my head, telling me not to give up, to keep fighting.

"Is it that you prefer older men?"

She looked confused.

"Why do you ask that?"

"Well, it's just that I think I might be a bit younger than you. Some women don't like to be with younger men."

"What age have you?"

"I'm twenty-seven. What age have you?"

"*Treinte et un*," she said, holding up three fingers with one hand and one finger with the other.

"Thirty-one? Ha. That's nothing. My last girlfriend was thirty-four."

"So, you like old women? So, you have many girlfriends? It is not me you want. For you I am a type."

151

"No, I swear, I've never known anyone like you. Your age doesn't matter to me. I want to be with you. I have never been so sure of anything in my whole life."

She was torn.

"I did not expect you to be so serious. I thought this was, *tu sais, pour nous amuser. Tu es trop sérieux.* I think I must go now."

"Please don't."

"We talk tomorrow. I must to think, much to think."

"Do you have to go?"

"*Oui.* But I see you tomorrow. *À demain.*"

We got to our feet and shook the sand off our clothes as best we could. I took the camera from my bag.

"I have to take your picture."

"*Comment? Non. C'est impossible.* I will not allow it."

"I am afraid I must insist. No one will ever again be as beautiful as you are in this moment. I must preserve this vision."

I began shooting. She refused to give me a proper smile, but it did not matter. The embarrassed look on her face was more beautiful than most people's smiles.

Finally, she forced me to stop snapping by exclaiming, "*Arrête!*"

I walked her back to the Casino. She hurried off alone into the night. I had told her so much, confessed so much. There was still much more to tell her, but at least I had made a start. I was determined this time not to hold anything back. I was not going to lose my nerve or allow myself to be overcome by doubts. I was in love. From this point on, I would only do and say things that led me directly to being with this woman.

20
Declan

I HAD always known I was not an ideal employee. I could never be bothered to play the political games at work to get ahead. I never kissed up to the boss or anyone else. Keith was the go-getter, not me. Climbing the corporate ladder and getting the big promotions was never going to be my thing. NO fancy title or huge salary for me. I was content to put in my five days a week and get drunk on the weekends.

None of that, however, meant I did not take my work seriously. I was good at what I did, and I made a point of not turning in work I was not proud of. People could say what they wanted about my attitude or the way I dressed or anything else, but they could not say I did not always do my best when it came to my photography.

Since I had been in Deauville, however, I was painfully aware that I was only going through the motions. Sure, I showed up when and where I was supposed to—most of the time anyway—and, once I was there, I just shot the same photographs as everybody else. A robot or a monkey could have done what I was doing. Maybe not quite as good as me, but probably good enough. I did not know exactly what my problem was. Was it being in an unfamiliar place? Was it the way the festival press people tried to control everything we did? Was it the jet lag? No, I was pretty much over the jet lag by now, but it was disorienting to be in a place where most people either were not speaking English or they were speaking it strangely. I got tired of never being certain of what someone actually meant—or actually did not mean.

This was not just a problem for my work at the festival. It was also a problem when it came to Valérie. Her English was good enough for us to communicate, but I could not shake the persistent feeling I was missing something important. I never felt I was getting the entire meaning behind her words. If I had been French, would I have understood some signal she was sending me between the lines? Could it make the difference between being with her and not being with her? As Tuesday dragged on, I could think only about seeing her again and making her understand me. I had four more days.

By now we had something of a routine. In the evening I looked for her at the Casino. This time I spotted her deep in conversation with an older couple. They were dressed formally, and I guessed they were bigshot donors to the festival. She was laughing at all their jokes, maybe a little too enthusiastically. Apparently, keeping people like them happy was part of her job. I raised my camera and began shooting photos of the three of them. The old guy spotted me and nudged Valérie. She turned and saw me. She gave me a pretend look of exasperation. Then she made her excuses to the couple and came to see me.

"There are much better people here to photograph than me."

"None of them is as beautiful as you, though."

"*Flatteur! Tu me flattes honteusement!* I do not believe you."

"Do me a favor. Find someone famous and stand next to them for a picture."

She did her best to look annoyed as she scanned the crowd. Finally she settled on a man with longish hair and glasses happily talking to a few other people. She grabbed his arm and presented him to me.

"*Voilà.* Here is a very talented director. He is like you. He is American. He has made a very pretty film about a woman who lives alone in the woods and who marries a very bad man. It is a lesson for all women."

He smiled good-naturedly for the photo and then went back to his conversation.

"That was good. Now find someone else."

"I am not here to do your work for you."

"Want to go for a walk? Maybe go to the beach again?"

She gasped in mock shock.

"*Comme tu es villain!* You are very bad for my work."

"Aw, come on. Isn't everybody else watching movies now anyway?"

"*Arrête.* I have to be serious."

"Okay, if you're busy now, then let's meet later. What time can you meet me?"

"This is not a good idea."

"No, this is a great idea. I will not take no for an answer. Give me a time and a place."

She sighed as if she was exhausted.

"Okay. I will meet you in the bar in our hotel at eleven. *D'accord?*"

"*D'accord!* See you at eleven."

Alone again, I proceeded to kill time wandering between the Casino and the other theater, looking for anyone or anything interesting. When I got tired of that, I walked down to the beach. The waning moon was in its last quarter, and I shot its light reflecting ever so faintly on the breaking waves.

Finally, eleven o'clock rolled around. I had been sitting in the bar since ten-thirty. Valérie wandered in around a quarter past.

"You came."

"Do you think I would not?"

"I don't take anything for granted. What'll you have? Pernod or Calvados?"

She looked at my glass.

"What do you drink?"

"Scotch. *Whiskey ecossais.*"

"I too shall have Scotch."

I got her drink and said, "Let's take these up to my room."

"You never stop."

"I just want to talk. We'll have more privacy in my room."

"I think there is something else you want in your room."

"No, I promise. We're just going to talk."

"Okay. Just talk. Nothing else. Understand?"

"Yeah, yeah. Just talk. Really."

Even though my room was the size of a postage stamp, she managed to sit on the bed so as to be as far away from me as possible.

"So. What do you want to talk about?"

"How serious is it with your boyfriend?"

"I do not know if that is your affair."

"I just want to know. Have you been with him for years or for weeks? Do you live together? Are you planning to marry him?"

"You pose too many questions! No, I do not live with him, but I am with him for a long time now. I like him very much."

"As much as you like me?"

"I know you only two, three days. One cannot make a comparison."

I edged closer to her. She noticed.

"You said only talk."

"That's right. We're just talking. That's all."

"This is a bad idea."

"What's his name?"

"*Mon petit ami?*"

"Yes, your little friend."

"Why do you want to know?"

"I need to know the name of my competition."

"It is not a competition."

"You're right. You're going to see there's no competition at all."

It was feeling more and more like Lonnie was doing the talking and not me.

"His name is Michel."

"Michelle? Is that your boyfriend or your girlfriend?"

"Not Michelle." She emphasized the end of the name, making it sound as if it had three syllables instead of two. "Michel. In English it is Michael."

"Michel, huh? So, will Michel have any trouble finding another girl-friend?"

I had edged close enough to give her a kiss.

"You said only talk."

"That's what we're doing."

I rubbed my nose on her cheek.

"We're talking."

"This is not talking."

As much as she sounded like she was protesting, she did not make me stop.

"And where is Michel right now?"

"He is at Bordeaux. That is where he lives. That is where we live."

I kissed her neck. I could not get enough of her perfume. I wondered if I could believe her. I was still suspicious about her and MacCaul, although I told myself I was misinterpreting that. I wondered if Michel truly existed or if she was just making him up because the real story was too embarrassing. I kissed her on the mouth. There was no more protesting. She moaned slightly. We did *la galoche*.

"You would like him."

"Like who?"

"Michel. He is like you. *Il est très beau.*"

"I am not *très beau.*"

"Yes, you are. Do not pretend you do not know it. *D'ailleur*, his English is very much better than my English. He has lived in your country. He speaks English perfect. I think you would like him better than me."

"Baby, if he is a he, then he is definitely not my type."

I couldn't believe I had called her "baby." That was a real Lonnie thing to say. Strangely, the more she tried to shift the topic away from us and to her boyfriend, the more excited I got.

"This is not right."

"Oh, yes it is."

We were lying on the bed. I pulled her sweater over her head and her black hair flowed in every direction on the bed cover. I ran my hands up and down her back. She enjoyed it. Then she turned sad.

"I am a disaster."

"You're not a disaster. You're wonderful."

"*Non.* I am a disaster. I should not be here."

"It's okay. It's not like you're married, right? Or engaged? Women break up with their boyfriends all the time. It's certainly happened to me. He'll get over it. He'll find someone else."

"He loves me. He loves me very much. And I love him. We—*comment dit-on?*—amuse ourselves very well together."

She was starting to make me feel guilty. I found myself feeling bad for this Michel, a guy I had never met.

"You will leave soon. You will go to America. Michel is here. You will be there. What you say is crazy."

"Listen. I have no reason to go back to the States. I will stay here with you. I will do whatever I have to. I'll learn French. I'll find a job. I'll make a life here with you. I just need you to tell me that you'll give it a chance. I'll do the rest. Just say the word."

"To talk, to think, they make me *fatiguée*. Why do I meet you? Why are you this way? I do not want to talk. I do not want to think. No more. Not now."

She embraced me with a surprising amount of strength, and I hugged her back. We kissed for a very long time, not wanting the moment to end. I began to undo her skirt, but it was clear I had crossed a line.

"*Non. Non.* I go. I am a disaster."

"Don't go. Stay. Stay the night."

She put her sweater back on.

"Do you have a cigarette?"

I gave her one of my Gauloises. Her fingers trembled. She put it in her mouth, and I lit it. She took a puff. She looked like she was having a nervous breakdown. I put my arm around her.

"Hey, it's going to be okay. I promise. It'll all work out."

"I am sorry. My life is very complex now. It is difficult to explain. There are many things. So many things. I am sorry."

She made short work of the cigarette and smashed the stub in the ashtray on the desk.

"I go. We shall talk another time."

I felt defeated. She put her arms around my neck and kissed me on the mouth. The kiss was full of feeling and passion.

"Thank you," she said.

She opened the door and was gone. I was desperate and alone. I wished I could figure her out. I wished I knew more French. I thought seriously about going down to the bar for another drink or two, but for once I did not feel like it. I got undressed and went to bed. I lay there for hours unable to sleep. For the first time since arriving in France, I felt the extreme dread of night closing in on me, as it had on so many nights before. This time, though, there was something like a small miracle. As long as I focused my thoughts on Valérie, I could keep away the worst of the dread—at least for this one night. I had only my loneliness and and heartache to contend with, and that was plenty.

In the morning, my only thought was of seeing Valérie again. I was determined not to let her go. Not her. Not this time. At least now I had a name for my competition. Michel was my enemy. I would show no mercy to Michel.

It was Wednesday, and there was no reason to think this day would be much different from all the other days I had been in Deauville. In the afternoon I rewarded myself with a drink in the Casino bar. I liked sitting at the bar because I enjoyed eavesdropping on other people's conversations. Obviously, I did not pick up much from people speaking French, but I could pick out a word here and there. I had less of a clue about the other languages except, of course, English. The English speakers' accents were from everywhere. A lot of people sounded British. Quite a few were from the States. It was fun to guess what part of the States they were from. Some sounded like New York. A few were definitely from the South. I was pretty sure some were from California.

That particular afternoon I happened to hear a guy a few stools down from me. He definitely sounded British.

"You know, this sort of carry-on simply isn't on. You definitely have to sort something straight away. Cop on, mate. It's bloody serious now."

I've heard people talk like that in movies, I thought. *but it's weird to hear someone talking like that in real life.*

Then I heard the guy he was talking to.

"Aw, fer feck's sake, Clive, don't go losing the head now. I'm good for the few bob. You know I'm sound. I haven't let you down before, have I?"

"That's not a question you want to be asking, mate. Anyway, it's out of my hands now, idn't it? When it comes to their dosh, those lads are about as serious as a bloody heart attack."

"I'm not trying to be funny here, Clive. I will sort it out. Just leave it with me another day. That's all I need."

"You don't have another day. Can you not get that through that thick head of yours? Time has run out."

"Well, that's just feckin' lovely. I cannot feckin' believe it. There's always a sting in the tail with you, isn't there, Clive? Well, we made a hames of it this time."

There was something oddly familiar about the man speaking to Clive. I had heard that accent before. I had heard that voice before. But where?

"There's no 'we,' mate. It's just you. This is on your head alone."

"Feckin' hell…"

I craned my neck to have a look at the two guys. Clive was heavyset and bald and had overgrown eyebrows. The other guy was turned away from me. When he turned to order another drink, I got a look at his face. It was a face I knew. He was older now, but the curly black hair was the same, apart from a bit of gray mixed in. I walked over.

"Help me out here, Clive. You're not just going to leave me in the shite, are you?"

I stared. It really was him. After all these years. The two of them noticed me standing there with my mouth open.

"Are you all right there?" he asked me. "Do you have a problem?"

"Séamus?"

Clive looked at me curiously. Séamus looked as if he might get sick.

"You've confused with someone else, mate," he said firmly.

Clive was intrigued.

"Why did he call you Séamus?"

"How the feck should I know? I never saw this tool before in me life."

"I know you," I said. "I knew you in Mexico. You drove me to the Guatemala border."

He hunched defensively over the bar.

"Aw, yer off with the fairies, Yank. I haven't got a feckin' clue what yer on about."

"He certainly seems to think he knows you, Declan."

"Aw, you know yerself, Clive. These Yanks are pured cracked. He doesn't know what he's on about."

Could I be mistaken? Was it just someone who looked like him? Was I that mixed up? It had been nine years after all. I went back to my stool and ordered another drink. After a while, Clive left. The other guy approached me.

"Fer feck's sake. You had to set the cat among the pigeons, didn't you?"

"So, it *is* you."

"Maybe I remember you and maybe I don't. I'm only saying your timing could have been better."

"You do remember me, Séamus."

"Keep yer feckin' voice down, wouldja? The name is Declan now. We won't use that other name if it's all right with you. Yeah, I remember you, Austin."

"Austin?"

"Isn't your name Austin?"

"No, my name isn't Austin. Where the hell did you get Austin?"

"Okay, Houston then."

"Houston? What the hell?"

"Okay, not Houston. Your name can't be Corpus Christi, can it? All I remember is you were named after some place in Texas."

"Corpus Christi? That's right. You were the one who told me all about Corpus Christi. I mean, the Corpus Christi Massacre. In Mexico City. Remember?"

"Yeah, yeah. It's coming back to me, all right. It has been a while. Just remind me of yer name again. San Antonio?"

"It's Dallas, asshole. After the situation you left me in down there, the least you could do is remember my fucking name."

"Dallas. Yeh, that's it. Dead on. So, how're you keeping, Dallas? Jayzus, it's been donkey's years."

"Yeah, yeah, I'm fine. No thanks to you. You left me down there to rot in a cell in Guatemala. You sent me walking across the border, and then you just left me there. It was no big deal, you said. Just walk across the border, you said. Deliver the package and walk back again, you said. I could have been thrown in prison for the rest of my life. I could have been shot in the back and buried in an unmarked grave. It was a miracle I even got out of there alive. You set me up. You hung me out to dry. You used me."

"Steady there, Dallas. Janey Mack, we're getting a tetch dramatic here, aren't we? Okay, I take yer point, but you have to hear my side of it."

"I'm listening."

"Well, you see, it's complicated like."

"I got nowhere to be right now. Take all the time you need."

"C'mere. It's like this. I did wait for you. I swear it. But things went pear-shaped fast. Sudden like there were patrols along the border. Something was definitely up. I waited as long as I could, but I had no choice but to do a runner. If there had been any way, I would have waited.

That's the feckin' truth. You know, I've never slept right since. I was absolutely gutted, so I was. I always wondered what became of you."

"Yeah, well, that wasn't much comfort when I was sitting in that jail cell and getting interrogated by that CIA guy. I was just lucky he decided to let me go. I was scared shitless that I was going to disappear like Tommy Dowd. So, what about your friend Peter? Is he here too?"

"Who?"

"Peter. Your friend in Mexico City. The guy from Berkeley. Don't you remember anything?"

"Oh, right, Peter. Jayzus, I haven't thought about him in yonks. The last I heard about him he was in New York. I heard he was working on Wall Street. He's probably a millionaire by now."

"You're joking, right? I'm talking about Peter, the Marxist guy. The one who told me the whole capitalist system was going to crash by the end of the century?"

"Yeah, well, maybe it still will. In the meantime, Peter got married and needed to make a few bob. He found he had a gift for investments. I think he said he was into high-yield bonds or some such. Anyways, he and I don't keep in touch much anymore."

"Great. So, not only did you almost get me locked up for the rest of my life and possibly tortured and maybe even executed—and all in the name of the poor and the working class—now I find out the two of you have gone completely capitalist?"

"Fair enough, but the problem is this. Ol' Karl Marx had some grand ideas, but they just don't pay very well. You have to have something to live on while you're making the world fair for everybody. You know, it's lovely seeing you again. What are you drinking?"

He reached into his pocket.

"Feck it," he said. "I must have left my wallet in my hotel room."

"It's okay," I said. "I'll buy."

"Good man yerself."

When his fresh pint came, he lifted it happily and said, "*Sláinte.*"

"You know," I said, "it's funny the things you remember. Do you remember teaching me the only Gaelic I ever knew? I didn't even know it was an actual language."

"Really? I taught you some Irish?"

"Yeah. Don't you remember? I remember it clear as day."

"You're not taking the piss, are you? Did I really teach you some Irish?"

"Really."

"And what did I teach you?"

I searched my memory and then said proudly, "Pug mah hone."

Séamus jerked forward. He literally spat some of his beer on the counter. He could not stop laughing.

"Was my pronunciation that bad?"

"No, no," he chuckled. "The pronunciation was spot on. *Pog ma thon.* Did I happen to tell you what it meant?"

"You never actually said. You just said I should say it if I ever met an Irishman."

He was still laughing.

"It means, kiss my arse. Now that did my heart-een good, so it did. You know, it's grand we met up again."

"Yeah, it's an amazing coincidence, isn't it? That we'd meet again after all these years, and here in Deauville of all places?"

In fact, too much of a coincidence, I thought.

"It's a small world all right."

"Yeah, too small sometimes," I said. "So, what are you doing here anyway?"

"Well, there's another long story. There was a horse race at the hippodrome here a fortnight ago and, well, let's just say things did not go exactly to plan. In fact, it's a feckin' disaster. I think I might be catching the next train out."

"Tell me the truth, Séamus, I mean, Declan. Did you know I'd be here? Are you here because of me?"

"What are yeh on about? How was I to know you'd be here? I'm as gobsmacked as you are."

"Is that true? Or did Marty send you?"

"Who the feck is Marty?"

"Now that's a long story too, but he said someone would be contacting me here in Deauville. Something about taking a photo for him. I'm just now thinking maybe it's you. Come to think of it, he asked me about you. He seemed to know a lot about you. Are you working with him now?"

"Fer feck sake, who is this Marty and how does he know about me? You haven't been talking about me to people, have you, Austin?"

"Dallas."

"Sorry. Dallas. You haven't been shooting your gob off about me, have you?"

"I didn't tell him anything he didn't already know, but he seemed to know quite a bit about you. He said your last name was COS-tello. Is that true?"

"Jayzus, this does not sound good at all. Yes, it's definitely time to move on. Look, if anybody asks, you didn't see me. Especially if it's anything to do with the ponies."

"So, Marty didn't send you to talk to me about a photo I'm supposed to shoot for him?"

"Are you slow or what? For the last feckin' time, I don't know any Marty. Just do me a favor. When yer talking to him again, tell him I died. Tell him you didn't see me. Tell him to forget all about me."

"Sure, whatever, Séamus."

"Declan."

"Right. Declan."

"I'd like to hang on and trade a few stories, Dallas, but I really have to catch a train right about now."

He walked away nervously. As he slipped into the crowd, he said, "Maybe I'll see you again and we can catch up proper like. We'll have the *craic* next time."

As I lost sight of him, I yelled, "Hey, Declan! One more thing!"

"Yeah?"

"*Pog ma thon!*"

I could not see him, but I heard him laugh.

The day had turned out much stranger than I had expected.

21
Dino

SEEING SÉAMUS had put me in a weird mood. All kinds of thoughts and feelings went through my head. I struggled to make sense of any of it. The only thing I knew for sure was that I wanted to see Valérie. No, it was more than that. I *needed* to see Valérie. In the course of just a few days I had gotten to a point where nothing felt right unless I was with her.

It was getting late and usually by that time I would have seen her at the Casino. I wondered if she was avoiding me. I finally gave up waiting and left to wander until it was so late there was nothing left to do but return to the hotel and go to bed.

I had a terrible feeling that my time with Valérie was over. I had ruined things by telling her how serious I was. I had forced her to choose between me and Michel, and she had obviously chosen Michel. Who could blame her? For her I was only someone to have a fling with.

I was dead tired and only wanted to sleep. I got as far as taking off my shirt when there was a knock on the door. I opened it too see Valérie trembling in the hallway. She did not look like a thirty-one-year-old woman. She looked like a child who was lost and afraid. I quickly put my arm around her, led her into the room, and closed the door.

"Are you all right?" I asked her. "What's wrong? I looked for you all day."

"I was not coming here. I was not going to see you. It is all crazy. I do not know what to do. I... I... *Je me rends.* You tell me what to do. I do what you say."

I hugged her and kissed her. I could not be happy as long as she was so miserable. I wanted to see her smile again. My only thought was that she was unhappy and it was my fault. All I wanted was for us to get past the unhappy part and get to the happy part.

"I think, I hope you know what I want, Valérie. I just want to be with you. Always."

"Okay. I be with you. We do what you want."

"It should be what *we* want."

"Okay. We do what *we* want."

She said nothing while I removed her jacket. She sat on the bed. I took off her shoes. She still said nothing. Slowly, I removed her sweater and then her pants. I slipped out of my jeans and under the covers, pulling her in beside me. I kissed her gently on the lips.

"I do not resist anymore. No more resisting."

"Don't worry," I said. "I'll take care of you. You can trust me."

Our hands explored every part of our bodies. The kisses came faster and then more frantic.

Finally, I thought. *Finally I have found the woman I am meant to be with.*

The kisses and embraces became desperate. I wanted to taste every inch of her. I wanted to breathe in her perfume until it filled my entire body. My heart pounded. I breathed in short gasps.

I froze.

"What is wrong?"

There was something mechanical about her motions. It was as though, somehow, she was not actually there. As if her body was there but not her soul.

"You need to want this. You need to be okay with this."

"I am okay with this."

"And you have to understand that this is not just for one night. We are going to be together now. No more Michel."

I was determined not to make the same mistake with Valérie that I had with Lana. I was not going to do this in secret. This was not going to be something hidden away. Something to be ashamed of.

She remained motionless for an entire minute before speaking.

"I am sorry. I cannot forget about Michel. I still love Michel."

"Why can't you forget about Michel? Is it so hard to leave him and be with me? What is the problem? Is it because I am younger than you?"

She laughed. It was good to hear her laugh, but it confused me.

"Why would that matter?"

"I don't know. Some women just feel weird about being with a younger guy."

"This is not a problem for me. Michel is younger than me."

"He is? Really? Michel is younger than you?"

She laughed again.

"Yes, he is younger than me. *Effectivement*, he is younger than you."

"Younger than me? You're kidding."

"No, it is true."

"How much younger?"

"Um, he has *vingt-trois ans*."

She held up two fingers on one hand and three on the other.

"He's only twenty-three? You're kidding."

"*Non.*"

She was half-amused and half-embarrassed.

"Well, you really are a little cradle robber, aren't you?"

"What is cradle robber?"

"Never mind. You mean, I have been going crazy with jealousy over this Michel guy, and he's just a 23-year-old punk kid? How do you even know him? Were you his babysitter or something?"

"*Non*," she said a bit crossly. "I was not his babysitter. He comes into my shop, where I work."

"And what does this kid do?"

"He is a student. He is a student at *l'Université de Bordeaux*."

She looked even more embarrassed.

"But he will finish soon," she added defensively.

I could not help but laugh.

"*Ne te moques pas de moi. Ce n'est pas drôle.* You know, you and he could be good friends."

"Somehow I don't think that is going to happen."

"I have told him about you."

"What? You told him about me? Was that a good idea?"

"Do not worry. I do not tell him everything. I just say I have met a very bizarre American who is *photographe. C'est tout.*"

For a brief moment I felt nervous. Was this Michel guy going to ambush me late some night like Lana's husband did?

"So, what do you two do together? Go to school dances?"

"I go to see him play football. He is a very good footballer. He plays for the BEC."

"The beck? What's that?"

"*C'est le Bordeaux Étudiant Club.* He has a match on Sunday. He is not happy that I shall not be there. I will not be back in Bordeaux until the next week."

"So, you go to his football games. That's really nice. You could be a cheerleader."

"*C'est quoi* cheerleader?"

"Never mind. Look, trust me. A guy that age, who is still in school, is not serious about anything. He will be okay if you break up with him. There is nothing to worry about. It will be okay."

"Michel is different. *Il est très sérieux.* He is in love with me. *C'est grave, tu sais?* You do not understand. We are very, um, close. He and I have been though many things together."

"What sorts of things?"

"The last year my mother has died. It was very difficult for me. Michel was with me always. I could not do it without Michel."

"Sorry, I didn't know. That's tough. What happened?"

"It was, um, cancer."

"Cancer, huh? That's tough. I'm sorry. What about your father?"

"My father is not well. He is in, um, *maison de repos à Bordeaux.* He is not well."

She made a circle with her finger at her temple, indicating his mind was not all there.

"Wow, that's tough. You've been though a lot. I had no idea."

"My mother. I have her *cendres* still."

"Her cinders? You have her ashes?"

"Yes. I am still not able to, you know, *je n'en ai déjà pu disposer.*"

"You haven't been able to dispose of her ashes. Valérie, I had no idea. What can I do to help you?"

"There is nothing you can do. Only *faire l'amour avec moi. Je n'y résiste plus.*"

There was nothing I would not have done for her in that moment. As much as I wanted to, though, there was no way I could make love to her. Not now, like this.

"I know I'm going to regret this, but we are not going to make love tonight. I want to so bad—in fact it's killing me—but when it happens, I have to know it won't be our only time together. Do you understand? I am *très sérieux. C'est grave.* See? I can learn a thing or two. I'm not as dumb as I look. I love you, Valérie. *Je t'aime.*"

"*Alors juste me tenir.*"

I put my arms around her and held her tight. We lay like that all night. We fell asleep in each other's arms, and neither of us moved until we woke.

In the morning she jerked awake with a start.

"*Dieu! Quelle heure est-il?*"

"It's okay. It's only seven. You're not late for anything."

"I did not intend to be here all the night. I am a disaster. Look at me."

I kissed her on the cheek.

"You are anything but a disaster. You look better than anyone has a right to look first thing in the morning."

It was true. Her long straight hair fell naturally into place. She did not wear makeup, so her skin looked every bit as good as it had the night before. She slipped into her clothes. They did not look like they were being worn for the second day in a row.

We went downstairs for breakfast together.

"Thank you for last night," she said as she sipped her coffee.

"Did I do something last night?"

"You were *très sympa*. You were very nice. You did not exploit me."

I put my hand on hers.

"*Je suis très sérieux*," I said.

"This is the final day of the festival."

"Yeah, that's right. I can't believe it. What a week."

Melanie and I were scheduled to be on a plane the following night, but there was absolutely no way that I could leave.

"Will I see you tonight?"

"Yes. I cannot say good-bye to you at breakfast. I have to say good-bye to you at night."

"I don't plan to say good-bye at all. I intend to stay. I just need you to say it's not completely hopeless. That's all."

She smiled sadly.

"We shall talk tonight."

"Okay. See you tonight."

She stood up and leaned down to give me a kiss. Then she went off to start her day.

I was determined to make the last day count. It was my last chance to get some photographs I could really be proud of. The early morning did not look hopeful, at least at first. Then, when I walked out of the Casino shortly before lunch time, I noticed the other photographers walking quickly toward the beach.

"*Q'est-ce quíl y'a?*" I asked one of them.

"Clint Eastwood!" he said, as he picked up his pace.

I followed. They were all gathering on the grassy area just before the sand. Sure enough, I saw a tall man crowned with an impressive sweep of hair, good-naturedly grimacing with a woman at his side. I was surprised at how tall he has. Most of the actors I had seen were surprisingly short. Not Clint. He was nearly a half-foot taller than I was. I would have recognized his steely stare anywhere. He still looked like the impetuous cowhand

Rowdy Yates from *Rawhide*. He wore a sport coat over a paisley shirt and padded around in running shoes. The woman with him had long blonde hair. She wore a long dress and no shoes. I recognized her. She had been in his latest movies, starting with *The Outlaw Josey Wales* if I remembered right. They did some friendly clowning around together for the benefit of the shutterbugs, who kept shouting at them.

"*Monsieur Eastwood! Monsieur Eastwood!*"

I walked in a different direction from the rest of them and circled in from behind.

"Clint!" I yelled. "Over here!"

I was not sure if he actually heard me, so it may have just been a coincidence that the two of them turned in my direction. I snapped the shutter and was pleased.

At least that one will be different from everyone's, I thought.

I walked back to the Casino, thinking, *Maybe that one shot will redeem me. Maybe that one will make the whole week worthwhile. No, what made the week worthwhile was meeting the one true love of my entire life.*

I became aware of a slow traveling car keeping pace with me as I walked. It was one of those little Citroëns, the ones that looked like tin cans. The driver was trying to get my attention. I thought maybe he was lost or something. He certainly had to be lost if he thought a tourist like me could give him directions anywhere.

He stopped the car. I walked over and leaned in the passenger window.

"Can I give you a lift?"

He was American. He had curly black hair and kind of looked Italian. I guessed he was maybe around forty.

"I'm just going to the Casino, but thanks anyway."

Why on earth would he offer me a ride? Did I look like a male prostitute or something? It was the middle of the day in a very public place, for goodness sake. Who tries to pick up somebody in a car in broad daylight? Yes, it had happened to me a time or two in the city, but always at night.

"Get in," he said. "It's okay."

"No thanks, pal," I said, walking away.

"Your name Green?"

He had my attention.

"What if it is? Who are you?"

"Get in. It will be easier to talk."

"I'm not getting in your car, mister. I don't know you."

"I'm a friend of Marty's. You know Marty, right?"

It still felt weird, but the guy had said the magic words. I got into the passenger seat. He drove out of town.

"So, you're the photographer, huh?"

"Yeah, I'm a photographer."

"When did you get to Deauville?"

"A week ago today."

"When do you go back?"

"I'm supposed to fly back tomorrow night."

"Can you put off your flight?"

I did not bother telling him I was already thinking of not showing up for my return flight.

"I suppose anything's possible."

"You understand you shouldn't be talking to anybody about any of this, right?"

"I wouldn't even know what it was I was talking about anyway."

"Yeah, that's the idea. Do you have a good memory, Green?"

"Okay, I guess."

"Because I can show you things, but I can't give them to you."

He pulled over to the side of the road. From a brown manila envelope he pulled out a glossy photo. The man in the picture had a narrow face with sunken cheeks and a weak chin. His crop of black hair looked like it was made of iron wool. His nose was as sharp as a knife blade.

"Will you be able to remember what this guy looks like?"

"Yeah, I think I'll be able to remember him."

He quickly put the photo back in the envelope.

"Do you know any German?"

"German? No, why?"

"Doesn't matter really. It would be good if you did, but English will do you okay. Actually, come to think of it, it's probably better if it's obvious you don't know any German."

"This is starting to sound kind of complicated. I don't know if I'm really the guy you want for whatever it is you need."

"Look, there's absolutely no risk in this. We just need someone who looks like they don't have a clue, you know, a typical young American hanging out and looking like they're just taking a few tourist photos. What we really want you to do, though, is, if you spot this guy, just get him in the photo. Him and anybody he is meeting with. Now here's the hard part."

I thought about asking him his name, but I was pretty sure he was not going to tell me. In my head I decided to call him "Dino" because he looked a bit like Dean Martin, the singer my dad liked to watch on TV.

170

"Dino" pulled out a city map and a piece of paper.

"You need to find your way to this spot," he said, putting his finger on the map. There's a café there. That's where you will hang out. Drink as much coffee as you have to. This is the name of the place and the address. Can you remember it?"

I was not so sure. It was all in German. The name was Zu Tisch, and I figured I could manage to remember that at least.

"What is this a map of ?"

"It's Berlin. The Soviet sector."

"Berlin? You mean, behind the Iron Curtain?"

"Yeah, technically it is. Don't worry. Americans cross from West Berlin to East Berlin and back again all the time. Have you got this place memorized?"

"Yeah, I should be able to find that. How do I get into East Berlin?"

"You'll figure it out. Just ask when you get there. You'll be going through Checkpoint Charlie."

"Checkpoint Charlie? You're kidding."

"No, that's where Americans cross. Why are you looking at me like that?"

"No reason. I was just thinking of a song. Go on."

"Okay. Now let's see your camera."

I pulled my Nikon F2 out of its bag and proudly showed him. He shook his head.

"That's no good," he said. "It's too expensive. Looks too professional. You have to look like a tourist. Don't use that one."

He pulled out a little Kodak Brownie.

"Here. Use this. We don't need great quality. We just need the photo. You won't attract anyone's attention with this."

Being told I had to use a crap Brownie camera was definitely a letdown.

"So, that's all I need to do?"

"Yeah, that's all. Just hang out for a few hours at Zu Tisch on a Wednesday morning. It has to be a Wednesday morning. Do not attract attention. Take a picture as casually as you can, and make sure this guy is in it—along with anybody he is talking to. That part's important. Afterwards, just cross back into the American sector. Then make your way to a club called Risiko and hang out there for a while. You shouldn't have to wait too long."

"Risiko? How will I find it?"

"Don't worry about that. You'll find it. Just ask anybody your age or younger. You won't have to wait too long until someone will come take the camera from you. Then you're done. Any questions?"

"Just one."

"What is it?"

"Just tell me that I'm doing this for the good guys."

"Yeah, it's for the good guys. Your country will be in your debt, though your country won't have a fucking clue about what you did."

"So, I'm going to Berlin."

"Yeah, you're going to Berlin."

He handed me two brown letter-sized envelopes.

"Take these. This one has French francs. This should be more than enough to buy a train ticket to Berlin. This other one has Deutschmarks. This should cover your stay in Berlin and the fees for crossing into the Soviet sector. There's some extra for any expenses that come up. Not too bad a deal, huh? It's like a free holiday, and you get to do your country a little service."

"This is definitely different than I thought my first trip to Europe would be."

By now he had driven back into town. He pulled over on a street not too far from the Casino.

"Nice meeting you, Green. Just one more thing."

"Yeah, what's that?" I said as I got out of the car.

"This meeting never happened."

22
Logan

I WAS desperate to see Valérie. I wanted so much to tell her about the strange turn my day had taken. I wanted to ask her to come to Berlin with me, to share my strange adventure. I wanted moral support. I had no idea what I had gotten myself into. How had my life become so damn interesting?

That evening the Casino was full of people dressed even more elegantly than they had been before. Everyone was drinking champagne. I felt completely out of place. I wandered around, looking for Valérie. I worried she had decided, in a fit of guilt and remorse, to leave the festival early and head back to Bordeaux. I panicked to think she might be there at that moment, confessing her sins to Michel and begging his forgiveness.

I gave up looking for her. I walked back to my hotel. I wondered how I was going to break the news to Melanie that I would not be on the plane home with her.

When I got to the hotel, things were buzzing. I did not want to drink alone, but I decided to have one anyway. When I walked into the bar, I saw her. Valérie was sitting alone at a table in the corner. I went straight to her.

"Buy the lady a drink?"

She smiled.

"*Enfin.* I am afraid you would not come."

"If I had known you were here, I would have come a whole lot sooner."

"Do you have a good day?"

"It was an amazing day. I got a great shot of Clint Eastwood and Sondra Locke. And guess what, I got a job as a spy. I'm going to be the next James Bond."

"You are very funny. I think about you all the day."

"I think about you all the day too. Let's get drunk."

"You have the good ideas."

I ordered two double scotches at the bar. My Basque friend was overworked by the milling crowd.

"*Señor. Mucho gusto verle a usted de nuevo,*" he said with a genuine smile.

"*Mucho gusto verle a usted también,*" I said.

He gave me a sly wink as he glanced in Valérie's direction.

"*Su compañera es muy bella, señor.*"

"Yes, she definitely is beautiful. I mean, *sí. Ella es la mujer más bella del mundo.*"

"*Felicitaciones.*"

Even though my relationship with him consisted entirely of me buying drinks, I felt we had become friends. He was entirely focused on his job, but he did not miss much either.

I took the drinks back to our table and stared at the beautiful woman I was with. If she went up to my room again tonight, I would definitely not be as stupid as I was the previous night. As much as I enjoyed sleeping beside her, I could not believe had passed up the opportunity to make love to her. At this point I was through worrying about doing the right thing or the wrong thing. I just wanted her.

"I cannot stop thinking about Michel."

Not what I wanted to hear.

"What is so special about Michel? What is so great about him?"

"I do not have the words. There is something important between us. That is all."

"Is it because he's French?"

"What?"

"First I thought the age difference was standing between us, but that's obviously not it. So, maybe it's the fact that he's French and I'm not. Is that it?"

"Did I say that he was French?"

"Yes. No. I don't know. I just assumed he was French. I mean, with a name like Michel what else would he be?"

She laughed.

"He is not French. His true name is not Michel. That is what I call him. His true name is Miguel."

"Miguel? What is he then? Spanish?"

She laughed again. Confusing me seemed to cheer her up.

"*Non. Il est du Chili. Il est Chilien.*"

"Did you say he was from Chile?"

"Yes. I have one man from *l'Amérique du Sud* and one man from *l'Amérique du Nord.*"

"Let me get this straight. The guy standing between you and me being together is a 23-year-old guy from Chile?"

"*Il est mon copain*," she said with a determined look on her face.

Following Valérie's love life was like riding a rollercoaster. In the space of a few days my mental image of my rival had gone from an old French guy to a young French guy to a young Chilean guy. It was hard to keep up.

Now I had a whole new—completely unexpected—interest in Valérie's love life. Because this Michel guy—or Miguel or whatever his name was—was from Chile, there was a chance, however slight, he might know something about Antonio. He was even the right age to have maybe gone to school with him or know him. Sure, it probably would be too much of a coincidence for the two of them to have met, but these days my life seemed to be full of unlikely coincidences. After all, what were the odds of running into Séamus in Deauville? As much as I wanted this Michel out of my life and, more importantly, out of Valérie's life, I now desperately wanted to meet him and talk to him. I wanted to see if he could provide any clues as to what happened to Antonio.

"You are now silent," she said. "I am sorry."

"No, no, it's okay. Say, remember when you said that you thought Michel and I could be friends? I'm starting to think you were right. I want to meet him."

This took her by surprise.

"I was joking. *Non*, you cannot meet Michel. That is not a good idea."

"No, it's okay. I'm not going to try to fight him or anything. It doesn't actually have anything to do with you and me. I'd just like to ask him some questions about a friend of mine who went to Chile several years ago. I never heard from him again, and I need to find out whatever I can about what happened to him. Michel might know something that could help me. Maybe he knew him. Tell me, where in Chile does Michel come from?"

"He is from Santiago. This is very bizarre."

"Santiago! Antonio sent me a postcard from there. That was the last time I heard anything from him. I have to talk to Michel. I have to meet him."

"*Non. Ce n'est pas possible.*"

She was adamant.

"It is just too bizarre. It cannot happen. It is impossible."

"Just think about it, okay? Please. It's important. I have spent so many years wondering what happened to Antonio. I can't pass up a chance to find out about him."

"I must to go to bed. Tomorrow is very busy. We leave tomorrow."

"Are you going back to Bordeaux tomorrow?"

"*Non.* I told you I do not go back there until the next week. I must to do something else first."

"Will you stay with me tonight?"

"That is not a good idea."

"Please."

She leaned over and kissed me. It felt like a goodbye kiss.

"I cannot. I am sorry. But I will see you tomorrow. I may have a surprise for you. We shall see, okay?"

"A surprise?"

"*À demain.*"

"*À demain* then."

As I watched her walk out of the bar, I kicked myself again for not having made love to her the night before. If only I had realized it would be my only chance. Trying to be noble and responsible sucked. It killed me to see her walk away and to go to my room alone. I was in for another difficult night.

In the morning I looked for her at breakfast. I ate alone but, as I was about to go, she appeared.

"*Bonjour, mon beau.*"

"*Bonjour, ma belle.*"

"Are you prepared for your surprise?"

"I guess I'm as ready as I will ever be."

"Come."

I picked up my camera bag and followed her. We walked to the Hotel Normandy. I followed her down a corridor to a room on the far end. She knocked on the door, and it opened. Inside we were greeted by the man I had seen her with on Sunday night. I now had a good look at his face, especially the eyes. There was no doubt. It was him. He greeted Valérie warmly but looked at me suspiciously.

"Dallas, this is Monsieur Logan MacCaul. Logan, *je te présente* Dallas Green."

My brain was numb. None of this seemed real. Somehow I managed to shake his hand.

"Mr. MacCaul, I am so impressed by your work. I…"

He cut me off.

"Have you actually seen any of my films?"

He spoke with a deep New York accent and a New York attitude.

"I, well, I…"

I looked at Valérie. It seemed stupid to lie in front of her when she knew the truth.

"No, sir, I haven't seen any of them. But I have a friend who says that *Tristan's Passage* changed his life. He said that…"

"It's crap."

"What?"

"*Tristan's Passage* is crap. If your friend had a brain in his body, he would know that."

"It's not just him. Everyone says it's a great movie."

"But you haven't seen it yourself. Do you always get your opinions from what you hear other people say?"

"Well, no, but if so many people say the same thing…"

"Then it must be true, right? People are like sheep. Especially film critics. *Tristan's Passage* is crap. I'm the one who made it, so I should know. I should know if it's crap or not, and I'm telling you it's crap."

"I'm sorry. I guess I need to watch it. Then I will tell you what I think."

"I wouldn't bother. It's crap. Show me your camera."

As if under a spell, I held out my camera. He took it from me and examined it closely.

"Nice. This is one of those new Nikon cameras, isn't it? How do you like it?"

"I like it a lot. It was expensive, but it is easy to use. It has all the settings, but I don't waste a lot of time if I need to shoot something in hurry."

"Tell me how you compose your frame."

It was like a pop quiz in a college photography course.

"I don't like to make it too symmetrical. If there's a horizon, I always put it well above the midway point. Sometimes I focus on something other than what the viewer would expect to be the main object—even if the main object is slightly out of focus."

"Good. What about portraits?"

"What about them?"

"How do you approach your subjects?"

"I try to keep them from posing too self-consciously. I hate it when people mug. I always go for the candid shot when I can."

"Good. Good. Do you touch them?"

"What?"

"Do you ask them to let you feel their skin so that you can get a better feel for the texture? It makes a better photograph if you know yourself what their skin feels like. People can be kind of strange about that, but it's worth doing. In the end, all that matters is the picture."

"Uh, yes, as a matter of fact, I have done that."

He turned to Valérie.

"I like him. He's young, but he has good instincts. I'd say he has a natural eye."

"Sir?"

"Yes?"

"If you don't mind me asking, can you tell me about your new movie?"

"What new movie?"

"The one you were going to show here in Deauville. The one that got canceled. The one everyone has been waiting for, for years. I'm sure it's a great movie."

"There is no new movie. Where did you get that idea?"

"There was a rumor. Everyone was talking about it. You mean, there's no new movie?"

"There's no new movie. And there won't be any more movies. I'm done making movies. Do you know what it's like to make your very first movie and everyone goes crazy telling you you're a genius and you know it's crap but they keep telling you you're a genius anyway? And then they keep pestering you for your next movie and they insist that it be as good as they thought the first movie was? A person can't work that way. It's absolutely fucking crazy. That's why I had to get away. The whole fucking world is crazy."

"There's really no new movie?"

"No."

"Then why are you in Deauville?"

"I came to see Valérie."

He put his arm around her. She blushed at his embrace.

"Uh, why?"

"You didn't tell him?"

"*Non.*"

"Shall I tell him then?"

She nodded.

"Let's sit down," he said. "Valérie, *ma chère*, is there any lemonade left?"

We all sat, and Valérie poured us glasses of fresh-squeezed lemonade. It was delicious. MacCaul told his story.

"As you may know, Mr. Green, there was a time years ago I lived in France. I rented a small farmhouse in Brittany. During that time I met a woman. She was living in Brest at the time. We fell in love. Unfortunately, she was married. Her husband was in the French navy and was away much of the time. She and I had a very intense relationship over several months, but in the end there was no future in it. She was not going to leave her husband. Eventually, I returned to the States and bought a little farm in California. I went on with my life, but I never forgot about Marie. Last year, out of the blue, I got a letter from her. She was dying of cancer. In the time she had left, she wanted me to know she had a daughter. Because of the timing and the fact she and her husband never had any other children, she was certain the daughter was mine. She thought I had a right to know. I came back, hoping to see Marie. Unfortunately, by the time I tracked her down in Bordeaux, she had died. I did, however, meet her... our... daughter."

He rested his hand on top of Valérie's. Her head was bowed, a single tear resting on her cheek. Slowly, she lifted her head, and I looked into her beautiful dark eyes. I should have seen from the beginning that they were the same as his.

"I think it has taken Valérie some time to adjust to all of this. It has taken some time for both of us. Anyway, for some reason it was important to her that I meet you. You may take a photo now if you like."

"Really?"

"Yes," he said impatiently. "But I suggest you hurry in case I change my mind."

I wasted no time. I put my eye up to the viewfinder and composed my shot. He sat there quietly with a mournful look. As many times as I clicked the shutter, his expression did not change.

"And you don't mind if this is published?"

"I'm not crazy about the idea, but I've decided it may be my only hope of discouraging journalists from knocking on my door in the middle of the night. Feel free to write whatever you want about this interview, but..."

"This is an interview?"

"Of course, it is. Didn't you know you were conducting an interview?"

"No, sir. I thought *you* were."

"This is your big scoop, young man. Make the most of it."

"But I'm not actually a writer. I'm just a photographer. I should get our writer over here so she can talk to you."

"That's not going to happen. No more talking. That's the interview. Write it up any way you want, but if you mention a word about Valérie or her mother or any of that part of it, I will track you down and kill you. Do you understand?"

"I understand."

"The main thing is that you tell the world that my movies are crap. Tell them to leave me alone. Tell them to move on and torture some other poor goddamned filmmaker for a change. I'm tired of it."

"Yes, sir."

He turned to Valérie.

"You were right. I like him. I think he's okay. Or at least I think he will be. Now tell him to leave. We have to finish packing. It's time to go."

"Go? Where are you going?"

"We go to *Bretagne*," said Valérie. "Logan wants to show me where my mother and he passed their time together. There is a place on the sea. We shall scatter her ashes there. *Enfin.*"

"Cremation is rather unusual in France," explained Logan, "but it was what Marie wanted. I like to think it was her way of going back to Brittany. I find that touching. I am planning to put the same instruction in my own will."

I wanted to ask if I could go too, but I knew that this was too personal. This journey was meant for just the two of them—Marie's daughter and Marie's lover. I thought how terrible it would be to spend so much of one's life regretting a love that never worked out. It made me deeply and unexpectedly sad.

"When will I see you again?"

"*Je ne sais pas.* It is all too complex. I must see Michel again. I have to discover how I feel. It is all so difficult."

"Don't take all day saying goodbye," said Logan grumpily as he went into the bathroom and closed the door.

I held Valérie. We kissed.

"This is not goodbye," I said. "I promise you that. I will never give up. We're not going to end up like Logan and Marie. You and I are meant to be together. I know it."

"Yes," she said. "We will not say *adieu*. We will say *au revoir. Dallas, mon amour, je t'aime vraiment, mais je n'ai aucune idée ce qui va se passer.*"

I did not want to let go of her. On the other hand, I knew it would be better if I were gone before Logan came out of the bathroom. I gave her one last kiss. I made it last as long as I could. Then I forced myself to leave.

I walked down the hotel corridor, absorbing everything I had just learned. Things had continued to get stranger and stranger. It was early in the day, but I felt like going somewhere for a few stiff drinks. That would have to wait, though. I had some other things to do quickly, and then I would leave Deauville. I had committed to go to Berlin, but there was someplace else I was determined to go first. I had made up my mind to go to Bordeaux.

I was going to talk to Michel.

23
Bordeaux

BACK AT my hotel room, I carefully removed the roll of film from my camera. In the closet there was a plastic bag meant for leaving laundry. I put my precious film roll—as well as all the other rolls I had shot—inside it. Then I sat down at the desk, grabbed a sheet of hotel stationery, and wrote everything I could remember about my conversation with Logan MacCaul.

As best I could, I described what he looked like and what he sounded like. I wrote everything he had said to me about his films being crap and how he was tired of people trying to talk to him about his work. I wrote that he had no new movie and that there would never be another movie. I wrote that he had come back to France for purely sentimental reasons without saying what those reasons were. I made no mention of Marie or Valérie. After finishing, I folded the paper and placed it in the bag with the rolls of film. Then I picked up the phone and dialed Melanie's room number.

"Dallas! Where were you? I was trying to call you earlier. We have to get going."

"Sorry, Melanie, but we need to talk."

"We don't have time now. We can talk on the train to Paris."

"No, we need to talk now. Can I come to your room?"

"Okay, but just make sure you're packed and ready to go."

"I'll see you in two minutes."

I grabbed the bag and rushed down to her room. When she opened the door, I saw her clothes all over the bed. She was in the middle of packing.

"I need to apologize to you," she said.

She was talking fast. She was stressed about making the train back to Paris.

"I meant to spend more time with you during the week. Things just kept coming up. I got some good interviews. I can't believe how many people are over from Los Angeles."

I waited for her to stop for a breath, but she just kept talking.

"I never did have any luck finding out anything about MacCaul. I don't think he was even here. I wonder how that rumor got started. David and his advertiser are going to be very disappointed."

"Melanie."

"Did you get lots of good pictures? I hope you weren't just shooting actors. It's important to cover the filmmakers as well."

"Melanie, I need to give this to you."

I handed her the bag.

"What's this?"

"There are about a dozen rolls of film in there. You need to guard them with your life."

"Why are you giving them to me? Here, you keep them."

"No, you have to take them. Melanie, I don't quite know how to tell you this, but I'm not going back with you."

"What?"

"I'm not going back."

"Is this about your fear of flying? You don't have to worry about that. I'll get you through it. We can get you something at a pharmacy. Don't be silly. You have to go back."

"Just listen," I said. "You have to take care of this film. Do not open the containers. Do not let them get wet. For God's sake, do not let them get exposed to light. When you get back to the office, give them to someone reliable, someone who won't screw them up. Give them to Ken. Definitely do not give them to Bill. It's killing me that I'm not going to get to develop them myself. You just have to stress to whoever does it to be very careful and not get it wrong."

"What are you talking about? You have to go back with me. How else will you get home?"

"I'm not going home. That's what I'm trying to tell you. That's why I'm giving this to you."

"Dallas, this is crazy."

"I know. You're absolutely right. Anyway, I've written some notes. They're here in the bag with the film. Do whatever you want with them. Re-write them in your own words. Put your own by-line on them if you want. I don't care. I did my best to write everything down. It's all there."

She pulled the notes out of the bag and looked at them.

"What is this?"

"I know you're not going to believe me, but I met him. I met Logan MacCaul. I talked to him. Well, more accurately, he talked to me. I've written it all down. You'll see. It's all there."

She scanned my notes as fast as she could.

"Is this a joke?"

"It's no joke. I know it sounds crazy, and you're probably thinking I made it all up but, when you look at the photos, you'll see. It's really him."

She sat down on the bed, looking as if she was in shock.

"What am I supposed to say to David? How am I supposed to explain that you didn't come back?"

"You don't have to explain it. You just have to say that that's what happened. Look, there's a pretty good story there. It's what he wanted. There's no new Logan MacCaul film, but we did get an interview with him and photos. He should be pretty happy with that."

"I can't believe this."

"Tell him I'm sorry. Tell him I said thanks for giving me a job and that I'm sorry for not giving him more notice about quitting. Tell him that I stayed here because there was something I needed to do. Hell, tell him whatever you want. Anyway, you better hurry up if you're going to catch the train."

"I can't believe this," she said. "I just can't believe this."

She stared at my notes with her mouth open. I did not know what more I could say, so I just said, "Thanks for everything, Melanie. Have a good flight home. Take care of yourself."

I headed for the door. She seemed to have lost awareness of me while she stared trance-like at my notes. I was nearly out of the room when she said, "Wait."

She grabbed her handbag and pulled out a couple of envelopes. She looked at them and then handed one to me.

"Here," she said. "This is your return ticket. Just in case you change your mind and there's still time. Even if you don't make the flight today, you should be able to exchange it for another ticket when you do go home."

I took it from her.

"Thanks, Melanie."

She said nothing else. She continued to be transfixed by my notes.

I went back to my room and thought about what to do next. Going to Bordeaux by myself was a crazy idea. Would I manage to get there with my non-existent knowledge of French? How would I find Michel? What would he do when I found him? No doubt Valérie would be furious with me. In spite of it all, I could not talk myself out of going. If there was any chance at all—no matter how slim—of finding out something about Antonio, I had to go for it. I would always regret it if I didn't.

I took some time to make a plan. My best hope of finding Michel was to go to his football game on Sunday. Today was Friday. If I traveled there on Saturday, it should give me time to find out when and where exactly the game was. So, I would stay in Deauville one more night. We were scheduled to check out of the hotel, so I went down to reception. The guy at the desk told me that the bill for my room had been paid. I had Melanie to thank for that. She was in charge of the expense account. It was extremely decent of her. Another person might have gotten seriously pissed at the way I blindsided her and left me with the expense—especially since there were quite a few charges from the bar on the tab. I asked the guy if I could keep the room one more night, and he said there was no problem. Now that the film festival was over, the town was clearing out.

The rest of that day turned out to be surprisingly lonely. Melanie was gone. Valérie was gone. I knew nobody else there. I ended up wasting a lot of time walking around and thinking about everything that happened during the week. I wondered what people at work back in the city were doing. I wondered what Justin was up to. I wondered if Marty had any customers to cook for. Did he know that Dino had made contact? Was he wondering anxiously if I was going to get his photograph for him?

I walked to the train station. After standing in line, I had a long talk with the man in the ticket window. Either he did not speak a lot of English or else he just did not want to. Eventually, I did manage to buy a ticket from Deauville to Bordeaux. With a lot of pointing and making notes with a pencil on a printed schedule, he managed to make me understand I would be taking a train to Paris. Once there, I would have to make my way from the train station I had been in before, Saint-Lazare, over to another train station called Montparnasse. That is where I would get the train to Bordeaux. It sounded like a long day of traveling. I put my tickets in my pocket and did some more walking.

By the time evening came around, I was pretty darn homesick. I was tired of hearing people speak French. I wished there was a place to get a decent hamburger. I would have paid anything for just one thing off the menu at Hamburger Mary's. I went to the hotel bar and sat down in front of the closest thing I had to a friend in Deauville, my Basque bartender.

"*Buenas tardes, señor.*"

"*Buenas tardes.*"

"Scotch on the rocks?"

"Yeah, *gracias*. The usual whiskey *escocés con hielo*."

"*Muy bien, señor.*"

185

When he came back with my drink, I asked if he had ever been to Bordeaux.

"*¿Burdeos? Sí. Muchas veces.*"

I asked him what it was like. He said it was very different from Deauville. It was a lot bigger and a lot older. Unlike many French cities, it had suffered little damage during the war. Many of the buildings were hundreds of years old.

"*Es una ciudad muy conservadora, pero el vino es excelente. Sobretodo el vino tinto.*"

"Conservative and lots of wine grapes, huh? Sounds to me like Bordeaux just might be the Bakersfield of France. You know what I wish I had right now? A good Mexican meal. There just aren't any Mexican restaurants in this place. Hey, you know what would be even better. A Basque restaurant. I would give anything to be at Wool Growers in East Bakersfield right now. I mean, absolutely anything."

I talked his ear off for a good hour or so. When I finally got up to go, he reached for my tab.

"*¿Le cobrará esto a su habitación, señor?*"

"I'll be paying you in cash tonight."

I counted out the money and added a generous tip.

"*No es necesaria la propina, señor.*"

"That's nice of you, *amigo*, but I want you to have it. You've earned it."

"*Gracias. Muchas gracias, señor.* I hope you return."

It was the first time he had spoken to me in English, apart from learning to say Scotch on the rocks.

"Thanks. I hope so too."

"I hope you return with *su muy bella amiga.*"

"Me too. Man, I hope so too."

The next morning I got up early. I did not want to take a chance on missing the train. I did not have much packing to do, but I took my time. I was now lonelier than ever. I did some calculating in my head and figured that Melanie was already back in the city. Valérie and Logan would be in Brest. They might be scattering Marie's ashes at that very moment.

There was a radio in the room. I turned it on for the first time. It played "Everybody's Got to Learn Sometime" by the Korgis. The lyrics were a little too appropriate for that moment, and I changed the station. This one played a song in French. It made me feel more homesick, and I turned the dial again. This time I got "Video Killed the Radio Star" by the Buggles.

I checked out and walked to the train station. On the train I got a window seat and watched the countryside roll by. At each stop more people got on. There were couples who looked like they were going home after a vacation and students who looked like they were going back to school. Eventually the green fields gave way to the outskirts of the city and then the city itself. Finally, we got to the end of the line.

Saint-Lazare was buzzing with activity. Deauville had been relatively quiet, and it took a while to adjust to a big city again. The guy at the Trouville-Deauville train station had told me to take *le Metro* to Montparnasse. I followed the signs which led me downstairs to a crowd of people pushing their way through a set of turnstiles. There was a big map on the wall of the whole Paris underground train system, and it was awfully confusing. I looked around and spotted a young guy with long hair and a backpack.

"Excuse me, do you speak English?"

"Yes."

"Can you tell me how I get to Montparnasse from here?"

He looked at the map and, after a moment, put his finger on a blue line.

"Line number 13. Take number 13 in the direction of Châtillon-Montrouge. That way."

He pointed to a sign on another wall that indicated that name and number.

"You buy a ticket there."

"Thanks, man."

He disappeared immediately into the crowd. I bought a ticket and followed the signs until I got to the train platform. The tracks disappeared into tunnels at either end of the platform, and a warm rubbery smell wafted through the concrete cavern. Advertising posters lined the painted brick wall.

A few minutes later a train pulled in. People crowded up to the doors. The doors opened, and a horde of people pushed their way out of the train car and through the crowd of people waiting outside. Then the scramble was on to get onto the train. I pushed my way in along with everybody else. There was a loud warning sound, all the doors closed simultaneously with a loud hiss, and the train began to move. There was no place to sit. At each stop I had to hunch over to look out the window to see where we were. Seven stops later, I spotted the sign that said "Montparnasse-Bienvenüe."

I joined the crowd that pushed its way through the door and out onto the platform. I climbed the stairs—I felt as if I was rising from the bowels of the earth—until I emerged into a bigger train station than Saint-Lazare. By following signs and looking at the big constantly changing boards displaying train arrivals and departures—and again asking somebody for help—I eventually made my way to the platform for the Bordeaux train. I breathed a sigh of relief. Getting from one train to the other had seemed like a huge ordeal. I looked forward to finally being able to settle into a seat on the train and do nothing but sit for a few hours. I also looked forward to reading the paper. Along the way I had spotted a news kiosk and splurged on a copy of *The International Herald Tribune.*

When the train finally arrived, I asked the conductor twice if this was definitely the one for Bordeaux.

"*Oui, Monsieur,*" he said both times.

I found my seat, shoved my backpack onto the luggage rack above, and collapsed into my corner by the window. After what seemed like a very long delay, the train finally moved. It went slowly at first, then gradually faster. It did not pick up speed until we were nearly out of the city. It was a relief to be out of Paris.

Someday, I thought, *I will have to see more of that city besides just the train stations and the Metro.*

I glanced through the newspaper. While I was having my adventure in France, the rest of the world had continued with all its usual problems. The Ayatollah in Iran issued demands to be met in exchange for releasing the American hostages. There was a military coup in Turkey. Post-Labor Day polls predicted President Carter would beat Ronald Reagan in the November election. (*That will definitely make James happy*, I thought.) There was also an article about Chile. It said there had been a constitutional referendum and, as a result, General Pinochet would continue running the government. I wondered if Antonio was still in Chile after all these years. Could he have possibly voted in the referendum?

A woman came by with a food cart. I bought a ham and cheese sandwich and a bottle of beer. I had not eaten all day. I had not bothered to have breakfast before I left the hotel. Still, I was not particularly hungry. The sandwich was good, though. In fact, it was the best ham and cheese sandwich I had ever had. There was not much to it. Just a slice of ham and a slice of white cheese stuffed inside a hunk of French bread. Nothing else, no mayonnaise or mustard or anything, but the bread was incredibly fresh and crunchy and the cheese had a strong taste that made me wish there was more of it.

As the train made its way south, I watched the fields, rivers, towns, and cities pass by. We traveled through places with names like Orléans (*the old one*, I thought, *not New Orleans*), Tours, Poitiers, and Angoulême. For the fiftieth time I wondered if I was insane for making this trip, and for the fiftieth time I told myself that it was not a crazy thing to do if, against all the odds, I learned something about Antonio. Even if I learned nothing, I told myself, at least I would know I had tried.

The sun set, and the world outside the train grew dark. I thought about what an amazing coincidence it was that I would fall in love with a French woman who just happened to have boyfriend from Santiago. And that Santiago just happened to be the very same place Antonio was the last time I heard from him all those years ago. Not only was Michel from the same city but he was around Antonio's age. Even if Michel did not know Antonio directly, there was always a chance he had heard of him or knew someone who knew him. There was at least a chance. That's all I wanted—just a chance.

The coincidence was all the more amazing, as I kept thinking about it.

Valérie had said Michel lived in the United States for a time. Just as Antonio had lived in the U.S. when I first met him.

Come to think of it, I thought, *in a way, the two of them have kind of the same name. Michel's name is actually Miguel. And Miguel is also the name Antonio used to travel to Chile. He took the name Miguel Pérez Rivera, which had belonged to Daniel's dead brother. They used it to get him a Mexican passport. Antonio had signed the postcard from Santiago Miguel Pérez Rivera.*

Finally, it hit me like a ton of bricks. What an incredibly stupid idiot I was.

All the details lined up perfectly. Too perfectly. What if Valérie's boyfriend Michel and my friend Antonio were one and the same? I felt dizzy.

No, I said to myself. *There's no point getting my hopes up. Sure, these coincidences keep adding up, but they are still probably just coincidences. I am sure there are lots of guys that age in Santiago named Miguel. They can't all be Antonio. I'm sure a few of them have lived in the States and know English. Okay, that seems less likely. Hell, I don't know how likely it is or it isn't.*

I was now desperate to know why Michel had come from Chile to study in France. I had read that a lot of Chileans, who were opposed to the Pinochet regime, were forced into exile. I had met some of them in the city. Daniel Pérez and his cousin Gustavo had been politically active. Gustavo had to leave Chile once before because of his politics. Maybe that is what happened to the three of them after Pinochet's coup. Maybe Daniel, Gustavo, and Antonio had to go into exile. Maybe they went to France.

I told myself not to get carried away. I told myself I was just setting myself up for disappointment. No matter what, though, I could not get the image out of my mind of me going to that football game on Sunday and finding Antonio there and seeing the look of surprise on his face when, after all these years, he saw me again. I imagined all the stories we would tell each other about everything we had done for the past nine years. I would have to tell him that Lonnie died, that I never saw Marisol again, that I moved to San Francisco, that I got sent to France to shoot photos at a film festival, that I met a French woman and fell in love with her. I would have to tell him she was the same French woman he was in love with.

Suddenly, my imaginary reunion got a whole lot more complicated.

It did not matter. At this point the only thing that mattered was that I saw Antonio again. How had he been living all this time? How did he end up going to school in France? I needed to hear him tell me all of it. God, how much I had missed him. I never stopped thinking of him since the day Lonnie and I left him in that little village of San Ramón.

The train slowed as it crossed a wide river and then came to a stop. Out the window I saw a sign that read "Bordeaux St Jean." I grabbed my backpack and hurried off the train and onto the platform. I looked around.

Okay, I thought. *Here I am. Now what?*

It was late. I needed to find a place to stay for the night. I walked out of the train station and down the street. There were some hotels close to the train station, but I did not care for the look of them. I kept walking. I followed the river until I came to a large arch at the end of a wide street called Cours Victor Hugo. I followed it past shops and other businesses, which were all closed. I passed sidewalk cafés, a few open but most closed. I passed a very old church with two pointy towers. It looked like a castle at Disneyland. It had a large clock. I came to a very narrow street and saw its name was rue Sainte-Catherine. I remembered this was the street where Valérie worked in a shop. I walked its length. There were many shops on that street all right, but they were all closed. I wondered which one was Valérie's.

Every few yards there was a woman standing on the sidewalk. The way they dressed told me everything I needed to know about why they were there.

This may be the main shopping district in the daytime, I said to myself, *but at night it is definitely the red light district.*

"*Ça va?*" said one of them as I passed.

"Yeah, *ça va*," I said before I had the chance to think better of it. Normally, I would have known better than to answer at all.

"*Veux-tu aller avec moi, mon beau?*"

I picked up my pace, the same as I always did when walking through the Tenderloin. Then I did something strange. I do not know how to explain it except to say in that moment I did not recognize myself. It was as though Lonnie had taken over. I stopped and turned around. I spoke, but it was as though someone else was speaking.

"*¿Hablas tú español?*"

"*Sí, guapo, yo hablo. Cómo tú que quieras. Cualquier cosa que tú quieres.*"

"*¿Cuánto?*"

She gave me a price in French. I had no idea what it was, but it did not matter. Nothing mattered. I was on automatic pilot. I nodded to let her know we had a deal. I followed her off the street. We went into a building and up to a dark room.

24
Ángel

WHEN I woke in the morning, I was alone.

When I had asked if I could stay the whole night, she had protested. She had naturally planned to work until dawn, bringing other customers to her dark room. I offered to pay extra. She took the money but only grudgingly. She could have earned more if I had not been taking up the space in her little room. On the other hand, she could have thrown me out if she really wanted to. After I paid her, she was tough and business-like, but at some level I know she felt sorry for me. It was not as though I was homeless or destitute. I am sure I seemed to her just another privileged American tourist. She must have somehow seen I was going through a weird confused experience. She took pity on me, probably against her better judgment.

So, there actually are whores with hearts of gold, I reflected.

I had never been with a prostitute before in my life. Unless you count that time in Tijuana with Lonnie, and there was no way that should count. Lots of guys I had known were fascinated by prostitutes. For some of them that was their first sexual experience. I never had any interest. Among my male friends, I was the odd duck. I think I was the only one who had never been with a woman I was not in love with. Marisol, Linda, Lana. I was in love with all of them. Yes, I had had two one-night stands during my first year in the city, but I was in love both times. I may have been in love for just one night, but it was still love. And just because I was drunk out of my mind both times does not mean it was not true love.

This was the first time ever I had paid for sex. I do not know why it was important she spoke to me in Spanish. Maybe I did not want her speaking French because it would have reminded me of Valérie. Maybe it was because I wanted her to remind me of Marisol. Maybe it was some strange way—that I did not actually understand—of preparing myself to see Antonio again.

All I knew for sure was that I could not be alone that night. During my time in Deauville, for whatever reason my usual fears at night had stayed away from me. I felt certain, though, they would come back for me if I slept alone in Bordeaux. I had been scared to sleep alone.

The prostitute—in my mind I called her "Cher" because of her long black straight hair and jaded eyes—must have thought I was crazy. Not only did I require her to speak Spanish and not only did I insist on staying the whole night but, when push came to shove, I could not perform. I do not know why I could make nothing happen. It was not because of alcohol. All I had had all day was just the one beer on the train. Or maybe that was the problem. They always try to tell you alcohol is bad for your sex drive, but maybe in my case I had no sex drive without it.

The real problem, of course, was that I was not in love with "Cher." No matter though. She still gave me what I *really* needed. As long as I touched her, the dread stayed away. It did bother me that I could not perform. I even closed my eyes and pretended she was Valérie. I pretended she was Marisol. When it was clear nothing was going to happen, I gave up. I might as well have pretended she was Antonio. After all, the more I thought back on it, the more it was apparent after that night with him in the forest in Michoacán that contact with another person could keep away fears in the night.

I had to hand it to "Cher" though. She was a true professional. She did not tease me or make any kind of fuss. She acted as if it was something that happened regularly, and maybe it was. She simply and calmly took matters into her own hands or, more specifically, into her own mouth. Her lips and tongue did all the work for me. She did what Antonio had offered to do that night in Michoacán and which I had refused because the idea appalled me. I thought, *Things have come full circle*.

I walked out of "Cher's" dim room and into the cool morning light. I was as ready as I would ever be to meet Michel or Miguel or Antonio or whoever he turned out to be.

I walked down the rue Sainte-Catherine. It was quiet. The hookers were long gone. I remembered it was Sunday morning, and I found I was starving. I walked to the Cours Victor Hugo and found an open café. I sat down and ordered a large café au lait and two croissants. I noticed a thin young man at a nearby table. He scribbled furiously on a notepad between puffs on his cigarette. I figured he was a student.

"Excuse me," I said to him. "Do you speak English?"

He looked up through stray locks of black hair dangling on his forehead. He was so slight a strong gust of wind might have blown him away. I still could not get over how scrawny most young French people were.

"Yes?"

"I'm here to see a football match today. I think it is at the beck?"

"Yes, *le BEC*. It is at the *Domaine Universitaire*. In Talence."

"Can you tell me how to get there?"

He looked at his watch.

"I will be going there soon. I can show you then if you like."

"That would be great. *Merci beaucoup*."

He went back to scribbling. I pulled out my newspaper from the day before. I read the comics and took a stab at the crossword. After a while, the young man stood.

"We can go now if you like."

We walked down the street.

"You are American?"

"Yeah."

We came to a large square with another large arch. He took me to a specific spot and stood next to a curb.

"We have to, um, *faire le stop*," he said, holding out his thumb.

"We're going to thumb a ride?"

"Yes."

"Is it far?"

"A few kilometers. Not far. People always take students from here to the *Domaine Universitaire*. This is Place de la Victoire."

He pointed to a large old building across the square.

"That is University of Bordeaux. The School of Medicine. But we go to the new part. In Talence."

Sure enough, before long one of those little Citroëns pulled over and we got in.

"*Merci bien*," said my young friend to the driver.

As the car sped off at excessive speed, the driver nonchalantly pulled out a pack of cigarettes.

"*Vous fumez?*"

"*Merci*," said the student as he took one.

I took one too. With a well-practiced one-handed maneuver, the driver slid one out for himself and grabbed it in his mouth. He pulled out a plastic lighter and lit all our cigarettes while speeding down the narrow twisty street with a single hand on the wheel.

Eventually the car slowed and the driver asked, "*Ça va ici?*"

"*C'est parfait. Merci bien*," said my student friend.

We got out, and my friend pointed. I saw the stadium in the distance.

I shook his hand.

"*Merci beaucoup*," I said. "I appreciate it."

He shrugged and said off-handedly, "*Pas de problème. Bon chance.*"

Then he walked away. My impression of French students so far was that they were extremely laid back.

I walked to the stadium. People were already filing in for the game. I had a plan in mind. I took out my press pass from the film festival and hung the strap around my neck. I took my camera out of its bag and walked up to the entrance. I had learned a long time ago you could get into just about anywhere if you had an expensive-looking camera and acted like you belonged there. I just hoped no one looked too closely at my press pass. Appearing as serious and business-like as I could, I walked through the entrance. I nodded knowingly at the students collecting tickets. They looked at me curiously but let me through. I walked through various corridors until I emerged at the edge of the field. I dropped my backpack on the ground and scanned the bleachers. Seats were starting to fill up. My timing was perfect. While waiting for the game to start, I shot a few photos of the crowd, just to look like I was there working.

After a while, the visiting team came running out onto the field. I looked at the scoreboard. Apparently, they were from someplace called Yvrac. They ran around in their shorts and jerseys, and I was glad this was soccer and not American football. Since they did not wear helmets, I could see their faces clearly.

The home team ran onto the field to enthusiastic cheers. I studied the players to see if any of them looked like Antonio—that is, the way I would have expected Antonio to look at the age of twenty-three. The game began, and one player stood out. His skin was a shade darker than his teammates', and he had a mop of black hair that waved in one direction and then another as he zigged and zagged down the field. His legs were extremely muscular. He chased the ball more energetically than the others. As the game played out, his arms and legs glistened with sweat. When he stole the ball from an opponent, his teammates called out, "*Miguel! Miguel! Bien joué!*"

I took as many photos of him as I could, not only to have them but to get a better look at him through the zoom lens. I hoped the coach would pull him out of the game, so that I could wander near him and get a better look. That did not happen because Miguel was indispensable. He played the entire first half. He would have played most of the second half too if the manager had not pulled him out for nearly getting into a fight. I watched him catch his breath as he stood on the sideline. He leaned forward with his hands on his knees. His brown eyes followed the action intently. He was desperate to return to the game. He did not have to wait long.

I asked myself, *Is it him? Is it really Antonio?*

I was surprised how much I enjoyed the game. I had played some soccer in elementary school, but I had not spent much time watching other people play it. Certainly not at this level. It was easier to get emotionally involved when players were not covered in protective gear like in American football. You could see them straining as they ran up and down the field. You could see the determined expressions on their faces. They were like actors in a drama, and none of them showed more passion than the shorter but powerful Miguel.

I compared him to the Antonio I remembered as a fourteen-year-old kid. Miguel was mature and muscular. I could see why Valérie would fall in love with him. The game drew to a close, and it was not going well for the Bordeaux team. They played their hearts out, but the disappointment and frustration was evident in their faces. I was focused on only one face. I had been confident I would recognize Antonio immediately, but I was still not certain. The more I watched the way he moved, the expressions on his face, the way he sometimes smiled, the more I was convinced, yes, it was Antonio. There were just too many coincidences for it not to be him, and this man now in front of me fit my image of how Antonio would have matured.

I prepared for our long-delayed reunion.

At the final whistle, the teams retreated to the locker rooms. I considered following them but decided against it. Instead I picked up my backpack and walked out of the stadium. Though most of the spectators had soon disappeared, a group of young people—friends and girlfriends, I surmised—gathered around one of the exits. I stood nearby. Eventually, the team emerged. Their sweating arms and legs were no longer exposed. They all wore jeans, tee-shirts and windbreakers. They strode with the easy, relaxed confidence of athletes—especially young male ones. Despite their loss, they talked and joked among themselves.

The players' friends greeted them, gave them pats on the back, and congratulated them on a hard-fought game. Still laughing and joking, the group walked past me. I wondered if Miguel would notice me standing there. I thought perhaps he would stop suddenly and stare with the shock of recognition. Instead, he passed by as if I did not exist.

I called out after him.

"Miguel!"

He turned and looked at me. His expression was one of curiosity. I stepped closer to him and stared into his face.

"Hi. Do you remember me?"

A smile crept across his face. There was the barest glint of recognition in his eyes.

"You're from the U.S.?"

"Yes, I am. I think we knew each other."

His smile broadened into a grin. He looked happy to see me.

"Were you in my high school?"

"No, we weren't in school together. I met you in Los Angeles. In Benedict Canyon."

He shook his head.

"I've never been to California. Are you sure we didn't know each other in Virginia?"

"Virginia? No, I've never been in Virginia. No, it was California. We went to Mexico together."

"No, I've never been to Mexico. You must have me mixed up with someone else."

My heart sank. He was not Antonio. I had had myself so convinced. It felt like a punch in the gut. It felt like losing my friend all over again. I struggled for something more to say.

"Sorry, I mistook you for someone else. I thought you were a friend of mine. I haven't seen him in a long time. He went to live in Chile nine years ago. I've been wondering what happened to him ever since."

"Chile? I'm from Chile."

It may have been my imagination, but I thought I saw sadness in his eyes as he said the name of his country.

"Yeah, and he would have been about your age too. He kind of looked like you. I was sure you were him."

"What was his name?"

"Miguel Pérez Rivera."

"Hey, that is amazing. *My* name is Miguel!"

He reached out and shook my hand.

"Miguel Ángel Contreras Vargas."

When he said his name, his perfect North American accent vanished and was replaced by a South American one. He had gone from Michel to Miguel to now Mee-gale On-hale.

"Miguel Ángel?"

"Yes, like the painter," he said, once again sounding like a guy from the U.S.

"The painter?"

"Yes, I think you say Michelangelo."

197

Perfect. No doubt Valérie thought he was beautiful enough to be an angel in one of those old Italian paintings I had to look at in Art Appreciation.

"It's funny," he continued. "At home everyone always called me just Ángel, but here everyone calls me Miguel. Except my girlfriend. She calls me Michel. I think she is trying to make me French. What is your name?"

My mind froze with panic. I had been focused so much on the idea he would turn out to be Antonio that I had not actually thought about what I would say or do if he turned out *not* to be Antonio. All I knew in that moment was that I could not tell him my name. Valérie had said she had mentioned me to him. If she happened to mention my name, he would know immediately who I was. I could be pretty sure he had never heard of anyone named Dallas before. If he heard the name twice in the same week, he would know it could not be a coincidence. Maybe my reaction was stupid, but in that moment I only knew I had to come up with any name but my own. I just said the first name that came to mind.

"Good to meet you, Ángel. I'm Lonnie. Lonnie McKay."

"Nice to meet you, Lonnie. I wonder if I ever met this Miguel Pérez back in Chile. Did he live in Santiago?"

"Yeah, the last time I ever heard from him he wrote me from Santiago."

"Do you know where in Santiago. Did he live in Las Condes?"

By now Miguel's friends were impatient. Some pointed at their watches. Ángel waved them on.

"*Allez-y! J'y vais après!*"

He turned to me again and said, "This is amazing. I wonder if I know this Miguel. Tell me more about him. Where in Santiago did he write you from?"

"It was a postcard from the *Parque Cerro Santa Lucía.*"

"Yes, yes, that is very famous. Everyone knows it. Do you know where he lived?"

"No, I don't know anything else about what he did after he got to Chile. He and a couple of friends traveled there from Mexico."

"When was that?"

"It must have been 1971 or 1972. They went because of Allende."

Ángel's face darkened.

"Were they political?"

"Yeah, the other two guys were. They were students. One of them had been in Chile before. He had been involved in student protests in Mexico."

"Things got very bad for a lot of students mixed up in politics in 1973."

His face told me I might not want to get my hopes up.

"Lonnie, some of us are going to a café, you know, to have a drink or two. Why don't you come too?"

"Thanks. I don't want to intrude on you and your friends. I did what I needed to do. I just wanted to find out if you were my friend Antonio. At least now I know."

"Antonio?"

"Sorry, it's complicated. His name was actually Antonio. He was just using the name Miguel Pérez. It's a long story."

Ángel did some thinking.

"Antonio... Antonio... or maybe Miguel... from Mexico. Let me think. I know a lot of people in Santiago. I am sure if I think about it, I might remember something. I could write to some of my friends at home and ask them. You should come with me and have a drink. Besides, I do not get many chances to talk English with a *norteamericano*. Please come, Lonnie."

The smart thing would have been to say no. I felt guilty for misleading him, and it made me feel extremely weird every time he called me Lonnie. That was my own fault, of course, but there was nothing I could do about it now. I agreed to go to the café. After all, there was still some chance I could find out something about Antonio.

We walked several blocks to the café. The entire way Ángel talked a mile a minute. He definitely enjoyed talking in English.

"You know what I miss most about the United States? Root beer. You cannot get root beer in Chile—or in France. And you know what else I miss? Peanut butter. You can find it in France—*pâte d'arachide*—and also in Chile, but it is very expensive. And it doesn't taste the same. It's just not as good. It's too watery or something. Everything is just so much bigger and better in the U.S. Chile seems so backward in comparison. I was there during the whole Watergate scandal. We lived near Washington and that was all anybody talked about for months. I still cannot believe Nixon resigned."

I could barely get a word in edgewise, but I did not mind. I liked listening to him. It was obvious why Valérie would be in love with him. He was friendly and cheerful. He was enthusiastic about everything. I wanted to hate him, but it was impossible. It would have been easy to pretend he was Antonio after all.

"Tell me, Lonnie, who do you think is going to win the election?"

"The polls are saying President Carter will be re-elected."

"He is not well liked by the government in Chile. They think he talks way too much about human rights."

"I read there was a referendum in Chile."

"Yes, on Thursday there was a *plebiscito nacional—el once de septiembre*—the anniversary of the *golpe*, when Pinochet became president. We now have a new constitution. He will be president for at least eight more years."

"Is that why you are here and not in Chile?"

"What do you mean?"

"I know a lot of people had to leave Chile after the *golpe*. I thought maybe that is what happened to you."

We had arrived at the café, and our conversation was interrupted. The soccer players and their friends had taken over several tables. Most of them were drinking beers. Ángel introduced them all to his new friend Lonnie, and each one dutifully greeted me by saying, "*Salut.*" Cigarettes were passed around, and everyone went back to discussing the soccer match.

Ángel asked, "Do you speak much French, Lonnie?"

"I've picked up a little since I've been here, but not nearly enough. *Yo hablo mejor el español.*"

"*Ah, sí, tú hablas bastante bien el castellano. Dime, ¿qué haces tú en Burdeos?*"

That was another question I needed to avoid. What was I doing in Bordeaux? I made up a story about coming to France on a vacation. I said I was just bumming around the country.

"*¿Y para quién sacabas tú las fotos de nuestro match de fútbol?*"

He had seen me shooting photos at the game and, naturally, wanted to know why. I made up something about being a serious soccer fan. I prayed he would not test my actual knowledge of the game. My accumulation of lies continued to grow. Fortunately, he seemed to accept everything at face value. He was not the least bit suspicious.

He asked more questions about Antonio. I did not have much more to tell him. He was sure, if he could spread the word among friends and family in Santiago, someone would know something.

After a while people in the group began to leave. Ángel and I talked until there was no one else.

"I am in no hurry to go home," he said. "My girlfriend is away for a few days, and I am lonely. I miss her a lot."

"Believe me, I know exactly what you mean."

"*¿Tú tienes una polola? ¿Por qué no vino ella contigo a Francia?*"

No matter how much Spanish I learned, there was always one more word I had never heard before.

"What's a *polola*?"

"Sorry, that's our word for girlfriend. Your Spanish is pretty good, but I will have to teach you *chileno*."

Eventually it got dark, and I wondered how much longer the café would be open.

"Well, you probably want to go home, Ángel. It was good to meet you. Thanks for offering to help me find my friend."

"Wait, I must get your address—so I can write to you if I find out anything about your friend."

He went over to the counter for a piece of paper and a pencil. It was hard not to trip myself up with all my lies. If I wrote my address, I would have to write my name. What address should I give him? I was now technically homeless. I had come to France with the intention of not going home again. Of course, that idea was completely crazy. It had taken only a couple of days on my own to realize how unrealistic it was. I probably knew all along I would not be staying in France. After all, I never bothered giving notice to my apartment manager or closing the accounts for electricity and telephone. So much for fresh starts.

He came back to the table and put the paper and pencil in front of me. I wrote, "Lonnie McKay, c/o Green" followed by my address in the city.

"Green?" he wondered, as he looked at it.

"Yeah I'm, uh, subletting. I just wrote it like that to make sure it gets to me if you write. Well, I guess I'll be going now."

"Where are you staying?"

"Well, I don't exactly have a place yet, but I'll find something in the city."

"Why don't you stay with me? I have a room, not too far from here. It's not very big, but you can stay there tonight if you want."

"That's really nice of you, but I don't want to impose on you."

"*Huevón*," he said, "*no es ninguna imposición, yo te aseguro.*"

Another word I had never heard.

"*¿Qué quiere decir* 'way bone'*?*"

"Sorry, it's just a word I use sometimes with my friends. It is somebody with very big, you know…"

He gestured toward his crotch.

"*Huevos*. But I don't mean it like that. It's just what you call someone when you are, you know, *amigos*."

"That's nice of you, Ángel. Really. It's just not a good idea."

He had become emphatic.

"*No seas tonto, huevón.* You are going to stay with me tonight. You will keep me from being too lonely for my girlfriend."

I had no other place to go, after all, and I did not particularly relish the idea of checking into a hotel by myself. Against my better judgment, I went along with him. We walked several blocks to where he lived. He continued talking a mile a minute.

"You know, it's funny you thought I was someone you used to know in the U.S. because, when you called my name, I thought for a minute you were a guy I knew from my high school in Virginia. He and I were best friends. I always wondered what happened to him. So, it was strange you thought I was your friend from long ago. *Es bastante extraño, ¿no?*"

"Yeah, I can't believe all the coincidences in my life. But they never quite turn out to be the ones I think they're going to be."

We arrived at the place where he lived. It was a large house, but he had just one of the rooms. It had its own entrance from a side garden. The room was small. There was one bed, its size about halfway between a single and a double.

I said, "Thanks for letting me crash here. I'll find someplace on the floor to sleep."

"*No seas tonto, huevón,*" he said. "The bed is big enough. There is room for both of us."

I had learned from Antonio how relaxed Latin Americans were about being close to one another. My night with Justin aside, I still found it weird to be in a bed with another guy, especially one I had met only a few hours before.

"It's okay. I'll be fine on the floor."

"What is your problem, *huevón*? Sleep in the bed like a civilized person."

"Doesn't it make you feel strange to sleep so close to someone you barely know?"

"No, why should it?"

"You don't know me that well. Did I tell you I live in San Francisco? How do you know I'm not gay or something?"

He laughed.

"*Huevón, tú no eres ninguna cola.*"

"How can you be so sure?"

"Because I can tell. If I was exciting you, I would definitely know it."

"Maybe you're just not my type."

He lost patience with me. He pulled his tee-shirt over his head to reveal his perfect shoulders and chest.

"*Huevón,*" he laughed, "I am *everybody's* type."

God, how I wished I had his confidence.

I gave up. We lost our jeans and got into the bed. I hugged my edge, trying not to brush against him accidentally. Ángel had no such concerns. As he fell asleep, he stretched in every direction at once. One of his hairy ankles landed on top of mine, and it tickled. I wondered if he did it deliberately as a way of teasing me, but it was more likely simply random. He was not the least bit self-conscious about sharing the bed. He was only making himself comfortable.

As I fell asleep, I did not mind the weight of his leg on mine. It kept away my dread of night. Moreover, I got an unexpected charge from the physical contact. As I drifted off, I could only think about how my leg was touching a leg that on numerous nights had touched Valérie's leg.

25
Armagnac

"LONNIE!"

I tried to figure out where the voice was coming from.

"Hey, Lonnie! Wake up! Are you dead or something?"

I mumbled. "Who wants to know?"

"*¡Hombre, despierta!* I have to go to class. Are you going to be okay here by yourself?"

"Yeah, yeah, no problem."

"Okay. I will see you later. I should be back in a couple hours. Help yourself to *desayuno*. Have anything you can find. *Tú tienes tu casa acá, ¿entiendes?*"

"Yeah, I understand. Thanks for everything, Ángel."

"And don't leave before I get back."

"I won't."

I had been exhausted. I had slept the entire night without waking even once. That was unheard of for me. I must have needed to catch up on a lot of sleep. I got dressed and checked out the tiny kitchen in the corner of Ángel's room. After some trial and error, I finally figured out how to work the little Italian coffee maker sitting on the stove. I made myself a small cup of inky black coffee. I munched some crispy fresh bread. I could still not get over the incredibly rich taste of French butter. The strawberry *confiture* was better than American jam.

I thought, *My life just keeps getting weirder. How in the world did I end up sharing a bed with Valérie's lover? This is just asking for trouble. I have to get out of here while the getting is good.*

The strange thing was that I liked Ángel a lot. I wished things were different and that he and I could be friends. In ways, being around him was a little bit like having Lonnie back and a little bit like having Antonio back. Against my better judgment, I decided that I would not take off just yet. I would hang around just a bit longer and hope that he did not find out who I was and that I had lied to him.

I killed the time as best I could, waiting for Ángel to come back. In addition to the plate and cup I had used for breakfast, there were a few dirty dishes in the sink. I decided to wash and dry them. The dish soap had a nice lemon scent.

I snooped around his bookshelf, looking for something I might be able to read. Judging from his textbooks, I guessed he was studying architecture. I could not find any books not in French. On a shelf there was a folder full of papers. I flipped through them. A lot of them seemed to be class notes, but there were also quite a few pencil drawings. Many were sketches that all seemed to be of the same guy—a muscular hero type in a loincloth and a red cape. He had long black hair and wore a cap with feathers. The drawings depicted him in various heroic stances, always holding a spear. Sometimes there was a medallion hanging from his neck. Some handwritten pages were interspersed among the drawings. They were poems in Spanish. Only one appeared completely finished. Its title was *La Lanza de Lautaro*.

I sat a long time, looking at the sketches and reading the poems. I was impressed by how good the drawings were. They reminded me of superhero comic books Lonnie and I read as kids and took me back to a time when we worshipped bigger-than-life heroes. I wanted to know about the man in the cape. Who was he and what was his story? Obviously, he was a warrior, but who was he fighting and what was he fighting for? In one drawing he embraced a woman. At the bottom of that sheet was written, *Lautaro y Guacolda*. Maybe it was just my own imagination, but I thought the two of them bore a resemblance to Ángel and Valérie. As much as I hated to admit it, the two of them looked good together.

My snooping was interrupted by a knock on the door. I opened it, and a short, round, white-haired woman jabbered at me. I had no idea what she said, but she was very cross about something. My limited number of French words were no help, so I played a game of charades in an effort to let her know Ángel would be back soon. Frustrated by my inability to understand her, she left.

Not long after, Ángel appeared.

"Good," he said. "You are still here. I was afraid you would go before I returned. *¿Cómo te ha ido?*"

"Great," I said. "I appreciate you letting me stay here. Oh, by the way, your landlady came by a little while ago. She seemed to be really unhappy about something."

"Yeah, she's always unhappy about something. Don't worry. I will talk to her. Do you want to have lunch?"

"Okay, but only if I can buy."

"We can go to the *restaurant étudiant*, you know, the school cafeteria."

Ángel enjoyed remembering his American high school days.

We walked to the campus and joined the lunch line. The cafeteria was on the second floor of a modern, almost futuristic-looking, building. They were serving sauerkraut with some kind of strange black sausage and boiled potatoes.

"What's this?" I asked, not sure if I could eat it.

"It is *boudin noir*," he said. "*Pudín negro, en castellano.* I'm not sure what it's called in English."

"¿*Pudín?* Pudding? Black pudding? It sure doesn't look like pudding to me."

There were endless amounts of bread in large metal bowls in various locations. There was also water in glass pitchers, but I bought us a couple of small bottles of wine. I thought this was great. You definitely could not buy wine on campus at Cal State.

"Is this where you always eat?"

"Mostly. It's not the greatest food, but it's very cheap."

Being on campus with him only highlighted how young he was—not only compared to me but compared to Valérie. I wondered if he ever took her to the student cafeteria.

"I keep trying to remember anything that might have to do with your friend in Santiago. I just cannot remember meeting anybody from Mexico—at least not someone my age."

"Thanks for trying, Ángel. At least you have my address. If you do remember something later or if you hear anything from someone in Chile, you can write me. I should be moving on now. Thanks again for letting me crash."

"*Huevon, ¿por qué tanta prisa?* What's your hurry? Stick around for a few days. I can show you some places in Bordeaux. We can eat tonight at l'Entrecôte. You get a very good steak there. Besides, my *polola* will be back in a few days. You should meet her."

"That's nice of you, but I don't think you'll really want me around when you and your girlfriend have your big reunion."

He laughed.

"Hey, I would not kick you out because of that. Besides, she and I can go to her place. Seriously, you should stay. You are curing my loneliness. You don't have anywhere else you have to be, do you?"

"Yeah, as a matter of fact I do. I have to go to Berlin. In fact, I should have been there already."

His eyes lit up.

"Berlin? Really?"

"Yeah. I told someone I would do them a favor there."

"That's amazing."

"Why?"

"I have something that needs to be delivered in Berlin. I should go with you."

This was unexpected.

"Sure, just give it to me. If I know where to take it, I can deliver it for you."

"That would be great. This is something I should have done already, but I needed someone to deliver it for me. I cannot deliver it myself."

"Why can't you deliver it yourself?"

"It has to be delivered in person, and it has to be delivered someplace I cannot go."

"You're being kind of mysterious."

"Sorry, I do not mean to be. Are you finished eating? Let's go for a walk."

We went outside

"Let's walk into the city," said Ángel. "It's a nice day, and I do not have any more classes today. It takes about an hour to go there on foot. I can show you some of the sights of Bordeaux."

"Sure. Sounds good to me."

I thought the purpose of the walk would be to discuss his mysterious delivery in Berlin, but instead he talked about anything and everything other than that.

"You know, Lonnie, life is funny," he said. "What are the chances you and I would meet here in Bordeaux? I am glad we did, though. When I lived in Virginia, I had a very good friend. He and I could talk about anything together. He was the one person I would never have to keep a secret from. We never had to be embarrassed around each other. You know what I mean? It was like we always knew what each other was thinking. I am sure you have a friend like that."

"Yeah, I do know what you mean."

"I miss him very much. The same way you miss your friend Antonio. We said we would keep in touch always. We wrote to each other a few times after I moved away from there, but after a while, the letters were less frequent and finally they just stopped. I always regretted that. I think about him and wonder where he is or what he is doing now. It is sad to leave friends behind."

"Do you still have his address? Why don't you write him?"

"I should. Maybe I will. The funny thing is, you remind me of him—a lot. Being around you is almost like having him back. Is that strange?"

"No, I understand. Even though you aren't Antonio, you still remind me of him. Being around you is kind of like having him back."

"That is good. Since I have lived in France, I have not had a best friend."

"What about…"

I barely caught myself. I nearly said Valérie's name, which would have been awkward since he had yet to mention it to me.

"What about your girlfriend?"

He smiled sheepishly.

"Yes, you are right. She is my best friend. An *amiga* is definitely better than an *amigo*."

He winked at me.

"There are some things a woman cannot understand about a man. Just like there are things a man cannot understand about a woman. A good friendship between two men is special, just as a good friendship between a man and a woman is special. There are some things a man can only say to another man. There are also things a man should never say to a woman. *¿Me entiendes?*"

"Yeah, I understand. I understand you exactly."

When we got to the city center, he took me everywhere. He showed me a very tall, very old Gothic tower and joked, "That is my tower. *La Flèche Saint-Michel.*" He showed me the church with the big clock I had seen after arriving and told me it was called the *Grosse Cloche*. He took me down la rue Sainte-Catherine and said quietly, in a seriously confidential manner, "At night this is where you find *las putas*." He paused in front of a glass window and announced, "*Mon amour* Valérie works here."

It was the first time I heard him say her name. It broke a spell. Until he had actually said it, I could hold on to the crazy hope his girlfriend's name would turn out not to be Valérie. I could fantasize it was all some misunderstanding and he was not really Valérie's lover.

He showed me the Palais Gallien, the ruins left over from Roman times. As we looked at it, the sky opened up and dropped buckets of water on us.

"It must be five o'clock," he said.

We ran to find a place that was sheltered. I looked at my watch. It was indeed just a few minutes past five.

"Why five o'clock?"

"I don't know. For some reason, it always rains at five o'clock. After a few minutes, it will stop. It is very strange."

He was right. About ten minutes later the driving rain stopped suddenly and the sky was again blue. If not for the wet sidewalks, it would have been hard to believe it had rained at all. Ángel and I walked a few blocks. We came to a wide open area dominated by a large building with columns.

"This is le Grand Théâtre," he said. "You can see plays here. And ballets and opera and all the culture you desire."

He led me across the street to a restaurant nestled tightly between a brasserie and a bank.

"This is l'Entrecôte. This is where we will have dinner."

There was a line all the way out onto the street. I wondered how long it would take to get in and whether it would be worth the wait. It did not, however, turn out to be that long. We were bustled into a crowded room and seated at a long table with everyone else. It was not unlike a Basque restaurant in East Bakersfield.

"When we get our menus," I said, "maybe you can suggest something for me to order. I don't have much experience with French restaurants."

"There are no menus."

"No menus?"

"No menus. You have only one decision to make. *À point* or *saignant*."

"What does that mean?"

Ángel laughed.

"Medium or medium rare. There are no other choices."

"I want mine well done."

"And ruin an extraordinary cut of meat by overcooking it? *¡Vergüenza!*"

"Hey, I'm sorry, but I can't eat meat that's still bleeding."

"*Ay, sobre el gusto no hay nada escrito.*"

"There is nothing written about taste? What does that mean?"

He laughed.

"It is something we say. Like the French say *à chacun ses goûts*. What do you say in English? To each his own? We agree to disagree? You know, the great thing about the English language is that it has so many clichés. I am amazed I remember so many of them."

Ángel had not lied. The only question we were asked was how we wanted our steaks cooked. At Ángel's urging, I agreed to have mine *à point*. Soon after, I had one of the best steaks I had ever had in my life.

"Amigo, I have to admit you were right. I don't think I will be ordering my meat well done after this. At least not if the steak is as good as this."

"Yes, if you can eat the meat only when it is over-cooked, then you should be eating different meat. Or you should learn to cook it yourself."

There was also an endless supply of French fries, and the bottles of red wine were bottomless.

"This is a great place!" I said.

"*Es fantástico, no?*"

"I like this wine. I see why everybody always goes on about Bordeaux wine."

"Yes, it is good, but in my heart I would prefer a nice *vino tinto* from *el Valle de Colchagua*. Chile has some of the best wine in the world."

"That right? Well, they grow quite a few wine grapes where I am from too. The San Joaquin Valley may not have any famous wineries like Napa Valley, but they sure grow a lot of grapes."

Ángel raised his glass. I did the same.

"To good wine," he said, "wherever we can find it—Chile, California or Bordeaux."

We stuffed ourselves on red meat, *pommes frites* and claret. Afterwards we wandered down the Allées de Tourny to a café. Ángel said we needed a *digestif.*

"You have to have an Armagnac."

"What's that?"

"It's brandy. A very nice brandy. Better than Cognac. Armagnac is a place not too far from here. Actually, Cognac is also a place not too far from here. First we will have an espresso. Then we will have Armagnac."

The espresso was indeed followed by a brandy. That was followed by another brandy.

"I'm really starting to like France," I said, enjoying a nice feeling of lightheadedness.

"Yes," said Ángel. "There are so many nice things in France. And they are all nicer when you are with someone who appreciates them with you."

After the third Armagnac, we somehow had the sense to know we should go back and get some sleep.

"We have a choice," said Ángel. "We can wait at the Place de la Victoire and go *a dedo…*"

He held up his thumb.

"Or, if we want to waste our money, we can take a taxi. It would be very far to walk the whole way back."

"I say, we go *a pie*. I think the walk would do us good."

"*A pie* it is," said Ángel.

We made our way down the narrow winding streets to Talence. Along the way, Ángel became more talkative than ever.

"Did I mention my *polola* is eight years older than me?"

"No, I don't think you mentioned that."

"Well, she is. That is a big difference between us, don't you think, Lonnie?"

"Well, yes, but did I mention my last girlfriend was seven years older than me?"

"Really? How did it work out?"

"It was great while it lasted, but it was not very good at the end. None of that had anything to do with the age difference, though. It had more to do with the fact she was married."

"Married? You were with a married woman? *¡Ay, huevón! ¡Qué atrevido estuviste!* You are more dangerous than you look."

We were now so tired and drunk we were practically leaning on each other to keep from falling over. We made a couple of stops along the way to relieve ourselves on the walls of buildings. We passed down a particularly dark street. Ángel looked up to the sky, and I did the same. The clouds had cleared, and we could see stars.

"That's Ursa Major and Ursa Minor, and that's the North Star. I learned to recognize them when I lived in Virginia. We cannot see them in Chile."

"You can't see the dippers in Chile?"

"No, they're too far north. Just like here you cannot see *la Cruz del Sur*. Sometimes when I look up at the sky and I cannot see it, it makes me lonely. It reminds me how far away from home I am."

He had that slightly sad, faraway look again, the one he got when talking about his country.

"Lonnie, I think she might be tired of me."

"Valérie? Why?"

"I don't know. She went to Deauville to a film festival. She goes there every year. This year for some reason she stayed longer. Then she went to Bretagne. She lived there when she was a little girl. Somehow I just know she did not go there alone. I don't know how I know, but I know."

"She didn't tell you why she went there?"

"No. She was very mysterious about it."

"Well, if she used to live there, she probably went to Brest to see old friends or something."

Ángel was starting to wobble as he walked.

"How did you know she went to Brest?"

"Didn't you say that's where she went?"

"No. At least I don't think I did. *Ay hombre*, I am so *borracho* I can't remember what I've been saying now. Maybe we are such good friends now you can read my mind. All I know is I am very much in love with this woman. I do not want to lose her. *¿Me cachas?*"

He used my shoulder to steady himself.

"Yeah, I catch you. Trust me, I know exactly what you are feeling. Don't worry. You're the one she really loves."

"So, you think there is someone else?"

"I think, when she comes back, she will have a very good explanation why she went to Brest. I think you can count on that."

"You are a very good friend. You say the right things to make me feel better. I cannot wait for her to come back."

"Don't worry *amigo*. She'll be back before you know it. You'll feel silly you were ever worried about any of this."

I could not bear to see him sad. In any case, I had no doubt I was telling him the truth. Of course, she would come back to him and the two of them would continue as before. Boy did my life suck. At least I had discovered Armagnac. My time in France had not been a complete waste.

I struggled to stay awake while we walked. Ángel, on the other hand, still had plenty of energy despite being drunk. He looked ready to go on all night.

"Aren't you tired, amigo? I feel like I'm walking in my sleep."

"*Los chilenos somos como los gatos.* We are like cats. Night is our time."

It took forever to get to Ángel's place. Once there, we collapsed onto the bed and fell asleep.

26
Trains

"HEY, LONNIE! Wake up!"

I was by now so very sorry I had ever told Ángel my name was Lonnie. I should have picked a name at random. No, I should have just told him my real name and dealt with the consequences. Did I not realize how much being called Lonnie would get on my nerves? I imagined the real Lonnie out there somewhere having a really good laugh at my expense.

The room was dark.

"I'm sorry," I said, "but didn't we go to bed, like, only five minutes ago?"

"No," he laughed. "It's been a couple of hours. We need to get up early."

"We do? Why?"

"If we go to the train station early, we might be able to travel to Berlin today."

"Today?"

"Yes. Why wait? You said you should have been there already. The sooner we go, the sooner we will come back. By the time we get back, Valérie will be home."

After all the walking the previous day and the Armagnac, I did not feel like getting out of bed.

"We? Are you going too? Don't you have classes?"

"They're no big deal. They are only beginning now. I can miss a few days."

"What about soccer, I mean football? Don't you have practices?"

"No, Sunday was our final match. We have finished for the year. In fact, I am finished with soccer forever now—at least at this school."

"Don't you want to be waiting for Valérie when she gets back?"

"Yes, but I have been thinking. Maybe it is a good idea if I am not here when she arrives. I should not act too eager to see her. After all, she has been keeping me waiting. She is the one who did not come home after the film festival. She should learn how it feels to be kept waiting."

"Man, if it was me, I'd be down there at the train station an hour early waiting for her to get in. I wouldn't be taking off for Germany and giving her more time for second thoughts."

"*Huevón*, she's my girlfriend, not yours, but you are probably right. The thing is, this delivery to Berlin is important."

"If it's so important, why haven't you delivered it already?"

"Because I cannot deliver it myself. I need you to do it."

"Why me?"

"You have a U.S. passport, right?"

"Yeah."

"You can cross from West Berlin to East Berlin to visit for a day. That is something I cannot do."

"What do you need delivered in East Berlin?"

"It is personal, a family matter. Will you do it for me?"

"Okay, I guess, but if I'm the one delivering it, why do you need to come?"

"Because I have to take it as far as I can. I am the one responsible for it. *Es un deber.* It is a duty."

"And what is 'it' exactly?"

"It is a letter. A letter that cannot go through the mail."

"A letter to who?"

"It is a long story. Like I said, it's a family thing."

"And you're bound and determined to do this?"

"Yes. It should have been done already."

I had mixed feelings. The smart thing would definitely be to separate myself from Ángel as quickly and distantly as possible. At the rate I was going, it would be only a matter of time before he found out I was not Lonnie McKay, that I was the guy doing my best to steal his *polola* in Deauville. The problem was that he had become almost instantly the best friend I had made in a very long time. We were having a great time together, and I did not want it to end. Traveling to Berlin with him would definitely be a lot less boring and lonely than going by myself. He also knew French and was obviously familiar with traveling in Europe.

"Okay. So, the two of us will go. Let's see about getting those train tickets."

Ángel broke into a grin.

"This is going to be great. *¡Lo vamos a pasar regio!* When we come back, you can meet Valérie."

He grabbed one of the books on his shelf. It was *Martín Rivas* by somebody called Alberto Blest Gana. He opened it and retrieved some cash stashed between the pages, explaining it was there for just such a contingency.

He threw his toothbrush, razor, passport, and a few clothes into a backpack. We took the bus downtown and walked the rest of the way to the train station. As usual, there were lines of people everywhere. When we finally got to a window, I let Ángel do all the talking. After several minutes of conversation and counting out cash, we walked away with our tickets.

"The train for Paris departs in about one hour. We have tickets for the night train from Gare de l'Est."

"Man, we're going to spend a *lot* of time on trains the next twenty-four hours," I said, looking at the printed details on the tickets and belatedly appreciating the distances involved. "What are we going to do all that time?"

"Drink!" he said with a grin.

Yes, in some ways Ángel was definitely more like Lonnie than Antonio.

The trip to Paris was uneventful. We passed through all the same places I had seen three days earlier—Angoulême, Poitiers, Tours, Orléans. We had bought a deck of playing cards in the train station's shop, and we spent much of the time drinking beer and playing cards. I taught Ángel how to play hearts. He taught me how to play carioca. I taught him how to play gin. When we were tired of those games, we played a few hands of poker. Ángel was surprisingly good at it. Luckily, we had decided to keep the stakes low. Otherwise, he would have totally cleaned me out.

"There's an interesting version of this game," I said. "It's called strip poker. With your talent for cards, you should definitely try it."

"Yes, I remember that from my time in Virginia. I only got to play it with guys, though. You and I need to have a game with some *niñas*. That would be *fantástico*. Hey, want to hear a joke?"

"Sure."

"I don't know if it will be as funny in English as it is in *castellano*."

"I'll be the judge of that. Just tell the damn joke."

"Two men are on a train, going across the Andes from Chile to Argentina. One man asks the other, 'Are we in Argentina yet?' The other man looks at his wristwatch and says, 'No.' Ten minutes later the man asks the same question again. 'Are we in Argentina yet?' The other man looks at his watch and says, 'No.' Ten minutes later he asks the same question."

"Yeah, yeah. I get the idea. Hurry up with the joke."

"Okay. Finally the man asks, 'Are we in Argentina yet?' And the other man looks at his wrist and says, 'Yes, we are in Argentina.' And the first man says, 'And you know that because of the time?' And the other man says, 'No. I know because my watch has been stolen.' "

"And why is that funny?"

"*Huevón*, it is funny because everyone knows *argentinos* are thieves!"

"Yeah, right. That's good to know."

As we continued to play our card game, I asked him, "Who's Lautaro?"

"You know about Lautaro?"

"I saw your drawings and poems in your room. I hope you don't mind. The sketches were very good. Is he someone you made up?"

He laughed.

"No. Your question confused me at first because I didn't know why you were asking. You see, my father's name is Lautaro."

"Your father goes around half-naked with a cape?"

He laughed again.

"No, the drawings are of the real Lautaro, I mean the first one. My father was named after him. A lot of boys in Chile are named after him. He was a leader of the Mapuches who fought against Spanish invaders in the sixteenth century. He won many battles against the Spaniards, but he was not able to liberate his country. They ambushed him. They cut off his head and put it on display in the middle of Santiago. He died exactly four-hundred years before I was born. On the very same day, April 30."

"Did you write the poem?"

"*¿La Lanza de Lautaro?* Yes, I wrote it. It is not very good. Pablo Neruda wrote a much better poem about Lautaro. There's also a very long poem that tells about him—*La Araucana* by Alonso de Ercilla. Every student in Chile studies it. I have always been fascinated by Lautaro. Maybe it's because of my birthday, or maybe it is because of my father's name. Lautaro spent his whole life trying to liberate his country—even to the point of pain and death. For me, that is what it means to be a hero."

Ángel's face again had that look of sadness and regret. For me, events in Chile seemed very far away and kind of unreal. For him, it was reality. I felt bad for him.

Once again my thoughts turned to Antonio. What was his life like in Chile? Did he go to school? Did he learn about Lautaro? Did he become inspired by him? I wondered when Antonio's birthday was.

It felt like forever before the train pulled into the Montparnasse train station.

"Now what?" I asked Ángel as we stepped off the train.

"We take the Metro to Gare de l'Est. I hope you are ready for a long walk. The Metro line is a long way from here."

It was good to travel with someone who knew his way.

"This place is huge. So, we'll get to the other train station without having to go above ground?"

"Yes."

"I can't believe this is my third time in Paris and I've still barely seen anything at all above the ground. I feel like I haven't seen any of this city at all. About the only thing I knew about Paris before I came here was that Jim Morrison is buried here. My friend Lon..."

I caught myself just in time.

"A friend of mine always used to say, if he ever got to France, he would go find Jim Morrison's grave and get drunk there. I kind of had it in my head that I would do that at some point while I was here. You know, in his memory."

"There will be lots of time for things like that on the way back," said Ángel sympathetically. "We can do whatever we want after finishing our business in Berlin."

"Yeah, I suppose, but it just seems weird I still haven't even seen the Eiffel Tower."

"You have never seen *la tour Eiffel?*"

"No, I haven't seen much at all. For all I have been able to see, Paris is just a bunch of tunnels and underground trains."

Ángel looked at his watch and made a calculation.

"Okay. I am changing the plan. Follow me."

I raced to keep up as he went off in a different direction. Our long walk ended at another train platform. We waited for the train to arrive.

"This will take longer to get to Gare de l'Est," he said. "Line 4 would have taken us there directly. Now we will have to change two times."

The train pulled in. We pushed and shoved our way into the train car.

"So, why are we going this way? What difference does it make which underground train we take to get where we are going?"

He smiled.

"Because not all of these trains are underground. At least not all of the time."

The train made its way through the dark tunnels, stopping every few minutes at a station. I was delighted when the train emerged into the early Paris evening. There was not much of a view at first because of the surrounding buildings, but then we crossed a bridge over the river. Off to the right, it was there as big as life. Looking just like every photo I had ever seen of it, the Eiffel Tower was all lit up. It was an amazing sight.

"I finally feel like I've been in Paris," I said. "*Un millón de gracias, amigo.*"

Soon the train descended back underground. When we got to the Trocadéro station, Ángel led me to another station to get on another train. I hoped it would go above ground like the other one, but it didn't. A bunch of stations went by, but they didn't mean anything to me—except one. The second station after we left Trocadéro was called Franklin D. Roosevelt.

"How the heck did an American president get a Paris train station named after him?"

"I think it might have had something to do with the Second World War."

After five more stops, we changed trains again. Four more stops after that, we were at Gare de l'Est. We made our way up the stairs.

I muttered, "I think it's taking longer to get from one end of Paris to the other than it will to go from Paris to Berlin."

Ángel had worried about taking time for our scenic tour of the Paris Metro system, but in the end we had about a half-hour to spare once we got to the platform for our train to Germany. Once it pulled in, we engaged in the usual pushing and shoving to board our designated car. Ángel scanned the numbers to find our compartment. Two seats were already taken by women in their early twenties. We nodded politely and shoved our backpacks onto the overhead racks. After we took our seats, there were still two empty seats in the compartment. I hoped that they would stay empty. I had gotten tired of being surround by so many people. At the last minute before the train pulled out, a young guy rushed into the compartment and took one of the remaining seats. He was tall and skinny with an unruly mop of curly blond hair and a bad case of acne. He had barely sat when the train began to move slowly.

The compartment was quiet at first. I suppose everyone was self-conscious since anything that anyone said was heard by all of us. Finally after a while, the two women began to talk quietly. Ángel and I looked at each other and laughed upon realizing they were speaking Spanish.

With the ease of a natural flirt, Ángel asked them, "*¿De dónde son ustedes?*"

"*Yo soy de California,*" said the black-haired one.

"*Y yo soy de Alemania,*" said the blonde one.

"California? Really? I'm from California."

"Really? Where?"

"Near Bakersfield. Where are you from?"

"L.A., the valley."

"So, why are you two talking in Spanish?" asked Ángel.

"Annaliese speaks hardly any English. We both study Spanish, so that is how we have always talked to each other. Where are you from?" she asked Ángel.

"*Yo soy chileno.*"

"Chile? Really? Cool."

"*¿Y cómo te llamas tú?*"

"Yolanda. *¿Y tú?*"

"Miguel Ángel."

"*Qué lindo nombre.*"

Ángel and Yolanda were really hitting it off. I prayed silently they would fall in love and solve all my problems. It would be perfect. He could go off with her, and I could have Valérie for myself.

Yolanda turned her attention to me.

"And what's your name?"

I had "Dallas" halfway out of my mouth before I froze. Using a false name was increasingly inconvenient.

"Lonnie. Lonnie McKay."

She looked at me curiously.

"There's something familiar about that name. I'm not sure why. Have we ever met before? Maybe somewhere in California?"

"I don't think so. I'm pretty sure I would remember you."

"You're right. I don't recognize you from anywhere. I probably just met someone once who had the same name."

Could she actually have met Lonnie—my Lonnie—sometime? The odds seemed pretty slim but, given the weird coincidences that sometimes happened to me, it could not be ruled out entirely.

"*Es tut mir leid,*" laughed Annaliese. "*aber ich verstehe fast nichts.*"

The teenaged guy, who had said nothing up to this point, perked up.

"*Bist du aus Deutschland?*"

"*Ja! Und du?*"

"*Ich bin Schweizer.*"

A strange kind of conversation among the five of us had begun. It shifted from one language to another, as we animatedly discussed anything and everything through the evening. There was no one language we all understood, so the train compartment became a self-contained Tower of Babel. All of us except the Swiss guy—we learned his name was Andreas—could speak Spanish, but I had trouble keeping up with Ángel and Yolanda.

Annaliese's Spanish was better than mine. If we spoke English, three of us had no problem but then Annaliese had trouble keeping up. Ángel and Annaliese were close to fluent in French, but that did not help Yolanda and me. No matter what language we spoke, Annaliese had to translate everything for Andreas. Consequently, the language being spoken shifted continually, depending on who was talking and who else was most interested in the current topic.

Yolanda and Annaliese, we learned, had been friends for years. They had met as students in a summer abroad course at the University of Seville. Yolanda was now nearing the end of a summer visit with Annaliese and her family in Munich. The two friends had spent the holidays working in a restaurant owned by Annaliese's parents. With the summer over, the two women had gone to Paris for a Peter Gabriel concert. Now they were going to Berlin to check out the music scene there.

Talking about the restaurant in Munich led to a discussion of European food.

"You know what I miss here?" said Yolanda. "Menudo and tamales."

"I know exactly what you mean," I said. "I would give anything for a plate of enchiladas de mole poblano right now. Or some chile rellenos."

"What are enchiladas?" asked Ángel.

"What? You have to know what enchiladas are."

"Why?"

"Because… I don't know… It just seems like you should. How do you not know what enchiladas are? You know about tacos, right?"

"A taco is the thing on the bottom of your shoe."

"This doesn't make any sense. How do you not know about…"

"About what?"

"You know, Mexican food."

"Because I'm not a Mexican."

Yolanda was laughing at the two of us.

"What do you eat in Chile then?"

"*Cazuela de ave, empanadas*, things like that."

"You must eat chiles," I said. "After all, that's the name of the country."

"Chiles? You mean, *ají*?"

"Man, it's weird to think of a country where they speak Spanish, but they don't have Mexican food."

"There are lots of countries that speak Spanish besides Mexico, *huevón*."

"And you never had Mexican food when you lived in Virginia?"

"Not that I remember."

220

Yolanda and Annaliese had been exchanging looks. Finally Yolanda asked her, "*¿Deberíamos sacar la botella?*"

"*Sí,*" said Annaliese, "*¿cómo no?*"

Yolanda reached into her bag very carefully, almost nervously. She pulled out a bottle.

Studying the label, she said, "Has anybody heard of Strathspey?"

27
More Old Scotch

I THOUGHT I was hearing things.

"Did you say Strathspey?"

"Yes. Do you know it?"

"That is actually Scotch from Strathspey?"

"Yes. You must be some kind of whiskey expert. I never heard of it before."

"Where did you get it?"

I looked around apprehensively. I half-expected Marty to appear out of nowhere and tell me this was part of a set-up.

"Annaliese's father gave it to us. It was our reward for working in the restaurant all summer. It's supposed to be very expensive."

"Is it twenty-five years old?"

She looked at the label.

"No, it's only twelve years old."

"What proof is it?"

She looked again.

"Eighty-four."

Okay, so this was not the super-expensive stuff Marty had let me drink at his house, but it was no doubt still pretty pricey.

Yolanda said, "You definitely must know your whiskeys. Want to try some?"

"That's some really good stuff. I mean, *really* good. Are you sure you want to open it here?"

"*Warum nicht?*" said Annaliese.

She winked at Andreas, who was keenly trying to follow the conversation about the bottle.

Yolanda handed me the bottle.

"Here. You open it."

I removed the foil from the top of the bottle. It had a cork, like a bottle of wine. I stared at it, wondering how I would get it out. Eager Andreas, however, was at the ready. As quick as a flash, he reached into his pocket and produced a Swiss army knife. Among its several blades was a corkscrew. Clutching the bottle between my knees, I yanked the knife's handle with both hands. With some persistence, the cork was freed.

"*No tenemos vasos,*" said Yolanda.

"*Podemos pasarlo no más,*" said Annaliese. "*Boca a boca. ¿Alguien tiene miedo de las bacterias?*"

So, it was decided, in the absence of drinking glasses, we would pass the bottle around.

"You first," said Yolanda to me, sounding a bit apprehensive.

"No problem," I said. "*¡Salud!*"

I lifted the bottle and took a few drops in my mouth. Though this whiskey was thirteen years younger than the Scotch Marty had given me, I could tell no difference. The smoky, burning sensation was as painful yet pleasurable as before. I shuddered involuntarily.

"Man," I said, "that's some fine liquor."

I passed the bottle to Yolanda. She opted to pass it instead to Annaliese. With no hesitation, she took her swallow. A pleasant smile came over her face.

"*Mein Gott, ist das gut!*"

It next went to Ángel who, being a gentleman, passed it instead back to Yolanda.

"*Yo no tomo hasta que tú tomes,*" he said firmly.

Obediently, she raised the bottle cautiously to her lips. She coughed as if she were going to choke. Then she laughed.

"It burns!"

Ángel took back the bottle and had his sip. His face glowed.

"*¡Regio! ¡A la pinta!*"

He tentatively offered the bottle to Andreas but then paused.

"*¿Tiene edad suficiente para tomar?*" he asked Annaliese.

Andreas had been following the whiskey discussion and subsequent partaking with fervent interest. His face darkened with disappointment as the bottle stopped just out of reach. Annaliese asked him his age and was satisfied.

"*Está bien,*" she said to Ángel.

Without a moment's hesitation, Andreas happily grasped the bottle. He took a swallow probably larger than he intended. His face turned red, as he recovered from his coughing fit.

"Thank you for generously sharing your whiskey," said Ángel to the two women. "That was very nice."

"*¿Tendremos otra ronda?*" offered Annaliese.

No one protested. We passed the bottle around again. The whiskey loosened our tongues even more. Our chaotic multi-language conversation was now more enthusiastic. We learned Andreas had recently disappointed his parents by deciding not to go to university. They had dragged him along to Paris, a trip he had not wanted to make. This had resulted in a huge fight. In anger, he made a snap decision to head for Berlin by himself. He had heard the music was really good there. He hoped to see David Bowie. Yolanda asked him if his parents knew where he was at that moment. He shook his head.

We each took a turn trying to convince him, at the train's next stop, to leave the train for a few minutes to call his parents and put their minds at ease. He adamantly refused our advice. Unfortunately the whiskey, which continued to be passed around, only added to his stubbornness. We each made our pitch in our own way, and Annaliese translated all of them. Yolanda told him his parents would be worried sick. Ángel told of a time when his brother did not come home before the *toque de queda*—the military curfew—and his grandmother nearly had a heart attack. I told him about the time I went to Mexico without telling anybody and how upset my mother had been. None of these testimonials made any difference. I had to admit they would have made no difference to me either at his age.

The conversation and the Scotch made the time fly. I became a bit apprehensive watching the bottle get passed around time and again while the glorious golden liquid inside shrank in size.

It's probably a really bad idea to drink the whole thing, I told myself.

That brief flash of good judgment was quickly quashed. I continued to take my sip each time the bottle came to me. I was enjoying it too much to stop. I liked the sensation in my head. I felt euphoric.

I wonder if this is what heroin is like.

The women had more sense than I did. I noticed they took a sip only every second time—if that often. After a while Yolanda stopped drinking altogether. Andreas, on the other hand, worried me. He obviously enjoyed the whiskey a lot. It was also obvious he was not used to it. I could see where he was headed, like watching a movie of a train wreck in slow motion.

As we all laughed uproariously at someone's joke, two very serious-looking men in uniforms stepped into the compartment.

"*Pässe bitte,*" said one of them sternly.

Their abrupt appearance and grim look caused me to panic. Being drunk off my ass did not help.

"Huh? What?"

"They want to see our passports," said Yolanda. "We've crossed the border."

Ángel, unlike me, was perfectly calm. He had already stood to retrieve his passport from his backpack. I felt as though I was watching everything from a distance. It was all I could do to grasp the fact we had crossed a border. Ángel helpfully reached into my backpack and grabbed my passport as well. He looked at the front of it, comparing it to his. He opened his passport so that his photograph would be visible to the border guards. He was about to do the same with mine. He must have thought I was crazy because I sprang up and grabbed it away from him. All I knew was that I could not let him see the name on the passport. I could not let him find out I had been lying to him since the moment we met. He looked at me strangely but did not make an issue of my behavior. The Germans had a good look at each of our passports. They stamped each one with the exception of Annaliese's. Then they handed them back and moved on.

"So, we're in Germany now?"

"Yes, West Germany," said Yolanda. "This is an easy border to cross. Crossing into East Germany will be a bit more serious."

With that intrusion over, we went back to our good-natured multi-lingual chatter. Despite the good time I was having, a somber thought inevitably crossed my mind.

I'm actually now in the country where Lonnie died.

Yolanda held up the bottle for all of us to see. There was only a small amount of the glorious liquid remaining.

"We've drunk practically your whole bottle," I said. "Something this excellent should have been enjoyed and savored over a long period of time. It was too good to guzzle in a single night. I'm sorry."

"It's all right," said Yolanda. "Sharing it with new friends was better than drinking it by ourselves. There's so little left now, we may as well finish it. You and Miguel Ángel should drink it."

Annaliese said something in German.

"She says we can't have any alcohol with us when we cross into East Germany," translated Yolanda, "so there's really no choice. You *have* to finish it."

I looked at the others. By this time Andreas was slumped in his corner. The expression on Annaliese's face made clear she would have no more.

"You have some too," I said, offering it to Yolanda.

She smiled.

"I think there is enough for only two. Anyway, I reached my limit a while ago."

I looked at Ángel. He looked back at me with a devilish grin. The look in his eyes said he was up for it if I was. The look in my eyes told him he was out of his fucking mind. I handed him the bottle. I was impressed by how much he could drink. No matter how much he had, he seemed able to handle it, but now he was acting pretty silly. He stuck out his tongue, which was surprisingly long, and licked the bottle's neck lewdly. He laughed, watching for my reaction.

"Are you going to put it in your mouth or just play with it?" I taunted.

"You first," he said.

Instead of drinking, he spit into the bottle and passed it to me.

"You idiot," I said. "That whiskey is way too good to waste."

"So, drink it."

It was a dare. Knowing how much the bottle had cost, I could not bear not finishing it. Besides, I was too drunk to care about drinking his spit anyway. I drank exactly half the remaining amount. Then I gathered all the saliva in my mouth that I could and dropped it into the bottle. I handed it back to him.

"There. You get the rest."

He did not hesitate. He took the bottle and massaged the neck again with his tongue. He laughed loudly. He seemed to think he was the funniest comedian ever. Finally, he raised the bottle above his head and drained every last drop. He continued laughing as he settled deep into his seat. Almost instantaneously he closed his eyes and fell asleep. At first I thought he was pretending, that it was part of his comedy act. I prodded him a few times, but there was no reaction. He was thoroughly and soundly asleep. Yolanda and Annaliese had fallen asleep too.

I watched Ángel's breathing. He looked like a child. Why does that happen when people are asleep? His black hair fell over his forehead. I envied his long black eyelashes and his athletic frame. I think he deliberately wore a tee-shirt one size too small just to show it off. Yolanda and Annaliese had looked at him differently than the way they looked at me. Of course, Valérie would choose him over someone like me. That tongue of his alone was probably enough reason. He was lucky his life was so uncomplicated. He could talk openly about the woman he loved. He was not lying about his name. He would never pretend to be someone else. He was happy to be himself.

I felt dizzy. My head felt like it was going to float away. My stomach was doing sickening backflips. It was impossible to ignore the rolling motion of the train car. It seemed to be accelerating and was becoming overwhelming. The unsettling sensation reminded me of the 1971 San Fernando earthquake that made the earth sway all the way up in Kern County. I wanted desperately to make the train stop. Instead the swaying seemed to increase. It was only a matter of time until I would vomit. I stood and then nearly fell. I made my way to the corridor but it was a struggle. It was like trying to walk on a boat in rough seas. I headed for the toilet and prayed it would be unoccupied. Luckily it was. I stepped inside and closed the door. I leaned over and waited for the inevitable convulsion. I felt like I was back on the airplane but the turbulence was a lot worse.

After an endless amount of time, it was finally over. I flushed the toilet a few times and then struggled to my feet. I did my best to wash the awful taste out of my mouth. I could only get a small trickle of water from the tiny sink's tap. I looked in the mirror. I looked like crap. At least I felt better.

Damn, I said to myself. *It's been a long time since I drank so much I actually got sick.*

I opened the door to find Andreas standing there. He was as white as a sheet, his eyes bulging in panic. He had been standing there for who knows how long, waiting desperately to get into the bathroom.

"Sorry, man" I said. "I didn't know you were there. Looks like we both have the same problem."

I stepped out of the way and let him go in. I thought he would close the door, but he didn't. He just stood there, looking helpless. His chest heaved in and out, and his face became increasingly panicked. It was all too apparent, if I did not help him, he was going to throw up all over himself. I stepped back into the bathroom and put my hand on his shoulder. I gently guided him down to his knees. Then I leaned his head over the bowl. If the whiskey in his stomach did not make him vomit, the smell in the tiny bathroom certainly would. His long curly hair hung down over his face, and I took it in my hands and held it back behind his neck.

"Just let it come," I said. "Don't fight it, Andreas."

I have no idea what he thought I was saying, but he was definitely glad to have someone with him. Finally, he began to cough and spit. Then came the full-blown heaving.

"It's okay, man," I said, steadying him as best I could. "It'll be over soon."

It was definitely not over soon enough as far as he was concerned. His misery seemed endless. Every time I thought he had coughed up everything, there would be a pause and he would start again. In between, he wheezed and tried to catch his breath. When it was finally over I helped him to his feet. I could think of nothing but getting out of there, but he did not want me to leave. It must have been the first time he had gotten sick from drinking. It may even have been the first time he had gotten drunk. I soaked some paper towels and wiped his face.

"You going to be okay, man?"

He nodded.

"*Danke.*"

"I'm sorry, man. I should never have let you drink so much. You going to be all right?"

He nodded again. He looked like death warmed over but, like me, he clearly felt a lot better having gotten it all out of his system. We walked back to the compartment and settled into our seats. The other three were sleeping peacefully. With any luck they would not be sick. Yolanda and Annaliese had been more sensible than me. Ángel had seemingly drunk as much as me. Though he was a bit smaller than me, he was able to handle it better. Like I said, he was lucky.

I was dead tired and ready for sleep. I closed my eyes and dropped off immediately.

I jerked awake. The train shuddered. It had stopped on the track. There was a jolt, as if it had run into something. There was another jolt.

"What's that? What's going on?" I wanted to know.

I felt like crap. Suddenly there were two uniformed men in the compartment. I had thought the previous pair—when we crossed into West Germany—had been hard asses, but they were sweethearts compared to these two. They were as serious as a heart attack. Huge black pistols hung from their belts. I decided to do whatever they wanted.

"*Pässe. Jetzt.*"

He did not ask nicely. It sounded like a threat.

We scrambled to get our passports. The train car shook again.

"What's going on with the train?" I asked.

"We're at the border," said Yolanda. "They have to change engines."

"*Schweigen!*" he barked.

The soldiers took a good look around the compartment. They examined our backpacks thoroughly. They also pulled the shades down over the windows.

As one of them held my camera in his hand. He stared at me sternly and said, "*Keine fotos. Verstehen?*"

"Got it," I said. "No photos."

After a while the train moved again. The mood had changed completely. It was hard to avoid the feeling of being watched, though we probably weren't. I remembered the talks we had gotten in primary school about communism and the Iron Curtain and how grim things were in eastern Europe. It was strange to realize I was behind the Iron Curtain now. I wondered how safe I was.

One by one we all went back to sleep.

"*WIR SIND angekommen,*" said Annaliese.

"This is Zoo Station," said Yolanda. "We're in Berlin."

I felt as if I had been on trains forever. For Ángel and me it had been about twenty-four hours of non-stop rail travel. None of us looked as fresh as the night before—especially Andreas.

"*¿A dónde irá él?*" I asked Annaliese, wanting to know what Andreas would do now that he was on his own in Berlin. "*¿Qué hará él ahora?*"

She put my questions to him in German. He shrugged and mumbled something.

"*Él va a buscar a David Bowie,*" chuckled Annaliese.

"I don't think he is here anymore," said Ángel, slightly amused. "I heard he left to record an album. I think he's in Switzerland. Andreas should have stayed there."

We got off the train and out of the station. We continued a couple of blocks to a major street. Annaliese said it was called Kurfürstendamm. It was full of modern-looking restaurants and stores. I was surprised how normal it looked. I don't know what I was expecting—maybe bombed out buildings from World War II or maybe barbed wire to keep the communists out—but it was a modern city. More modern than Paris had looked. I could nearly have thought I was back in the States.

"Maybe we will see you in one of the clubs?" said Yolanda, sounding like she was not quite ready to split up.

"Sounds good to me," said Ángel gamely, "although I will probably stay away from scotch for a while."

We said our goodbyes. The two women headed up the street. Andreas went off in a different direction. Kurfürstendamm was big and wide and looked like it went on for miles. A thought occurred to me.

"Damn. What day is today?"

"It's Wednesday. Why?"

"This is when I was supposed to be in East Berlin. Good thing it's still early. I should get there as soon as I can. Where do I go?"

Ángel shrugged.

"We can ask somebody," he said. "Do you know any German?"

"*Nein*. Do you?"

"*Tampoco*. We will have to find someone who speaks English—or Spanish."

"Damn. I wish I thought of this before Annaliese and Yolanda left."

We walked down the street. We came to a very old church. It stuck out because everything around it was modern. The roof was damaged. It was probably from the war, and for some reason it had never been repaired. Lots of tourists were milling around. I stopped a man and a woman who were around my parents' age and looked like they were American. I asked them if they knew how to get to East Berlin. On hearing my voice, the man's eyes lit up.

"Hey! Where are you from?" he wanted to know.

"California. How about you?"

"Pittsburgh, Pennsylvania. I tell you, this place sure is different now. I was here in '45 and, boy, it was a whole different story then, I'll tell you."

"So, do you know how I can get to East Berlin?"

"It's easy. You just have to go to Checkpoint Charlie. It's a couple of miles that way. You can get a bus over there."

"Thanks."

I could tell he would have liked to tell me a few stories about the war, but I got away from him as quickly and politely as I could. Ángel and I headed for the bus. There was some fuss figuring out how much to pay and getting the driver to make change for some of the Deutschmarks Dino had given me, but in the end we managed to get where we needed to. On the bus, Ángel handed me an envelope. A name and address were written on the front. The name was Paulina Muñoz Rojas. Ángel was now very serious.

"This is important. *¿Me entiendes?*"

"Yeah, I understand. Who is she?"

"She is my aunt. I mean, *más o menos. Ella es la cuñada de la hermana mi madre.*"

I did my best to work it out in my head.

"She is your mother's sister's sister-in-law?"

"Yes, the sister of my political uncle, I mean, my aunt's husband. That does not matter. The important thing is that she and my mother were best friends since they were children."

"And why can't you take this to her yourself?"

"I cannot go to the *sector soviético*. I have to be absolutely certain it is delivered into her own hand by someone I trust."

"Why? What's it about?"

"I will tell you when you come back."

"What are you going to do while I am on the other side? I have no idea how long this other thing will take. I could be gone a few hours."

"I don't know. I guess I will walk around Berlin. Maybe I will look for a place we can stay tonight. Don't worry about me, though. Just please deliver the letter."

"Is it from you?"

"No, it is from my mother."

We got off the bus and walked to the checkpoint. I got my first look at the Berlin Wall. I was surprised it was not bigger. It looked like an ordinary concrete wall. It was not that high. It did not look like an Iron Curtain. It just looked like an ugly wall.

If the wall made an underwhelming impression, so did Checkpoint Charlie. It was just a wooden shack surrounded by some sandbags. Above, a sign said "U.S. Army Checkpoint." To one side, another sign said "You Are Leaving the American Sector" in English, Russian, French, and German. I thought again of the Elvis Costello song. When I first listened to it, the name Checkpoint Charlie meant nothing to me. Now I was here. I said goodbye to Ángel. I made a joke about him getting in touch with the U.S. government if I did not come back. I hoped it would still be funny at the end of the day.

Crossing over was not that big a deal, at least on the American side. Lots of people were going back and forth. They were all westerners like me, mostly tourists. When I got to the East German checkpoint, things were more serious. They had guard towers and cement barriers. Cars heading toward the western side were being pulled to one side and getting the once-over. My passport and my backpack were thoroughly examined as well. I tried not to be nervous, but I had seen too many Cold War spy movies not to be apprehensive. A guard took my four-day-old *International Herald Tribune* and did not give it back. I worried they would take Ángel's letter from me, but luckily it did not interest them. What did interest them was my wallet full of Deutschmarks. They demanded a hefty fee for going across. Eventually, I made it through and found myself standing in East Berlin.

It did not look a whole lot different than the other side. It did not, however, look nearly as bright and shiny as Kurfürstendamm. Generally, the areas close to the wall on both sides were drab and depressing. It was a strange feeling. I was further from home than I had ever been in my life. I was alone in a place where I did not speak the language and that was run by communists. I wished Ángel could have come with me.

I walked a few blocks and then began stopping people and asking if they knew English. I found a man who did, and I told him the address of the café Dino had made me memorize. He was nice enough to walk me there. I thanked him and then walked back to a bank I had noticed along the way. I changed a few Deutschmark for Ostmarks and then went back to Zu Tisch. I found a seat and ordered a coffee. After my coffee came, I sipped it and tried not to look nervous. I stood out since I was a foreigner and by myself. I wished I had a newspaper to read or a cigarette to smoke or anything to occupy me so I did not feel so self-conscious.

As casually as I could, I scanned the place, trying to spot the guy I was looking for. I closed my eyes and summoned my memory's image of the photograph Dino had shown me. I reminded myself of his face, of his sunken cheeks, weak chin, black hair, and sharp nose. I opened my eyes and searched for a match among the other people drinking coffee. He was not there. What would I do if he did not show up? What could I do? If he was not there, he was not there. I replayed my conversation with Dino, making sure I had not forgotten anything he had told me. He had definitely said it had to be a Wednesday morning, hadn't he? If the guy was not there, Dino could hardly expect me to wait around and come back the following Wednesday. If he did not show up in the next couple of hours, that would be the end of it as far as I was concerned. I would feel bad about my promise to Marty, though. I would feel like I had let him down.

And what if he did show up? How was I supposed to snap a photo of him without being obvious about it? I mean, who randomly takes a photo of a stranger inside a coffee shop? That was strange behavior even for a clueless American tourist.

I made my cup of coffee last as long as I could but, since I did not have anything else to occupy me, it was no time at all before I drained the cup. I ordered another cup. Then another one. I looked at the clock on the wall. It was nearly noon. How much longer should I wait? My cup was again empty. I stared at the bottom of it. I wondered if it was a good idea to have a fourth coffee. Two heavy-set women walked into the place. There was no place for them to sit. One of them spotted me sitting there by myself with my empty cup. She walked over and began talking to me. I had absolutely no idea what she was saying, but it was a good bet she was suggesting I should be a gentleman and let the two of them have my table. I played dumb.

"Sorry, ma'am, but I don't speak German."

She was not dissuaded. She continued talking, more sternly than before. She seemed to think the more determined she was, the more understandable she was. I smiled weakly and shrugged.

Then I saw him. Finally. He was there. He was actually there. He looked just like the photo, right down to his nose that looked like a knife blade. He sat at a table with a bald man who, I had noticed about a half-hour earlier, had been sitting by himself reading a newspaper. They barely nodded at each other and did not speak. My guy pulled out his own newspaper and began to read.

Damn, I thought, *the way he holds the paper hides his face.*

The heavyset woman was still there. She stood over me and continued her lecture. The longer I sat there without moving, the more insistent she was likely to become. She might start to attract other people's attention. That was something I definitely did not want. Feeling desperate, I tried to think of way to use the situation to my advantage. I made a plan. I took a deep breath.

I stood and gave her a great big smile. I pretended I knew her.

"Hey, it's you. Good to see you again. Hey, remember those great times we had all those years ago in Visalia?"

She was dumbfounded. She had no idea what I was saying. I was afraid she might make some sort of scene, but she simply stared at me in disbelief.

"Hey, and you brought Beatrice! How are you, Beatrice? How great that we're all back together again."

The other woman seemed flattered to be brought into the conversation, though she was more confused than the talkative one.

"I really have to get a photo of you two. You know, to take back to the folks in California."

I reached into my backpack and pulled out the cheap dime-store Kodak Brownie. I hated having to use it.

"Say cheese, girls!"

Through the Brownie's crummy little viewfinder I could see the two men at the table across the room. The bald guy turned in our direction with a sour look. To my delight the knife nose guy lowered his paper to see what was going on. I pressed the button.

"That was great. Just one more for posterity."

To my amusement the two women straightened their posture and quickly brushed their hair. They liked having their photograph taken. They even gave me a pair of proper, if not exactly radiant, smiles. I pressed the button again.

"That was great. Definitely give my regards to Ferdinand and the boys. Tell him that no one makes wiener schnitzel like he does. I wish I could stay, but I have to get going. Here, take my table. I'll be sure to send you prints after I get the photos developed."

I put the Brownie back in my backpack and then, on an impulse, gave each of them a hug. They were still confused, but they did not seem to mind the hugs at all.

"*Auf wiedersehen.* Let's not wait so long until the next time."

I hightailed it out of the place. I could not believe what I had done. I walked several blocks to calm myself down. Several times I looked over my shoulder in case someone had followed me. Was I insane or what?

With one mission accomplished, I pulled out Ángel's envelope. I walked down a main street called Friedrichstraße. In the distance was a tall futuristic-looking tower. As before, I stopped people at random until I found someone who spoke English. The first man I spoke to explained that I needed to travel a couple of miles on a bus. He was nice enough to take me to the bus stop and made sure I got on the right one. After I got off the bus, I had to stop a few more people until someone could give me directions to the address on the envelope. I finally found the apartment building I was looking for.

I pushed the button for the apartment number. A woman spoke through the tinny speaker.

"*Ja?*"

"Sorry. Do you speak English?"

"*Hä was?*"

"*¿Habla usted español?*"

"*¿Español? ¡Sí!*"

"*¿Señora Paulina Muñoz Rojas?*"

"*¡Sí! Soy yo. ¿Quién es?*"

"*Yo soy un amigo de Miguel Ángel Contreras Vargas.*"

"*¿Miguel Ángel? ¿De veras? Suba no más. Por favor.*"

The buzzer sounded, and I opened the door. I walked up three flights of stairs until I found the apartment. The door was open. Inside stood a short woman with wispy gray and white hair. Her jaw was determined. Her eyes flashed fiercely, but there was something kind in her smile. We spoke in Spanish, which put me at a disadvantage, but she made a point to speak slowly and clearly.

"How do you know Miguel Ángel?"

"I met him in Bordeaux, where he is a student."

"You are North American?"

"Yes."

"And how are you called?"

I was not sure what name to tell her, but I ended up using the same name I had told Ángel.

"I am called Lonnie. I have a letter for you. Ángel asked me that I give it to you."

I handed it to her. She looked at the handwriting on the front of it, and her eyes began to moisten.

"I do not believe it. I do not believe it."

"I think he would have liked to have given it to you himself, but he could not come all the way. He is in West Berlin."

She wiped her eyes and regained her composure.

"Please forgive me. How badly mannered I am. Do you want coffee, Lonnie?"

I was full of coffee from Zu Tisch, but I said yes anyway. She filled a kettle and put it on the stove to boil. From a shelf she took down two cups and saucers and set them on the table along with a jar of instant coffee called Rondo Kaffee. She put out a jar of sugar, a small pitcher of milk, and a small plate of cookies.

"It is not very much," she said. "I am sorry. I do not have many visitors."

"That is all right. I do not want to take up much of your time. I have already done what I came to do."

"How is Ángel? Is he well? Is he happy? He had six years, no more, the last time I saw him."

"He is doing great. He plays football at the University of Bordeaux, and he has a *polola*."

She was impressed I used the Chilean word for girlfriend.

"Have you been to Chile yourself?"

"No, never. But I would like to go someday. I have a friend there. At least I think he is there."

She opened the letter and began reading. She looked overwhelmed. She put it down without finishing the first page.

"It is from a very dear, very old friend of mine. It makes seventeen years back I have not seen her. My husband's sister-in-law was her sister."

"Yes, Ángel explained that to me."

"I miss my country very much. Tomorrow is our national holiday, the 18th of September. It saddens me that I may never set foot on Chilean soil again."

"Can you never go back?"

"No. Not with the current government. Many friends died when it came to power. Many disappeared. Many were tortured. It was a terrible time. My own son…"

"Yes?"

"My son Matías disappeared. He was walking down the street in Santiago. He was only nineteen years old. There was a car. Three men forced him into the car. We never saw him again. The *carabineros* said they do not have him. We do not know if he is alive or dead. He is gone, no more. This is hell for a mother. You never get over that."

"But why? Why did they do that to people? What made them do it?"

"I was part of the Popular Unity. I was with Allende. We were all targets. They were determined to wipe out all of us, to crush anyone who wanted justice for Chile, to help the people."

I said, "A long time ago I talked to a man who said that things were very bad under Allende, that there was chaos in the streets and the economy was ruined."

"Lies. All lies. It is reactionary propaganda. Allende was elected democratically. Chile never had dictatorships or military governments until Pinochet. The fascists could not bear to see the people rise up and improve their lives."

"And how did you come to be in East Berlin?"

"I am a guest of the East German government. They have been supportive in the struggle against fascism. East Germany, Cuba, the USSR—they are our friends."

"But aren't they all communists?"

"Yes, of course. What is wrong with communism? Is it wrong to want people to be equal, to want the resources of society to be shared fairly? Is that so bad? That is what the capitalists are afraid of. They are greedy. They want everything for themselves."

"But if communism is so fair, why do they look underneath cars at the checkpoint? Why do they have to look for people trying to escape?"

"No one tries to 'escape,' as you say. Only the capitalists. They do everything to sabotage the future. I do not say socialist countries are perfect, but at least they try to make things better for everyone. The capitalists do not even try."

I looked around at her tiny, modest apartment, at her hard cookies, and at her bitter-tasting coffee. I wondered if I should feel guilty about the good life I had in the United States. Would the world be a better place if we all lived like her?

I stood to leave.

"I should go back now. I hope there is only good news in your letter. Is there anything you would like me to tell Ángel?"

"Tell him I love him. Tell him to tell his mother I love her. I pray to God someday we can be together again."

"You pray to God?"

"Yes, of course."

"I was taught that communists do not believe in God."

"Well, I do. I would never stop believing in God. I would never stop being a Catholic. Does that surprise you?"

"I guess. I was taught in school atheism was part of communist theory."

"Officially maybe. Do you want to know why I will always be a Catholic?"

"Why?"

She leaned close to me and lowered her voice, as if she were telling me a closely guarded secret.

"Communists do not have very good holidays," she laughed with a twinkle in her eye. "Christians have much better ones. I would never give up Christmas! Or my *onamástico*."

"Your what?"

"*El onamástico*. The day of the saint I am named for. It is what we celebrate like a birthday. *Un abrazo, joven.*"

She gave me a big hug and a kiss on the cheek.

"I will give Ángel your message, *señora* Paulina. I promise."

"*Gracias*," she said with tears in her eyes. "*Mil veces gracias.*"

I walked down to the street and back to the bus stop. I felt sad for Paulina and for her son Matías and for Ángel and for all the Chileans who had to live in other countries. I understood better now why Ángel had a sad look when he talked about his country. I understood why he went to school in France and not in Chile.

I rode the bus back to Friedrichstraße. I walked back to the checkpoint and endured the examination of my body and my backpack. I was glad there were no questions about my cameras. A short distance away, soldiers were going over every inch of cars headed to the American sector. I wondered if they would find any capitalists hiding in the trunks or behind the back seats or under the chassis or in any of the other various places they were searching. I walked across to Checkpoint Charlie. It was a relief to hear the soldiers' American accents. They let me through with no problem.

Across the street I spotted Ángel. He had been standing there for God knows how long. He had a big smile on his face. I think he had been feeling every bit as lonely as I had been.

"Lonnie!" he called. "*¡Yo te eché de menos!*"

"Yeah, man. I missed you too."

29
Fulda

"DID YOU find her?"

"Yeah, I found her. She was very happy to get the letter. She said to tell you she loves you. And that you should tell your mother she loves her too. And that she prays that you will someday be together again."

Ángel fell silent. It took a couple of minutes before he could speak again.

"*Gracias, amigo.* I can never repay you for this."

"You don't owe me anything, amigo. I was glad to do it. I sure learned a lot today. What were you up to while I was gone?"

"I got us a room. I found an inexpensive hotel not far from Kurfürstendamm. And I had the best hot dog ever. It is called currywurst. You have to try it."

"Sounds good. We can just kick back and enjoy ourselves from now on. There's just one more thing I need to do first."

"What is that?"

"I need to find a club called Risiko."

We asked around and learned we had to travel southwest to Yorckstraße. It was nearly dark by the time we got there. Risiko was nothing like I expected. It had a tiny storefront. It was part of the ground floor of a large apartment building. We never would have noticed it if not for the strange array of people hanging around outside. It looked as though it might have been a small shop once. It had a large window covered up from the inside. Its name was hard to spot. The sign for Engelhardt Pilsner was bigger than the sign with the club's name, a triangle with Risiko spelled out in letters made to look like lightning bolts. It was like a warning sign for high voltage—which made sense once I learned the word Risiko meant risk.

We went inside. The place was tiny. It was not too crowded, but I suspected it would not be long before it would fill up and become absolutely claustrophobic. Every inch of the walls was covered with graffiti, drawings, and incoherent scrawls. It smelled like a place that could do with a thorough cleaning. It reminded me of places I had been in the city, the kind of places where the music and the drugs could take you into a whole different plane of existence.

"Why did you need to come here?" asked Ángel.

"It's complicated," I said. "Just go along with it. I need to hang out here for a while. Then we can go somewhere else."

We found a couple of stools at the bar and ordered pilsners. Being Germany, it should not have been surprising the beer was excellent. Ángel was particularly appreciative.

"*Esta cerveza está bien buena,*" he said happily. "Much better than Escudo, which is what I would be drinking back home."

I had a good look around the place. There was just about every category of non-conformist you could imagine. There were guys with torn jeans, women with bald heads, men with earrings, leather jackets, jean jackets, men with eyeshadow and makeup, women done up in black leather, and people with long frizzy hair and headbands. It was the kind of place where you could see people wearing round black sunglasses even though it was night time. I wondered if I had understood Dino correctly. Was this actually where I was supposed to hand over the Brownie camera? It seemed like an unlikely place. On the other hand, that was probably the reason. I imagined someone like Dino or Marty walking into the place. He would immediately stand out like a sore thumb. He would look too old and too straight. A couple of guys with eyeshadow gave me looks. I did my best to ignore them. Ángel set his bottle down on the counter.

"I am going to the W.C.," he said. "I will be back in a minute."

I hoped he would not be gone long. I felt isolated, sitting there by myself. Sure enough, it took only a couple of minutes before things got uncomfortable. A tall skinny guy with tons of eyeshadow, purple lipstick, and an earring sidled up next to me. He had long, stringy, black hair.

"Come here off-ten, luv?" he asked.

He sounded English.

"No, first time," I said as matter-of-factly as I could, trying not to look at him.

"There will be music in a wee bit. Fancy a dance, luv?"

"Not much of a dancer," I said evenly, kicking myself for not just ignoring his questions.

I wished he would take the hint and move on. Instead he moved closer. I was about to stand and walk away when he put his lips so close to my ear I could almost feel his taste buds. He had the slyest of flirting smiles.

I was about to shove him away angrily when he whispered huskily, "Do you have the bleedin' camera, mate?"

I was definitely slow on the uptake.

"Yeah, it's right here."

"That's brilliant, luv," he whispered.

He still had the same lascivious look on his face. Any observer would see it as nothing other than an aggressive come-on.

"Just leave it on the bar. No fuss now. That's a good lad."

As nonchalantly as I could, I took the Brownie out of my backpack. I set it down next to my pilsner bottle.

"Lovely job there, mate," he said as he shifted his body so that he was facing me. "I'm just giving you a little peck on the cheek now. Not to worry. It's only to distract the punters. It's rather like being a magician."

It was more than a peck. He licked my cheek with his rough tongue. Then he was gone, almost like magic. I looked at the counter. The Brownie was gone. I had not even seen him take it. I doubted anyone else would have seen him take it either. Well, except for one.

Ángel appeared out of nowhere, looking agitated. He was about to run after the guy.

"He took your camera, Lonnie! Didn't you see?"

I grabbed Ángel and pressed him against the bar. It was the only way to stop him before he launched into pursuit.

I whispered into his ear, "It's okay. Let him go. It's all right."

"*¿Qué demonios pasa contigo?*" he said. "*Nada de esto tiene sentido.*"

"Don't worry," I said. "It's over now. He has the camera. It's all over. I'm free. I did what I promised to do. We can do what we want now."

"What is going on with you? Are you a spy or something? Do you work for *la CIA*?"

He pronounced it "la see-ya," the way people refer to the CIA in Spanish.

"You don't have to worry," I said. "I'm not part of the American government or anything like that. It doesn't bother me if you're a communist. Your politics don't matter to me. I don't give a damn about politics."

"Communist? What are you talking about?"

"It's okay, Ángel. I had a good talk with Paulina. I think I understand things better now. It doesn't matter to me if your family is communist."

"You think I'm a communist?"

"Communist, socialist, whatever you are, it doesn't matter. I don't care. You're my friend. That's all that matters."

"Are you working for my father? Did he send you here?"

"Your father? How would I know your father? Why would I be working for him?"

"He knows people in the CIA. Anything is possible. I don't know what to think. Everything about you is just too strange."

"How does your father know people in the CIA?"

"Because he does. He is in the government. That is why we were in Virginia. He spent two years working on training programs with your government."

"Wait. You mean your father is part of the Pinochet government? How is that possible?"

"Because it is. He was with Pinochet from the beginning. Ever since the *golpe de estado* in 1973."

"But Paulina, she was with Allende. I thought your family was with Allende."

"My mother and Paulina were friends since they were children, but their families were on different sides. Paulina's family was for *la Unidad Popular*. My parents' families always supported *el Partido Conservador*."

"But every time we talked about Chile, you always seemed so sad. I assumed it was because you were against the government."

"Yes, I am sad for my country. You have to understand. Allende was wrong. Yes, he was elected president, but it was not by a majority. He only became president because the Christian Democrats backed him. It was the biggest mistake ever. He ruined the country. He ruined the economy. There was chaos. Before the *golpe*, before we moved to Virginia, I missed two years of my education. The teachers in the *colegio* spent all their time leading political events. They never taught any classes. Allende brought in the Cubans. He ignored the constitution. He did not respect the laws of the country. He formed his own army. The military had to act."

"So, does this mean you support Pinochet?"

"*Mira.* I was sixteen when the *golpe* happened. Yes, I supported it. But they went too far. Yes, they had to get rid of Allende. He was destroying the country. But it went too far. They began killing people. They made people disappear. They tortured people. It was too much. They became the thing we were always told the communists were."

There were tears in Ángel's eyes.

"My country is a disaster. There is no one I can support. Both sides only want to kill the other side. I tried to say this to my father, but he did not want to hear it. He only does what Pinochet wants. I cannot talk to him anymore. When I realized you were CIA, I thought maybe he actually sent you to spy on me. Sometimes I think anything is possible."

"I'm not CIA. Why do you keep saying that?"

"Because you are American. Because you have so many secrets. Because you had to go to Berlin on your mysterious mission. Because you have a fake passport."

"Fake passport?"

"Yes. Forgive me, but I looked at your passport. Last night on the train I woke up when you and everyone else was asleep, and I took a look at your passport. I only did it because you acted so strangely when you had to show it to the border guard. I saw the fake name on it. Dallas Green. That does not sound like a real name. It sounds like a made-up name. Why would you have a fake passport if you were not a spy?"

I did not know what to say. I felt everything was closing in on me. My lies had gotten so complicated I did not even know myself what was true anymore. I was tired of it. I was through with the lies.

"Dallas Green is my real name."

"Stop making fun of me. That is not a real name."

"Why is it not a real name?"

"It's just a stupid name. Who names a child after a city in Texas?"

"I swear to you, it is my real name. My name is Dallas Green. I'm sorry I didn't tell you the truth from the beginning."

"It makes no sense. If you're not some kind of spy, why would you not tell me your real name?"

"I was afraid that you would recognize it."

"How would I possibly recognize the name Dallas Green?"

"I thought Valérie might have mentioned it to you."

"Valérie?"

"Yes. That is what I did not want to tell you. I met Valérie. I know her. I met her in Deauville during the film festival."

"You know Valérie?"

"Yes."

He looked like he had been hit with a ton of bricks.

"You were with her? In Deauville?"

"Yes."

"What are you saying? What do you mean when you say you were with her?"

"We were both working. She helped me get some photos. We became friends."

"I do not understand. Why did you not tell me this? Do you know why she did not come back after the film festival? Do you know why she went to Brittany?"

"Yeah, I do."

"Did she go there with someone?"

"She did, but it's not what you think."

"You don't know what I think."

He was angry.

"Tell me. Tell me who she went with."

I was torn between loyalty to Valérie and loyalty to Ángel.

"It's not my place to tell you. It's better if she tells you. You should hear it from her, but trust me, it's not what you're afraid of. She will tell you when you see her in Bordeaux. Then you will understand."

"Did you sleep with her?"

"Ángel, I'm done lying to you. As hard as it is for both us, I am only telling the truth from now on. Yes, I fell in love with her. I'm sorry, but that is what happened. It was before I knew you. It was before I even knew about you. But the fact is I fell in love with her. I'm still in love with her. But for what it's worth, I did not make love to her. I won't say I didn't want to, but it never happened. She doesn't want to hurt you. She truly cares about you."

Ángel was devastated. I was sick with guilt. He got angry again.

"I liked you," he said. "I liked you a lot. I thought we were friends. You were laughing at me the whole time."

"No, Ángel. Please believe me. I was not laughing at you. It was all so strange. I somehow convinced myself you were actually my friend Antonio. Then I found out you weren't. Then we somehow became friends anyway. We became really good friends. I didn't plan it. I wanted to hate you. But the truth is you're the best friend I have had in years. I have never had such a good friend since Antonio went to Chile and Lonnie died."

"So, Lonnie is a real person?"

"Yes, he is a real person. Or at least he was. He died here in Germany six years ago. Every time you called me by his name it was like a knife in my heart."

"What kind of person are you, Dallas Green?"

He said my name like it was a bad taste in his mouth.

"What kind of person uses the name of a dead friend to play a joke on someone? What kind of person does something like that?"

The intensity of his anger made me defensive.

"Look," I said, "you didn't exactly turn out to be who I thought *you* were either."

He got angrier.

"I never lied to you," he shouted. "Is it my fault you made up your own story about me? Am I supposed to be sorry my life does not fit nicely in the story you gringos tell yourselves about South America? The story people like you want to hear so you can feel better about yourselves. For you, things that happened in my country were maybe something you read in a newspaper. For us, these things are our life. We have to live it."

"I'm sorry, Ángel. I fucked up. I'm just so sorry—about everything."

My heart beat in my chest like it was going to burst. I was panicky. My heart beat faster and faster. If I did not do something, I was sure my chest would explode. In desperation I put my hand on Ángel's shoulder.

"What else can I say to you?"

Touching him was the wrong thing to do. With a force that shocked me, he grabbed my hand and shoved it back at me. He bent my wrist in such a way I thought it would break. He slammed his glass to the floor, shattering it to pieces. Everyone in the place was looking at us.

"*¡Hijo de puta!*" he yelled. "There is nothing for you to say because I do not want to hear it. You lied to me. You made a fool of me. What is worse, you lied to yourself. You have serious problems. How can you lie the way you do? How can you steal someone else's name? Someone else's life? Someone else's woman? You are pathetic. You need to solve your problems, but they are not my problems. Solve them yourself and leave me alone. You are nothing but trouble, *pico*. I gave you a place to stay. I tried to be your friend. What a joke. *Ándate a la chucа!*"

He pulled one of the train tickets out of his backpack.

"Here. This is your return ticket to Paris. You should go. I am finished with you. I do not want to see you again. Ever."

He threw his backpack over his shoulder and walked out of the club. I stood shaking as if the temperature had dropped below freezing. The pain in my chest was agonizing. I wished I could close my eyes and make it all go away. I looked around. Only a few people were still staring at me. No one had made a move to clean up the glass on the floor.

I took deep breaths and, with painful slowness, began to calm down. My feeling of panic turned to sadness. The thought of never seeing Ángel again broke my heart. His friendship had meant the world to me, and I had squandered it. At the age of 27 I wanted to burst into tears. He was right. I was pathetic.

I did not know what to do next. As embarrassed as I was, I stayed and finished my beer. I pondered my options. I was dead tired and did not have a place to sleep for the night. In the end, I could think of only one thing to do. I made my way back to Zoo Station. There was a surprising amount of activity in the city late at night. It was a place that kept going twenty-four hours a day. At the train station I found a bench to sit on for the rest of the night. Though I tried not to fall asleep, I kept dozing off. The night lasted forever. Eventually it was morning.

I caught the earliest train I could out of Berlin. As I joined the line of people waiting to get on the train, I spotted a familiar face. It was Andreas, as gawky and awkward as ever. When our eyes met, both of our faces lit up. He came over and gave me a hug.

"Heading back to Paris?" I said.

He nodded his head and said something in German I did not understand.

"Me too. Berlin did not work out the way I thought. Did you find David Bowie?"

He smiled ruefully and shook his head. He said something else. We looked at each other awkwardly. Without Annaliese to translate for us, neither of us had any idea what the other was saying. We communicated the best we could with gestures and facial expressions. In the end we had to accept that we were not going to have a meaningful conversation. We sat together on the train but in near total silence.

The train made its way extremely slowly across East Germany. When we crossed the border with West Germany, the atmosphere changed. The window shades were raised, and sunshine was allowed into the train. People around us began to talk more freely.

At the first stop in West Germany, I said goodbye to Andreas. We hugged awkwardly, and I got off the train. There was someplace I needed to go. I went to a ticket window and asked for a map. I found what I was looking for and pointed to it. I asked for a ticket. It took a bit of doing. It would have been easier if I had known German or if the ticket agent had been more understanding. In the end I succeeded in exchanging what was left of my ticket to Paris for where I really wanted to go.

Luckily, I did not have to wait long for the next train and, even after having to change trains twice, I arrived before evening in the city of Fulda. Walking out of the train station, I looked around, scarcely believing I was actually there. The city looked like something from another age, full of old churches with tall sharp spires. I made my way to the edge of the city and found the army base. It was a strange feeling knowing that, just a short distance away, was the border with East Germany. In Berlin I had been on a small island in the middle of the communist world. Here I was on the border between East and West. I was in the shadow of the so-called Iron Curtain.

I walked to the base entrance. Above the road was a large sign in the shape of an arc. I approached the shack off to one side. The American soldier inside was all business.

"Can I help you sir?"

"Hi. I was just wondering if I could talk to someone who was here six years ago."

"Say again, sir?"

"Sorry, this probably sounds kind of crazy. A friend of mine was stationed here six years ago. He died in a road accident. I just wanted to find out what happened. You know, just maybe see the place where it happened. It's something I've wanted to do for a long time. Is there someone here I could talk to?"

The soldier, who looked to be about eighteen years old, appeared totally confused by my question.

"I am sorry, sir. I don't know if that is something we can do. Do you have an appointment with someone on the base?"

"No, I don't know anyone here. I was just trying to, you know, understand better how my friend died. His name was Lonnie McKay and he was a private. He and I grew up together in California. He was the best friend I ever had, and he was only twenty-one when he died. I just thought maybe I would feel closer to him if I could see the actual place where it happened. Maybe talk to someone who was around at the time. Sorry, it was a crazy idea."

"Sorry, sir. I don't understand how I can help you. Perhaps if you wrote to the base commander…"

"It's all right. Like I said, it was a crazy idea. At least I got a look at where he lived for the last part of his life. You can forget about it. Thanks anyway."

By this time another soldier had come to see what was going on. He was older than the guy I was talking to and had sergeant's stripes. I decided I was causing too much of a fuss and should just leave.

I walked back toward the city, feeling tired and depressed.

"Sir. Hold up a minute please, sir."

I stopped and turned around. The sergeant had followed me. He looked about thirty years old and had a shaved head. His eyes were pale blue.

"Sir? You said you were a friend of Private McKay?"

"Yeah. Lonnie and I grew up together. I knew him better than I ever knew anyone in my life."

He pulled a pencil and a notepad out of his shirt pocket.

"Look. I shouldn't be doing this. And if anybody asks, I didn't do it."

"Do what?"

He scribbled something on the notepad. He tore off the sheet and handed it to me.

"This is an address here in Fulda. I don't know if I'm doing the right thing, but I think maybe Private McKay would have wanted me to give this to you."

I looked at the paper and the address written on it.

"What is this?"

"Like I said, I probably shouldn't be doing this. Whether you go there or not is up to you. Good luck, sir."

He turned and went back to the shack. The strangest thought came into my head. I had fantasized many times Lonnie had not really died, that he had faked his death and was living in secret somewhere. After all, he had a closed casket at his funeral. Anything was possible, wasn't it? Stranger things had happened, hadn't they? Just in my own life, a lot of weird things had happened. Was the sergeant trying to tell me Lonnie was still alive and living in Fulda under a new identity? Of course, it was a crazy idea, but I desperately wanted to believe it.

Clutching the paper, I walked back into the city. By now I was an old hand at finding German addresses. I stopped people on the street and showed them the address. Different ones kindly pointed me in this direction and that direction. Finally, I found myself standing in front of an apartment building.

I pressed the button next to the apartment number. I held my breath.

30
Lukas

A WOMAN'S voice came out of the speaker.

"*Wer ist es?*"

"Hello. Sorry to bother you. My name is Dallas Green."

There was silence.

"I'm a friend of Lonnie McKay. I was given this address."

There was more silence and then, "Lonnie?"

"Yeah, Lonnie McKay. He was my friend."

I waited for what seemed like half a minute. I heard the buzzer release the door. I went inside and walked up the stairs to look for the apartment number. At the top of the stairs was a woman standing in the hallway.

"*Bist du Amerikaner?*"

"Yeah. I grew up in California with Lonnie."

She led me into an apartment. She stared at me curiously. She did not seem to speak English. I felt I should explain what I was doing there, but the truth was I had no idea what I was doing there. I hoped that, miraculously, Lonnie would pop into the room, laughing, and saying, "Hey, man, you finally found me! I sure pulled one over on everyone, didn't I?"

The woman was about the same age as me. We just looked at each other awkwardly. I glanced over at her shelves and saw a small photo in a frame. I went over to have a closer look. In the photo was the woman standing in front of me. She was with a man. It took a moment to recognize him, but there was no mistake. It was Lonnie. He looked strange because he was in his army uniform with his head shaved in a military cut. The two of them were laughing.

I pointed at the photo and said, "You knew Lonnie?"

She nodded quietly.

"I don't suppose you speak any English."

"Little. Very little."

I held out my hand, and she held out hers.

"My name is Dallas. It's nice to meet you."

"Renate."

I pointed to the photo again and said, "So, you and Lonnie were... close?"

She said nothing and then turned her head in the direction of an open door.

"Lukas," she called. "*Komme.*"

Slowly a small child walked into the room. His hair was blond. He looked like he was five or six years old. My heart froze. It was like seeing a ghost. He looked exactly like Lonnie at the age when we were in kindergarten. For a moment it was as though twenty years had never happened.

"*Lukas, meine Liebe,*" she said softly, "*dieser Mann ist ein Freund deines Vaters.*"

"Lukas?" I asked her, just to make sure I had his name right. She nodded.

I shook the little boy's hand. He was shy. He would not look at me directly.

"Hello, Lukas," I said. "I am a friend of your father's. I grew up with him. I knew him very well. We were friends our whole lives. I think he would be very proud to see what a fine young man you are."

Lukas looked at his mother, silently asking if he could go back to his room. She nodded. He ran off without giving me another look.

"It's amazing," I said to her. "He looks exactly like Lonnie. It's as though Lonnie has come back to life."

She smiled and nodded, to let me know she understood what I had said.

There were a lot of things I wanted to ask her. I wanted to know how she and Lonnie met, how much time they had spent together. Did he know he was a father before he died? In that moment I would have paid a million dollars to be able to speak and understand German for just ten minutes. I was not sure what to do next. I felt like an intruder in the lives of this woman and her child. Did she want me to stay longer and try to find a way to communicate? Would it be easier if I just left? She seemed as confused as I was.

The only thing I could think to do was take out my wallet and hand her some Deutschmarks. It was a strange thing to do, but I thought that was what Lonnie might have wanted me to do. The gesture horrified her. She firmly refused to take it. To show I could be just as stubborn as she was, I left the money on a table. I pulled out the scrap of paper with her address on it and turned it over. I indicated to her that I wanted a pencil. She gave me one.

"What is his birthday?"

"*Geburtstag?*"

"Yeah."

She took the pencil and wrote, *Lukas Wolf – 11. November 1974.* I put the paper in my pocket and said, "Every year for the rest of his life, Lukas is going to get a birthday present from America. Even though he can't have his father with him on his birthday, he will get something from his father and me. I know Lonnie would have wanted me to do that. He would be very proud of that little boy."

I wanted to do and say more, but I did not know what. In the end, this was Lonnie's story, not mine. As usual, I was just a guest star in someone else's movie.

"*Möchtest du Kaffee?*"

"Thanks, but no. I should be going. I've taken up enough of your time. Thank you for letting me meet Lukas. He's a great little boy. Lonnie would have loved him."

She gave me a kiss on the cheek and watched solemnly as I left.

I walked back to the train station. I wondered if I should let Lonnie's mother know she was a grandmother. I had heard she divorced Don a few years earlier. She had re-married and moved to Fresno. I decided to let Lukas remain Lonnie's and my secret. I did not want to be responsible for complicating his and Renate's lives unnecessarily. I do not know if it was right or wrong, but that seemed right to me.

I could not get another train until the morning, so I found a hotel for the night. I bought a pint bottle of Scotch and took it to my room. I drank the whole thing. I was very lonely. I had been with Ángel nearly a week, and I missed him a lot. I was sad for him and the problems I caused for him. I thought about Lonnie, Renate, and Lukas. They might have been a happy family. It was amazing Lonnie had a kid. A part of him had survived after all. Maybe my dreams about Marisol and little Antonio were supposed to be about Renate and Lukas.

I dreaded the coming night. By some miracle I had not been consumed with my nighttime terror since being in Europe. I wondered if it would come back on this night. I was dead tired from all the train travel and I hoped that plus the whiskey would make me sleep so soundly the fear would continue to leave me alone.

I got my wish. I did not wake or dream the whole night. In fact, in the morning I had to struggle to wake up. I felt like crap. I promised myself, for the fortieth time since I had arrived in Europe, that I would definitely stop drinking.

I spent another entire day on trains—first one to Frankfurt and then one to Paris. By now I was tired of sitting on trains. I wished Ángel was there to play cards with or to just talk nonsense with. The hours passed slowly. There was plenty of time for thinking. The more I forced myself to put Ángel out of my mind, the more I could think only about Valérie. I wondered where she was at that moment. Was she still in Brittany with Logan? Was she back in Bordeaux? Was she wondering where Michel had gone and why he was not there waiting for her? It was possible Ángel was already back in Bordeaux. If not, he would be there soon. Or maybe he decided to stay in Berlin a while longer and lose himself in the clubs.

The train pulled into Gare de l'Est in the evening. I was in a mood to indulge myself. I found a map of the Metro system. By now I had a pretty good idea how it worked thanks to Ángel. I worked out I was only five stops from the Père Lachaise station and would only have to change trains once. Once there, I climbed the stairs out of the Metro station and onto the street. One of the streets radiating from the traffic circle was lined with a stone wall. There were trees behind the wall, and I knew it was the cemetery because I could see the tops of monuments. I had to walk a long way down the street before finding an entrance. When I did, I realized I had wasted my time. The cemetery was closed. I would have to wait one more day.

I headed back to the Metro station. I decided to go to the Champs Elysées. It was a long train ride, but it only required one change. I got off at the Place de la Concorde. That turned out to be the biggest, craziest traffic circle I had ever seen in my life—at least until I got to the Place de l'Étoile where the Arc de Triomphe was. The Place de la Concorde was wide and surrounded by old columned buildings with a million cars driving every which way. There was an ancient Egyptian obelisk right in the middle of it all. By now it was dark. I walked along the big wide street through the adjoining park. It went on forever. Eventually, I could see the Arc de Triomphe in the distance. It seemed smaller than I thought it would be, but I soon realized this was only because I was so far away from it.

The trees lining the wide avenue gave way to buildings. The farther I went, the more shiny and glittering the shops, cafés and restaurants. Everything looked expensive. People were dressed to the nines. While a long line of people waited to get into a movie theater, a street mime entertained them. I looked at the marquee to see what was playing. It was *Bronco Billy*. As I continued walking, the Arc de Triomphe grew more massive. As I got close to it, I happened to glance across the street and spot something weirdly familiar. It was a McDonald's.

I had not eaten at a McDonald's in years. After all, why would I go there when I had Hamburger Mary's in my neighborhood? Now, however, the sight of it made me suddenly homesick. I risked life and limb to get across the street, and I went in. It was eerie how it made me feel I was back in the States. There was at least one difference, though. It served beer and wine. I debated for a few moments between *Le Big Mac* and *Le Royal Cheese*, but in the end I went for *Le Royal* with a side of *Les Frites*. As tempted as I was to have a beer, I went for a chocolate *Frappé*. It had been a long time since I had had a milkshake.

If West Berlin had been a capitalist island in a communist sea, McDonald's on the Champs Elysées was like an American island in the middle of French waters. They had even thoughtfully posted pages from the latest *International Herald Tribune* on the wall. Unfortunately, the news was as depressing as ever. The Pentagon was accusing the Soviet Union of violating a nuclear treaty. A plane had been hijacked to Cuba. A nuclear waste dump was leaking radiation into San Francisco Bay. The former dictator of Nicaragua had been assassinated in Paraguay. There was still no progress on the Iran hostage situation. I gave up on news and focused on the sports and comics.

After my meal I walked back out onto the street and remembered I was still in a foreign country. I walked the entire circumference of the Place de l'Étoile and studied the massive Arc de Triomphe from every angle. Then I retraced my steps down the Champs Elysées.

Is that it? I wondered. *I have come all this way across the world, and that's it? All I can find to do in Paris is go for a burger at McDonald's?*

A couple of weeks earlier, France had seemed the answer to everything. A new country. A fresh start. Leaving behind all my accumulated problems. Escaping my dread of night. What a laugh. I was in a place where I did not know anyone, where I hardly spoke the language and, most importantly, I was still the same idiot as always. Whenever I started to connect with another person, I screwed everything up. Why was I incapable of having a simple normal relationship with a woman or a friend? Why did I always make a mess of everything?

It was getting late, and I had absolutely no idea where I would spend the night. I had no interest in finding a place to stay. I did not want to go through the frustration of trying to communicate with some French person at a reception desk. I did not want to sleep in another hotel room. I decided to just keep walking. I walked all the way back to the other end of the Champs Elysées and across the Place de la Concorde. I walked through the Tuileries garden and along the Seine past the Louvre. I walked until I crossed a bridge and had a good look at Notre Dame cathedral. I walked up and down the Boulevard Saint-Michel. Then I did it all again in reverse, winding up back at the Arc de Triomphe. Then I walked down Avenue Kléber until I came to the Chaillot palace. I stepped out onto the wide flat expanse. In front of me across the river, as large as life, was the Eiffel Tower. It was lit up and looked like a vision out of a movie.

There was definitely something magical about Paris. It was beautiful and exciting. It made you feel you were at the center of the world. It also made me sad. All the beauty and teeming life made me feel very alone. I would have given anything to have Valérie with me, to be able to share it with her, to have her explain what it meant to her, what this city meant to all French people. It was the best possible city for being in love. It was the worst possible city for being alone.

Should I try to see her? To talk to her? How could I? As much as I was in love with her, I also cared about Ángel. There was no doubt in my mind she preferred him. Even if she did not, how could I bear to hurt him more than I already had? It was an impossible situation. I was under some sort of curse.

It was now late enough there was definitely no point looking for a place to stay. I spent the early morning hours walking the same streets I had already walked. Then I found new ones to walk. By the time the sun began to rise, I was again approaching the Champs Elysées. I found a café that was open early. I sat at a table on the sidewalk and ordered a café au lait with a croissant. It cost a fortune, but I had earned it.

By now I knew the city so well I could have found my way back to Père Lachaise on foot. Unfortunately, my feet were killing me. I had blisters on both of them. I took the Metro.

Luckily, the cemetery opened at eight o'clock. For a while I wandered around aimlessly, naïvely thinking I would simply come across Jim Morrison's grave. The place was massive. It was also creepy. It was like an entire city of dead people. It had lanes lined with crypts and mausoleums the way a town has streets lined with houses. There were no simple graves with modest markers like the cemetery in my hometown. Everything was big and ornate. I had to ask people for directions more than once, but it was no problem. People were accustomed to directing tourists to the final resting place of The Doors' front man.

Finally I found it. It was just a rectangular block on the ground with his bust on top. The name Morrison was etched in large letters with the dates 1943-1971. He had died shortly before Lonnie's and my star-crossed adventure in Mexico. Flowers filled the pots next to the bust and anywhere else people could find to put them. There were also more than a few bottles. Lots of different kinds of beer and whiskey, including at least one bottle of Jim Beam. Like the interior of Risiko, there was scrawled writing all over his tomb and all other adjoining surfaces. Some of it was in French. Some of it was in German. A lot of it was in English. Someone had written in huge letters *Lizard King*. Many people had simply written their own names.

So, this is what it is like when a rock star goes out at the age of twenty-seven, I thought.

I had less than three months to go until I was not twenty-seven anymore.

I had meant to bring my own bottle and have a drink there on Lonnie's behalf, but I was still not totally recovered from my bender in Fulda. Besides, nine in the morning was a little early—even for me.

I sat there a while, pondering the meaning of it all and coming up with nothing profound. Finally, I said to myself, *Dallas, I think it's time to go home.*

It was a shame to leave now that I was such an expert on the Metro. I made my way to the Paris Opéra, where I had first set foot in Paris, and then caught a bus to Charles de Gaulle Airport. I found an agent for the airline and presented my unused return ticket. I gave her a long sob story about not being able to go home on schedule. Either I wore her down or she just took pity on me, but in the end I had a boarding pass for a flight back to San Francisco for early the next morning. I spent the rest of the day and night hanging out in the airport terminal, sometimes sleeping across a few chairs whenever I found a quiet waiting area. The time dragged, but eventually the departure time arrived. I boarded the plane with everybody else. I collapsed into my seat and almost did not wake up when the plane took off. I slept most of the way back.

Shortly before we were due to land, a flight attendant woke me to give me a pre-packaged breakfast with orange juice and coffee. As usual the city was clouded over. When we emerged from the clouds, it looked as though we were headed straight for the bay. At the last minute the runway appeared, as if from nowhere, and we skidded to a halt.

I was home.

31
Fall

I HAD lost track of time, but I finally managed to figure out it was Sunday. Luckily, I had enough American money to get a taxi home from the airport. I made a mental note to go the bank the next day and exchange my leftover francs and Deutschmarks. Though I had done nothing for the previous day and a half other than hang out at an airport and sit on an airplane, I was exhausted. The same old seagull watched me as I went into my building. I climbed the stairs to my apartment and found everything exactly as I had left it—except maybe for the bad smell in the refrigerator from some milk I left. The mailbox was full, but it was just the usual accumulation of junk mail and bills. I felt I had been gone for months. In fact, it had been only two and a half weeks. It did not appear anyone had missed me.

I set my alarm and went straight to bed. I decided I might as well go into the office at the usual time in the morning and face the music. Though I no longer had a job, I would still be owed one or two paychecks. I would pick them up in person. I owed David the chance to chew me out face to face. He had been a good employer after all. I owed him that much.

In the morning, when I was nearly at work, I had second thoughts. Being a man and taking responsibility had seemed a good idea the night before, but now in the cold morning light I was nervous. I swallowed hard and kept going. Time to take my medicine, as my father would have said. I kept my head down as I headed to David's assistant's desk.

"Hi, Marla," I said sheepishly.

She looked up. Her eyes grew wide, as if she had seen a ghost.

"I was wondering if you had my paycheck."

"Dallas! Hold on a sec. David wants to talk to you. We've been trying to get a hold of you for the past week."

"You don't need to bother him. He's probably busy."

"Don't you dare go anywhere. Stay right there. *Do not move.*"

She never once took her eyes off me as she picked up her phone. She said evenly, "David, it's Dallas. He's here."

I thought she would send me in to see him, but instead he came out.

"Dallas Green! We have been trying everything we could think of to get in touch with you. Where in the hell have you been?"

"I'm sorry, David. It's a long story. Actually, it's not that long a story. I don't have a good reason. It's just that…"

"You've caused quite an uproar, Mr. Green. We've been getting phone calls from all over. Not just the *Chronicle* and the *Examiner*, but the wire services, the national papers, the news magazines. Even one of the networks."

"Sorry, what?"

"It's been amazing. We've licensed your photos to magazines and newspapers all over the country, and abroad as well. They're a sensation. Thanks to you, there is now more interest in Logan MacCaul than ever before. He's the most famous filmmaker in the world right now."

Logan was right. Journalists did not have a fucking clue.

"Your article and photos hit like a bombshell. Everybody wants to know how you found him. How did you get the interview? Did he have anything else to say? Will you be talking to him again?"

"*My* interview?"

"Yes, your interview. You wrote it, didn't you?"

"Well, yeah, but it wasn't very good. I told Melanie to rewrite it and put her own name on it. I didn't expect it to have my name on it."

"She did do some polishing all right, but Ms. Francis insisted on the two of you sharing the byline—with your name first."

"Well, that was pretty nice of her. She didn't have to do that. So, the photos turned out okay? I felt bad I didn't get to develop them myself. Were they really all right?"

"They were great. They were amazing. We had to have an extra print run. How on earth did you do it?"

I did not know what to say. There was no way I was going to tell anybody about Valérie or her connection to Logan. I would not do that to them. That meant I had no good way to explain how I met Logan MacCaul.

"I just got lucky, I guess. Just a case of being in the right place at the right time, I suppose."

"That's it? You just happened to run into him—the most reclusive, publicity-shy filmmaker in the world—you just happened to run into him in Deauville and he decided to give you an interview—just like that?"

"Yeah, pretty much. Even I get lucky sometimes."

David eyed me skeptically.

"Mr. Green, I was not born yesterday. Mark my words. I am going to have you over to the house for dinner soon, and I'm going to ply you with Chablis until I get the full story."

Only then did it finally occur to me I might not be fired.

"So, you're going to let me keep working here?"

"Let you? Mr. Green, I am going to hire a bodyguard to follow you around to make sure you do not disappear again."

I had been so convinced I no longer had a job that it was hard to get used to the idea of still working there. Did I still want to work at the paper? Since I had absolutely no other plans, the easiest thing was to go back to what I knew.

"Thanks, David. I'm sorry about what I did and I appreciate you giving me another chance. I won't forget it."

"I should not be telling you this, but you're in a position to write your own ticket. You will be able to dine out on this MacCaul coup for a long time. By the way, you may want to spend your first morning back going through your mail and messages. You have quite a pile waiting for you."

I went to look at my inbox. David had not exaggerated. There were a ton of letters and phone messages. I did not know where to begin. It was all too much. After a half-hour of staring at it, I gave up. It was time for coffee. I walked to Flaubert's. I was surprised to see Carrie on the espresso machine. She always worked the counter.

"Your usual?" she asked.

Even though it felt like I had been gone for ages, it was obviously not so long that the staff at Flaubert's had forgotten my usual.

"Thanks, but I'll have an espresso today. Where's Justin?"

"He's gone."

"Gone?"

"Yeah, he quit. He said his parents gave him an ultimatum. He had to choose between going back to school or moving out. I heard he found a part-time job closer to home while he's going to school."

"What about his band?"

"Didn't you hear? I guess you have been gone a while."

"Yeah, I was in Europe for a couple of weeks."

"Nice. Anyway, the band broke up. I think one of them wanted to go solo, and someone else got a new job that was going to have a lot of overtime."

"Wow. I missed a lot while I was gone. Do you have Justin's phone number?"

"Don't you? I thought you and he were friends."

"Yeah, but I never had any reason to call him at his parents'. I always just talked to him here."

"I'll see if I can get it for you. Here's your espresso."

She came back with his number on a piece of paper.

"Something wrong with the coffee?"

"No, it's just that the espresso was so good in France."

"I see. You went to Europe for a couple of weeks and now you're a coffee snob."

"No, it's not that. It's just that... Never mind. Thanks for the number."

I downed my shot of coffee and headed back to the office. I wondered whether I should bother calling Justin. It sounded as though he was trying to get his act together. The fact was I was not exactly the best influence on him. He might be better off without me around. All I ever encouraged him to do was waste time and drink.

Back at the office David came looking for me. He had an envelope.

"I almost forgot," he said. "There were some photos on one of your film rolls. They were of a woman. Nobody here recognized her. We thought they might have been for your personal use."

I took the envelope into the darkroom for privacy. I knew immediately what photos they were, and I wanted to look at them alone. One by one I pulled them out of the envelope and stared. The sight of Valérie's laughing face was more than I could bear. There she was on the beach in Deauville in the darkness of the evening. She looked embarrassed and amused at the same time. It was the evening she taught me the word *galoche*. I missed her so much. I loved her so much.

I wanted to immediately get on a plane and fly back to her. I wanted to fight for her. But there was no point. I was once again in an impossible situation. It was time to accept my entire life was one long continuous impossible situation.

The following Sunday I walked to the Mission District. I passed by Marty's restaurant. It was closed. It looked like it had been closed for a while. The padlock on the door made the closure look long-term if not permanent. It made me sad. I had really looked forward to one of Marty's meals. I had hoped to get the chance to tell him about Berlin. Maybe he would know about it already. I had hoped he might answer some questions. I guess I should have known that was never going to happen.

For the next couple of months I fell back into my old routine. I took photographs for the paper. I went on my long walks around the city. It was a lonely time. I missed Valérie. I missed Ángel. I also missed Justin. It felt like I did not have a friend left in the world.

Baseball was a distraction when October rolled around. I had always loved watching the World Series as a kid. Lonnie and I always watched the games together, arguing over who was the best player and who wasn't. This particular year, for a change, I had a team to root for. It was not the Dodgers. They had not been in a World Series for a couple years. It was not the Giants either. They had not been in a World Series since I was nine years old. No, this year I rooted for the Philadelphia Phillies. Not only was it the first time they ever won a World Series, but their manager actually had the same exact name as me. Now maybe people would stop making fun of it.

After a campaign that had gone on forever, the election was finally held in November. To the surprise of a lot of people, Ronald Reagan won. Everyone I knew in the city was depressed. James lost it completely. He ranted and railed about how stupid most Americans were. He talked about emigrating to Canada.

"I'll never get financing for my business in Seattle now," he complained. "This country will be completely ruined. He's going to cut programs right and left. He'll destroy the economy. But it won't matter because nobody will care about the economy because he is going to get us into a war with the Soviet Union."

Personally, I was sick of politics. I was glad the election was finally over. People still insisted on talking about it, though. I did my best to tune it out.

Looking at the calendar, I remembered I had a promise to keep. I went to a toy shop and brought home a set of twenty-four *Star Wars* mini-action figures. I gift wrapped it myself and then wrapped it in parcel paper for mailing. I stood in line at the post office where I filled out a custom form and paid a fortune to send it to West Germany. I hoped it would get there in time for Lukas's birthday.

My time in Europe now felt like ancient history A couple weeks later, though, that history came alive in a totally surprising way.

Every afternoon the *Examiner* was delivered to the office. I always leafed through it before leaving for the day. I liked to see what photos they used and maybe get ideas for my own assignments. One particular evening, as I flipped through the pages, my eye was drawn to something I unexpectedly recognized. I saw a face I knew. The image quality was not great, but I would have recognized that knife-blade nose anywhere. It was the guy I had photographed at Zu Tisch in East Berlin. In fact, the photo was of him at Zu Tisch. It was the very photo I myself had taken. It had obviously been cropped and enhanced. I was disappointed in the quality, but

I told myself it was not my fault. I could only do what I was told to do, and I had to work with the crap camera Dino gave me. I stared at the photo for a long time. Like magic I was transported back in time to that day in Berlin in September. The photo was uncredited, and I was glad. I did not want anyone knowing it was my work.

The headline above the photo read, "British Double Agent Arrested in Germany." The cutline did not have a lot of information except to say the guy had been working for years for both British intelligence and for the East Germans—until he had been caught in the act in East Berlin.

Well, how about that? I thought. *So, that's what it was all about. I wish I knew how to get in touch with Marty. I sure would like to talk to him about it and ask him some questions. And maybe have some of his enchiladas de mole poblano.*

On one of my Sunday walks I actually went all the way to Russian Hill and found the house where I drank Scotch with him. There was no answer when I knocked on the door and rang the doorbell. There was no sign anyone was living there.

When Thanksgiving came around, I went home as usual for dinner with my family. Most of the attention was on my brother and his wife and their kids, and that suited me fine. This year the conversation was more awkward than usual. My mother wanted to know how things were going with my girlfriend. I had to tell her we had broken up. At least she would stop pressuring me to bring Lana home to meet them. They were interested to hear about my assignment in France. The only actor they were impressed by, though, was Danny Kaye. Mom asked if I was going to church on Sundays, and I lied and said I was. Dad asked suspiciously if I was still sometimes going to "the Roman churches." That was how he referred to Catholics. I lied and said I wasn't.

Looking disapprovingly at my hair, he said, "Son, you are going to be twenty-eight soon. Don't you think it is time you stopped looking like a hippie?"

I listened respectfully and said nothing. I looked at his bald head and promised myself I would wear my hair long for as long as I could.

Before we could eat dinner, we had to sit through Dad's customary twenty-minute prayer. Mom asked him to include an extra prayer for Linda's family.

"They are going through a rough time," she said. "Their son Michael is in the hospital, and it doesn't look good. The doctors can't seem to figure out what's wrong with him."

That was bad news. I made a mental note to phone Linda after the holiday was over.

In contrast to people in the city, my family was positive about the recent election.

"Maybe Reagan will be able to do something about all this inflation and high unemployment," said Dad. "And maybe he will be able to bring our hostages home from Iran since Carter hasn't been able to."

It amazed me how people living just a few hundred miles apart could see the world so differently from each other. Political arguments made me uncomfortable. Still, as combative as politics sometimes got in the U.S., at least it was nowhere as bad as having a military coup like what happened in Chile. Or having a wall running through the middle of a city like Berlin. It could never get that bad in America, could it?

After church on Sunday morning, Dad drove me to Bakersfield to catch the Amtrak train to Martinez. I sat by a window watching endless flat fields pass by. I thought about how different riding a train in California was compared to traveling on one in Europe. It was a relief to be going home. The city was home now. Kern County was now a place where I used to live.

I was not back in my apartment very long when the phone rang.

"Dallas!"

"Yes?"

"I've been trying to get a hold of you all day."

It was James. He had never phoned me at home before. I was surprised he had my phone number.

"Yeah, I was out of town for Thanksgiving. What's up?"

"Did you hear about Keith?"

"No. What about him?"

There was a pause.

"James, you still there?"

"I'm sorry. Dallas. It is just that I know you and he were good friends."

"What are you talking about, James? What happened."

"Sorry. I don't know how else to say it. Keith is dead."

"What?"

"Keith's dead."

"If this is a joke, James, it isn't funny."

"I wish it were, Dallas. I'm truly sorry."

"There has to be some kind of mistake. How can Keith be dead?"

"They found him Friday morning. In his garage."

"What happened to him?"

"The car engine was still running. He died from carbon monoxide poisoning."

"This is crazy. What happened? Did he fall asleep or pass out or something before he could turn off the engine?"

"It was not an accident, Dallas. They said he ran a hose from the exhaust to the car window. He did it on purpose, Dallas."

"No, that can't be right. That makes no sense. Why would he do that? It's crazy. He had a plan. Things were going great for him. He was doing great at work. He was on the rise. He loved being married. He loved his kid. It makes no sense. He had everything going for him. Everything."

"I know, I know. It makes no sense. I wish I had some explanation. No one saw it coming. No one. I don't know what to say. I'm sorry, Dallas."

"Do you know when the funeral is?"

"No. I don't know if they've made the arrangements yet. Everyone is still pretty much in shock. David is devastated. As you can imagine, Amy has taken it pretty hard. Sorry to be the one to deliver such bad news, Dallas."

I hung up the phone and sank into the cushions of the couch. I still refused to believe it. I tried to think of all possible ways for it not to be true. As the minutes passed, I gradually accepted it was true.

I felt guilty. I had not seen Keith for a long time. We had grown apart since working at the paper. After he got married—and especially after the baby was born—we had barely talked, only exchanging a few words at work. Had I missed something? Had there been some warning sign? If I had not been so consumed with my own life and my own problems, would I have seen something? I should have made an effort to spend more time with him after he got married. I could not stop the questions from flooding my mind, though they were all completely useless.

I thought about Amy. My heart ached for her. I could not imagine what she was going through. I thought about their little daughter Jennifer. She would grow up without a father. It was such a waste. It was not fair.

As I adjusted to the shock, I knew I had to do something. I had to find some way to help. I needed to find a way to make a difference. I could not fix it, but I had to find a way to make it better. I needed to go to Amy and offer her my help. I had to find out what she needed. I looked at the clock. It was too late to see her tonight. I would go in the morning. They would understand at the office. In fact, the office might not open tomorrow.

I barely slept. I tossed and turned. I dozed in fits and starts. It was not my usual night fear. It was worse. It was not the dread of what *might* happen. It was the dread of what *had* happened. It was a relief when morning finally came.

I got up and found some halfway decent clean clothes. I knew I should take something to Amy, but I did not know what. If this had happened in my hometown, my mother would have immediately made a casserole and sent me over with it. I did not know how to make a casserole. Instead I went to a florist and got flowers. I hopped on a bus to Marin.

Sitting on the bus, I stared out the window and struggled with my thoughts. Nothing in the world made sense anymore. People died for no reason. People were left behind and had to cope. What was the point of anything? At least some people tried to help out. Some people tried to make things better. What had I done? All I had ever done was think about myself. What was the point? What was the point of anything? Not only was I not doing any good for anybody but I was not making myself happy either. I needed to change my life. But how?

I thought about Amy and her new situation. She was a widow with a small baby. She had to be overwhelmed. I had to help her somehow. I got a crazy idea. I could offer to stay in the house with her for a while. I could help out. I could watch the baby while she went shopping or just wanted time for herself. I could learn to cook and make dinners. It could not replace Keith, but at least she would not be alone. She would not have to bear her burden alone. And who knows? I always kind of liked Amy. Maybe over time we would grow closer. Maybe the three of us could become a family. Yes, I still loved Valérie and always would, but the reality was that I had no future with her. Why not offer myself to someone who needed me? Maybe this is what I was meant to do. Maybe this was my life's purpose.

I walked from the bus stop to the house. It was a nice neighborhood. I could get to like living in Marin. It would be different than living in the city. Maybe it was time I grew up and moved to the suburbs. Maybe it was time I took on some responsibility.

There were several cars parked outside Keith and Amy's house. I wondered who was in the house. I was nervous going to the door. I told myself this was no time to be a wimp. It was time to grow up.

I knocked on the door. After about a minute, it opened. I saw the last face I expected to see.

"Justin?"

32
Birthday

"WHAT ARE you doing here?"

"Hey, man! It's good to see you! When did you get back from France?"

"I've been back a while now. In the end I was only over there for less than three weeks."

"Why didn't you call me?"

"Sorry, man. I heard you quit your job at Flaubert's and that you went back to school. I thought maybe you might be too busy to see me."

"Hey, man, you should have called. Didn't I tell you that you were my best friend?"

"Yeah, and didn't I tell you that nobody says that once they're past the eighth grade?"

He had a plate in one hand and a towel in the other. He leaned forward and gave me a hug. He smelled of dish soap, but it was not lemon scented. It had only been three months since I had seen him, but he had changed a lot. His hair was cut short. He had put on a little weight and did not look as scrawny as before. On his upper arm was a tattoo. It was the ÜberVenge logo that had been on his bass drum.

I pointed to the tattoo and said, "I heard the band broke up."

"Yeah. It was time. We weren't going anywhere. Johnny decided to go out on his own. Terry and Rick just lost interest. But it's cool. It was a blast while it lasted."

He lowered his voice and leaned closer to me, "And I did get laid, like, a million times."

"I was in a club you would have liked a lot. It was in Berlin. I didn't get to hear any music there though."

"Wow. You were in Berlin? I would give anything to go to Berlin. Man, you're so lucky."

I pointed to his chin.

"Nice beard you got going there."

He stroked it.

"Yeah, I thought I would give it another try. I was never able to grow one before, but now it's coming in pretty nice. I guess I'm finally becoming a man."

"So, what are you doing here?"

"I came as soon as I heard about Keith. I came two days ago and haven't left since."

"Really? I didn't realize you knew Keith that well."

"Yeah, it's actually kind of strange. I saw a lot of him and Amy lately. One evening after I quit my job in the city, I was wandering around the local supermarket and I ran into Keith out of the blue. It was so weird to see him here. It turned out they bought a house only a few blocks from where I lived. He invited me over sometimes to watch movies with the two of them."

Justin suddenly remembered something and his face lit up.

"Hey! I saw your article about Logan MacCaul! You found him. I was so proud of you. I couldn't believe you got to meet him, that you got to talk to him. I was so jealous. You must be the luckiest guy in the whole world."

"Yeah, there's a whole long story behind that."

"You're going to have to tell me all about it. I have to hear everything. Some night we have to go out drinking and catch up. I've really missed you, man."

"Yeah, I've missed you, too. I should have called you. There have been some times lately when I could have used a friend to talk to."

"Hey, anytime, man. I'm always here. Anyway, what are we doing standing here talking in the doorway? Come in. Amy will be glad to see you. You brought flowers!"

Quite a few people were in the house. Amy's mother and her sisters were there. I spoke to Amy briefly, but she was mostly keeping to herself in her bedroom. She looked wrecked. I felt so bad for her. I wished I had something to say that did not sound stupid. To my relief, Lana was not there. I had been afraid that she would be. I spent most of the time hanging out with Justin in the kitchen. He had an endless supply of dishes to wash, and I dried them.

I heard Amy's mother in the other room talking to someone on the phone.

"I know. I know," she said. "It's just so senseless. He was only twenty-seven. Imagine. Only twenty-seven."

"I still can't believe Keith did that," whispered Justin. "You knew him better than anyone. Do you know why he would have done it? I mean, the guy had everything."

"I don't know, man. I sure can't figure it out. It just makes absolutely no sense."

"Amy told me I could stay in the guest bedroom while I'm helping out. I don't know how much help I am, but at least I can wash dishes and do some cooking. And I can make a pretty mean cup of coffee."

"That you can," I smiled. "Flaubert's isn't the same without you."

He lowered his voice further.

"Just between you and me, I'm hoping she will just let me keep staying here. Frankly, school's not working out. Things aren't working out at home with my parents either. It will only get worse when I quit school. I figure I can get a full-time job and pay Amy rent. That will help her out with her mortgage."

"Sounds like you got it all figured out."

Justin managed to make his voice softer still.

"I know this is an inappropriate thing to be saying right now, but the truth is, I've always kind of had a thing for Amy. I'm not trying to take advantage or anything, but being here feels so right to me. Does that seem weird?"

I put my hand on his shoulder and said sincerely, "You're a good man, Justin. You're doing a good thing being here for her. Just take things one day at a time. I'm sure over time everything will work out the way it's supposed to."

"God, you're so wise. Thanks, man. I just have this feeling, you know, that this is what I'm meant to do. You know?"

"Yeah, I know."

After a while I could see there was not much point in hanging around anymore, and I said my goodbyes. Justin and I promised after the funeral the two of us would go out for a night in the city—like old times. On the bus home, I had a good laugh at myself. Justin had naturally and effortlessly stolen my crazy plan. I was going to have to find some other purpose for my life. It was just as well. It was silly of me to think of any long-term plan without Valérie in it.

After the bus crossed the Golden Gate, I got off at the first stop. I went for a walk on the bridge. At the midway point I looked down at the water below rushing out of the bay and into the Pacific. I remembered the evening I made the same walk a few months earlier. I remembered thinking about throwing myself off. I remembered giving myself permission to come back and jump the day before my twenty-eighth birthday. That was now only five days away. It was just another of my many plans that was never going to happen. There was no way I could think about it after what Keith had done.

I had seen how it devastated everyone around him. I remembered Jim Morrison's tomb. I recalled all the empty bottles and the graffiti. Dying at twenty-seven might be okay for a rock star, but it was not okay for people like Keith and me. I definitely knew I was not a rock star. I was stuck having to face whatever life was going to throw at me. I was too chicken to take the coward's way out.

The next few days at work were pretty grim. The office was closed the day of the funeral, but otherwise David did not take any time off. He put up a brave front, but we could all see he was devastated.

There was one bit of good news in the middle of it all, though. On Friday morning James grabbed me and insisted I go to Flaubert's with him. He had news he wanted to share.

"The financing came through! I got the green light from the bank. I can finally start my own business. I have to tell David I'm leaving. I'm not looking forward to that. He's had such a tough time lately. But I can't wait. Seattle, here I come!"

"That's great, James. I'm happy for you."

"I tell you, those idiot bankers actually seem to think that Reagan will be good for the economy. The morons. But I'm not going to look a gift horse in the mouth. I'm going for this. I am going to make this a success no matter how much Ronnie boy screws up the country."

"That's the spirit, James. Best of luck to you."

"My offer still stands. It would be great to have you with me while I'm getting started. I wouldn't be able to pay as much as you're getting here—at first. But I'd be willing to cut you in for a stake in the company. If it works out, it could mean a lot of money for both of us. And it would be a real coup for me. To get the famous photographer who broke the Logan MacCaul story."

"I'm flattered. I really am."

"I'm dead serious. Take the weekend to think about it. You can tell me on Monday if you want to accept. This could be that fresh start you wanted. We could be the toast of Seattle."

"Thanks, James. I'll let you know on Monday."

The more I thought about it, the more James's offer made sense. A new city, a new job, new people, new friends. As much as I liked working at the paper, it was never going to be the same now that Keith was gone. Yes, Seattle was the right place for me. I did not need the weekend to think about it.

It was a depressing weekend. Friday was Lonnie's birthday, always a bad day for me. That night I went to a bar by myself and drank too much.

Saturday was a complete waste. In the evening I went by myself to see the new movie version of *Flash Gordon*. They had obviously spent a lot of money on it, but it wasn't great.

Sunday was my birthday. Not one single person remembered. No, that is not true. Early in the morning my mother called. She wished me a happy birthday. She wanted to talk about the day I was born and what I was like as a child. She also told me to be sure and not miss church. That was the extent of my birthday wishes. I was now twenty-eight. No more pressure to flame out like a rock star. I had survived longer than Jim Morrison, Jimi Hendrix and Janis Joplin. I might have called Justin and gone out for a night on the town, but it was still too soon after Keith's funeral.

Instead I made my own plan. I went to the liquor store and bought a bottle of José Cuervo—the good stuff, *Especial* Gold—and stopped by a grocery store to buy a fresh lime. I already had salt. I put a Led Zeppelin LP on the turntable and downed my first shot. Time to get this party started.

I held up the shot glass and said, "Happy birthday to me!" and swallowed it all.

I poured another one. "Here's to Lonnie!" Down the hatch and another taste of lime and salt.

"Here's to Keith!" and another gulp.

"Here's to Antonio!"

I was feeling good and happy now. When "Stairway to Heaven" came on, I poured another shot.

"*À toi, Valérie, mon amour. Je t'aime. Yo te quiero, mi amor.*"

I had not felt this good in a long time. Before I knew it, I realized I was not alone. There was an old face I had not seen in years. Sitting on the chair across from me was Lonnie's ghost. He had not stopped by since my days in Bakersfield.

"Hey, man. What's up?"

"It's my birthday, man. Didn't you remember?"

"Nah. You know I don't remember things like that. Happy birthday."

"Thanks, man. Happy birthday to you too. Two days ago, I mean."

"Yeah, we were almost twins. Born two days apart. How have you been, man?"

"Where to begin? So much has happened. And you missed it all. I really resent that you keep missing so much of my life. You should have been here, man. You should have been part of it."

"Hey, sorry, man, but somebody has to be eighteen forever. Might as well be me."

"You aren't eighteen forever. You're twenty-one. You were twenty-one when you died."

"No, man. I'm eighteen forever. I'll always be the same age I was when we went to Mexico."

"Hey!" I said, suddenly remembering something important. "I met your kid!"

"I have a kid?"

"Yeah, you have a kid. Didn't you know?"

"Nah. How would I know that?"

"I don't know. It just seems like you should. He's a cool kid. He looks just like you. It's amazing how much he looks like you."

"Cool."

"It was his birthday a few weeks ago. Don't worry. I got him a gift from the two of us. I got him some *Star Wars* action figures."

"What's *Star Wars*?"

"Shit. You don't even know about *Star Wars*. This isn't fair. This just fucking isn't fair."

"Hey, take it easy, man. Don't start crying on me."

"I'll never forgive you, you know. I'll never fucking forgive you. You're off there in the afterlife or wherever you are, having a great time being eighteen forever, and I'm here and I can't have a normal life because I'm too messed up because of you. It's not fair."

"Hey, don't put that on me, man. I didn't ask you to be messed up because of me. That's your deal."

"Why are you here, Lonnie? Why now? Why today of all days?"

"I don't know. You figure it out. You were always supposed to be the smart one."

"Am I dying?"

"What?"

"Is that it? Did I finally drink so much that I gave myself alcohol poisoning? Is that why you're here? Did you come to help me cross over to the other side?"

"You need to fucking ease up, man. God, you were always such a damn worry wart."

"You should have been here, Lonnie. You should still be here. You should have come to the city with me. We would have had a great time here."

"How come you always do that? You always call it the city—like it was the only city in the world. There are lots of cities."

271

"Everybody here does that. San Francisco is too long to say every time. Anyway, you should have come here with me."

"I was in Frisco once."

"They don't like it here when you call it Frisco."

"Is that right? Well, bite me. Like I said, I was in Frisco once. I didn't like it. The place was full of fags."

"Don't say that."

"Don't say what?"

"Don't say that word. Some of the people you're talking about are my friends now."

"Yeah, well, I always knew you were a little soft. I guess I'm not surprised. You know, I always suspected there was a little something going on between you that Antonio kid."

"Do you know where Antonio is?"

"Where he is? How the hell would I know where Tony is?"

"I thought maybe you would have come across him in the afterlife. Do you know if he is alive or dead? Did Pinochet kill him?"

"Listen, if I ever see Tony again, I'll…"

Lonnie was interrupted by a buzzing sound. I jerked awake. I had been sleeping on the couch. I heard the buzzing again. It was the intercom. I got up, went to the door, and pressed the button.

"Yes?"

A voice came through the speaker.

"Is Lonnie there?"

I pinched myself because I was sure I was still dreaming.

"What?"

"Is this Lonnie? Sorry. I mean Dallas. Is this Dallas Green?"

"Who is this?"

"It *is* you. *¡Huevón!* Open the door. *¡Yo me hielo!* I am freezing out here."

I pressed the button to release the front door. I ran out of my apartment and down the stairs. Halfway down the stairway I saw him. His mop of black hair hung over his forehead. His face was tired. Underneath his windbreaker he wore a Bordeaux Étudiant Club tee-shirt that was a size too small. His backpack was slung over his shoulder.

"Ángel? What the hell are you doing here?"

"I came to see you. What do you think?"

We climbed back up to my apartment.

"But how? How did you get here? How did you find me?"

"You gave me your address, remember? In care of Green. I just gave it to the taxi driver."

"But what are you doing in the city?"

"*Hombre, ¡tú andas con el mono!* What are you drinking?"

"Tequila."

"Tequila? I have never tried that. Give me some."

"You've never had tequila? How is that possible?"

"There you go, trying to make me a Mexican again. I have never seen tequila in Chile. What's it like? Is it like pisco?"

"What's pisco?"

"You'll find out."

"Whoa. Back up. What the hell are you doing in San Francisco?"

"Pour me some tequila first."

I poured him a shot.

"Here, give me your hand," I said.

I took his hand. I licked the part between his thumb and his index finger. That was not something I normally would have done, but I was drunk and it was easier than trying to tell him what to do himself. I shook some salt on his hand where I had licked. I cut a wedge of lime.

"Okay," I said. "Lick the salt on your hand. Then down the shot of tequila. Then suck on the lime."

"This is very complicated—and I do not think very sanitary."

I licked my own hand, put salt on it, and licked the salt—to show him how it was done. He imitated me, and then we downed the shots together. Then we sucked our wedges. Ángel shuddered.

"I think I like this," he said. "I like San Francisco."

"So, what are you doing here?"

"I have always wanted to see this city. It is named after my favorite saint, Saint Francis of Assisi. What little I saw of it on the way from the airport looks nice. It reminds me of Valparaíso."

"So, you're here on a whim? Just because you wanted to see San Francisco?"

"I decided I could not continue with school. Not in France anyway. I told my father I was coming home. I told him to send me a ticket home and that I needed an extra ticket for a friend who was coming with me from the States."

"Me?"

"Yes. You."

"That must have cost a fortune."

"I don't know how much it cost. My father is paying for it."

"I didn't think you ever wanted to see me again."

"I didn't. I was very angry with you. Very, very angry. I called you many bad names after you left."

"You also called me many bad names *before* I left."

"Then, after you left Berlin, I missed you. And that made me more angry with you."

I was afraid to ask my next question, but I did anyway.

"And Valérie?"

"Valérie was waiting for me when I returned to Bordeaux. She was annoyed I had not been there waiting for her. She was very upset. She explained the whole story, about her father, I mean, her real father and about her mother's ashes. The fact that you knew all about it before I did only made me more angry with you."

"Is she okay?"

"I think so. I don't know. Things have changed. Things were not the same with us anymore. I do not know if that is because of her father or because of you. She would not talk about you, but she was angry when I told her that you had come to Bordeaux. She said she needed time to—how did she say it? *organiser ses pensées*—to organize her thoughts. We did not see each other for a while. Then she wanted to see me again, and we went back to how things were before. Except they were not the same. She was very preoccupied. Her father—I mean the man she thought was her father—has not been well. I think he is dying."

"Dying? Man, you should be there with her. Or I should. One of us should. She shouldn't be alone now."

"I think he has been dying for a long time and is going to be dying for a long time more. She said that she did not want me around during this time. She is spending more time with her sister and her brother and their father. She said she did not want distractions right now and I was a distraction. I did not like it, but it is what she wants. Besides, I was homesick. My country's new constitution was announced in October. That and your visit with Paulina made me realize I needed to go home. I was not able to vote in the referendum in September because I was outside the country. There will be another referendum in eight years. I want to be there for that one. I want to be in the country and help make sure that Pinochet keeps his promise to let democracy be restored. I want to be part of what happens from now on."

"What about your father?"

"I do not know if he will agree with me. I don't know if he will want Pinochet to stay in power forever or if he will think it is time for him to go. But it will not matter. I have to do what I think is right."

I still could not believe he was there. I stared at him. I could see every detail of his torso through his stretched tee-shirt. He looked like his own drawing of Lautaro.

Yes, I thought, *he will go back to Chile, and he and his generation will be the heroes that liberate their country.*

I poured two more shots of tequila.

"*¡A Chile!*" I cried.

"*¡A Chile!*"

"So, your trip from Paris to Santiago just happened to pass through San Francisco?"

"I told my father I was bringing someone from here with me. There are seats booked for the two of us on a flight tomorrow morning. I came to find you and invite you to come. Luckily, I still had my green card from when I lived in Virginia."

"But why? After I tried to steal your girlfriend and I lied to you, why would you make your father pay all that money to take me to Chile with you?"

"Because I missed you. You may be a *pico conchetumadre*, but you are also my friend. It was too difficult to make myself keep hating you."

"But what about Valérie?"

"I love her too. I always will."

"But how does this work? How can the two of us be friends when we are both in love with Valérie?"

"I don't know. We will work it out somehow. Maybe I will be with her for a while. Then you will be with her for a while. Somehow I think our three lives are going to be tangled up for a long time. It will be like that Truffaut film. The three of us will be like Jules and Jim and Jeanne Moreau."

I shook my head and poured two more shots of tequila.

"Wait a minute," I said. "Didn't Jim and Jeanne Moreau die in that movie?"

He downed his shot and thought for a moment.

"Yes, you are right. You are absolutely right. Okay, that settles it. You get to be Jim."

"No way, *huevón*. If we're going to live our lives like a movie, then we're going to be Butch Cassidy and the Sundance Kid. We can go out shooting at the whole goddamned Bolivian army—together."

"Sorry, I do not know that movie. Anyway, there is another reason you have to go to Santiago with me."

"What's that?"

275

"We are going to find Antonio."

"We are?"

"*Mira*, there is nothing I can do about what happened in 1973 or all the things that happened afterward. I can do nothing about all the people who died or who were tortured or who disappeared. But maybe I can do something at least about one person. We can find your friend Antonio."

"How?"

"I don't know. I will make my father help. He is in a position to find out things. He knows people. If there is any way to find out, he will be able to help. We will find out once and for all what happened. Was he arrested? Did he leave the country? Has he simply been living there in Chile all these years? If it is possible to get the answer, I promise you we will get it."

The tequila made me want to cry.

"I don't know what to say."

"Say you will go with me."

"I... I have to think about it. I am supposed to work tomorrow. I have a job. They are counting on me. And I have to tell someone tomorrow if I will take another job—in Seattle. This is a lot to take in—especially when I have been drinking tequila all night. Tell me, do we really have to fly there."

"Why? Do you not like to fly?"

"I'm not that crazy about it, but I can manage. No, that's not it. It's just that, well, years ago I had a crazy idea."

"What was your crazy idea?"

"I had this idea that a friend and I would drive a car all the way down to Chile."

"That would be a very long journey, amigo. That would take weeks or months."

"You're right. I know I'm still pretty crazy, but I guess even *I* have to grow up eventually and leave some of my crazier ideas behind."

"Let's sleep on it, *huevón*. I am exhausted. I will leave in the morning and you can come with me on the plane or not."

The two of us fell into my bed next to each other, just as we had slept in his room in Talence. It was so good not to be alone. I could tell by his breathing Ángel would be asleep in no time.

"Can I tell you something, Ángel?"

"*Desde luego*, Lonnie," he muttered tiredly. "Sorry. It will take me some time to get used to your real name, Dallas Green."

"This is important. This is something I have never told another living person in my whole life."

"Yes?"

"When I am alone at night, everything becomes very black."

"You mean, because the light is turned off?"

"No, I mean really black. Like the darkness of death. I spend the whole night afraid."

"Really?"

"Yeah. Does that ever happen to you?"

"No, not like that. Not at night. But I have my own *demonios*. Some of them you know about already, but there are others. I will tell you about them some other time. Right now, though, I need to sleep."

He rolled over and laid his arm over me. The magical feeling of peacefulness flowed from his body into mine. It was blessed relief. Ángel was the perfect name for him.

He woke me early in the morning. My mouth was bone dry. I had yet another epic headache. I threw some clothes in my backpack and grabbed my passport.

"I should get some money from the bank."

"There may not be time. I can lend you what you need."

"I guess I can call David from the airport and explain what's happening. I hope he'll understand. And I better call James. I told him I would give him an answer today."

I called for a taxi, and within a few minutes we were on our way to the airport.

As we settled into our seats on the airplane, I tried to ignore my head's throbbing. I made myself a promise. As of today I would finally clean up my act. I would stop drinking once and for all. I would not smoke anymore—not even occasionally. From now on my life would be healthy and sane. I would be mature and sensible. As I went through my new resolutions in my head, I realized Ángel was talking to me.

"This is going to be great, *hombre*. We are going to have such a good time in Santiago. I am going to take you to all my favorite places. I am going to take you to the best clubs and to the best parties. *¡Lo vamos a pasar regio!* And you know what the best part will be?"

"What's that?"

"*Huevón*, we are going to drink liters and liters of pisco!"

About the Author

A native of California's San Joaquin Valley, Scott R. Larson has also lived in Ohio, France, Chile, and for many years in and around Seattle, Washington. He currently finds himself in the West of Ireland, where he writes one of the internet's longest running film blogs. His previous novels are *Maximilian and Carlotta Are Dead*, which introduced the character of Dallas Green, and *The Three Towers of Afranor*, a fantasy adventure.